Singles vs. Bridezillas

Linda Fausnet

Published by Wannabe Pride 2015
Editing by Lisa Winders and Zann Wasiljov
Cover Design by Evan Lerman
Formatting by Polgarus Studio

FIRST EDITION.
Library of Congress Control Number: 2015903402
ISBN 978-0-9916525-4-9

For my parents, Cecelia and Bernard Wasiljov, and my fabulously single and sassy sister, Zann Wasiljov. They have provided a lifetime of unflinching support of my dreams.

CHAPTER ONE

Imogene Hart stared at the casket being lowered into the ground. Somberly, she bent down and gathered a handful of dirt. She took a deep breath, then fired the fistful of dirt at the casket where it landed with a satisfying *splat*!

"Peace out, you old bat," Imogene said.

"Immy!" cried Faye. She looked around to make sure no one heard her sister's outburst. "Jeez, show a little respect."

"Oh, she was a horrible old woman and you know it," Imogene said. She wiped the sweat from her forehead. There was no escaping the Florida heat, even in early October. The fresh funeral roses on the grave would be roasted into potpourri by the afternoon.

"She was not. She was just…worried about you," Faye said. She tucked her shoulder-length brown hair behind her ear. *Mommy hair*, as Imogene thought of it. Kind of boring and ordinary. At least Faye didn't wear those awful *mom jeans* with the elastic waistbands. Imogene shuddered at the thought. It was easy for her younger sister to defend Great Aunt Maddy. Faye was married with two kids, so the old lady had no reason to torture her. Maddy, her grandmother's oldest sister, had acted like being single was a crime.

She had felt like a loser watching her younger sisters march down the aisle, and then she had Aunt Maddy's constant warnings about her *spinsterhood*. She had actually used the word "spinster"...

"You'd better find a man and settle down, Immy. You don't want to die alone..." Imogene said in a singsong voice. She shot a smug look at the casket. "You *were* married and you still died alone..."

"Imogene! Seriously."

"Everybody obsesses over single people dying alone, but what are the odds that you and your spouse are gonna kick it at the exact same time?"

Faye glanced around nervously, clearly hoping no one overheard Imogene's commentary on the not-so-dearly departed. It wasn't likely, though, considering the average age of the funeral goers was ninety. They had trouble hearing people standing right next to them.

Imogene looked at the casket and sighed. If anybody was watching, it would look as if she was mourning the lady in the box. Instead, she was mourning the sad state of her own life.

"Good thing Aunt Maddy bought it before she found out Nathan and I broke up."

Faye winced and nodded.

"If she hadn't, the news probably would have killed her," Faye said.

"No doubt."

Imogene had dated Nathan for a year and a half and it looked to everyone, including Imogene, that she had finally found her future husband. That was, until Nathan took some boring but prestigious finance job in California. A long-distance relationship didn't make sense for a woman who had just turned thirty. She didn't have that kind of time if she hoped to have children someday.

What a horrible, disappointing, waste of time that relationship had been. And now she was back to square one. Again. The idea of going back to blind dates, Internet dating, and the bar scene made Imogene want to lie down and take a nap right next to one of the gravestones.

She didn't know what was so wrong with her. Sure, she might not be gorgeous, but neither were most women. She wasn't skinny, but she wasn't fat either. She was average. In every way. Her hair was brown, but at least it was a pretty, light brown. When she stood in the sun it almost looked blonde. Almost. If you squinted a little. She'd been told she had pretty brown eyes. Okay, it had been her father who said it, but still…There were lots of less attractive women who were married, that was for sure.

A sudden surge of renewed rage took hold of Imogene as she remembered Aunt Maddy's commentary at her sister Chrissy's wedding, captured forever by the videographer. Rather than express her best wishes for the happy couple, Maddy had gone on and on about how shocking it was that Chrissy, the youngest, was married while Imogene remained single.

"Such a shame Imogene hasn't found a husband. It's bound to happen for her eventually, I suppose," Aunt Maddy had said loudly to the camera and to anyone in earshot. "I hope so. She's not getting any younger, you know."

"What's the matter?" Faye asked. She looked rather alarmed at Imogene's furious expression.

"Nothing." Imogene didn't want to talk about it. She was sick ᶜtalking about it. And if she got one more pitying look…

ⁿe turned and walked away. She looked at the
ⁱng every time she came across a grave containing
who'd been buried with her parents. *Spinster.*

That ridiculous, outdated term was all she could think of. She felt like she was staring into her own future. Husbandless, childless, buried with her parents, and survived only by a bunch of cats. Not that she had any cats.

The problem was, Imogene happened to adore cats. She'd never owned any growing up because her mother was allergic, and she always thought she would get one when she lived on her own. Instead, she refused to get one on principle. She simply couldn't bear to be the stereotypical single cat lady.

Just when Imogene was beginning to look forward to being the newest member of the underground party, she spotted a grave like no other she'd ever seen. It was a medium-sized tombstone, but rather large for a gravesite that contained only one person. The lettering was quite fancy, almost like calligraphy. It read:

Here lies Agnes McCann,
A lady who never had time for a man,
She had a good life,
Was never a wife,
But how fine did she sing with the band.

Imogene sank down into the soft, warm earth as she stared at the gravestone. She was surprised at how much the words touched her, and she took a few moments to contemplatively pay her respects to Agnes. Funny how she had more reverence for this unknown woman than she ever had for Aunt Maddy.

"Wow," Imogene said softly. She ran her fingers over the engraved words on Agnes' tombstone. This lady must have been incredibly cool. She was never married and died in 1954. Sure, it was tough now for women to be single, but *damn*. Back then, it must have been practically unheard of. What a brave woman Agn must have been. Imogene imagined her as a wonderfully glamorous, classy lady wearing an evening gown and singing in a jazz band. This woman had a fabulous life without a man, and Imogene admired the hell out of her.

A sudden realization—a true epiphany—struck Imogene like a sharp jolt of electricity. She realized she could give up on looking for a man.

Imogene assumed that after she broke up with Nathan, she would have to get right back on the whole nightmarish woman-desperately-seeking-a-husband kick.

But she didn't have to do that. After all, where had it gotten her? Nowheresville. She was a thirty-year-old secretary who lived in an apartment. No husband. No kids. Not even a damn cat.

Imogene suddenly felt liberated. Free. She imagined the time she would save if she finally quit her practically full-time job of searching for a man. Instead of reading Internet dating sites, she could read actual books. She could learn how to cook! Like cook for real, not just the hastily prepared meals she threw together because she felt it was useless to bother cooking for one. She could go back to school. Hell, she could become a doctor! Not that she wanted to. Not in the least. But still, she could if the urge struck her. She could do whatever she wanted.

Imogene thought of her bare apartment. She'd lived there for years but had scarcely decorated it. She'd always figured she would get married and buy a house, so why bother dressing up a stupid little apartment? Well, it wasn't just a stupid little apartment. It was her *home*. She had to start treating it as such, not just a place to keep her stuff while she waited for something better to come along. Sure, maybe she could buy her own house one day, but for now this was where she lived and she planned to make the most of it.

She decided to redo everything in the apartment, starting with those horrible dishes she'd had since her college days. They were off-white with little green rings around the edges and looked like something from a greasy spoon diner. Now that she knew there would be no bridal registry and no significant other whose opinion she had to consider, she could pick out whatever dish pattern she liked.

"I'm gettin' new dishes, dammit!" Imogene shouted.

Faye rushed over to see what her sister was getting all worked up about.

"Immy, what the hell?" Faye asked in a hushed voice. Imogene's shout had gotten the attention of some of the old biddies getting into their cars.

"Faye, check this out," Imogene said, as she gestured to Agnes' grave. Faye scanned the grave, looking unimpressed.

"What? Somebody you know?" She read the stone. "Well, 1954...I guess not."

"No, but look. Even in the 1950s this lady was single. And she was a singer. Don't you think that's cool?" Imogene asked, her eyes lighting up with excitement. Faye shrugged and looked at her sister quizzically. "I mean, she was single and she had a good life. It says so right on her grave."

It was back. That look of pity that Imogene hated so much. She could hardly blame her sister, though. Imogene had made herself an object of pity as a single woman. She shuddered with shame when she remembered the times she had begged her friends to set her up on a date with somebody. *Anybody.*

Thirty. She was thirty years old and had done nothing with her life. If she died today, nobody could write on her tombstone about what a wonderful life she'd led. As she looked around at the rows and rows of dead people, some of them so young when they died, she knew she had to change her life. Starting now.

CHAPTER TWO

Imogene wrinkled her nose at the smell of Mrs. Ettles' house. It had that old lady stench, that weird combination of mothballs, sickly-sweet perfume, and dusty furniture. It was mostly elderly women who were gathered for the funeral luncheon. They had all outlived their husbands, some by as many as twenty years. Imogene chewed on her dry turkey and cheese sandwich, debating the merits of throwing it away and stopping at McDonald's on the way home.

Home. For once, she couldn't wait to get back to her apartment. The decision to stop husband-hunting and to finally be her own person made her eager to get on with the proverbial first day of the rest of her life. She thought of the bare white walls and visualized hanging beautiful art prints of the sea or maybe a painting of one of those country cottages surrounded by a flower garden. She began to prepare a mental shopping list of all the new stuff she would get for her place.

It was amazing how free she felt. Imogene was no longer a slave to the dating scene. For the first time ever, she was going to live life on her own terms. Her happiness was no longer up to fate and she couldn't wait to tell everyone.

"So, I've decided I'm done with the whole dating scene. I'm so over it. I'm just gonna be single and embrace it," Imogene said to her sisters.

By the horrified looks that followed her declaration, you would think she'd just said she was planning to quit her job and become a stripper.

"You cannot be serious," Chrissy said. She sank back into the worn cushions of the couch and stared at Imogene.

"Damn right I'm serious. Nathan was the last straw. I'm tired of the disappointment. Tired of seeing everybody else get married while I'm left behind."

The look of pity—and guilt—that Chrissy gave Imogene was worse than the one Faye had been shooting her all day. Chrissy, blonde and petite, still looked like the cute little cheerleader she'd been in high school. Faye got married first, but being only two years younger than Imogene, it wasn't that big of a deal. But Chrissy was the baby. She wasn't supposed to beat Imogene to the altar.

Chrissy's wedding had been a humiliating experience for Imogene. She had felt like everyone was staring at her, pitying the poor, older sister who couldn't find a husband. But Imogene had sucked it up, put on her best face, and dealt with the usual nosy questions from annoying relatives. She didn't have to fake her excitement for Chrissy, though. Her husband, Liam, was a sweetheart and Imogene was genuinely happy for them. Her sister had looked radiant up there on the altar, and she could tell by the way Liam looked at her that they belonged together.

Still, it hurt. Imogene's little sisters had looked up to her their whole lives. They had begged to borrow her clothes, her shoes, her makeup, and had been desperate to grow up and be just like her. Now, it seemed they had surpassed her; Imogene was nothing to envy anymore.

"You're just saying that because you're upset," Chrissy said. "I know Aunt Maddy was rough on you, but she meant well. She just wanted you to be happy."

Imogene should have known nobody would believe her when she said she was done with man-hunting. Even though it had been her life's mission to find a man, she'd announced she was giving up a million times. Whenever a date didn't work out or she felt depressed about being alone, she'd say she was done looking for a guy. But this time was different. It felt different. This time, she wasn't giving up out of desperation. She really wanted to quit searching for a man and start living on her own terms.

"Is this about that dead woman?" Faye asked, then blushed when several people turned and gave her disapproving looks. She shifted uncomfortably on the couch next to Chrissy. "No-no. Not Aunty Maddy…God rest her soul. I mean the gravestone you saw?"

"So what if it is? She had her life together without a man. If she can do it, so can I," Imogene said. She crossed her arms stubbornly.

"She was probably a lesbian," Faye whispered, so as not to scandalize the old ladies.

"So what if she was?" Imogene said, dismissively waving her right arm in the air. "She still refused to get married when I'm sure everybody told her she should. Especially back then, that's what women were expected to do."

"You don't know that she refused to get married," argued Faye. "She could have been butt ugly."

Imogene was about to argue when their father, Nicholas Hart, wandered over to check on his daughters. He was in his early 60s, too young for any of the gals at this gathering, but that didn't stop the old broads from looking. Her dad had worked in construction most of his life, and had the rugged good looks of a man who spent most of his time outdoors,

"How we doing, girls?" he asked.

"Why don't you tell Dad about your grand plan to be single and lonely for the rest of your life? I'm sure he'll be jazzed about that," Chrissy said.

Imogene glared at her. She was confident in her decision to move on with her life without a man, and she didn't feel like arguing about it.

Imogene's father looked at her with a touch of sadness. Great. More pity. Chrissy and Faye weren't the only ones who felt bad about their getting married first. Imogene knew it kept her dad up at night, worrying about her lack of a spouse. Her parents had been married for twenty-six years before her mother died. They'd had a wonderful marriage, and her dad seemed lost without her. He probably figured Imogene was lost without a partner, too.

"I'm *not* gonna be lonely. I just decided to quit wasting my time looking for a husband."

Mrs. Ettles gasped loudly. Imogene jumped at the noise, nearly spilling her paper cup of Diet Coke all over the doily covering the splintered end table.

"You don't want to get married?" the old lady asked. "What happened to that cute fella you were with for so long? Billy? Bobby? Barnaby?"

Imogene frowned. "Nathan."

"Nathan! What happened to him?" Mrs. Ettles nearly shouted. "He could have been a husband for you!"

A husband. She said it like Imogene could just select any random guy to fill in the empty blanks in her life. Imogene sighed so deeply that the sound seemed to come from the depths of her soul. Aunt Maddy might be gone, but she had plenty of friends to carry on her legacy of torture and judgment.

"We broke up. He moved out of state and I am way too old to do the long distance thing," Imogene answered. Why should she have to justify her love life to this lady? She wasn't even family.

"Oh, no! That's awful!" Mrs. Ettles looked traumatized. Imogene summoned every ounce of willpower not to roll her eyes at the crazy lady. Drama queen much?

Aunt Maddy's friend and neighbor, Mrs. Mortimer, ambled over.

"It's okay, Ellie," Mrs. Mortimer soothed. "She's in a better place now."

"Who-what? Oh, no. Not *that*. June, Imogene broke up with Bil- I mean Nathan."

Mrs. Mortimer turned to Imogene, eyes wide.

"Oh, dear Lord!" she exclaimed in horror.

Chrissy giggled and nudged Faye as she tried to suppress her laughter. Her father looked worried.

"Yeah, it really was a shame that he took that job and you broke up," he said, shaking his head sadly. "I really thought you two would get married."

"Yeah, well we didn't," Imogene grumbled, trying to keep her temper in check. "It's fine. I'm fine. Look, I just realized that I've spent way too much time sitting around and waiting to find a man. I don't want to do it anymore, okay? I'm gonna be fine as a single woman."

"Oh, honey," her father began. "You're still young. You-"

"Dad, I'm not young! I mean, I am compared to-" She stopped herself before she said something to offend the truly ancient ladies in the room. "I mean, I'm thirty now. Thirty! I'm too old for getting married and having kids."

"Thirty is not old! You still have plenty of time to—"

"Sure, if I had any prospects! But by the time I meet somebody, plan a wedding…"

It made Imogene weary just thinking about it. She'd been over the math a million times. If she met somebody today, they could get engaged within a year, plan a wedding for the next year, and then start trying for a kid. Yeah. So far it hadn't happened that way.

"I'm done. I'm over it. Seriously, I know I can have a rich, full life even if I don't get married and have kids."

Faye shook her head. She had two little boys at home and her whole life revolved around them. She clearly couldn't imagine having a happy life without her kids.

"Immy," Dad said softly. "You've always wanted to get married and have a family. That's all you've talked about for years. I don't want to see you give up on it if that's what you really want."

It was true. For a very long time, all she wanted out of life was to get married and have kids. But she'd changed her mind. Was that so hard to understand?

"I mean, honey, what kind of life is there if you have no family?" Her father asked, his forehead worry lines deepening.

Like Faye, his whole life revolved around his children. Imogene had no idea what her father did when she and her sisters weren't around. He loved having the family over for visits. Other than that, he pretty much just hung around the house by himself as far as Imogene knew.

"I do have family. You guys! And I have friends and hobbies. Well, okay, I really don't have any hobbies, but that's exactly what I'm going to start working on. I'm done putting my life on hold waiting for some stupid prince to show up. What if he fell off his horse or got maimed or died or disowned by the king?"

"At least you'd be married-"

"I said screw the prince!"

Mrs. Ettles gasped and Mrs. Mortimer put her hand over her mouth.

"Maybe your standards are too high," her father said, oblivious to Imogene's rising fury. "Forget Prince Charming. You just need to find a nice, stable man who can take care of you."

Chrissy sucked in her breath and Faye literally backed away. That was exactly the wrong thing to say.

"Dad, I *do not need* a man to take care of me. And I am not going to settle for some stable, boring guy and spend the rest of my life washing his socks and underwear just so I can have a shiny ring on my finger. Agnes did just fine as a single woman and *so will I*!" Imogene slammed her hand down on the wooden end table.

Her father was startled by Imogene's outburst. He furrowed his brow. "Who's Agnes?"

"Never mind," Imogene grumbled. He wouldn't understand anyway. Nobody did.

He reached out and took his daughter's hand. "I didn't mean to upset you. And of course you don't need a man. That's not what I meant and I think you know that."

Imogene took a deep breath and nodded. Her dad had sounded terribly sexist just a moment ago, but that's not who he was. He was always proud of his wife and three daughters. Imogene's mom always took care of him and not the other way around. Living in a house full of women, he knew firsthand how strong they could be and he didn't harbor any antiquated notions about a woman needing a man to survive. He was just worried about her.

"It's just that having a family is the most important thing in the world. It's what life is all about."

"So my life has no meaning unless I get married and have kids?" Imogene asked.

"Imogene," her father said gently. "That's not what I said. I-"

"Dad, don't…" Faye said, shaking her head. "There's no reasoning with her right now."

"That's exactly what you said. That's what everybody says," Imogene yelled, getting more worked up by the minute. No wonder she felt so horrible about being single. Everybody, including her own family, treated her like a social reject. "I've heard it my whole life and to tell you the truth, I'm getting pretty damn sick of it!"

The old biddies gasped, clucked, and shook their heads, pitying the poor little dear. Ugh.

Imogene stomped out of the room and slammed the door, rattling the walls and sending a framed photograph of the dear departed Maddy crashing to the floor.

CHAPTER THREE

Ignoring her family's unsupportive attitude, Imogene quickly moved forward with her new life as a happy, independent single lady. Making such a dramatic 180-degree turn in her life, going from planning a future as a wife and mother to learning to embrace being alone, wasn't anywhere near as difficult as she had expected. She sure as hell didn't miss the dating scene and all the disappointment that came with it. The breakup with Nathan had been hard, especially because she had convinced herself he was The One. They had dated for a long time and things were going well enough. She had fun with him. Sometimes. Nathan was really sweet and had a good job. Definitely husband material. When he drove off to California in his rented BMW, Imogene felt like she was watching her dreams of marriage and family drive off with him. Imogene was determined never to let anyone else take control of her life, her dreams, ever again. She was in charge of her life now.

Imogene currently worked as a secretary in a family law firm. The firm, ironically, specialized in divorce. She liked her boss, Attorney Camille Towers, but it was a dead-end job. Imogene did her job well, but had no passion for it. There was no question in her mind that it was time to make a career change, but she had no idea what she wanted to do.

Imogene decided to start her new life with something simple. She was excited about the idea of learning to cook, so she sat down in front of her computer to find a cooking class to attend. She found an evening class at one of the local colleges, and felt a surge of excitement as she signed up for it.

By the time the cooking class started a few weeks later, Imogene was well on her way to reinventing herself. Her apartment looked totally different, complete with a new set of dishes with a girly, rose pattern on them, soft pink curtains for the windows and sliding patio door, and cat figurines placed strategically throughout the apartment. She also had a kitten calendar in the kitchen and cute little dish towels with cats on them. She had everything but an actual cat. As much as she loved them, she simply couldn't bring herself to be a single, cat lady. She was working so hard to be taken seriously as a modern, single woman who was doing fine without a man, and she feared the crazy cat lady stereotype would ruin that image.

Imogene practically skipped up the steps to the community college when it was finally time for the cooking class to start. She had arrived fairly early. The room was set up with two rows of counters, six counters in all. Each one came equipped with two tall chairs, so you'd be paired up with a partner. The counters were prepared with a roasting pan, some cooking utensils, and measuring cups and spoons. There were already some people paired up, so Imogene took a seat behind an empty counter. She scanned the room and saw a couple in their 30s, an older man in his 60s, and a few girls who were in their 20s. The room filled up quickly, but so far no one sat next to her. Just before the class was set to begin, an attractive woman with dark brown skin and friendly brown eyes walked in. She wore dangling earrings, skinny jeans, and a dark blue silk blouse, looking glamorous and casual at the same time. She glanced around the room, looking for an empty seat. Imogene smiled warmly at her, and the woman gratefully smiled back and slid into the seat next to her.

"Hi, I'm Imogene," she said, offering her hand.

"Adrienne," the woman responded, shaking her hand. "Nice to meet you. You know anything about cooking?"

"Yeah, a little. I know how to cook the basic boring stuff, but I'd really like to branch out. You?"

"Not a damn thing," Adrienne said, shaking her head. "But I need to start. I just got married a few months ago. I know it sounds so old-fashioned, but I'd like to be a wife who knows how to cook. Truth is, I always wanted to learn and he didn't have any interest, so we made a deal. I'll learn to cook and he promises to do all the dishes and clean up."

"Fair enough," Imogene said.

The classroom door opened and the teacher walked in. She was a little old woman who looked like she'd just gotten off the boat from Italy. She was short and squat with gray hair piled up on top of her head.

"Oh my God, it's Mama Celeste," Adrienne said, making Imogene laugh.

"Hello, class!" The old lady screamed.

"Mama Celeste on crystal meth," Imogene murmured, causing Adrienne to giggle.

"I'm skeered," Adrienne said under her breath.

"Me, too…"

"My name is Mrs. Letrillo," she said, still talking quite loudly.

"And I am hard of hearing…" Adrienne added for her. Imogene chuckled, and so did the older gentleman behind her.

"Who here knows how to roast a whole chicken?" asked Mrs.

Letrillo. Not one hand was raised. "Well, shame on all of you!" She glared around the room, which was so quiet all you could hear was the soft hum of the ceiling fan. Then she broke into a huge grin. "That's what you're here for. Let's get to it!"

The class broke into laughter. Mrs. Letrillo was a feisty little firecracker.

"Think we'll have to kill and pluck the chicken, too?" Imogene asked. Adrienne laughed again. The two of them giggled their way through that class, and pretty much every one that followed. Mrs. Letrillo was kind of a nut, but she knew her stuff. Imogene learned a lot quickly and had even more fun than she had expected.

Imogene also enrolled in a cake decorating class that met on a different night than the cooking one. It wasn't quite as entertaining without Adrienne by her side, but it was a blast nonetheless. Imogene was shocked to discover she had a real flair for cake-decorating. Who knew?

When the two-month *Intro to Cooking* class was over, Imogene and Adrienne decided to show off their new skills by throwing an old-fashioned dinner party. Imogene thought it would be the perfect opportunity to reconnect with some of her married friends. They had fallen out of touch after many of them had gotten married and the kids came along.

When she invited her friends to the dinner party, Imogene was sure to make two things clear: 1) their husbands were more than welcome to come and 2) she would not be bringing a date. She'd been prepared for her friends to hassle her in the same way her family had. To her surprise, she only had to provide a brief explanation which her friends readily accepted. Their attitude was, "If you're happy, more power to you!"

Imogene was bubbling over with excitement the day of the dinner party. She sang along with the radio as she set the table.

She'd bought a white lace tablecloth and eagerly put out her new dishes and silverware. She'd been in a rut for so long, it felt good to shake things up. Doing new things and seeing people she hadn't seen in a long time was great. She couldn't remember the last time she'd felt so enthusiastic.

Adrienne and her husband, Carl, arrived early so the two women could prepare the meal. Carl was a warm, friendly guy who was content to sit on the couch and watch TV while Imogene and Adrienne worked in the kitchen and the dining room.

No sooner had Carl settled comfortably on the couch, than Adrienne squealed and yelled for him to come back into the kitchen.

"Carl! You gotta come see this!"

Groaning good-naturedly, Carl obligingly heaved himself up from the couch and headed in to the kitchen.

"Damn," he said, genuinely impressed when Adrienne showed him the cake that Imogene had crafted for dessert. It was a three-tiered cake delicately frosted to look like a woven basket full of flowers.

"Right?" Adrienne exclaimed, sounding equally as impressed. "Imogene, that looks incredible! Let's eat it now." With that, she grabbed a fork and feigned an attack on the cake.

"Back off, you!" Imogene said, wielding a butter knife and waving it at Adrienne.

"Them's fightin' words!" Adrienne countered.

Carl smiled and shook his head. "I'm going back to the couch." He headed for the living room.

"Seriously, Imogene, this turned out amazing!"

"Nobody was more surprised than me. Just figured I'd take the class and try it out. It's really not that hard."

"Maybe not for you. I couldn't do it," Adrienne said, still

admiring the cake.

"All right," Imogene said, clapping her hands. "Let's do this thing!"

The two of them worked well together, in sync in Imogene's kitchen just as they had been in class. Everything was prepared and in the oven when the other two couples arrived.

Imogene felt a little nervous about being the only single person there, but she was determined not to feel awkward. You were only a third wheel if you acted like one. These people were her friends, and if she was comfortable with them bringing their spouses, then everyone would be at ease. She was the hostess, and would set the tone for the evening.

"Hey, girl!" Imogene exclaimed when her friend from college, Susan, arrived with her husband, Tim. Imogene couldn't help but notice that Susan sported the same *mommy hair* as her sister, Faye. Still, she looked great. Her dark brown hair touched her shoulders, and she wore a black cocktail dress. Even though it was an informal evening, they'd all decided to dress up for the occasion, lamenting that nobody threw dinner parties anymore, and maybe it was high time they started. Imogene was more than happy to be the one to restart the trend.

Tim looked good, if a bit tired. He wore a white, button-down shirt and nice slacks, but no tie. Imogene could understand why he looked exhausted. Susan and Tim had an infant and a two-year-old at home. She was sure they welcomed a night out of the house for some adult conversation, not to mention adult beverages.

"Margarita?" Imogene asked, holding up a glass.

"Hell, yeah!" Susan said.

"Tim, there's beer in the fridge." Imogene said.

"Say what?" Carl said, venturing back into the kitchen.

"Sorry, Carl! I should have offered you a beer a long time ago,"

Imogene said.

"For real!" Carl said with a grin.

"Hi. I'm Tim," he said, offering his hand.

"Carl." He shook Tim's hand, then grabbed two beers from the fridge.

"Carl, you're my new best friend," Tim said, eagerly accepting the beer. The two exchanged the usual "so what do you do" pleasantries, while Susan, Imogene, and Adrienne sipped margaritas and chatted about dinner.

The last couple, Kate and Robert, arrived a little later. Imogene was thrilled to see Kate. They'd been friends since grade school, but hadn't seen each other in months. Imogene had been the maid of honor at their wedding almost ten years ago. They looked slightly less tired than Susan and Tim, as their kids were six and eight. No doubt it was still tiring being parents, but at least kids that age were toilet-trained and could sleep through the night.

After downing a few margaritas and beers on empty stomachs, everyone was in a festive mood by the time they took their seats at the table. There were lots of oohs and ahhs over the fanciness of the table, followed by even more compliments when Adrienne brought out the dinner: roasted rosemary and garlic chicken, sliced and fried potatoes, and broccoli with cheese sauce. The meal turned out wonderfully, tasting as good as it looked and smelled.

"Tell you what, the money we spent on that cooking class was worth every penny," Carl said after eating a third helping of chicken and potatoes. "Little woman can really cook."

"Call me little woman one more time," Adrienne dared.

Carl laughed and put his arm around her. "You know I'm just messing with you."

Adrienne laughed and relaxed comfortably in his arms. Susan and Tim also touched each other frequently throughout the meal, but Imogene noticed that Kate and Robert didn't seem quite so intimate. Robert was a nice enough guy, but he looked bored throughout the evening, as if he were eager to get the night over with. It was a shame, because Kate seemed to be enjoying herself.

Imogene had never been crazy about Robert. He was okay, but he was hardly the type of man that she and Kate had dreamt of in high school. They'd spent countless hours on the phone and at the mall, talking about the guys they thought were hot and what kind of guy they thought they might marry. Kate ended up with Robert, and Imogene was still single. Imogene was starting to think maybe she'd gotten the better deal. Robert was nothing like the future husband Kate had envisioned. He was so ordinary, and there seemed to be little spark between them. Imogene knew it must be hard to keep the magic alive when you had little kids screaming and puking on you, but she'd always thought there should be more to marriage than what she saw between Kate and Robert.

"You almost ready to go, hon?" Robert asked Kate quietly the moment the last bite of dinner had been consumed. Kate didn't look like she was ready to leave.

"Oh, you have to see the dessert Imogene made!" Adrienne said. She jumped up from the table. "Want me to bring it in or do you want to?"

"You can. Just don't drop it," Imogene warned.

"Yeah, butterfingers," Carl said. Adrienne stuck her tongue out at him.

Imogene cleared a spot on the table and Adrienne, slowly and carefully, carried the three-tiered cake into the room.

"Daammnnn!" Kate exclaimed.

"That's what I said!" Carl said.

"That looks totally professional. You really did this?" Kate asked. Imogene nodded proudly. "That's incredible. You should go into the cake business."

"Really? You think?" Imogene asked.

"Oh, yeah. You know, you could start it as a side business and see how it goes. I know you're sick of the law firm."

"You got that right. I don't know. I'll think about it," Imogene said, feeling fairly excited about the idea.

"Think about it, Immy. Really," Susan added, admiring the cake. She laughed and looked at Tim. "Remember the cake I made for Hayley's birthday?"

His eyes opened wide. "No. No, I do not."

Susan laughed again and rubbed his back. "Good man. It was freakin' awful." Imogene began cutting into the cake, and Adrienne passed out slices.

"Ooh! Speaking of horrible cakes," Kate said. "I mean, not yours, Immy, I meant..." She looked at Susan who raised her eyebrow. "You know what I mean!"

The group dissolved into laughter. "Anyway, have you ever seen Cake Wrecks?" Kate continued. Imogene shook her head, and so did Susan. "You have *got* to see it. It's hilarious! Immy, do you have an iPad?"

"Sure!" Imogene jumped up to get it. She couldn't help but notice that Robert looked annoyed that his wife was prolonging the evening. Couldn't he just let Kate have fun for a while? There'd be plenty of time for him to sit on the couch watching TV and drinking beer later. At least, that's what Imogene figured he did at home, judging by the size of his belly. It had grown since the wedding.

Imogene got her iPad from the living room and brought it into the dining room. Ignoring Robert's annoyance, she also brought the pitcher of margaritas in from the kitchen. She topped off everyone's drinks and sat down next to Kate.

"Okay, check this out. It's this whole website dedicated to horrible cakes. Seriously, look at this." She pulled up the website, which showed page after page of cakes gone horribly wrong. A number of them were unintentionally X-rated, with everyday items like palm trees and coconuts or candlesticks resembling certain parts of the male anatomy. There were also cakes that were beautifully decorated, but contained messages like *Congratulations On Your Boob Job* or *Happy Birthday in Pink Frosting!!* It was funny anyway, but being loaded on margaritas made it even funnier. Adrienne, Susan, Kate, and Imogene were reduced to tears while Carl and Tim watched with great amusement. The men had slowed their drinking a while ago so they would be in condition to drive the women home. Tim and Carl seemed to enjoy watching their wives have fun, while Robert still looked tired and bored.

They ended the evening with hugs and promises to stay in touch. Imogene collapsed into bed, exhausted and still half drunk. The evening had been so much fun. It was wonderful to hang out with old friends and new friends, and it gave her a sense of peace to know that she really could be happy even if she wasn't married. It occurred to her that love and relationships really were what life was all about, but romantic relationships were just one kind of love. Family and friends were what made life worth living.

Imogene mentally congratulated herself on having such a profound revelation, especially since her head was still spinning from all the margaritas. She just hoped she would remember her epiphany in the morning....

CHAPTER FOUR

Imogene awoke the next day in a good mood, despite a slight hangover. The winter sunlight spilling into her bedroom was a little too bright for her condition. She got out of bed and headed to the kitchen for some ice water. She surveyed the damage from last night's festivities. The place was a mess, but that was okay. That was the price she paid for having a fun party with great friends. She put the radio on so she could sing along while she cleaned up.

Fortunately, she remembered her revelation from the previous night. It was hardly earth-shattering news, but it was significant. There was so much emphasis on romantic relationships these days, especially here in Florida, where you practically choked on Disneyfied fairydust. Everybody was so damn eager to find their perfect soulmate and ride off into the sunset, people forgot the other relationships in their lives. So many people lost themselves when they got married. It's fine to be a wife, but that didn't mean you stopped being a daughter, a sister, an aunt, and a friend. Those relationships were often neglected, even abandoned, after people got married.

Imogene found herself looking forward to Sunday dinner at her father's house. So often, she'd felt out of place there. Faye always had stories to share about what her kids were up to, and Chrissy and her husband, Liam, always seemed to have some exciting trip planned or some news about a job promotion. Imogene rarely had anything new to share about her dead-end job and non-existent love life.

Not anymore. Her family knew she had taken cooking classes, but she hadn't mentioned the cake decorating one. She wanted that to be a surprise. After she finished cleaning the apartment, she was going to bake a fancy cake to bring to dinner. She could hardly contain her excitement. She loved having so many things to look forward to now. She used to just sit around her apartment watching television on the weekend. It was much more fun to spend the day baking and decorating a cake and singing along with the radio. It felt so good to have accomplishments and goals to talk about at Sunday dinner. She didn't have to be the weird, unmarried aunt anymore.

Her father greeted her warmly when she arrived at the house. She felt the familiar pang of sadness when she walked into the room. The house still smelled faintly of her mother's perfume, even though she'd died more than three years ago. No matter how many husbands and children were added to the Sunday gathering, the place still felt slightly empty without her. Nobody ever sat in her place at the table next to her dad. That seat still belonged to Mom.

"Hi, baby. How you doin'?" her father asked.

"Fine. Really good actually," Imogene responded. It was amazing how making a conscious decision not to feel bad could actually work. She saw her sisters snuggling with their husbands on the couch and, for the first time in a long time, she didn't feel jealous or lonely. She was just fine.

"Aunt Im'jean!" cried her four-year-old nephew, Marcus.

"Come here, stinker," Imogene scooped up Faye's little boy in her arms and whirled him around. He giggled madly and Imogene's heart soared. It rocked being an aunt. All the fun of having kids and none of the responsibility. She'd play with the kids today and then sleep soundly through the night once she got home. According to Faye, it was a rare night that one or both of her kids didn't wake up. Two-year-old Allen toddled over and Imogene put Marcus down on the kitchen floor.

"Okay, you're old news. Come here, Allen!" She grabbed the toddler and kissed his cheek.

"Hey!" Marcus yelled and grabbed Imogene's leg.

"I'm just kiddin' ya, cutie pie. So, how's life, Faye?" Imogene asked. Faye laughed as she tried to have a conversation with her sister while her two sons clung to Imogene's legs. Kids still attached, Imogene staggered over to where her sister sat on the couch.

"Oh, you know. Same as ever. Lots of noise. What's new with you?"

"I finished my cooking class."

"That's nice," Faye said, sounding bored already.

Imogene tried not to notice how her family members never seemed to be excited about what she was up to. Husbands and grandchildren always took precedence. She hoped they might take her a bit more seriously once they saw the cake she'd crafted for dessert. It had turned out pretty amazing, if she did say so herself. It was so strange; until she'd taken the cooking classes, she'd had no idea that she'd possessed any kind of talent like that. Maybe she really could make a career out of it. She certainly loved it as a hobby.

It took a while to wrangle the two kids and get everybody settled at the dinner table. Her dad wasn't a bad cook. He tended to make simple recipes like her mom did, but the food was pretty good. Today's menu was spaghetti and meatballs with garlic bread.

"So Allen, tell everybody your big news!" Faye said to her toddler in a booster seat next to her. He shot her a clueless look, so she whispered something to him.

Allen's eyes got wide. "Oh yeah! I went poopy in the potty!"

"All right, 'lil man!" Chrissy said as she high-fived him.

"Nice job, kiddo!" Dad said enthusiastically. "You're a big boy, aren't you?"

"Yup!" Allen said, then proceeded to stick a green pea up his nose. Big boy indeed. Faye grabbed a napkin, retrieved the pea, and scolded her son.

"So, Liam and I went out with Jenna and Anthony the other night," Chrissy said.

"Oh, yeah? How they doing?" Dad asked with great interest. Jenna had been one of Chrissy's best friends in high school, and Imogene's parents had both been quite fond of her. All of their friends had always been welcome in the house, and their dad had enjoyed watching them grow up and seeing how they turned out.

"She's pregnant!"

"Wow, that's great! Tell her congrats from me," Dad said, smiling as grabbed a big hunk of garlic bread.

"Me, too. That's really great," Faye said.

"When's she due?" Imogene asked. It was hard to imagine silly little Jenna being a mother. She still pictured her as the teenager with too much eyeliner who was obsessed with Coldplay.

"Sometime in May," Chrissy responded.

"That's nice. Tell her I'm very excited for her!" Imogene said. She was amazed when she realized how much she meant it. Just a few weeks ago, the notion that Chrissy's goofy little high school friend was not only married but was knocked up would have severely depressed her. Yet another girl in her twenties was happily married with a baby on the way while Imogene had remained single. Now, Imogene was so busy doing things she loved and having fun that it just didn't bother her like it used to.

"Speaking of old friends, I had dinner the other night with Kate and Susan," Imogene said.

"Oh, that's great. How are they?" Dad asked.

"Good. Very good. They came to my place with their husbands. It was so much fun. My friend from cooking class, Adrienne, and I made this incredible dinner for everybody. I can't believe how well it turned out! I'm so glad I took that class. Shoulda done it years ago," she said as she twirled pasta on her fork.

"Isn't that girl Adrienne married?" Faye asked.

"Yeah. Her husband is so nice."

"Soooo, you were the only one there who was…" Chrissy began.

Imogene narrowed her eyes. "Without a husband. Yes."

"Did you bring anybody?" Faye asked.

"You mean did I bribe a homeless guy at the bus station to pretend to be my date? No. No, I did not. There is nothing wrong with hanging out with married people without bringing a date," Imogene informed them.

"Wasn't it, you know, awkward?" Chrissy said. She wrinkled her nose at the thought.

"You mean did they make me feel like a total loser like you guys are doing right now?"

"Jeez, don't get all defensive," Chrissy said.

"It's natural to get defensive when you're being attacked," Imogene replied frostily. She took a bite of spaghetti before she said anything she might regret later. *Might* regret.

"I'm done!" Marcus announced as he jumped down from the

table.

My sentiments exactly, Imogene thought.

Faye chased Marcus down so she could hose him off before he spread spaghetti sauce all over the living room. He got a lot more on his face than in his mouth. Kids could be great tension-breakers, that was for sure.

After the adults finished eating, it was time for dessert.

"I have a cool surprise for you guys. I brought dessert. Lemme go get it." Imogene had stashed the cake in the fridge in the garage so she could keep it hidden until after dinner.

"Dessert! Yaaaaaay!" Marcus said as he ran back into the dining room and hopped back into his seat. Perhaps he wasn't done after all.

Imogene carried the cake into the dining room and set it down in the middle of the table.

"Wow!" Marcus said, his eyes growing huge.

"Wow is right," Faye agree. "That is beautiful!"

A thrill of excitement shot through Imogene as she watched her family survey her handiwork. The 9" x 13" cake had white frosting with delicately-sculpted pink ribbons and roses. She still couldn't believe how well it had turned out.

"Why'd you get something so expensive just for Sunday dinner?" Chrissy asked.

Imogene smiled at her. "I didn't buy it. I made it."

"No way! You made this?" Chrissy looked astonished.

"Yep. After the cooking class was over, I took a cake decorating class and it turns out I don't suck at it."

"That's an understatement. This is really impressive!" Dad said. He kissed his daughter on top of her head.

"It's so pretty. I hate to cut into it!" Faye said.

"I want some! I want some!" Marcus hollered.

Imogene chuckled and said, "I don't think you have much of a choice." She handed a knife to Faye, who quickly cut a piece of cake for her son to shut him up. It didn't work.

"Dis is good, An Imjean," he said with a mouthful of cake.

"Don't talk with your mouth full, kiddo," Richard corrected.

"K, I won't," Marcus said, spilling cake out of his mouth. Richard and Faye exchanged a weary but genuine smile.

"This is incredible, Immy," Chrissy said. "So this is what you're doing with your time these days, huh?"

Imogene shot her a questioning look. It was hard to tell what her sister had meant by that, but it didn't sound complimentary.

"Yeah. Learning to cook and bake and getting back in touch with friends," Imogene said with an edge to her voice. Faye and Chrissy shared a look that gave Imogene the distinct impression that they'd been talking about her behind her back. "What? What is that look about?"

"Nothing," Faye said in a tone of voice that meant the opposite. "It's just, we've been thinking that lately you've been kind of in denial…"

Richard and Liam exchanged a weary look as if to say *Here it comes…*This was a catfight in the making and there was nothing they could do to stop it.

"Denial about what?" Imogene asked as she chopped off a huge slice of cake. She had a feeling she was going to need comfort food to get through this conversation.

"I don't know. Life in general, I guess," Chrissy said, glancing at Liam who refused to make eye contact with her. He wasn't about to get involved. "I mean, all these little projects of yours are cute…" She gestured toward the cake.

Imogene slowly put down her fork. "Cute little projects…."

Chrissy looked alarmed at Imogene's tone. "I don't mean

anything by it."

"Oh, you never do."

"It's just...I don't know. Is this really what you plan on doing for the rest of your life?"

"Maybe. I was thinking of maybe starting a cake business on the side. You know, see what happens."

"Well, okay, yeah," Faye chimed in. "That's fine, you know, for a hobby."

"Oh, thank God you approve," Imogene said.

"You gotta admit, it's not exactly a life plan."Chrissy said.

"Oh, and you know what my life plan should be?" Imogene asked, eyes blazing. She looked at Chrissy, then at Faye. "What exactly are you trying to say?"

"We're just...concerned," Faye said. "We're concerned that you're throwing your life away by refusing get married. You're gonna regret it, Immy. You just are. You're gonna get older and you're gonna regret it."

"Since when is refusing to settle refusing to get married?" Imogene demanded. She wished she hadn't already put her fork down so she could slam it down onto her plate.

"Well, you've totally given up on trying to find a husband."Faye said.

"So what? I'm a total loser just because I'm not married?" Imogene said, stunned at how hurt she felt when just moments earlier she had felt so proud of herself and her accomplishments.

"Of course you're not a loser, baby doll." Dad said gently. "Nobody thinks that."

Imogene couldn't help but notice that Faye and Chrissy remained silent.

"We just don't want you to regret not getting married and having children. It's like the most important thing in life," Faye said.

"*Like* says who?" Imogene said mockingly.

"It's just a fact," Chrissy said as if she were stating that the sky was blue. Imogene half-expected her to add the word "duh."

"It really is, though, Imogene," Dad said softly. "Family is what's important."

"Yes, family and friends are what's important in life, but that doesn't mean just husband and wife and kids. Quit acting like I'm some superficial career-oriented bitch with no respect for family. That is not who I am!"

"Of course not!" Dad exclaimed. He looked worried about his daughter, but clearly didn't understand what she was getting all worked up about.

"Look, don't get all huffy," Chrissy said. "We're just concerned. You always said you wanted to be a wife and mother."

"I also said I wanted to be a Power Ranger. Things change when you grow up!" Imogene said.

"I wanna be a Power Ranger!" Marcus said. He swung his fork around, spraying cake crumbs everywhere.

"Kiddo, you can be whatever you want to be and don't let anybody tell you different!" Imogene told him.

"K." Marcus said nonchalantly.

"Imogene," Faye began gently. "Your entire life, you've always wanted to get married and now you've changed your mind and decided to stay single."

"Did it ever occur to you that maybe I've had my mind changed for me?" Imogene said softly. "I'm thirty years old and I haven't met anyone that I want to spend the rest of my life with. I figured I could either be sad and depressed, or I could celebrate my life and feel good about myself. And I *was* feeling good. Until I came here."

"Honey," Dad said soothingly as he reached across the table to hold her hand. "We didn't mean to make you feel bad. We just don't want to see you give up."

"I am *not*...you know what? Never mind. Just...never mind. I don't want to talk about it anymore. Change of subject. Allen? What's new with you?"

"I ated a bug yesterday," replied the two-year-old proudly.

"Good for you, buddy. Good for you." Imogene told him.

CHAPTER FIVE

After spending a particularly mind-numbing eight hours at the law office on Monday, Imogene was more determined than ever to get a new job. She sat at the computer in her living room perusing job listings while sipping a glass of wine. She half-listened to the television for background noise while she searched. So far, nothing in the online classifieds had taken her fancy. Most of the jobs listed either seemed as boring as her current job or were completely out of her league.

Imogene felt a tingle of excitement when she stopped googling full-time jobs and started looking for information on starting a small business. It would be so much fun if she could actually sell designer cakes for a living! She felt so optimistic every time she imagined a future in which she was a successful businesswoman with a full social life filled with friends and hobbies.

She felt happy, that is, until she thought of all the terrible things her sisters had said to her. They were convinced she would become a bitter old woman if she never married. Imogene did her best to push thoughts of her sisters out of her mind so she could focus on the future. She managed to do just that until she started paying attention to the television.

"As everyone knows, a woman's wedding day is the single most important day of her life. It's every little girl's dream to find her handsome prince and live happily ever after. Her whole life has been leading up to the moment when she finally walks down the aisle."

Imogene slowly turned her head toward the TV to see what idiotic female was spouting this offensive, outdated garbage.

"I should have known." Imogene said as she stared at the television.

The idiotic female was Lindsay Saga, wedding planner for minor celebrities and anyone else rich enough to afford her services. She orchestrated ridiculously lavish affairs that rivaled royal weddings. In fact, after Kate and William had tied the knot, there was no shortage of brides-to-be planning copycat services. Weddings often included a knockoff royal gown, a crown, and even a horse and carriage. Imogene wouldn't have been surprised if some couples actually hired throngs of admirers to stand outside and wave to them as if they were actually royalty.

Imogene couldn't stand Lindsay Saga. She'd seen her on a few talk shows and Lindsay seemed to think that a wedding was the most important thing in every woman's life. Even when Imogene was still on the husband-hunt, she'd thought the woman was an idiot.

"The bride is the envy of every girl in the world!" Lindsay continued, further fueling Imogene's rising anger.

Imogene stared at Lindsay's fake, red-lipsticked smile. She was in her late forties at least. She could be a lot older, but it was hard to tell, given the amount of plastic surgery she must have had. She had shiny brown hair that was too long for whatever age she actually was. She was always impeccably groomed with elegant fingernails, diamond earrings, and designer suits. Imogene pitied whatever hapless assistants might work for her, as Lindsay likely had the whole Devil-Wears-Prada thing going on. She exuded a bossy chilliness and probably loved lording over her underlings.

"A beautiful, white wedding is such a wonderful, happy event not only for the bride, but for her bridesmaids and women everywhere. It gives other women hope for their future. Every single girl out there can dream of her own blessed wedding day when she truly becomes a woman."

Imogene's jaw dropped open. *She did not really just say that.* A jolt of rage-fueled adrenaline shot through her.

She shouted at the television. "Oh, so not only am I pathetic, but I'm not even a *woman* now?"

The friendly interviewer talking politely to Lindsay was undisturbed by her offensive comments. In fact, the moron was sitting there smiling, nodding, as if Lindsay was spewing forth brilliance instead of the sexist, corrosive nonsense that was her credo.

Imogene was so incensed that she hardly knew what to do. She could scream and yell at the TV, but what good would that do? Nobody would hear her except her neighbors. She knew she had to do something, anything, to vent the anger and heartbreak that had been building since she'd announced her decision to quit manhunting and be happy. Though her friends were supportive, she'd gotten nothing but grief from her family and now here was this wedding-obsessed woman on television telling the world that single people should be ashamed. If she didn't do something, Imogene felt she might have a stroke.

Imogene turned back to her computer. A blog entry. Yes! That would do it. Like 98% of the population, she had her own blog. And, like 95% of *that* population, she had grown bored with it and let it languish for months. Nobody ever read the damn thing anyway and they probably wouldn't now. Still, it would at least make her feel like she was *doing* something.

Imogene typed the headline of her blog in all capital letters: *WHY I HATE MARRIED PEOPLE AND WHY YOU SHOULD, TOO!!*

> *Somewhere along the line, married people decided that single people were vastly inferior to them, and somehow, we singles started agreeing with them.*
>
> *Married people decided that you must be married or your life simply doesn't matter. Your life doesn't truly "begin" until you march down the aisle. I am sick to death of that condescending attitude from couples, forever trying to fix my life. Who said my life needed fixing??*

Imogene jumped up from her computer.

"Yeah, who the hell asked you?" she yelled out. She paced for a second, then ran back to the computer, leaning over to type instead of sitting down.

> *Who the hell asked you?*

Imogene paced back and forth again, trying to quash thoughts of the numerous times she had asked, begged even, her friends to set her up with guys in an effort to "fix" her life. Still, now that she had decided she was done with all that, nobody respected her choice. And that wasn't fair, dammit. She took a deep breath and sat back down in the chair.

> *Believe it or not, there are women who actually think about things other than rings, weddings, and running off into the sunset with some jackass who's only going to grow a*

beer belly and man boobs before we've paid off the second mortgage we took out to pay for our overblown, freak show, circus of a wedding.

Maybe if married Americans spent more time working on the high divorce rate rather than trying to force the rest of us into their little club of failure, marriage wouldn't be such a mess right now.

So, as an American woman, I should be free and able to make my own decisions, so I hereby say to married and otherwise coupled America – BACK OFF!

Imogene yelled that last line out loud. She sat back in her chair. She thought she was done with her rant, but was suddenly seized with more anger and realized she had more to say.

It's perfectly acceptable to be married and then divorced—even multiple times. NOBODY questions that. I've got nothing against divorced people, but why are we single people criticized for not making that mistake in the first place? WE didn't marry the dumbass. YOU did!!!

Imogene jumped up and paced some more.

"Let's see, what else, what else…" she muttered to herself. "Kids!"

Imogene plopped back down in her seat.

I am so tired of people telling singles that our lives are worthless if we don't get married and have kids. They say that the whole point of life is to procreate and if we don't, well, we're just a waste of oxygen and carbon dioxide, now, aren't we? Too bad. That Mother Theresa could have really made a difference in this world if only she had popped out some kids.

Imogene was about to jump up and start pacing again, but then something else occurred to her.

It's time to STOP treating weddings like they're royal events reserved only for chosen, special people. Anybody with ten bucks can get a marriage license. Get a pilot or taxidermy license, then maybe I'll be impressed.

Imogene stopped typing for a moment. She realized that it wouldn't be enough to just complain about how badly single people were treated. She wanted to do something to make a difference, and not just for her own sake, but for every other woman out there who was made to feel like she wasn't good enough without a man. No matter how liberated people thought they were, everyone still thought there was something wrong with a woman who didn't get married. Imogene couldn't help but wonder…What would Agnes McCann do?

Then Imogene got an idea. There had to be millions of single people out there who felt just as abused and mistreated as she did. She just had to find them and get them together.

It's not enough to just complain about the abuse we endure as single people. It's time we banded together and had our single voices heard. We need to show the world our power and our strength. We need to show everyone that our lives do matter. NOW. Not when or if we get married, and not when or if we have children. We are people NOW and it's time we formed a group to show our singles power.

Imogene thought for a moment, then got a better idea. She deleted the last two words from her blog, then replaced *singles power* with *solo power*. She liked the play on solar power.

"Solo Power! That's it. We'll form a group to show our Solo Power. And now, to send this little blog entry to every human being I know. Facebook! Twitter! My whole address book!"

Imogene took a moment to think before hitting send. Maybe she needed to cool off a bit before sending her rant out into the world. She took a deep breath and considered waiting at least a few hours until she was sure she wanted to do this.

"Screw that. I'm mad now!"

She hit send with a flourish.

CHAPTER SIX

The more Imogene thought about it, the more fired up she got about forming a singles group. She decided to get started immediately. She arranged for the first Solo Power meeting to be held in a library conference room set aside for book clubs and other small gatherings. It was a cozy room with fuzzy, soft blue carpeting. There were long tables and folding chairs set up, but there were also some comfy armchairs. The place reminded her of a lounge in an old folks' home.

Imogene was both nervous and exhilarated at the same time. It thrilled her to think of meeting other women who were in the same boat she was. To hear her family talk, you'd think she was the last unmarried thirty-something woman alive. She was eager to meet like-minded single ladies that she could befriend and even commiserate with. Imogene was serious about embracing being single, but that didn't mean it would always be easy. She knew there were bound to be single women who still felt the way she used to feel—like there was something wrong with her because she didn't have a significant other. Forget what her stupid sisters said. Imogene couldn't wait to inspire other single people to be happy just like she was. She moved to the blackboard, picked up a piece of chalk, and wrote SOLO POWER in large letters as she wondered how many people would show up.

Three. The answer was three.

The three people who showed up arrived at the same time and at first Imogene thought they had come together. As it turned out, they didn't know each other.

Imogene tried to smile warmly, but her stomach sank as she surveyed the three, none of whom was a woman her age. There was an old lady, probably in her sixties, an obese teenage girl, and a man. It never occurred to Imogene that a man might show up to one of these meetings. Sure, there were lots of guys who were single, but nobody gave them a hard time. If you were a single guy, you were a hero and the envy of all your married friends. If you were a single girl, you were a charity case.

Imogene's heart ached with disappointment as she looked at the meager group. She figured the older woman was probably widowed. She was tall, fairly thin, and had short gray-white hair that she wore straight instead of having one of those little-old-lady type perms. She sported large, white plastic earrings, a light pink pastel shirt, and white pants. The outfit was the type retired people wore when they went on cruises. She'd probably been married for forty years and was newly single. Imogene worried that the old broad would be just like Aunt Maddy and preach to her about how she should get married, just like her and her dearly-departed Edgar, or whatever her dead husband's name was.

And what about that… big girl? She couldn't have been more than sixteen or seventeen years old. So what if she was single at that age? Lots of teenagers were. Imogene felt a stab of sympathy for her, as the girl must have weighed at least 250 pounds. She had shoulder-length brown hair, brown eyes, and was rather short, compounding her weight problem.

The man was about Imogene's age, average-looking, tall, and

on the skinny side. He had light brown hair, blue-grayish eyes, and had a friendly, warm look about him. Imogene wondered if he was gay.

Imogene surveyed the tiny group and took a deep breath before addressing them.

"Well! I want to thank you for coming tonight in support of singles everywhere." She felt her earlier enthusiasm waning. Tonight's meeting would be a complete waste of time. She would have to work harder on publicity for the next gathering, but for now she was stuck with what she had. She had no choice but to soldier on. "My name is Imogene Hart, and I started this group to change the way we're treated as single people. I mean, everybody acts like there's something wrong with us, like we have a disease or something, and that needs to stop."

"Damn right!" the older woman called out.

Imogene blinked. Wow, that was unexpected.

"Uh, yes! What's your name, Ma'am?" Imogene asked politely.

"Don't call me Ma'am, and we'll get along fine," the woman said with a smile. "My name's Paula. Paula Flandey."

"Nice to meet you," Imogene said. She looked over at the man.

"I'm Matt. Matt McFarland."

"Hannah Wanderling," the heavy girl said.

"Well, welcome Paula, Matt, and Hannah. So glad you came out tonight," Imogene said, feeling her spirits lift slightly. "I don't know about you, but I'm sick and tired of being treated like I'm crazy because I'm not married!"

"Me too!" Paula said. "I've been single, by choice mind you, my entire life and nobody can understand that I'm happy this way! I got nothing against men—dated a few in my day—but I never had any interest in getting married. I knew that from the time I was very young and I never changed my mind. Nobody can accept that. Nobody! Got nothin' but pity and condescending comments my whole life because I don't have some old, fat, balding man lyin' in bed next to me. Don't tell *me* I got nothin' to offer this world just because I don't have a wedding ring on this old finger!"

Imogene just stared at Paula for a moment.

"Oooh, I like you..." she said, offering Paula her fist. Paula bumped it eagerly. Imogene was impressed with Paula's outlook. This chick was nothing like her Aunt Maddy. She was much more like Imogene imagined Agnes must have been.

Imogene turned toward the lone male in the room. "So, what's your story?"

"I'm not gay!" Matt said, a little too loudly.

"Um, well. Okay..." Great. A homophobe. Just what she needed. Imogene was prepared to hear him out and then unload on him for his prejudicial and judgmental ways.

"Look, I have *no* problem with gays. I've marched in dozens of parades in support of their rights. Rights we shouldn't *have* to fight for, since they *should* be guaranteed by the Constitution!"

Imogene's eyes widened. Okay. Once again, that was unexpected. She was starting to realize that maybe *she* was the judgmental one. So far, Paula and Matt were totally different from what she'd first assumed.

"My little brother's gay, so..." Paula and Hannah nodded, understanding. Imogene was happy to note that Paula seemed to be totally on board with the whole gay thing. You never knew how older people would react when it came to that subject. They were from a different generation after all. "He's getting married soon!" Matt's eyes twinkled with pride, and Imogene found herself warming toward him. Too bad he wasn't her type, because he seemed sweet. "Anyway, just because I'm over thirty and unmarried, people assume I'm gay."

Imogene nodded, feeling guilty since that's exactly what she had assumed about him.

"I mean, it doesn't offend me if people think I'm gay, it's just...you know..."

"People thinkin' you're gay puts a crimp in your love life," Paula finished for him.

"Yeah, exactly!" Matt said, laughing. "But you know, people assuming I'm gay isn't the worst thing about being a single guy. I swear, if one more person tells me to *settle down* and get married, I'm gonna punch 'em." He ticked off his points on his fingers. "I have a steady job. I have a nice, reliable car. I own my own home. How much more *settled* and *responsible* am I supposed to be?"

Imogene nodded and was about to respond when Matt continued his spiel.

"I just hate the stereotype that single guys are totally aimless and irresponsible. Like I've got beer bottles and empty pizza boxes all over my place. Not a chance. I'm actually a very good housekeeper. My house is neat as a pin, thank you very much."

"But you're not gay," Imogene said, laughing.

Matt laughed too, and shook his head. Imogene was glad to see that he had such a good sense of humor. "No. Not gay. Just neat and responsible."

"So, if you don't mind me asking, why don't you want to get married?" Imogene asked. She had wound up single by default, so it was hard for her to understand why anyone would choose to be single. She made a mental note to ask Paula the same question at some point.

"No, no, I don't mind. Okay, don't get mad or anything..." Matt looked anxiously at the three females in the room. Poor guy was outnumbered. "It's just that so many of my friends got married to these well, bit- I mean, you know, *shrews* who try to control everything they do. I don't want to ask for permission every time I want to go fishing or something. I just want to be able to go when I want to."

"Makes sense," Paula said.

"And the way some of these wives talk to their husbands," Matt said, shaking his head. "I mean, look. I'm not saying it's all the women's fault. Of course not. But sometimes they say such mean things to their husbands. And in public! I'm like, you know, embarrassed for my friends. Who needs a wife who belittles you and makes you feel like less of a man?"

"I know what you mean," Imogene said. She'd always thought a spouse was supposed to be supportive and be your best friend. Lots of times it just didn't work out that way. "I work in a family law firm and I've seen some pretty awful stuff."

Matt nodded. "Yeah, I guess you have. I mean, you wonder how you go from happily walking down the aisle, to, you know, *that*."

Imogene shook her head and then turned to Hannah. "What about you, Hannah? What brings you here?" Imogene spoke softly to the girl. She was so young and there was an air of vulnerability to her. Being so heavy, it couldn't be easy for her. High school was rough enough as it was.

"Look at me. I'm never getting married," Hannah said softly with a touch of bitterness. She looked down at the floor. The others exchanged nervous glances, a silent agreement passing among them to don kid gloves when dealing with Hannah.

"What do you mean?" Imogene pressed gently.

"I'm fat," Hannah said bluntly. "I'm huge. I'd have to lose like 100 pounds, minimum, for any guy to give me even half a chance."

"Oh, sweetheart, that's not true!" Paula said. "You're a lovely girl. And so young! If you don't want to get married, sweetie, I can certainly respect that, but you shouldn't give up because you think you're not good enough for a man."

"Exactly!" Imogene agreed. Her heart went out to the girl. "Besides, if guys don't think you're good enough, that's their problem, not yours. If some shallow idiot only wants a size eight woman, you don't want him anyway." She thought about all those idiots with nasty bumper stickers like NO FAT CHICKS on their redneck-mobiles and she felt a new rage build up inside her. There certainly were lots of fat men who still expected to be able to date supermodels.

"Well, I happen to think you're very pretty!" Matt chimed in, smiling at Hannah. He looked as if he really meant it, too. Hannah blushed. Those words obviously meant a lot to her coming from a man.

"You're all so nice. Really. But I'm just being realistic." Hannah said. She was clearly resigned to her fate and trying to make the best of it. "My mom is as big as I am and she has a boyfriend, but she was just plain lucky. I'm gonna spend the rest of my life alone, so I might as well get used to it."

"See? This is exactly what we need to change," Imogene said. "*If you don't get married*—and I'm not saying you won't—it's not a bad thing and it doesn't mean you'll end up alone! You can lead a very full life with family and friends and whatever makes you happy. Ugh! I can't stand that young girls grow up thinking that a wedding is the ultimate victory and that they're miserable failures if they don't land themselves a stupid man!"

Matt cleared his throat and folded his arms.

"No offense," Imogene said. Matt grinned at her to show there was none taken. Imogene noticed that Hannah looked depressed. "That's what you think, isn't it?"

Hannah shrugged, which got Imogene more fired up. She thumped her foot on the floor and stood up with a loud sigh. She grabbed a blue dry erase marker and wrote *SINGLE PEOPLE ARE NOT LOSERS!* in big letters on the white board attached to the wall.

"Okay, what else do we hate about the way people treat us?" Imogene asked the others.

Paula was the first to respond. "I hate how people act so shocked that I'm a lifelong single. When people find out I never married, they look at me like I just told them I never heard of pancakes," Paula cocked her head to the side and, with an exaggerated expression on her face "What?! You've never…*what?!* You can't be *serious!*" That got a big laugh from everyone in the room. Certainly, everyone could identify with that experience. "I think they'd feel better if they found out I was a widow. To them, that's perfectly acceptable. Do you know people actually bring me casseroles and food like I'm in mourning? Do I look like I can't take care of myself?"

Imogene wrote *Shock and Pity* on the board.

"I really hate that people think marriage equals adulthood," Matt said. "Just because I'm a single guy doesn't mean I'm some overgrown frat boy. I'm doing just fine. I don't need a wife to take care of me."

Imogene nodded enthusiastically. "I know exactly what you mean. My dad's always saying he hopes I'll find a man to take care of me. And here I thought he was just being sexist. I guess it's not just me."

"Nope. I know my family means well, but…" Matt rolled his eyes and shook his head.

Imogene wrote: *MARRIAGE DOES NOT MEAN RESPONSIBLE AND BEING SINGLE DOES NOT MEAN*

IRRESPONSIBLE!

"This is great stuff, guys," Imogene said, looking proudly at her new group. "I think what I hate, hate, *hate* the most is that everybody assumes that having a wedding is every girl's dream come true!"

Imogene was happy to note that Hannah nodded eagerly at that one and looked just as annoyed as she was.

"I never sat around dreaming about the day when I would dress up like a Fairy Princess and lord over everybody on *my* day," Imogene said. She may have spent an awful lot of time imagining her future life with a husband and family, but she really never dwelled that much on the wedding itself. Sure, she had thought about it, but it was never a huge deal to her. Still, it would have been nice... "A wedding is not a goal! It's a huge, overglorified, self-indulgent party!"

"Amen to that!" Paula shouted.

The door to the conference room swung open as Imogene wrote *A wedding is not a goal!* on the board. A library employee, a woman in her fifties, frowned at Imogene. Her name tag read JUDY.

"I'm afraid you'll need to keep it down in here," Judy said.

"Oops, sorry. We'll be good!" Imogene promised. Judy nodded, glared at the other three, then left the room.

"Ha-ha. You got in trouble," Matt teased in a singsong voice. Imogene chuckled. She turned around and wrote *dying alone* on the board.

"If had a nickel for every time I heard that one," Paula muttered.

"I know," Imogene said "It's so stupid. Having a spouse in no way guarantees that you won't die alone. Most people die in hospitals and nursing homes and whatever, so it doesn't even matter if you still have a living spouse," Imogene said.

She thought for a moment, then wrote *romance is a lie* on the whiteboard.

When she turned around, she noticed Matt raising an eyebrow.

"All my life, I've been fed the lie that some guy will come and sweep me off my feet," Imogene sighed heavily. "All those romance novels, romantic comedies, and bridal magazines that promised we could all meet some cute, charming guy who was witty and handsome and every girl's dream come true…" Imogene made a mental note to throw out all those corny, embarrassing romance novels she had in her apartment. Since she had decided to live her life man-free, she really had no use for them anymore.

Imogene tried to ignore the depressed look on Hannah's face. She didn't like that Hannah had already given up on meeting a man, but she figured it was probably best that she learned the truth about romance sooner rather than later.

Romance is demeaning to women.

"The idea that a woman needs to be rescued by a man is insulting. That kind of crap starts when we're kids. Fairy Tales and all that. God knows we're constantly fed all that princess garbage, especially living this close to Orlando," Imogene said.

Paula rolled her eyes and nodded. They were surrounded by Disney princess signs and billboards. This part of Florida was practically blanketed in fairy dust. Imogene hadn't really thought that much about it until now, probably because she had always enjoyed fantasizing about romance. She had to put all that behind her. It wouldn't be easy, but she could do it. It really was degrading, the idea that women were supposed to be sitting around and waiting for some guy to come along and make their lives complete. You certainly didn't see men doing that. They were too busy concentrating on their jobs, getting promoted, and actually doing something with their lives.

"Princesses," Hannah said, rolling her eyes. She spoke quietly, as if to herself. "Lazy bitches just sitting around the castle all day waiting for a prince to show up. At least Cinderella cleaned the joint once in a while, even if she did get the mice to do most of the dirty work for her."

Imogene, Paula, and Matt laughed, which clearly took Hannah by surprise. She looked as if she hadn't expected anyone to hear her, let alone find her comment amusing.

"Good point. Who wants a broad who just hangs around the house all day looking pretty? Bo-ring!" Matt said. He looked at Imogene. "Keep in mind the whole romance thing puts a lot of pressure on guys, too, ya know. I'm not a mind reader. How am I supposed to know what girls want?" Matt asked.

Imogene nodded. Fair enough. She wrote on the board: *Romance puts unrealistic pressure on guys, too.* She thought for a moment, and then could actually feel her blood pressure start to rise as she remembered one of the most insulting things of all that people said about singles.

Imogene wrote: *Your life is meaningless if you don't have kids. You don't know what life is about until you have a child.*

"Oh, man. You don't even want to get me started on that one!" Paula bellowed. Hannah sat up and looked interested in what Paula had to say about this particular topic.

Judy the librarian poked her head back in and shot them a disapproving look.

Paula held her hand up. "My fault."

Judy nodded sternly, then shut the door.

"People at my church love to say that. That the good Lord intended for us all to 'be fruitful and multiply.' Look, I was a pediatric oncology nurse for 38 years," Paula said. "I played games and told jokes to kids getting ready for chemo. I threw parties for them when they finally got to go home. I held weeping parents in my arms when they had to say their final goodbyes. Don't tell me my life had no meaning!" Paula spoke with a fiery passion. She glared at the door, as if daring Shushy Judy to poke her head in again so she could give her the what-for.

"Wow. Paula, that's incredible," Hannah said. Paula nodded, clearly proud of her work.

Paula turned to face Hannah. "Sweetie, whether you get married or not, your life will have meaning. Do you know what you want to be when you grow up?"

Hannah shook her head. "Not yet."

"Well, then, that's your mission right now. No rush! Take your time, but figure out what it is that you want to do. What gets you excited? What are your God-given talents? Figure out what you have to offer the world. That's your job right now. If you meet some nice young man who wants to share your journey - and you just might, darlin'," Paula said, affectionately tousling Hannah's mousy hair, "that's great. But don't you dare sit around waiting for him to show up. You've got a life to live. Now!"

"Paula, where have you been all my life? Can you go back in time and give me that advice about ten years ago?" Imogene said, laughing.

Paula smiled warmly at her. "Never too late, Imogene. Never too late." Imogene nodded, feeling cheerful about her life all over again.

"And now, perhaps the biggest lie of all…" Imogene said dramatically. She wrote on the board: *Marriage will make you happy.*

Hannah studied the words on the board intently. Matt nodded approvingly, as did Paula.

"Maybe it will and maybe it won't," Imogene said. "But the idea that getting a fancy diamond ring and hitching yourself to some other person will make you happy or guarantee that you won't be lonely is simply not true. Sure, lots of marriages end in divorce, but I'm not just talking about those marriages. There's also those ones of quiet desperation. You know, where one or both people are desperately unhappy, but they feel stuck. So many couples stay together because they think it's best for the kids. Or maybe because of financial reasons, they feel like they can't get out. Maybe they're just too stuck in their ways. Afraid they're too old to start over. Whatever the reason, it must be awfully depressing to be stuck in a marriage like that." Imogene eyed the dry erase board. She wrote a series of words and phrases as they occurred to her. *Spinster. Pathetic. Charity case. Always a bridesmaid. Everybody wants to set you up with somebody. Everybody wants to "fix" your life.*

Imogene turned around to see the others nodding.

"Anything else?"

They looked at one another, thinking.

Imogene remembered one more thing she wanted to address.

"Valentine's Day…" she said slowly.

Groans erupted from all four of them, the loudest coming from Hannah. Valentine's Day might be a stupid, phony, made-up holiday, but it could be very painful for single people.

"What an obnoxious, self-congratulatory alleged holiday designed for couples to parade around, acting superior to the rest of us, and engage in gross displays of public affection," Imogene said.

"Yep. Pretty much sums it up," Paula agreed.

"Couples already have a million stupid holidays of their own. Anniversaries of their first date, first kiss, first time they pick out matching socks…" Hannah said.

Imogene chuckled. "You are so right. It's ridiculous to have an official Couples Day. Every day is Couples Day. We need a Singles Day, that's for sure. Hmm. That's an idea." She wrote it on the board.

Imogene stood back and surveyed all the things they had come up with to discuss. She felt satisfied, happy. It was such a relief to be able to vent all her frustrations without people judging her, telling her she was crazy to embrace the single life. Finally, she had met some people who felt the same way she did.

"Whaddaya think? Meet again in two weeks or so?" Imogene asked.

"Works for me," Paula said.

"Uh-huh," Matt said. Hannah shrugged, then nodded.

"Okay! In the meantime, tell your friends and anybody else who you think might be interested. We need a big group if it's going to be successful."

Imogene left the first Solo Power meeting with a renewed zest for her fight for single people. The turnout hadn't exactly been what she had hoped for, but the meager group had more than made up for their number with their enthusiasm for the cause. Until now, no one had really been supportive of what she was trying to do, and it was great to finally find like-minded people.

The next day, Imogene found Hannah and Matt on Facebook and sent them friend requests. It would be good to keep in touch with them between meetings, and she wanted to make sure they stayed excited about the cause. Not only that, they were nice people and she was happy about having more single friends.

As an afterthought, she typed Paula's name into the Facebook search engine, though she doubted that a woman her age was on Facebook. She thought about Aunt Maddy and her elderly friends who barely knew how to plug in a computer. She felt immediately chastised when she not only found Paula's Facebook page, but realized that the woman had more friends that Matt and Hannah combined.

Paula accepted her friend request almost immediately, and within a few hours, so did Matt and Hannah. Paula wrote on Imogene's Facebook wall: *"Hey, Imogene! Was so great meeting you and I'm really excited about all the great things we can do with this group. It might be a good idea to create a Solo Power group on Facebook. You can invite people to join and you can keep everybody up to date on meetings and other events."*

Imogene chuckled to herself that Paula had outdone her on the tech front. She searched for instructions on how to create a Facebook group, and then created one for Solo Power. She sent out virtual invites to Paula, Hannah, and Matt. She also sent out invites to her married friends, Adrienne, Susan, and Kate. All three women joined the Solo Power Facebook group, and, to Imogene's surprise, Adrienne's husband Carl did, too. Adrienne posted on Solo Power's wall:

"Way to take on the world, baby! Love it!!!"

Imogene felt a surge of hope and optimism for her new group when she saw that her married friends were so eager to join. That just proved that not all married people thought single people were wrong for staying single. Imogene's dad wasn't on Facebook, but her sisters were. She considered sending them invites, but she knew they would just flip out because she was "giving up on marriage" and "wasting her life."

That was exactly the kind of attitude that Imogene was working to change.

CHAPTER SEVEN

68 Years of Unwedded Bliss
By Paula Flandey

I was truly honored when Imogene Hart asked me to write an article for her new Solo Power blog. The idea of a pro-singles group is long overdue and I am so proud to be a part of it.

I never wanted to get married. There's nothing wrong with marriage—if it's your thing—but the idea that becoming a bride, a wife, and then a mother should be every little girl's dream is a bunch of—well, to keep this blog PG-rated—let's say baloney. Sure, I've dated my share of men and had my fun, if you know what I mean…but the idea of being tied to one person never appealed to me. I like being free, being my own person, and doing what I choose. If I hear one more small-minded idiot telling me that I'm selfish because I chose not to have children, I swear I'll punch them in the throat. I could do it, too! I may not be physically strong, but I've got the element of surprise on my side. After all, you don't expect a five-foot-four, 68-year-old broad to punch you in the throat.

You've been warned.

You know what's selfish? Self-righteous people who think they're better than others because they have children and, even worse, spout off to everybody else about how they simply MUST have children of their own! In case you hadn't noticed, we have a bit of an overpopulation problem on this planet. Can you even imagine if EVERYONE procreated? And I believe there's a reason that some people are unable to conceive and that some people are gay. There are plenty of people out there who get knocked up and don't want the kid, so God created people who can't have children of their own who want to raise kids. Like God's own matchmaking service.

Don't tell me I'm selfish because I'm not married! I believe God put us all here for a reason. My reason was to spend 38 years as a pediatric oncology nurse, where I touched the lives of so many. At least I hope I have. Since I didn't have a family of my own that I had to take care of, I used all my emotional energy to care for my little patients and their families. Many a time I would come home from work utterly exhausted. I'd be physically and emotionally drained, so I'd just kick back with a glass of wine and watch my favorite sitcoms. Relax, unwind, and prepare to go through it all over again the next day. It's hard for me to imagine having a bunch of kids and a husband to tend to when I came home. Sure, lots of people work tough jobs like I did and then come home to be with their families. They find comfort in that. You deal with sick kids all day and then go home and hug your healthy ones extra tight. I think that's wonderful!

But not for me.

Sometimes I can't help but wonder how many hapless women wandered into that trap, that promise that having children would fulfill them. I imagine many women have given into that pressure and had children, only to find themselves leading lives of quiet desperation as mothers of exhausting children they never really wanted to have to begin with.

What do you think it's like to be one of those kids?

So before you go running your mouth off and acting like you understand the secrets of the universe just because you had children of your own, I implore you to take the sage advice of many a schoolyard child:

MIND YOUR OWN BEESWAX!

You do what works for you, and let everybody else figure out their own way.

Everybody warned me that I'd live to regret not marrying and remaining childfree.

68 years and counting. It ain't happened yet…

Paula was cool. No doubt about it. Imogene found it so inspiring that Paula was enjoying a very full life without ever having been married. She was living proof that Imogene's sisters were dead wrong. There were women who were husband-free, child-free, and never looked back with regret.

Imogene texted Paula to thank her for her beautiful blog post. She asked Paula what she was up to right now.

"Knitting and sitting in my rocking chair," Paula texted back.

"Now, why don't I believe that?" Imogene responded.

"Cause it ain't true."

Imogene grinned. Just as she'd suspected.

"Doing my exercycle and watching the Miami Dolphins."

"You like football?" Imogene texted her back.

"I like most sports. Football, basketball, hockey, baseball. You should come shoot hoops with me at the gym sometime."

Imogene laughed out loud and realized she would love to play basketball with this snazzy old broad. The more Imogene got to know her, the more she admired her new friend. She sure wasn't like any other old lady she'd met before. Imogene learned from the photos on Facebook that Paula had at least three dogs and participated in the Pets on Wheels program, where people bring therapy dogs to visit sick people. She also ran flea markets and charity drives at her church, among other things. The woman packed more into a day than most people half her age did.

It occurred to Imogene that if you had children, you probably didn't have time to contribute a whole lot to society as a whole. You were too busy rushing around to soccer practice, ballet lessons, and orthodontist appointments. Irritation welled up in Imogene as she realized that the people who accused single people of being selfish probably did less to help the outside world than anybody else. Imogene certainly didn't judge them for their choices. Why should they judge her?

Imogene was determined to change the world with her new Solo Power group, or at least that was the plan. The really cool thing was that, no matter what happened, she was getting some great new friends out of the deal. She'd been delighted when Matt posted on his Facebook status that he was watching a *Saved By The Bell* marathon on TV. Imogene had been indulging in the same guilty pleasure at the time. She posted on Matt's Facebook to tell him so, and he confessed his continued deep and abiding love for Kelly Kapowski, the dreamy cheerleader from the cheesy show from the 90s.

"You know Tiffani Theissan is on a show on the USA Network

now," Imogene posted.

"No way!!"

"Yes way!! It's called *White Collar*. Check it out, it's really good."

"I will!" Matt had responded on the Facebook thread.

Then Imogene wrote "I think Mr. Belding was totally hot" just to screw with him.

"I hope you're kidding!"

"You'll never know…."

Imogene smiled. Matt was such a fun guy. However, she was disappointed to find that she still wasn't attracted to him. Just as well, she supposed, since he was really hell-bent on staying single. That's why he'd joined the group. Still, it would have been nice since he was around her age and really sweet. She wasn't sure why she wasn't attracted to him, but she simply wasn't.

They wrote back and forth on Facebook about all the shows they loved to watch and discovered they both had a passion for crime shows like NCIS, CSI, SVU, and pretty much anything with initials in the title. After they'd built up a thread of more than 50 messages, Imogene realized how stupid it was that they weren't just talking on the phone already. Though she had Matt's phone number from the Solo Power sign-in sheet, it seemed like an awfully big risk to call him. She didn't want to give him the wrong idea and make him think she was interested in him romantically.

She decided it was worth taking the chance.

"Yel-lo!" Matt answered cheerfully, and just the sound of his voice made Imogene smile.

"I-I hope you don't mind that I called. This is-"

"Imogene!" Matt said, laughing. "I was just thinking how dumb it was that we weren't just talking on the phone. How awesome was it when McRuddy got knifed last night on CSI?" he asked, picking up the conversation right where it had left off on Facebook.

"I know! It was hysterical," Imogene said, marveling at how Matt was the only one she knew who would understand why she thought a fictional stabbing was hysterical. The dude had totally deserved it.

"Nine times. He got stabbed *nine times*. I counted. I should've done a shot for every one, I was so happy."

"So I'm not the only one boozing it up while watching these shows?" Imogene asked. "But I don't drink shots. I drink wine. You know. All ladylike and stuff."

"Oh, I'm sure." Then he added in a high-pitched imitation of Imogene's voice, "Stab him. Stab him good!" He laughed again. "Very ladylike indeed." He paused for a moment. "Hey, I don't suppose you'd ever want to hang with me on a Thursday night and watch some of the shows together. Just as, you know, friends."

Imogene was having such a blast talking to him that she couldn't imagine anything more fun than having a few drinks and shouting at the TV together. She really did want it to be a "just friends" thing, though, and hoped he really meant it when he said that was what he wanted.

"Sure. That would be fun!"

They ended up making a date—well, not a *date*, but they set up a *time* to meet on Thursday to hang out, drink, and watch their shows. Imogene couldn't wait.

She also made a date to see the latest Jim Carrey movie with her sisters. They met at the movie theater, then went to an early dinner afterwards at a local Italian restaurant.

"It's nice to have some adult conversation, I'll tell you that! And I won't even have to wipe spaghetti sauce off anyone's face after dinner," Faye said, smiling. She took a sip of wine and leaned back in her chair, relaxing.

"Yeah. Liam and I do want kids, but we're trying to enjoy some peace and quiet for a little while first," Chrissy said.

"That's a good idea. You guys are young. You have plenty of time to have kids. Just enjoy being husband and wife right now," Faye said.

"Oh, we are," Chrissy said with a giggle.

Imogene smiled at her sister, feeling genuinely happy for her. She felt a brief flash of sadness, that familiar feeling of disappointment that she didn't have a man in her life. A few months ago, she would have been completely dragged down by that feeling. Not anymore. Imogene was learning that she could be disappointed that she was unmarried and still love her life at the same time.

"I'm glad things are going so well for you guys," Imogene said sincerely. "Liam's a sweetheart. And how are things with Richard, Faye? Can't be easy with the kids underfoot all the time."

Faye sighed wearily. She took another sip of wine. "No, it's not. I mean, you want to make time to, you know, be together, but it's tough to find the energy. When the kids are finally settled, sometimes all I want to do is collapse in bed and sleep. Rich is great, though. He understands and doesn't pressure me…too much…when I'm just not in the mood."

"That's good. It'll get better once the kids are a little older," Imogene said.

"True. So what's new with you? Anybody in your life I should know about?" Faye asked.

Imogene decided to answer the question as if Faye had stopped after asking what was new with her. There was plenty new, but it had nothing to do with dating. "I really think my singles group is going to take off!" Just saying the words out loud made her stomach tingle with excitement. She had high hopes for Solo Power.

"Oh, yeah. How did your little meeting go?" Chrissy asked.

"It went great!" Imogene tried to ignore the niggling feeling of irritation she felt when her youngest sister referred to Solo Power as a "little meeting."

"That's cool, I guess. Did a lot of people show up?" Faye asked.

"Well, not exactly," Imogene grudgingly admitted.

"How many?" Chrissy asked.

"Three." Fine. So maybe it was a "little meeting," but it was only the first one. These things took time to build. "But everyone seemed really excited about it. It was so nice to meet other people who realize that there's more to life than getting married."

"Anybody your age?" Faye asked.

"Well, one guy was," Imogene said, and then stifled the urge to clamp her hand over her mouth. She hadn't meant to tell them about Matt.

"Really? Awesome! Tell me about him!" Chrissy asked, picking up her glass of wine and learning forward, ready to hear all the juicy details.

"There's nothing to tell and please don't get any stupid ideas, all right?" Imogene said.

"So, what's wrong with him? Lazy eye? He got a hump?" Chrissy asked. She would say that. Chrissy was incredibly shallow about guys, or at least she used to be in high school. She was the pretty, perky, cheerleader type who had her pick of boys. She'd settled down later when she wanted a more meaningful relationship. Her husband was a really nice guy. Still, Imogene doubted Chrissy would have married him if he wasn't cute.

"Fat? Too tall? Too short? His tie doesn't match his socks? What's your excuse now?" Faye asked, looking annoyed. Faye had always been reasonable when it came to picking men. She'd wanted a decent, responsible, family-oriented type of guy. She'd found him in Richard.

"There's nothing wrong with him! He's a nice guy and I like him, just not that way, okay?"

"Why not?" Chrissy asked.

"Because I don't. And it's my life and my choice, so stay out of it. I like him pretty much the same way I like Paula, one of the other three who showed up. She's awesome!"

"Could you sound any more like a lesbo?" Chrissy said.

"The term is 'lesbian' and no, I'm not," Imogene said irritably. "Matt just seems like he'd be a really good guy to be friends with. And that's all."

"Don't you think you might be a little bit too picky, especially at this stage in the game?" Chrissy asked.

"Oh, because I'm some old maid now?"

"Chill out, Immy. I didn't say that."

"I will not chill out!" Imogene shot a warning look at her sisters. "I just don't get why nobody can even pretend to be interested in a damn thing I'm saying unless it has to do with dating somebody. Yet, I'm expected to be totally fascinated by Allen's poop habits!"

"Immy, shush already!" Faye said, looking around. Imogene had spoken louder than she'd intended, and "poop" wasn't the greatest word to shout in a restaurant.

"And the thing is, I *am* interested in his poop habits because he's my nephew! I love him and I'm so proud of him. I'm proud of you, Faye, because I know it can't be easy trying to toilet train a stubborn two-year-old. I want to hear what's going on your life. Why don't you care what I'm trying to do with mine?"

"Just what is it that you're actually trying to do?" Faye asked.

"I'm trying to help other single people like me to stop feeling like total losers just because they don't have a significant other. I'm trying to help change the way society treats us, because it's not right!"

Faye nodded in a way that implied she understood what Imogene was saying but didn't necessarily agree with her. No doubt she preferred the old Imogene. The one who pored through the online singles ads and went on date after date in search of her future husband. Well, Imogene didn't miss that life. Not at all.

Well, maybe just one tiny bit.

She certainly didn't miss the awful disappointment that came with the realization that yet another guy just wasn't going to work out. What she did miss was the thrill of hope she felt just before she went out on a date. That anticipation that maybe, just maybe, this time he'd be *The One*. That wasn't the focus of her life anymore. She had so many other things going on. Things that nobody in her family seemed to give a damn about.

"I just wish you all would understand that it really is possible to have a good life even if you don't get married."

Faye glanced at Chrissy, who shook her head. Imogene shot her younger sister a death stare. She decided to tell them more about Solo Power's plans, if for no other reason than to make them as mad as she was.

"My singles group has decided that we should have a Singles Day this year. Kind of like Valentine's Day but for single people."

Chrissy rolled her eyes. Faye sighed.

"Do you really think that's such a good idea? I doubt it would work. Most people hate being single. Nobody wants to celebrate it." Chrissy said.

"So I should be ashamed of being single. That's really what you're saying," Imogene said.

"There's no use talking to you when you get like this, Immy," Chrissy grumbled.

"Like what?" Imogene demanded.

"All defensive and stuff."

"Everybody gets defensive when they're being attacked!"

Faye glanced around the restaurant. "Settle down. You're gonna get us kicked out."

"You've only got three people in your group. What can you possibly accomplish with three people?" Chrissy asked.

"We've only had one meeting," Imogene said through clenched teeth. "There will be a lot more people who want to get involved."

"Oh, sure they will," Chrissy said sarcastically. "You know, you-"

"Enough!" Faye said. "Enough. I get enough fighting with two little boys at home. Can we talk about something else please?"

"Oh, by all means. We should talk about something much more important. Like washing Liam's underwear or how many times Allen threw up on you today or that fact that Richard clipped his toenails last week. As long as it has to do with husbands or kids, it's automatically more important than anything I could possibly have to say!" Imogene practically shouted.

The poor, hapless waiter hesitated, then tentatively approached their table.

"Ladies, can I get you anything else?"

"More wine, please," said all three women, glaring at one another.

CHAPTER EIGHT

Lindsay Saga Weddings

A wedding is the single most important day in every woman's life. There isn't a girl alive who doesn't dream of the day when it's finally her turn to be the object of affection of the entire world. Every bride is a princess on her wedding day, and she deserves to have the best of everything that money can buy. The finest crystal champagne flutes, the most beautiful flowers, the most elegant and expensive gown will make her the envy of every single woman! Trust Lindsay Saga Weddings to make all your most extravagant wedding dreams come true. Your fantasy wedding is a priceless treasure! Wedding packages start at $75,000.

"You look utterly gorgeous, Katherine. Just breathtaking," Lindsay said as she fluffed up The Bride's gown. "You're the most beautiful bride I've seen in years. I just—I can't believe it!"

"Oh, I bet you say that to all of your brides," Katherine said, admiring herself in the mirror.

Well, of course she did. That was her job. Brides paid upwards of one hundred thousand dollars for her to kiss their ass all day long, and Lindsay was happy to oblige. She'd made a very successful career out of making brides feel like royalty on their wedding day. After years of practice, she knew exactly what to do and say to ensure that her brides were gushing about her services for years after their weddings, thus ensuring her a steady stream of affluent clients.

"Where's my flowers?" Katherine demanded.

Lindsay gently lifted the huge bouquet of white, yellow, and orange flowers and handed them to The Bride, who continued to preen in the mirror. The flowers were hideous, but they were a perfect match for the ugly yellow and orange dresses that the Queen for the Day was forcing upon her poor bridesmaids. Katherine was just one of innumerable brides who deliberately chose the most unflattering gowns possible for their sisters and friends, so as to make themselves appear more beautiful. She'd no doubt assured everyone that the dresses she'd chosen were the height of fashion, designed by some internationally renowned expert. It was amazing how often that tactic worked. Though the gowns were clearly ugly, people just assumed they didn't know current fashion trends well enough to know what was hot and what was not. Sure, every once in a while, a clueless elderly guest or a drunken family member would announce how awful the bridesmaids looked, but for the most part, brides got away with humiliating their attendants. That was part of the wedding game. It was usually payback for all the times The Bride had to suffer as a bridesmaid. When it was finally her turn, The Bride had every right to do whatever the hell she wanted to her friends and family.

"Ella, fix your hair! You've got strands escaping," Katherine told one of her bridesmaids. "In fact, all of you do a hair and makeup check. I want you to look your best."

Lindsay nodded as she continued to fuss over Katherine's dress, though it was perfectly fine the way it was. Lindsay knew The Bride didn't want her girls looking their best; she just wanted to order them around while she could. Might as well, for tomorrow Katherine would return to ordinary life and her reign as The Bride would be over. Forever. On the day of the wedding, everybody does everything The Bride demands without question. It was crazy how everybody worked together as a whole to ensure that she would suffer no disappointment on her special day. Everyone knew that if anything went wrong on a girl's wedding day, she would never, ever get over it so everybody cooperated to make sure that everything went according to plan.

Lindsay admired Katherine some more. "Stunning. You look simply stunning! I'm gonna go check and make sure the church is perfect and ready to go. Be right back."

Katherine nodded, and went back to looking in the mirror.

Lindsay walked down the long aisle, checking the oversized pew bows and gigantic sprays of lilies and roses that adorned the altar of the huge, stone church.

"Melissa!" Lindsay hissed to her assistant. "Check each of the pew bows and make sure they're perfectly straight. I can tell you right now at least two of them are crooked." That was the beauty of being a wedding planner. You still got to order people around, just like The Bride. Her young assistant snapped to attention and rushed off to inspect each bow.

The scent of the oversized bouquets of flowers was as pungent as heavy perfume. You could probably smell it from the church parking lot. They looked fresh and beautiful. Good thing, seeing as they'd cost more than ten thousand dollars.

Lindsay loved doing high-end weddings. In fact, those were the only weddings she planned anymore. Her website might say packages started at seventy-five thousand, but she rarely bothered with any wedding that cost less than two hundred thousand. Sure, many couples budgeted seventy-five to a hundred grand, but that always more than doubled by the time Lindsay was through making sure they had everything they needed to have a truly memorable wedding day. Her cut was fifteen percent of the total budget, so the more "necessities" she talked them into, the better.

Lindsay Saga had already made quite the name for herself in the wedding planning business. She wasn't exactly a household name yet, but that was her goal. Her ultimate dream was not only to plan celebrity weddings, but to become a celebrity in her own right. So far, she had only worked on weddings for C and D list celebrities. Washed-up child actors, reality show stars, and the occasional politician. She had her sights set on multi-million-dollar movie star weddings. Not only would she rake in a fortune, but her name would be in all the magazines, not just the wedding and style ones. Magazines with huge circulations, like *People* and *Entertainment Weekly* would feature story after story on the weddings she coordinated. They would include her name and maybe even a photo. The day she saw her name in *The National Enquirer* would be the day she knew she had truly made it. Tabloid writers might be the scum of the earth, but they didn't write articles about nobodies.

Lindsay was already a kind of quasi-celebrity. She had been on numerous daytime talk shows as a resident wedding expert. She'd even been on *Oprah*! That was the most thrilling day of her life and, sure enough, hits to her website soared. After that, Lindsay knew her days of slumming with weddings at local fire halls and American Legions were over. After *Oprah*, she'd hit the big time. Well, maybe medium-time. She had fantasized that Oprah would have her back on again and again until she was finally given her own show, like Dr. Phil and Dr. Oz. As it turned out, that was her one and only appearance on *Oprah*. Now the show was off the air, taking with it the chances of there ever being a *Lindsay Saga Wedding Show*. Still, she was invited to appear on other, smaller daytime shows and each one increased her celebrity level. It was only a matter of time until she hit it big. Weddings were never out of style, and shows about weddings never failed to get huge television ratings from both brides-to-be and pathetic, lonely, single gals still dreaming of the day when it would be their turn.

The wedding of Katherine and Michael was perfect and involved lots of tears. The Bride cried, her mom cried, and the bridesmaids, (probably due to the shame of wearing those eyesore dresses) cried too. Next it was time for pictures, which was always excruciating. No matter how many times she had warned them, couples always underestimated how time-consuming the post-nuptial photo shoot would be. Naturally, the bride and groom were ready to head over to the reception and drink, dance, and bask in the adoration of everyone they knew. Each minute the photographer spent on the pictures took precious time and money away from their long-awaited wedding day.

"Can we hurry this up please?" Katherine asked irritably.

"Yeah, we kinda want to get moving here," the groom agreed.

"I just said that, Michael," said The Bride irritably to her husband of ten minutes. "I can handle this."

"We will definitely keep this thing moving just as fast as we can!" said the photographer brightly. "I know you guys are eager to get going. After all, you have a lot to celebrate! Still, we wanna make sure we get all those precious memories captured for your wedding album. You all look gorgeous!" he said, and then snapped a quick photo that would be utterly unusable due to The Bride's fierce scowl.

"It's very important that we get these photographs wrapped up as quickly as possible," Lindsay said crisply. "Katherine and Michael have hundreds of friends and family members waiting to see and congratulate them." The fire in The Bride's eyes grew as she saw precious moments of her waning Day of Royalty ticking by.

Lindsay was no dummy. The Bride and groom would be pissed if they got a wedding album that didn't contain every possible photograph of them up on the altar, with their attendants, their parents, and so forth. But that would be the photographer's problem after the wedding. Right now, all The Bride would remember was that Lindsay came to the rescue and refused to let the photographer eat up all the reception time.

"Of course!" said the photographer, who was also no dummy. The trick was to keep acting as if they were moments away from finishing, while continuing to take as many photographs as he could get away with, without enraging The Bride. "Almost done! Now, let's grab a quick picture of The Bride with her dad…"

Lindsay shot him her most practiced impatient look as she exchanged a look of exasperation with The Bride. Lindsay had no problem throwing any wedding vendor under the bus when it suited her. Screw professional courtesy. Her entire business was built on happy brides.

The photographer had snapped only a few more pictures, then The Bride literally stamped her foot with impatience. "Come on, come on! Get it done already!"

"Just a few more minutes. I promise."

"We'll be done soon, hon. I want to get going, too, but we want to make sure we have all the pictures we need to make our wedding album perfect," Michael said soothingly.

"Oh, so you'd rather stand around here all day than go to our reception that we paid a fortune for! Typical man. In no hurry to do anything." Katherine rolled her eyes.

"If you're not done in five minutes, we're leaving!" Lindsay said authoritatively. That finally brought a smile to Katherine's face.

True to her word, Lindsay waited precisely five minutes before pulling the plug on the bridal photography session. "Okay, that's enough. Let's go!"

"Finally!" Katherine said, lifting her skirt so she could stalk out to the limo. The humongous stretch limousine was fully stocked with champagne and The Bride would hopefully have a glass or three and really be in a partying mood once they arrived at the reception.

Lindsay slid behind the wheel of her sleek, black Mercedes and flipped on the radio. She was always careful to follow right behind the limo so she would arrive at the same time the couple did. She worked hard to create the illusion that she could be everywhere at once, tending to any possible need that The Bride might have on her day.

Lindsay turned the volume up when the local radio station reported on the entertainment news. She daydreamed about hearing them report on some big-name celebrity announcing her engagement and how she simply *had* to hire Lindsay Saga to plan the wedding. She snapped out of her reverie when she nearly rear-ended the limo which stopped abruptly at a red light.

"Idiot. Just go through it!" If the limo driver had run the light, Lindsay would have blown through it, too. Screw the red light cameras. It was worth it to get a ticket so long as she arrived at the reception on time.

It turned out to be a good thing for Lindsay that the driver interrupted her daydreaming or she would have missed a news item of critical importance.

"The Estrogen Network has announced that its popular reality show, *Get the Ring, Ladies,* is on indefinite hiatus. *Get the Ring* is, of course, the reality show that helps women force their deadbeat, commitment-phobic boyfriends to propose by having the camera crew ambush them and present them with an ultimatum: Marry me or it's over! The host of the *Get the Ring, Ladies,* Janet Ferban, has actually been arrested for....wait for it...jewel theft," the radio reporter said, laughing. "I assure you, we are not making this up! Anyway, this leaves The Estrogen Network with a huge hole in its programming and they are reportedly going to open it up to viewers in their search for a new reality show. So, if you've ever dreamed of having your very own wedding-themed reality show, now's your chance!"

Lindsay damn near hit the limo again.

CHAPTER NINE

Getting Used to Being Alone
By Hannah Wanderling

It's a good idea to get used to being alone. I think everybody should, because we're all gonna be alone at some point in our lives. You gotta get comfortable with taking care of yourself. Even if you get married, you might be widowed someday, especially if you're the woman. Men just don't live as long, so it doesn't make sense to let the man handle everything and then be totally lost when he dies.

I don't think I'll get married, so I want to get used to being alone now. I'm not sexy. I'm not beautiful. I'm overweight. I'm not overweight in the way skinny bitches complain that they're fat so everybody will fawn all over them to reassure them how thin they are. I'm obviously, head-turningly, traffic-stoppingly fat. People stare. Some people make comments. It hurts most when guys comment. I know none of them wants to be with me, but I'd rather they treat me like I'm invisible than say out loud how ugly they think I am.

I like this Solo Power group so far. I'm kind of hoping it

will help me figure out who I am. I know who I'm not. I'm not the pretty, cheerleader type. I'm not stupid, but I'm not a brain either. I'm for sure not one of the Disney princesses who are so popular around here. I've been told that I'm funny. I'm definitely known to make a sarcastic comment or two, but I don't know how comfortable I am with being the funny fat girl. In the Disney animated cartoon of life, I'm just the amusing, fat, comic relief. I'm the sidekick in my own life. And everybody knows it's not the funny best friend character who goes home with the prince.

I'm still hoping Solo Power will help me accept being single, because that's what I'm gonna be. Forever.

Imogene sighed heavily as she sat at her computer and read Hannah's blog entry. This wasn't exactly the positive, upbeat message she was going for with Solo Power, but she couldn't very well tell Hannah she wasn't going to publish her blog entry. After all, the girl had a right to express her feelings.

Part of Hannah's problem was her family. Hannah's mother didn't approve of the whole singles pride thing any more than Imogene's family did. In fact, Mrs. Wanderling was constantly trying to drill it into Hannah's head that she needed to find a husband someday. Her mom was a single mother and apparently thought that her life would have worked out a lot better if Hannah's deadbeat dad had stuck around.

As much as she hated to admit it, Hannah reminded Imogene of herself. The girl was so much like Imogene had been just a few short months ago, always down on herself for being single and complaining that she didn't have a man in her life. Ugh. A wave of guilt and shame washed over her as she realized how much she had contributed to the stigma against single women. Well, she was done acting pathetic and lonely. Better yet, she was done *feeling* pathetic and lonely. Pride and optimism swept over Imogene, replacing the shame. She couldn't wait until Solo Power really starting taking off. There was no telling how many people she might be able to help. She wanted to reach out to all the people whose families had belittled them for being single. She wanted to welcome them with open arms so they could take on the world together.

After grudgingly publishing Hannah's blog on the Solo Power website, Imogene collapsed onto the couch and flipped on the television. She had baked a fancy birthday cake for a friend's daughter earlier and was tired from being on her feet half the day.

She groaned as she watched an entertainment news report about the ridiculous Estrogen Network and how they were searching for their next shallow, insipid, wedding-related reality show. The Estrogen Network was supposed to be a channel for women in general, but it was really just a channel for brides.

"Spokeswoman for The Estrogen Network, Becky Houston, says the network plans to fill the hole in their programming with a new, viewer-inspired, reality show," the reporter said.

"We want to hear from our viewers!" annoyingly perky Becky Houston cried. "Go to www.EstrogenNetwork.com and submit your proposal for the new reality TV show. Submit your very best wedding-related idea so that we-"

"That is so stupid," Imogene muttered.

"It could be a show about wedding apparel...maybe a show about getting engaged...it could be about honeymoons..."

"Why does it have to be about weddings? It's The Estrogen Network, not the wedding channel. They already have one of those. It's called *The Wedding Channel*. Nimrods!"

Becky remained unconcerned with Imogene's fury and

continued to prattle on about the new reality show. "Could be about wedding shoes…or how about reception themes…or even a show about bridesmaids and how they're still waiting for their special someone to come along."

"Oh, vom-MIT!" Imogene yelled. She jumped up and darted over to her desk. She rapidly flipped through all her papers to find the sign-in sheet from the Solo Power meeting listing everyone's phone numbers on it. She needed to talk to somebody now. She was way too mad to wait for a response on Facebook. She had planned on calling Matt, but spied Paula's name first and quickly dialed her number.

"Hey, Paula. It's Imogene."

"Imogene! How are ya, honey?" Paula's voice cheerfully greeted her and she immediately felt better. Damn, it felt so good to have single friends.

"I'm not like, interrupting a Tae Kwon Do lesson or something, am I?" Imogene asked.

Paula laughed. "No, why do you ask?"

"I just never know what you're up to, but it always seems to be something interesting. I think I wanna be you when I grow up."

"Well, you're on your way, kid. What's up?" Paula asked.

"Did you hear about *Get the Ring, Ladies*?"

"Are you kidding? I about fell off my chair. Jewel theft!" Paula cackled, which made Imogene laugh, too.

"I know. It's too funny. I hate that damn show." Then Imogene said in a whiny voice, "My boyfriend doesn't wanna marry me, so help me force him to!"

"Exactly. What a great way to start off a marriage. Nimrods!"

Imogene grinned, finding it delightful that Paula used the same word to describe the network that she had. "So did you hear The Estrogen Network is looking for a new reality show?"

Paula scoffed. "Yeah. They're gonna replace one ridiculous bridal show with another one. Can't wait…"

"I know. But what if we submitted a proposal for a reality show that was for singles instead? I'm sure they'll just ignore it, but it can't hurt. Worst they can do is say no. At least it might get them thinking, you know? Remind them that lots of women watch their channel and we're not all just brainless bridal bimbos."

"Or wedding wimps," Paula added.

"Fairytale freaks."

"Walkin' down the aisle-o-philes…"

"Matrimaniacs!"

"Hah!" Paula said. "Good one. But yeah, I say we go for it. What do you have in mind for a singles' reality show?"

"Well, I'm not exactly sure. I would love to get everybody's input. And by everybody, I mean the people who actually showed up to the first Solo Power meeting. I say we get Matt and Hannah and we can put together a proposal," Imogene said.

"Great idea!" Paula agreed.

Since they knew it would only be the four of them, there was no reason to meet formally at the library. They decided to meet at Matt's townhouse for pizza. As they all sat at the dining room table, Imogene looked around at Matt's lovely home. As promised, it was neat and clean. The house featured sleek, modern furniture, including a black leather couch and chair in the living room and a shiny, black dining room table. Imogene marveled at how comfortable the dining room chairs were. They were made of soft, cushy leather and were a far cry from the hard wooden dining room chairs at her father's table. Matt's kitchen featured a stainless steel refrigerator and a matching microwave oven and stove. Matt obviously did quite well for himself. Imogene couldn't help but be impressed. This wasn't the home of a lonely bachelor. It clearly belonged to someone who enjoyed his life.

"Another beer, Paula?" Matt asked.

Paula, who had almost half a beer left in her bottle, quickly downed the rest in one shot. "Yes, please!"

Matt chuckled, then looked at Hannah's empty glass. "You want some more Coke, Hannah?"

Hannah nodded shyly. "Thanks."

Matt went to the kitchen, then returned with a can of Coke for Hannah and a bottle of some fancy microbrew for Paula.

"This is soooo good," Imogene said after finishing another bite of the super-cheesy pizza. "You sure you don't want any money toward it?"

"I'm sure. My treat!" Matt said warmly. "So! Shall we get down to business?"

Imogene nodded. She picked up her notebook and pen from the floor and put them on the table.

"Now, I hate to say we're fighting a losing battle here, but we do have to be realistic," Imogene began. "I think we should put together the best proposal about a singles' reality show that we can, while knowing full well that The Estrogen Network will probably ignore us completely. They were very clear that they were only interested in wedding-themed proposals."

"Boooo!" Paula said.

"I know," Imogene shook her head. "I figure I'll write a cover letter telling them about our singles pride group and how we think it's discriminatory that they only want bridal shows. We'll ask them to at least consider our proposal. If nothing else, it will send a message to the network that not everybody is interested in wedding stuff and that they're missing out on an important demographic. Single people have money, too, ya know!"

"I'll say," said Hannah quietly, as she looked around at Matt's house. "Check out the bachelor Taj Mahal here."

Everyone at the table laughed. Hannah blushed and looked down at her plate. Imogene couldn't help but wish the girl would just speak up. *Stand tall*, Imogene wanted to shout. *Stop hiding!*

"Why thank you, Ma'am," Matt said, bowing his head slightly. "Glad you approve of my humble abode. So, what kind of format do you have in mind for the show?"

"Well, I think it needs to be positive and upbeat. Something to inspire people, kind of like *The Biggest Loser* or *Undercover Boss*. One of those shows where everybody cries at the end."

"Never seen any of those shows," Matt said.

"Neither have I," Imogene admitted. "But everybody cries on the commercials." Matt chuckled and Paula nodded her head.

"Yeah, I know what you mean. So how do we make people cry, Imogene?" Paula asked.

"Hmmmm," Imogene said, tapping her pen against her lips. "I think a lot of it depends on the contestants we choose. The whole point is to show people how great being single can be. That it's something to be celebrated. That even if your life turns out very different than you expected, it can still be wonderful. So we gotta pick people who are miserable being single so that we can show the transformation. In other words, we need to choose people who are the total opposite of *you*," Imogene said, pointing her pen squarely at Paula.

"Oh, I'm not good enough to be on your show, young lady?" Paula asked. She folded her arms dramatically.

"No, you're too good. You're happy being single so you already know everything that our contestants need to learn."

"Oh, all right then," Paula said brightly. She unfolded her arms and took a big bite of her pizza.

"We need somebody more like…" Imogene happened to glance

at Hannah, then quickly looked away. "We would need to find people who feel like failures because they're single. I want this show to be inspirational, to show everyone how rich and full your life can be even if you never get married."

"That sounds great. It wouldn't necessarily have to be just for people who never married. What about divorced people? Or widows?" Matt asked.

"That's a great idea!" Imogene said as she eagerly wrote down the suggestions in her notebook. "Basically, it could be anybody who's really down about being single. We want the viewers to be able to identify with them."

"So how do we magically transform them into happy singles?" Paula asked after taking a big swig of beer.

There was silence in the room for a few moments while everyone thought about it. Then Matt, Imogene, and Hannah all started to speak at the same time, causing the group to break into laughter.

"Hannah, what were you going to say?" Imogene said, hoping to encourage the girl.

"I was just gonna say what if you had some kind of big prize at the end? Like if you took somebody who always wanted to go to college and never got to go, maybe we could get a school to give 'em a scholarship in exchange for using their school name on the show," Hannah said.

"I think that's a fantastic idea!" Imogene said.

"Or if we had an older contestant, like some woman in her seventies who was never married or maybe is widowed, and she always wanted to see Paris or someplace like that, the prize could be an all-expense-paid trip. Now, *that* would make people cry!" Hannah said.

"Yeah it would!" Imogene said with great enthusiasm. She

wrote *Trip to Paris* in her notebook. "I really love the idea of getting people of all ages involved. It wouldn't have to be just women in their thirties who are worrying that they'll never get married."

"I like that idea, too. What if we got a bunch of people of all ages together and put them in the same house for a month or so? They'd start out as strangers, but then get to know each other and become friends. Kind of like we did here." Matt said with a smile.

Imogene looked around the table at her new friends who were indeed of all different ages. It gave her such a feeling of warmth, comfort, and contentment. There was something so wonderful about sharing a meal and good conversation with friends. She'd felt the same way when she threw the dinner party at her home. She looked around at Matt, Paula, and Hannah and marveled at how much she liked them even though she hadn't known them very long. It was so validating to hear them sit here and talk about how wonderful it was to be single. They shared her excitement about Solo Power, and their support gave her such a feeling of peace. Friends like these were what made life worth living. It was these tender moments of love and friendship that she simply could not find a way to articulate to her family. The way she felt so appreciated, so accepted, so *happy* even without a romantic relationship. Maybe their singles program could help show her family what she was trying so hard to express.

"I love it! They could all live together and share their stories. What their lives are like and how life turned out differently than they had planned." Imogene said. "Kind of like what we're doing here."

"Yeah," Hannah said softly.

"They might start out kinda sad," Imogene said. "They might talk about how they had all these plans to get married and have kids and it just didn't work out. We could encourage them to talk about their families and how society treats them. A big reason why singles are depressed and get so down on themselves is because of the way other people treat them."

"I wonder if we could get some of their family members to talk," Matt said thoughtfully. "We could do little segments about what their parents think about them being single. Maybe even some of their married friends who keep trying to set them up on dates."

"And siblings," Imogene offered drily. "Don't forget siblings."

"Your brothers and sisters give you a hard time?" Paula asked.

"Sisters. Two younger sisters. Both happily married," Imogene said.

"They're happily married and that works great for them, so naturally you're insane to want to be single," Matt said, summing it up perfectly.

Once again, that contented, peaceful feeling washed over Imogene. *Yes,* she thought. *These people totally get it.*

"I'm lucky my brother supports me unconditionally," Matt said. "He is head over heels in love with his boyfriend – I mean fiancé—but he's never judged me for wanting to stay single. My parents are another story. They're obsessed with getting me to *settle down.* I could announce that I was President of the United States and they would say 'Ooooh, is there a First Lady in your future?' "

Imogene laughed. "I believe it. My father and sisters are the same way. They don't care about anything I have to say unless it involves a guy."

"I'm sorry, Imogene," Matt said with genuine compassion. "That really sucks."

"It does," she agreed. "But that's just the kind of thing that this reality show could help change. We can show people's backstories, show what their lives are like and how they're treated, and by the end of the season they can have a complete turnaround and be really happy and excited about their lives."

"That gives me chills. The good kind, I mean!" Paula said.

"Me, too," Imogene said. "I love the idea that they can kind of have an emotional life do-over in addition to the vacation or scholarship or whatever they actually win."

"I'm sure it won't be possible to give every contestant a prize, though," Matt said. "I can't imagine The Estrogen Network would have the kind of budget that could make every person's dream come true. There would have to be some kind of winner at the end."

"Good point," Imogene said. "But how do we decide who wins? Should viewers vote people off?"

"No," Hannah said softly. "I don't think anybody should get voted off. It's mean."

"I think you're right, Hannah. I don't want this to be a mean, competitive kind of show. It's supposed to encourage people. The last thing I would want is for people to get kicked out, especially by hundreds of voters at home," Imogene said.

"Agreed. So maybe nobody gets eliminated along the way, but there is one big winner at the end," Paula said. "But who decides who wins?"

"I bet the network could get some kind of celebrity judge," Matt said. "Would be great if they could get a famous single person like Jennifer Arlington. Wouldn't that be amazing?"

"Yeah, it would!" Imogene said excitedly. "She would be perfect. The tabloids are always going on and on about how lonely she must be since she got divorced, but she never looks lonely to me!"

"You're not kidding. From what I hear, she's shacked up with a bunch of hot co-stars. And even if that ain't true, she's laughing all the way to the bank. She's incredibly successful, but that don't matter, does it? If she's single, she's gotta be miserable, right?" Paula said, shaking her head.

"I do have to admit," Matt said. "You really don't hear people talking that way about single male celebrities."

"Of course not. They're studs, but single women are lonely spinsters," Imogene said. "So I think we can agree that a celebrity who is female and single would be best. Jennifer Arlington would be ideal, but she's a huge star and it's really doubtful she'd do it. Still, there are bound to be other B or C list stars who might be interested. Now, the question is, what would the contestants actually do on the show? Like how do they score points so the celebrity judge can decide who wins?"

"Most reality shows have challenges they have to do. What could we make them do?" Paula asked.

"I like the idea of them teaming up to do something. In pairs." Matt said. "Not matchmaking pairs of course! Just like two of them have to work together to do something as a team. The team that does the best at the challenge wins that round, and it's the celebrity judge who decides the winner."

"Love it!" Imogene said. "Working together can create strong bonds. My biggest hope is that the people end up being friends at the end. Some of the challenges could be learning how to do something. Like I took cooking classes and I found I'm pretty good at baking cakes."

"Is that so?" Matt said. He raised an eyebrow. "You can make dessert for our next get-together."

Imogene smiled warmly."You got it."

"I think it's a great idea! Both you making us dessert and the whole challenge thing. They could have to learn how to cook or make something out of wood or something like that. Learn how to play a song on the piano! Some of them might discover a talent they never knew they had," Paula said.

Imogene nodded, scribbling in her notebook. She looked up. "What about a challenge that has to do with facing their fears? Not anything gross like *Fear Factor,* but fears about being single. What if they have to go to a wedding alone? Their challenge is to genuinely have a great time instead of feeling sorry for themselves."

"Or maybe they go out with another couple? Like you did with your dinner party, Imogene," Paula said. "I loved how you told me that you're only a third wheel if you act like it."

"Or maybe they go out somewhere on Valentine's Day? Like go see a romantic movie. The challenge is to do something they think might make them feel bad and maybe they discover that it's not so bad if they face their fears," Matt said.

"True," Imogene said thoughtfully. "And I hate to say it, but even if it doesn't go well, like if they do get sad about it, we can discuss that on the show. Overall, we want to show that being single can be great, but it's not realistic to say that it's always wonderful. Nobody's life is perfect, and I think it might be good to admit that being single can be painful sometimes."

"I like that," Paula said softly. "I've really never doubted my decision to stay single and I like being on my own, but I do feel lonely on occasion. Doesn't everyone?"

Matt and Hannah nodded.

"Of course. And, by the same token, I'm sure married people would like to have some alone time, too. No one's happy all the time," Imogene said. "No matter what my damn sisters say."

"Amen!" Paula said. She hoisted her beer and took a big swig.

"I think we got some great stuff here," Imogene said, skimming over her notes. "We get singles of all ages who are unhappy and feel like failures because they never married, have them live together for a month, do singles-related challenges and hopefully learn some great lessons along the way from a happy, single celebrity. Then, at the end, somebody goes home with an amazing prize."

"And everybody cries at the end!" Paula said.

"Yes!" Imogene said, laughing. She looked down at her notebook and sighed. "Oh, I just can't help but picture our proposal ending up in the recycling bin at The Estrogen Network."

"Could happen," Matt said. "But remember, the point is to get them thinking. At least ours will stand out from all the other wedding proposals. No pun intended."

"Hey, we still don't have a name for the show," Imogene pointed out. Hannah mumbled something under her breath, but no one could understand her.

"What'd you say, honey?" Paula asked.

"I've been thinking about a name for it," Hannah said. "How about *Single, Not Alone*?"

"Wow," Imogene said. The name so perfectly summed up what the show was about. "I think it's absolutely beautiful."

She looked at Matt and Paula, who both smiled and nodded their approval.

"I love it, Hannah," Imogene said, as she got up to give her a hug. "The show is making me cry already."

CHAPTER TEN

"On your wedding day, you realize that fairytales really do come true."
– Lindsay Saga

Lindsay Saga knew she was a lock to get her own reality show. She was already a famous wedding expert, so she was guaranteed to pull in huge ratings. She had the perfect idea for the show—it would essentially be a beauty contest for brides called *Beautiful Bride*. The winner would get an all-expense-paid wedding planned by Lindsay Saga herself. Brides-to-be would line up for blocks for a chance at that kind of prize. Most women couldn't come close to affording Lindsay's services, let alone all the fancy extras they could get on a two hundred thousand dollar budget, or whatever The Estrogen Network would agree to provide for the lucky winner. Audiences ate up any show that was even remotely related to weddings, and a cutthroat bridal competition would be a huge ratings draw.

Lindsay tried to concentrate on typing up her proposal, but it wasn't easy to do with a house full of people who refused to leave her alone.

"Mom! Where's all my hockey gear?" yelled her 15-year-old son, Cody.

"How should I know?" Lindsay replied testily.

She tried to block out the noise so she could keep working on the proposal. She had a feeling this could be her big break. If she got her own reality show, she would no longer be known only in wedding circles. She would be a household name. That idea thrilled her to no end. She had always longed to be the wedding planner to the stars, but more than that, she wanted to be a star herself.

"Mom!"

"Dammit, Cody. I don't know!" She loved her son and her seventeen-year-old daughter, KellieAnne, but they drove her crazy. Lindsay's work kept her so busy that she didn't have much time for her kids. She figured it wasn't her fault. Her wedding business wouldn't be so successful if she spent all her time at home with them. Most weekends, she was attending actual weddings, and planning for future weddings took up much of her time during the week. Besides, it wasn't like Cody and KellieAnne were toddlers. They were old enough to take care of themselves.

She suddenly remembered where his damn hockey stuff was. "I think Dad put your gear back in your closet!"

"Okay!" shouted Cody.

Lindsay groaned aloud. Her son's distraction had caused her to lose her train of thought.

"Crap, crap, crap, where was I… okay, yeah. Each contestant will model her dream wedding gown, with points awarded to the most attractive bride-to-be…" Lindsay typed.

"Hey, hon?" Lindsay's husband, Barry, bellowed. Lindsay tried hard to swallow her frustration.

"What?"

"Um, we got anything for dinner?"

"Yes. It's been kind of a busy day, okay? Got fish sticks and fries in the oven," Lindsay said. Barry accepted that answer and kept his mouth shut. He knew better than to cross her when she was in one of her moods. "Let's see, what else..." She thought about what she could add that would make the reality show more exciting, more challenging. What if the brides-to-be could vote each other off like in other reality shows? That would be great. Maybe even the viewers could vote people off? No, that was no good. They might just vote off the meanest brides, thus eliminating most of the conflict. Lindsay decided that she much preferred the idea of being the judge herself. It would be up to *her* to decide who got the fairytale wedding and who got sent home with her dreams crushed to pieces.

Lindsay felt a ripple of excitement when she thought about all the power she would wield as she lorded over the brides, their future in her hands. She relished the idea of putting the women through different challenges and then deciding the winner of each one. The contestants would have to kiss up to her constantly if they wanted to win.

Lindsay drummed her long, manicured fingernails on the desk as she tried to think of some challenges for the brides. Maybe she could give them a certain budget and they would have to find the best bargains for their weddings. It would have to be something specific, otherwise the women would wind up getting some used wedding gown from a thrift store. Lindsay grimaced at the thought. No. It would be better if they had to find a pair of Jimmy Choo shoes and a Versace gown for under a certain price. They'd be forced to race around town and beat each other to the best sales. Maybe she'd force them all to go to the same stores, where they could fight over the items.

Now that would be fun, Lindsay thought.

She could also challenge them to get the best deal on a hand-crafted designer wedding cake by encouraging them to argue with the baker. The old cliché of the squeaky wheel getting the grease was absolutely true. Lindsay knew firsthand; she'd gotten amazing bargains for brides by yelling at vendors.

Let's see, what else could I make them do? Lindsay thought. She grinned as a wonderful idea occurred to her. It was one thing to get the brides to model wedding gowns, which she was still going to do, but what if she made them wear bridesmaids' gowns? Lindsay laughed aloud as she typed up a challenge in which the brides would compete to see who could find the ugliest bridesmaid dress they could get their hands on. Then, they would have to model them. This time, the winner would be the one who looked the worst.

This was going to work. She could feel it. It had to work. Lindsay truly believed this was her last real shot at fame. She was pushing fifty and was still stuck doing mid-level weddings. She made a fair amount of money, but she wasn't exactly booking high society weddings in Manhattan. She was a fairly big fish here in Florida, but if she ever wanted to hit the really big time, she simply had to land her own reality show while she had the chance. She would do anything to be famous. Anything.

CHAPTER ELEVEN

Bachelor – CONFIRMED
By Matt McFarland

I'm an enigma. Or at least as I am as far as society is concerned. I'm a 34-year-old unmarried man who is neither gay, nor a lazy, worthless manchild. I just don't want to get married. I like my life. I'm content. I come and go as I please. I realize you're probably picturing days spent behind the counter at some minimum wage job, wild nights at strip clubs, numerous one-night-stands, and a filthy apartment with empty beer bottles and takeout containers. That's not exactly how it is…

I work as a Computer Systems Analyst for an engineering firm here in Florida. I own my own townhome, which is neat and clean. I do the best I can to keep it tidy myself, but I do have a housekeeper come in twice a month. No strip clubs (aside from the occasional bachelor party), but I do go out frequently for beers with my friends. Sure, I order takeout from time to time when I don't feel like making dinner, but I assure you that I am an excellent cook. In addition, kindly note that I neatly place takeout containers in proper waste receptacles at all times.

As for one-night-stands, well, all I can say is that I'm a red-blooded American male who enjoys—very much so—the company of women. I have been known to have a steady girlfriend now and then, though I've never lived with a woman. I always make it clear to the woman, by the third date if not before, that I have no plans to marry. Ever. Sure, lots of women think they can change my mind, but so far no dice and they can't say they weren't warned. If it's a husband you desire, you best keep looking, 'cause I'm not your guy.

So that's my story. Single, fun-loving and free-wheelin', yet a perfectly functional and contributing member of society.

Matt came over on Thursday night to watch crime shows with Imogene. Right before he arrived, she started having second thoughts. What if he got the wrong idea and thought she wanted to date him? Or worse, what if he thought this whole television-watching idea was really a booty call? Imogene shuddered. Sure, she'd slept with a few men in the past, but only when she was in a serious relationship. The idea of a one-night-stand seemed gross to her.

"Hey-hey!" Matt said, grinning, when Imogene opened the door. He sounded just like he had on the phone. Casual. So far so good. "I wasn't sure what you were drinking, so I just brought the beer I usually drink."

"No problem. I've got my usual wine chilling."

"Sweet!"

Imogene led him to the living room where he promptly flopped down on the couch like he was an old friend who'd visited her a million times already.

"Okay, what do we start with?" Imogene asked, picking up the remote.

"How about *Crime City: Los Angeles*? That's the one I'm dying to see. And I saved it just for you, my dear. I wanted to watch it so bad last night."

"Well, I appreciate the gesture," Imogene told him, laughing. She fired up the DVR and they settled in—but not too close—on the couch. It seemed strange to have a guy in her apartment again. She hadn't really hung out with a man since she'd broken up with Nathan. It was nice. Comfortable.

Matt cracked open his beer and Imogene sipped her wine. They laughed uproariously, if inappropriately, at the sometimes violent crime show.

"Dude, in that ugly-ass shirt, you deserved to die," Matt said. "Pink? Really?" He might be a huge proponent of gay rights, but he had a thing about guys wearing pastels. He did not approve.

"If fashion is a crime, that lady needs to be the next to go. Seriously, send that hairdo back to the 70s where it belongs," Imogene said. Of course, everything is even funnier when you've been drinking, and they reduced each other to tears on more than one occasion. Imogene could not remember ever laughing this much with *anyone*, not even her best girlfriends.

A nervous flutter stirred in Imogene's stomach when they'd watched the last program and it was time to call it a night. She'd had such a great time with Matt, but it was still so totally platonic. What if he tried to kiss her? Why didn't she want him to? If he did, what would happen to this wonderful friendship they were developing?

Imogene was afraid to let the evening end in case something happened.

Matt tossed his last beer bottle in the recycle bin and headed toward the door.

This was the moment of truth. Matt turned to face her.

Imogene took a deep breath. *Oh, please don't do it.*

Matt opened his arms and engulfed her in a huge bear hug.

"This was awesome! Can't wait to do it again next week!" Matt told her, grinning.

Imogene returned the hug with great enthusiasm. "Me, too!" Relief coursed through her. "You sure you're okay to drive?"

"Yeah, I'm cool. I know my limits. See ya!" He saluted her and headed out.

It amused Imogene to think how thrilled she was to receive a salute from her new guy friend rather than a kiss. She could barely suppress a giggle at the thought as she shut the door.

*****

The next morning at work, Imogene looked up from her desk to find a woman staring at her. Her face was tear-stained and her eyes red.

"Good morning. Can I help you?" Imogene asked her.

"Yes, please. I'm Donna Bridgeford. I have an appointment with Attorney Towers?" the woman said, sniffling and wiping her eyes. She was a thin, fairly attractive woman who was dressed professionally in a light gray skirt and a white blouse. At least she looked as if she would be attractive if her face wasn't swollen and red from crying. Imogene had the feeling that if not for this meeting with Camille, Donna would probably be at home wearing sweatpants.

"Of course. Right this way," Imogene said gently, getting up to lead Donna down the short hallway to the conference room. "Can I get you anything?"

"I want the last four years of my life back!" Donna wailed, before bursting into another crying fit.

Imogene nodded, understanding. Donna was hardly the first client here to say something like that. She gestured for her to have a seat at the conference room table, which was always set up with a pitcher of water, glasses, and a box of tissues. Donna settled into one of the cushiony chairs Camille had chosen for comfort as much as for professional appearance. The conference room was designed to be a deliberate mix of both a homey and business-like atmosphere. Camille knew her clients needed to be prepared for a possibly long and protracted fight with their soon-to-be-ex spouse, but she wanted to make them as comfortable as possible while they did it. There was a time to cry and a time to fight when it came to divorce battles, and this room had been designed to handle both.

"I'm so sorry! I don't know what's wrong with me. I mean, I do know what's wrong with me. A cheating bastard who used up four of my few remaining childbearing years." She sighed, and added, "I'm sorry. I don't mean to trouble you with my problems."

"Oh, please don't apologize," Imogene said kindly. She poured Donna a glass of water. "Unfortunately, we see a lot of unhappy people in here."

"Yeah, I guess you do," Donna responded wearily.

"Marriage doesn't always end up being the fairytale people told us about, does it?" Imogene said.

"Well, that's damn right!"

"Camille will be here in just a few minutes. Don't worry, she's very nice and will take really good care of you." Imogene paused for a moment. "You know, I run a new singles group called Solo Power. We kind of celebrate being single instead of being depre-"

"Oh, God, don't remind me that I'm single again! I'm thirty-four and single and I'm gonna die alone, surrounded by cats!"

Donna buried her head in her hands and Imogene stifled a groan. Here was yet another single woman buying into the whole "dying-alone-with-cats" stereotype. Donna was living proof that there were worse things than being thirty-something and single, like being thirty-something and divorced. The more Imogene thought about it, the crazier it seemed to pin all your hopes of happiness on one person, even if you were married. It's not up to your spouse or your kids to make your life meaningful, only *you* could make your life meaningful.

Only you can make your life meaningful. Wow, that was a good one. She'd have to try to remember that one for her next blog entry.

Imogene went back to her desk, leaving Donna to wallow in her misery. She supposed the poor woman was entitled to a little self-pity, but she knew Camille would whip her into shape. You can't have weepy, whiny clients if you wanted a chance at getting anything in the divorce settlement.

Just then, Camille Towers burst in. She never walked, she always burst. She was a busy woman, always in a hurry to get somewhere, do something. It made for a hectic workplace sometimes, but Camille was passionate about what she did for a living and her enthusiasm was contagious. She was always impeccably dressed, stylish, and sometimes wore clothes that were just a tad too young for her. Her chin-length hair wasn't gray, but probably should have been by now. If she dyed it, it was hard to tell. She reminded Imogene of Lindsay Saga by the way she dressed, but Camille was way classier. It was funny, Lindsay was in the business of weddings and Camille specialized in divorce. They were like opposite sides of a coin.

"Is my nine o'clock consult here yet?" Camille asked, breathless. Imogene opened her mouth to answer, but Camille held up a hand. "Wait! Good morning, Imogene."

Imogene laughed. "Good morning, Camille."

"Is my nine o'clock consult here yet?" Camille repeated, smiling.

"Yes. She just got here. It's okay. Take a breath."

Camille hurried into her office to put her purse away. When she came back out, she headed for Imogene's desk instead of the conference room.

"Imogene," Camille said.

Imogene looked up from her desk and blinked, surprised to see her boss.

"Uh, yes?" Imogene started to wonder if she was in trouble or something.

"I finally got a chance to read through your blog. I'm sorry it took me this long. I must say, I'm impressed."

"Really?" Imogene asked. Camille had been happily married for a long time, so Imogene wasn't sure how she would react to her singles pride crusade. But she was also childfree by choice and clearly didn't buy into the whole "kids are the meaning of life" idea.

"I think it's fantastic. Getting married and having kids is wonderful, but it's really not for everybody. I think your idea for a singles group is excellent! And long overdue. This is something that can really help people, Imogene. This could be your calling!"

"You think?"

Imogene stared at her, amazed. She'd always admired her boss for her success in life and was truly flattered that Camille had thought of her that way.

"When I hired you five years ago, I could see it. You had attitude. In a good way! Determination, drive, that kind of thing. I really thought you'd be running this place by now. It's about time you stopped waiting around for some goddamn man to come and save you!"

Imogene felt slightly embarrassed that it had been that obvious. She had done okay in her job at the law firm, but she certainly hadn't given it her all or really shown much initiative. She'd always viewed her work at the law office as just a day job to do while waiting to get married and have kids. She'd been waiting for her "real life" to begin, when in fact it had been in progress all along.

"Thanks. That's pretty much the same realization I've come to. I've been wasting my life waiting for the right man to come along."

Camille nodded. "And he still might. If some great guy shows up and you want to spend the rest of your life with him, great! But if not, so be it!"

Camille made it sound so simple. And it really was that simple, Imogene supposed. Simple, but not always easy. There would always be a little part of her that missed having a partner. She still felt sad when she thought of the wedding she'd never have, the long walks and talks she would never experience with her husband, the dinners alone instead of cooking for a family. It was hard to imagine being on her own forever. Imogene felt guilty having these thoughts, like she was betraying her new Solo Power friends. Then again, when she pictured her new friends, she didn't really feel lonely anymore.

"Keep up the good work!" Camille said as she hurried off to the conference room.

Imogene glanced at her phone, which she kept on silent mode at work. She saw she had one missed call but she didn't recognize the number. She typed the phone number into Google to do a reverse phone number lookup and gasped when The Estrogen Network came up. "Holy crap!" she exclaimed. She glanced toward the conference room and was grateful that Camille had already shut the door. Imogene clicked on the number that had showed up on her phone so she could call them back.

"Good morning, thank you for calling The Estrogen Network," a perky voice said.

Imogene realized, too late, that she had no idea who at the network had called her. They hadn't left her a message and she only knew it was the network by looking up the number.

"Um, somebody called me from this number and…um…" Just then, her call waiting clicked in. "Never mind!" Imogene quickly hung up on the poor receptionist and answered the other line. "Hello? Yes, this is she…"

"Hello, Miss Hart. My name is Jacqueline Torris, and I'm one of the executives here at The Estrogen Network. I have to say I was very impressed with your proposal for *Single, Not Alone.*"

"Thank you very much!" Imogene's heart was beating so hard she could hear it pounding in her ears. She couldn't wait to tell the Solo Power group that she had actually gotten a personal response from the network! She waited for Jacqueline to tell her that, though she liked the proposal, they couldn't consider it because it wasn't about weddings.

"I can't tell you how nice it was to receive a proposal that had nothing to do with weddings," Jacqueline said, the irritation clear in her voice.

"Glad to know I'm not the only one who's tired of that sort of thing. I mean, it's fine, but there are so many other topics out there for a show!"

"Don't I know it. Anyway, it took a lot of finagling, but I got some of the others at the network to at least consider it."

"Well, I guess – Wait. What? You're actually considering doing my show?" Imogene asked, feeling a bit dizzy.

"Yes. They've agreed to at least discuss it. We've got it

narrowed down to your show and a show that is all about brides. We need to move rather quickly, since we want to fill the hole in our programming. We had expected *Get the Ring, Ladies* to still be on the air, and we're losing a lot of ad revenue right now. Would you be able to come to a meeting at the network to discuss your show?"

"Oh my—Yes! Yes, of course!" Shakily, Imogene managed to write down the details of where and when the meeting would take place. "Thank you so much! Honestly, I never thought we would get this far with our proposal."

"Me neither, to tell you the truth. Well, I'm fighting for you, for what it's worth. I understand that ratings are critical, but I really think our audience is a lot more intelligent than our network tends to give them credit for. Thanks so much for your time. I look forward to meeting you."

"Same here. Thank you!"

Imogene hung up the phone. She pressed her fist over her mouth and screamed into it. Had she been anywhere else, she would have yelled at the top of her lungs. She knew she had to keep her enthusiasm in check, and not just to avoid being fired for screaming at work.

Maybe her singles crusade wasn't as crazy as her family thought.

When Camille returned to the reception area with a tear-stained but much calmer Donna Bridgeford, Imogene couldn't resist telling her right away about the exciting news.

"Camille! You won't believe this, but I just got a call from The Estrogen Network!"

"About the singles show you talked about on your blog? You're kidding!" Camille said.

"They want to meet me to discuss it! I mean, they're probably gonna go with another idiotic wedding show, but at least I've got a shot at them doing a show about single people!"

Camille grabbed Imogene and hugged her warmly. "Imogene, that's fantastic!"

Imogene noted the look of surprise on Donna's face and, lest she be imagining things, a glimmer of hope. The woman was clearly surprised to see how much Imogene had meant what she said. She really was happy being single. Imogene's heart warmed, thrilled that the very idea of the singles show was working already.

It was agonizing to wait until her lunch break to call Matt and Paula to tell them the amazing news.

"No kiddin'!" Matt said when she called him. "That's crazy. I thought they would ignore us for sure. The most I expected was a form rejection letter. That's really great, Imogene. Way to go!!"

Paula actually screamed with excitement when Imogene told her she had a meeting with the network about their singles reality show. Imogene laughed, loving her enthusiasm.

"Don't get too excited," Imogene warned her. "They were pretty clear that they are still leaning toward another dumb wedding show."

"I'll get as excited as I please, little lady, and I advise you to do the same. This is a wonderful accomplishment. I'm so proud of you! No matter what happens, you got them thinking. Isn't that what you set out to do?"

"True."

"And you've done it! You've got them second-guessing themselves about adding another wedding show to their network. I think we're gonna get our show on the air. I really do!"

Feeding on Paula's enthusiasm, Imogene allowed herself to fantasize about *Single, Not Alone* actually happening. Her stomach fluttered with excitement. Just thinking about lonely, single men and women watching the show and becoming inspired, feeling better about themselves, literally made her eyes tear up.

"Do you really think it could happen?" Imogene asked, her voice choking up a bit.

Paula must have heard the catch in her voice, because she spoke softly yet firmly. "Yes, Imogene. Yes, I do."

After calling Matt and Paula, Imogene sent a text message to tell Hannah. Imogene figured she would be in school and she didn't want to get her in trouble by calling her. She briefly considered calling her sisters to tell them what was going on, but she couldn't bring herself to do it. Even Faye and Chrissy would have to admit it was pretty incredible to be called into a meeting with The Estrogen Network, but Imogene feared they would just start in on her about getting married and tell her she was spreading evil singles propaganda. No. She would tell them later. She was way too excited to risk letting them ruin her happiness.

CHAPTER TWELVE

Lindsay arrived fashionably late to the meeting at The Estrogen Network. In reality, she had arrived early, but hid out in her car for about twenty-five minutes before heading into the network's building. She didn't want to blow this opportunity, but she had to make it clear that she was a celebrity (sort of) and worth waiting for.

The receptionist clearly recognized her, which pleased Lindsay immensely.

"Ms. Saga!" the young girl had exclaimed. "Come with me."

The receptionist led Lindsay to a large conference room with huge windows and a wonderful view of downtown Orlando. Lindsay felt a flutter of excitement in her stomach. This was really happening. Her big break. Her own reality show, which would make her a huge star, the reigning queen of brides everywhere.

A woman in a crisp navy and black suit rose to meet her. Lindsay recognized the suit right away—it was Degane—and it went for around $2500. Nice. Very nice.

"Ms. Saga, it's so nice to meet you in person. I'm a big fan of your work!" the woman said. "I'm Becky Houston."

"Of course. How wonderful to meet you," Lindsay said, shaking her hand warmly. She recalled seeing Becky on the news talking about the reality show contest. She was one of the chief executives of the network.

"I'd like you to meet Ms. Imogene Hart," Becky said.

Lindsay glanced at Imogene disdainfully, figuring she must be some sort of assistant. The woman was dressed in a simple black skirt and pink blouse, probably from JC Penny or Sears. Lindsay shook her hand and graced her with the fake smile she reserved for greeting nobodies.

"Wonderful to meet you!" Lindsay said.

"You, too!" Imogene said, nodding. Lindsay couldn't tell whether Imogene recognized her or not.

Another well-dressed woman (though not as expensively dressed as Becky) stood and offered her hand to Lindsay. "Good morning. I'm Jacqueline Torris, one of the executives here at The Estrogen Network."

"Please, everyone have a seat and we'll get started," Becky said. "The reason we brought you all together this morning is that, though we've received a lot of great proposal ideas for our new reality show, we've narrowed it down to your two."

Which two? Lindsay thought. She looked around and her gaze landed on Imogene. Oh, no. They weren't considering some kind of white-trash, low-budget wedding show, were they? Lindsay had taken a lot of criticism lately about the wasteful nature of big weddings and how nobody could afford them anymore in this economy, blah, blah, blah. But that was just the point of her reality show, wasn't it? Some poor bride who couldn't afford her services would win the grand prize of her dream wedding!

"We loved the idea of having a Lindsay Saga wedding show!" Becky gushed. "I think it would be an incredible ratings draw, as you're already a "name" in the wedding industry. I have no doubt whatsoever that our viewers would be very excited to see a show about the beautiful weddings you plan."

"Oh, I think so, too!" Lindsay said. "And I love the idea of helping some lucky bride have the wedding of her dreams. One she never thought she could afford, but we can make it happen! Everybody loves a dream wedding, and I believe women everywhere would tune in to see it!"

Was it her imagination or did that Imogene woman just roll her eyes?

"And I don't think it would be difficult to get lots of sponsors for a Lindsay Saga reality show," Lindsay continued. "The most prestigious wedding vendors in the industry would be willing to donate their products and services in exchange for being included in the final wedding show. I can just imagine the ratings for the finale of the season! Everything leads up to the wedding and so many people would tune in for-"

"That sounds great and I'm certain that a lot of people would love that," Imogene began. Lindsay slowly turned her head, stunned that Imogene had the gall to interrupt her. "But don't you think The Estrogen Network has enough wedding shows? I mean, they're very popular and that's great, but I think maybe it's time to try something totally different. You already have lots of brides-to-be who love your network, but you could start attracting a whole new demographic in addition to the one you already have if you tried something different."

"Yes, I agree that perhaps a little change of pace may be warranted," Jacqueline began tactfully. "We do have quite a number of wedding shows on our network and it might be refreshing to try something new."

Jacqueline was smiling, but you could see the contempt she had for wedding shows barely hidden beneath the surface. With her closely-cropped hair, she was probably some bitter lesbian who had a thing against weddings.

"Exactly! I think a show for single people about the singles life could really be a great success for the network," Imogene said.

Lindsay burst out laughing. It was unladylike and not in keeping with her usual cool demeanor, but she couldn't help it. "You can't be serious!"

Imogene stared at her, unblinking. Lindsay realized that Imogene must be one of those hyper-feminist, man-hating types who thought women were better off devoting their lives to a soulless career than to having a family.

"Why would anyone want a show all about single people? Oh, wait! You mean, like a matchmaking thing where-"

"Hell, no!" Imogene burst out. "Sorry. Sorry, I mean, no. That's not at all what I mean. It would be a show all about the single life and why you should embrace it. Everybody can make a difference in the world and have a meaningful life, even if they don't get married and have children."

Lindsay shot Imogene her patented death stare, the one that reduced her assistant and housekeepers pretty much to rubble. It didn't seem to have much effect on Imogene.

"A singles show..." Lindsay shook her head and laughed again. She looked at Becky, who shrugged apologetically. "You're thinking of putting on a reality show about lonely, single people instead of a show celebrating love."

"Single people are not lonely!" Imogene snapped. Lindsay leaned back in her chair and let out a sharp, sarcastic sigh. Then she glanced at Becky, who shifted uncomfortably in her seat. "Just because someone doesn't have a significant other, either because they choose not to or just because they haven't met the right person does *not* mean they're lonely. Single people do have family, friends, work, hobbies, and lots of other things to-"

"Fill the void when they don't get married!" Lindsay interrupted, leaning forward in her chair. She looked to Becky, waiting for her to back her up. Imogene drew a breath but Jacqueline spoke first to try to defuse the mood of the room, which was rapidly deteriorating.

"We're just trying to explore all angles available here. Certainly another wedding show would be great!" Jacqueline said, wincing on the word *another*. "But we thought it might be interesting to have a show about single people for a change. It would be sort of an inspirational show, sort of Oprah-esque if you will, one that shows you how to live your best life. Single people are often down on themselves, and this show would lift them up and show them what they could be!"

"And that would be wonderful!" Becky said. "But we're also quite interested in having a Lindsay Saga wedding show. As you mentioned, it would be a dream come true for these lucky brides just to be on the show. And the grand prize would be just glorious! To be able to see some poor bride's dream of a fairytale wedding realized!" Lindsay could almost see the stars in Becky's eyes.

"Wouldn't that be just beautiful?" Jacqueline said, her teeth clenched. "But it would also be beautiful to help people change their lives with the singles show. So empowering for women! It would be so inspiring to our viewers and it would have a lasting effect, you know, unlike after a wedding when that's pretty much it."

"Exactly!" Imogene said. "The singles show would have a lasting effect, whereas a wedding is just one day."

"One day," Lindsay scoffed. "Only the most important day in any woman's life."

"Not every woman's life. Not my life!"

"Well, obviously not. I mean, you've clearly closed yourself off to the idea of love. You'd rather spend your life alone, concentrating on yourself instead of-"

"Now, wait just a minute there, Lindsay!" Imogene said, leaning forward in her chair. Lindsay couldn't believe the girl had called her by her first name. She was Ms. Saga to everybody but her closest family and friends. "Just because I'm single doesn't mean-"

"Um, it seems we're getting a bit off track here," Becky interjected. "We clearly have two really fantastic ideas and only one slot. It will be so hard to choose!"

Not for her, it's not, Lindsay thought. Becky was clearly in the wedding camp, while Jacqueline was right up Spinster Alley.

"Right. Since we can't quite agree on which of these great ideas to go with, we've come up with kind of a solution on how to decide," Jacqueline said. "Since we've gotten such a great viewer response to our call for proposal ideas for the new reality show, we've decided to leave it up to viewers to decide which show they would like to see on the air!"

A slow smile spread across Lindsay's face. This was going to be even better than she'd thought. No way was the public going to vote for some depressing reality show about singles. All women were into weddings. Single women were desperate to have one of their own, so they lived vicariously through their friends' weddings and through the ones on TV until it was their turn. Engaged women were clearly obsessed with planning their own big day and loved watching wedding shows. Past brides loved to relive their day by watching other weddings, reveling in the fact that they were safely married and not desperately trying to catch the bouquet at the reception. As if that weren't enough to clinch the deal, Lindsay Saga was famous for the elegant and dreamy weddings she created. Nobody knew or cared who this Imogene person was.

Not only would Lindsay get her show on the air, she would

crush this upstart Imogene girl in the process. She would get the satisfaction of completely humiliating her when her singles show lost by thousands and thousands of votes.

"What a great idea!" Lindsay said, as she turned to look directly at Imogene. "Don't you think that's wonderful? We'll let the viewers decide."

"Oh, I can't think of anything I would like more," Imogene said smugly.

What was wrong with her? She couldn't possibly think her little show had a chance in hell. Let her dream. Her cockiness would only make this little competition that much more fun.

"Wonderful!" Becky said. "We'll announce the contest in a press release and we'll keep count on The Estrogen Network's website. The first show to receive 250,000 votes goes on the air!"

"Fabulous. What a fabulous idea! And it will be such great publicity for the network," Lindsay said. Sure, it would be great publicity for The Estrogen Network, but who cared? It would be excellent PR for Lindsay Saga Weddings. She would get her name out there even before her show went on the air. Lindsay couldn't wait to demolish Imogene and her ridiculous singles show, but the longer the fight dragged out, the more publicity there would be for Lindsay. It was a win-win.

"Okay then! So it will be *Beautiful Bride* vs. *Single, Not Alone*. Good luck ladies. May the best show win!" Becky said.

Oh, it will, thought Lindsay.

CHAPTER THIRTEEN

Imogene announced, via the blog, Facebook, and Twitter, that there was to be an important meeting of the Solo Power group the very next day. She sent out several social media messages entitled CALLING ALL SINGLES!! and encouraged single men and women in the area to attend the meeting.

So as not to get their hopes up too high, Imogene had texted Matt, Paula, and Hannah telling them that The Estrogen Network hadn't made any decisions yet about what kind of reality show they would produce. She told them that the meeting went well, and she would give them all the details tomorrow.

When she arrived at the library, she was pleased to see about a dozen people gathered. Hannah and Paula were already there. She didn't see Matt yet, but she knew he would be there. Imogene noticed that Hannah looked kind of down.

"You okay, hon?"

Hannah shrugged and said quietly "Rough day…"

Imogene's heart ached for the girl. She had noticed that someone uploaded a photo of an elephant on Hannah's Facebook wall the other day. Imogene had desperately hoped that it was some kind of silly inside joke between Hannah and a friend and not a horrific jab about Hannah's weight. Now Imogene was forced to believe the latter. She felt a tightness in her stomach and found herself balling her fists. She would love nothing more than to march into Hannah's school and confront all those cowardly bullies who harassed her.

Imogene couldn't help but feel slightly annoyed with Hannah, too, though she knew that was probably unfair. The girl was so bright and so funny. If only she would stop looking down at the ground and acting so shy. Imogene wished Hannah would speak up for herself and hold her head high!

Easy for me to say, thought Imogene. She couldn't imagine how hard things must be for Hannah at school.

Matt breezed in and took a seat in the front row of the conference room. He glanced over at Hannah, who was seated right next to Paula. He winked at Hannah.

"Hey, beautiful," he said.

"Well now, which one of us are you talking to there, sailor?" Paula asked flirtatiously.

Matt grinned at her. "Tell you what. You're 'hey, sexy' and she's 'hey, beautiful'," he said, looking at Hannah.

"Deal," Paula said. She fist-bumped Hannah, who was blushing.

Imogene smiled, as that familiar feeling of warmth and happiness washed over her. She really loved being around her new friends. Matt was sweet and charming, and she was so grateful that he'd said just the right thing to bring a smile to Hannah's face.

"Well, what about me?" Imogene asked, batting her eyelashes at Matt.

He lifted his head in acknowledgement and said "'Sup'."

Imogene laughed. "I'm touched..." She scanned the room and was excited to see that a few more people had come in, some of whom she knew. Squealing, Imogene jogged to the back of the room.

"I can't believe you guys came!" Imogene said. She hugged Susan and Kate, excited to see her married friends at her singles meeting. Imogene had also received a text message earlier in the day from Adrienne apologizing that she couldn't attend the meeting and demanding details on whatever the announcement was. Imogene had promised to fill her in after the meeting.

"Of course. We wouldn't miss it!" Susan said. "I know we've been horrible about keeping in touch like we promised, so we figured this would be a great time to catch up. I can't wait to see what you're up to with this group!"

"Nice turnout," Kate said approvingly as she looked around the room. "Didn't you say you only had a few people the first time?"

"Yeah, it's definitely getting better. I have a good feeling the group is going to get even bigger after tonight." Imogene said. "I better get started. Thanks again for coming! So nice to know that not all married people think I'm crazy."

"Don't listen to those bitchy sisters of yours, Imogene," Susan said. Imogene smiled and nodded, then headed back up to the front of the room. A flutter of nervousness and excitement went through her body as she faced the small crowd.

"It's great to see that we have some new faces here today. Welcome, and thank you so much for coming! For those of you who don't know me, my name is Imogene Hart. I started this group to help change the way society views single people and even the way we view ourselves," Imogene looked directly at Hannah when she said that last part.

"Hear, hear!" Paula yelled, which got a chuckle out of the people in attendance.

"I know that most of you are familiar with The Estrogen

Network, otherwise known as the All-Weddings, All-the-Time Network," Imogene said, eliciting groans of annoyance from around the room. "As you may have heard, they recently announced they were accepting proposals for a stupid wedding show to replace yet another stupid wedding show that is currently on hiatus."

"Yeah. On hiatus for five-to-ten for grand theft," Hannah murmured low enough that only a few people around her heard it. Those who heard her, including Imogene, chuckled.

"Pretty much," Imogene said, smiling at Hannah. "Anyway, we figured why should they only be open to wedding shows? Why couldn't they at least consider a reality show about singles? So the founding members of Solo Power and I put together a proposal for a show that would be an inspirational-type program to help single people embrace their lives and understand that they matter just as much as married people. We figured the network would ignore us. The plan was to at least get them thinking. We wanted to make them question their decision to broadcast so many wedding and bridal shows while ignoring all the single people out there. Much to our surprise, The Estrogen Network brought me in for a meeting." Imogene's stomach turned over as a jolt of fresh excitement shot through her. She could hardly wait to say the words out loud. "The network is considering putting our singles show on the air."

Imogene's excitement was contagious, as hoots and hollers erupted, the loudest coming from Paula and Matt.

"No way!" Paula shouted.

"That's amazing. Way to go, Imogene!" Matt said. He started applauding and everyone else joined in.

Imogene shouted over the noise, "I can't take all the credit. I had lots of help developing the proposal for our show. Paula

Flandey, Matt McFarland, and Hannah Wanderling, please stand up and be recognized!"

Paula stood up and curtsied, while Matt took a huge, theatrical bow. Both actions made the crowd laugh. Hannah stood up tentatively, looking like she was tempted to act as showy as the other two. As usual, she looked at the ground instead.

"And Hannah was the one who came up with the brilliant title, *Single, Not Alone!*" More applause, which made Hannah blush. Hannah sat back down and so did Matt and Paula.

The door to the conference room opened and a woman who was about Imogene's age slipped in quietly. She looked familiar. It took Imogene a moment or two to place her; then she recognized her as Donna, the weeping woman who was in Camille's office the other day.

"Paula, Matt, and Hannah came up with some wonderful ideas for the singles show and that's why The Estrogen Network is taking us seriously. We've come up with a great plan for a show that can really inspire single people so they'll know that they are *not* alone and they can be just as happy and fulfilled as married people. And that goes for people who never married or are divorced, separated, or whatever," Imogene said, looking at Donna and smiling. Donna smiled back, but there were tears in her eyes. Imogene could almost feel her pain. Imogene was so honored that she had come to the meeting. If anyone was in need of a singles support group, it was a woman going through a painful divorce. Imogene vowed to do whatever she could to help Donna, and she knew she wouldn't be the only Solo Power member to reach out to her and offer love and support.

Imogene also noticed that her friend, Kate, looked almost as sad as Donna did. Imogene had a feeling that Kate's marriage was a deeply unhappy one, and that could be much worse than being divorced.

"Okay, here's the deal," Imogene said. "The network executives have narrowed their search down to ours and one other reality show."

"Some wedding crap, no doubt," Hannah muttered. "Watch *Bridal Bitch* and see who's the last one standing!" As usual, she looked surprised that her comment garnered laughter from the group.

"Oh for the love of God, Hannah, *speak up!*" Imogene said a bit louder than she'd intended.

The whole room went deadly silent. Hannah looked like she'd been slapped in the face. Paula and Matt looked at Imogene wide-eyed. Imogene was about to apologize for her sudden outburst, then thought better of it.

"Many of you read Hannah's blog post, right?" Imogene asked. She looked at all the faces staring back at her. "She said she didn't want to be the funny fat girl." Imogene did her best not to wince when using the word *fat* in reference to Hannah, but that was what she called herself in the blog. "Well, that's not how I see this incredible, amazing young woman. This is a girl with fire in her. She's got such a quick wit, and she's so damn smart. I want to see her look up at the world, not down at the floor!"

Imogene could see by the smiles and nods from the audience that they understood where she was going with this, and they approved.

"I want to see you look at people when you speak. When you've got something to say, say it out loud. Don't hide! You are too important and you've got too much to give the world to stay hidden. Do you understand me?" Imogene said, looking defiantly into Hannah's eyes.

Everyone turned to the young girl to see how she would react.

"Yes, Sarge," Hannah responded, somewhat louder than she had spoken before.

"What did you say?" Imogene demanded.

"I said, YES, SARGE!!" Hannah shouted.

People laughed, then began applauding. Hannah laughed, too. She also blushed and looked at the floor. She realized what she was doing and quickly looked up at Imogene.

Imogene broke into a huge smile. "That's my girl!"

"Oooh, I do like a sassy woman," Matt said with approval.

"Slow your roll, Slick," Hannah said dryly. "Aren't you a confirmed bachelor?"

"Yeah, but you never know… a smart, pretty lady like you could make me change my mind," Matt said. Hannah chuckled and waved him off, but she didn't blush this time.

"Hannah darling, you're so close on your guess about the other show, it's not even funny…" Imogene told her. "The title is *Beautiful Bride,* but it might as well be called *Bridal Bitch* because that's what it comes down to. A bunch of stupid challenges for bridezillas to compete against each other so one of them can win an all-expenses-paid wedding."

"Oh, yuck," Paula said.

"Yeah, it's essentially a beauty contest for brides because, after all, that's what love is all about right? Who's the prettiest!" Imogene said, rolling her eyes. "The bridal proposal was submitted by Lindsay Saga."

This news was greeted with a mixture of annoyance and interest.

"Wow, she's pretty famous…" Hannah said, looking a little concerned.

"Yeah, she is. Those weddings she puts on…" Paula said, shaking her head. "When you think of the money people sink into those ridiculous affairs! It's sickening, it really is."

"I know. People call me irresponsible because I'm not married, but you don't see me squandering a downpayment on a house on some stupid party," Matt said. "Look, I know it's not just a party and there's more to it than that. I mean, my brother's planning his wedding and it's really important to him, but it really is a waste to sink all your dough into a friggin' ice sculpture and chocolate fountain." He paused and looked thoughtful. "Well, then again, a chocolate fountain might be kinda awesome…"

"Hell, yeah," Paula agreed.

"But yeah, Lindsay Saga weddings are all about way over-the-top spending and who has the best fancy napkins," Matt continued. "It's just dumb. My brother and his boyfriend are planning a really nice ceremony, writing their own vows and stuff, and it's way more about how much they love each other than anything else."

"Lindsay's weddings are all about who's the most beautiful and who has the most expensive stuff, and her reality show will be no different. Problem is, she's a celebrity, so she'll be hard to beat. She's also kind of a jerk," Imogene said.

"Did you meet her?" Susan asked, sounding impressed.

"Yeah. She was at The Estrogen Network meeting. She thinks our singles idea is the dumbest thing she's ever heard."

"Bitch," Susan muttered, no longer too impressed with Lindsay.

"So what happens now? Do we have to do another proposal or something?" Paula asked.

"No. The network has actually decided to leave it up to the viewers to decide. They're going to have a contest. The first show that gets 250,000 votes wins."

Matt whistled through his teeth. "That's gonna be tough."

"Yeah, it will be," Imogene admitted. "Lindsay's already

famous, and I know lots of women would kill to be on a wedding show with her. Not only that, but the grand prize is an all-expenses-paid wedding planned by Lindsay herself."

"Do you really think we have a shot?" Hannah asked softly. Then, remembering Imogene's orders to speak up, she spoke a bit louder. "I mean, it's Lindsay Saga! And look, I know singles stuff is really important to you—to us—but do you really think we can get people to vote for that over a wedding show?"

The room got quiet for a moment. It was obvious that this would be an uphill battle. There was a reason that The Estrogen Network was nearly nonstop wedding programs. Because people were watching. Lots of people.

"Yes!" Imogene said with more confidence than she actually felt.

She knew there was a distinct possibility that Lindsay Saga's show could get up to 250,000 votes before their singles show got even a few thousand, but she was determined not to let that happen. "I'm not gonna lie to you. It won't be easy. Lindsay is famous and people do love her weddings, but it's our job to show people how great being single can be. I totally get why brides-to-be would be interested in her show. They want to get ideas for their own wedding or they're just so damn obsessed with weddings while they're engaged that they don't think about anything else."

Nods from around the room. Everybody knew somebody like that. The Bride Who Wouldn't Shut Up.

"But don't forget why we're here today. Why we started this group in the first place! To help single people be happy being single *right now*. I hate to think of all the single women-" Imogene paused and looked at Matt. "-single *people* being bombarded with all this wedding stuff and thinking there's something wrong with them. Wedding shows are fine, I guess...for people planning a wedding, but there should be other shows for those who aren't."

"Damn right!" Paula said.

"And even if we can't get our show on the air, we can still get our Solo Power name out there and reach out to a lot of people. People will hear about our group and know there's an alternative for those who don't have a significant other."

"That's a really good point," Matt said thoughtfully. "We can really piggy-back on Lindsay's name. I mean, if we're her competition, we could make national news just for that alone."

"Yep. And I know she'll just love to have our little singles group right there beside her," Imogene said, smiling.

Lindsay obviously had nothing but utter contempt for the whole singles show idea. She made her living convincing women that they absolutely *had* to have a huge, overblown, princess wedding. She clearly bought into the idea that a single woman was a lonely object of pity. Not only was Lindsay Saga the competition for the singles show, she was the enemy of single people everywhere. It was people like her who made single women feel terrible about themselves.

"Just think, every step of the way, we'll be right there behind her. She'll be touting the importance of having some stupid, wasteful wedding and we'll be right there showing how great life can be without a partner. Finally, we can show the world that there's *nothing* wrong with us, that we're *not* losers. We are real people with real hearts and real minds and we have a lot to contribute to this world!"

Paula started applauding and others followed suit. Matt clapped and whistled. Imogene grinned, bolstered by the warm show of support.

"The next step is to spread the word to everybody you know. Tell your friends and family about our group and about the contest. And not just single people. We're lucky to have some great married supporters, too!" Imogene said. She gestured to Susan and Kate in the back of the room. "With our grass roots efforts and the publicity from The Estrogen Network, we can really get our name out there. But I think we can do more than that," Imogene said, adrenaline coursing through her. "I think we can actually win this thing."

CHAPTER FOURTEEN

After all the excitement from the Solo Power meeting, Imogene found she couldn't wait to share the news about the contest with her family. She hadn't told them about the proposal in the first place, knowing full well they wouldn't approve and they would just crush her enthusiasm. Now that she had the backing of The Estrogen Network, her family couldn't help but be impressed. It had nearly killed her to wait until Sunday dinner, but she desperately wanted to tell them in person and that was the only time everybody was gathered together in one place.

Faye was there with Richard and the kids, but they were still waiting for Chrissy and Liam. Where the hell were they? Imogene thought it was ridiculous that Faye could manage to get two young kids dressed and ready and arrive on time but Chrissy couldn't even get herself together.

The door opened and Chrissy and Liam came in.

"Finally! Where the hell have you been?" Imogene demanded.

"Jeez, chill out. We're like fifteen minutes late. What's the big deal?" Chrissy said.

Marcus came running in and grabbed her leg. "Hi Aunt Kwissy!"

"Hi, pookie!" Chrissy picked up Marcus and snuggled him.

Liam wandered into the living room to watch TV with Richard. The timer buzzed and Imogene's dad went to pull dinner out of the oven. Imogene looked around and saw family members scattered in every room in the house. She realized it would be impossible to get everyone together in the same place at the same time right now. She would have to wait until they were all seated around the dinner table. She sighed heavily. It was so frustrating. She had waited almost a week to share this news and she could hardly stand it a moment longer.

It seemed there was always somebody else who had a big announcement to share at Sunday dinner. Somebody got a new job, then a promotion. Then one of her sisters was dating a new man. The next thing you knew, she was engaged. Then married. Then the other sister was dating, then got engaged. Then the already married sister announced she was pregnant. Meanwhile, Imogene was always stuck in the same dead-end job and was still single. She never had anything new to share, but that didn't stop her family from constantly interrogating her about what was new in her life. Or, more accurately, *who* was new in her life. That's all they'd seemed to care about since she broke up with Nathan. Who was next on the horizon.

Well, this time she *did* have big news for her family. And it was just as exciting as announcing an engagement or a pregnancy.

Everyone eventually made their way to the table. It was painful to wait until everyone, especially the kids, sat down.

"Okay. Everybody settled? Good. Shut up. There's something I've been dying to tell you guys!"

"Oooh, are you dating somebody? Is it that Mark guy from your little group?" Chrissy asked. There were so many offensive things in that sentence that Imogene simply chose to ignore her sister altogether.

"It's about my singles group." Every face at the table fell, and not one of them had the decency to hide it. "I assume you've all heard of The Estrogen Network?" Nods from Faye and Chrissy, and a combination of blank stares and shrugs from Liam, Richard, and her father. "It's supposed to be a network for women, but really it's just a bunch of shows about weddings."

"I know! I just love the one about the wedding gowns…" Chrissy said.

"Oh, yeah! That mother-daughter show where they go to pick out the dresses and-" Faye began.

"*Anyway…*" Imogene continued. Her sisters looked suitably chastened. "The network was asking for suggestions from viewers for a new wedding show. I thought it was stupid for them to consider only shows about weddings, so me and some of the members of Solo Power put together a proposal for a singles show." Imogene drew a deep breath. "And The Estrogen Network is considering putting it on the air."

Chrissy gasped. "Are you serious?"

Imogene nodded and squealed a little. As far as she was concerned, this was way more exciting than announcing that she was dating some guy.

"Yes. They've narrowed it down to my show and another stupid wedding show. They're going to leave it up to the viewers to decide. Starting tomorrow, they're going to let people vote on their website for which show they want, so make sure you go vote tomorrow!"

"Immy, that's amazing!" Faye said. "The network actually called you?"

"Not just called. I went to a meeting there and met two of the executives."

"Wow!" Chrissy said, genuinely impressed. "What's your show

about?"

"It's called *Single, Not Alone* and it's all about how just because you're single doesn't mean you're some lonely spinster. It will be kind of like a life makeover show where we take somebody who's single and down about it, and show them how great their life can be even if they never get married. They can get a scholarship to go back to school or something, like really figure out what to do with their lives instead of feeling like giving up because they're not married."

Dad frowned. "So you're pretty much telling people that it's okay to not get married. That they don't need a family."

"Dad, just because you don't raise your own family doesn't mean you have no family. I have you! And I have two sisters, two nephews…"

"That's different."

"Well yeah, it's different, but that's just it. Everybody's life is different. It doesn't mean that married people with kids are better than single people."

"Just happier," her dad said.

"Says who?" Imogene demanded.

"That's just, you know, the way it is. People who get married and have kids are more fulfilled than-"

"That's not true!" Imogene looked around at her sisters and could see she wasn't going to get any support from them. "See, this is just the kind of attitude we're trying to change. Everybody thinks that single people are lonely all the time and have no lives. That's exactly what causes so damn many unhappy marriages. People think they have to get married, and half of them make a horrible mistake and then have to get divorced or live unhappily ever after. Well, I'm not buying into that garbage. I'm not gonna marry somebody I don't love!" Imogene shouted.

"Imogene," Faye said gently. "Nobody said you should marry somebody you don't love. Chrissy and I certainly didn't." She squeezed her husband's shoulder with affection.

Sure, Faye and Chrissy had good marriages. They were lucky. Not everybody was. "But do you really think it's such a good idea to encourage people to be single?" Faye continued. "You don't want people to give up on marriage just because they haven't found anybody yet. I don't want you to give up, either."

"I'm not *encouraging* people to be single. Lots of people *are* single. And there's an awful lot of married jerks out there who make them feel like crap about it!" Imogene said, glaring accusingly at her sisters.

"Yeah, but isn't your show kind of telling people if they're single, they should stay that way?" Chrissy asked. Dad nodded.

"Not necessarily. I'm not telling people not to get married. I'm just saying it's okay if they don't."

"Is it?" Dad asked. "I mean, don't you think people who don't get married will live to regret it?"

"NO!" Imogene was ready to throw a full-on tantrum. It was so damn frustrating that nobody seemed to understand what she was saying.

"So what is the other show? The other one they're considering?" Chrissy asked.

"Like I said, it's just another dumb wedding show. Lindsay Saga wants to run some ridiculous pageant-like thing where the winning bride would get a free wedding planned by her." Imogene shook her head in disgust.

Both her sisters gasped.

"Lindsay Saga? *The* Lindsay Saga? The one from TV?" Chrissy asked.

"Oh, yeah. I've heard of her. She does real expensive weddings, doesn't she?" Richard asked. "You wonder how anybody can afford that kind of wedding these days."

"I know. It's a total waste." Imogene said.

"Oh, her weddings are so beautiful!" Faye gushed. "She did this one where every table had these crystal vases of flowers that guests could take home and everything was by candlelight and it was so romantic!"

"Hasn't she been on *Oprah* and stuff?" Chrissy asked.

"Yeah. So what?" Imogene said, feeling defensive.

"Wow…So you're telling me that Lindsay Saga is your competition?" Chrissy asked. "I don't know Immy. I mean, your singles thing is a neat idea…"

"Don't lie to me. You think it's a terrible idea!"

Chrissy didn't argue. "It's just that….do you really think a lot of people will vote for a show about single people over a Lindsay Saga show?"

"Well, I guess I can't count on any of your votes," Imogene grumbled.

"Don't be stupid, Imogene. Of course we'll vote for your show," Chrissy said. Everyone else nodded. "I'm just afraid it's gonna be kind of a tough sell, you know? People love wedding shows and they love Lindsay Saga."

"She's a bitch," Imogene blurted out.

"Imogene," her dad said sternly.

"Sorry," Imogene said. Her parents had always hated bad language, especially in front of little kids. "But she is. She's really snotty."

"Yeah, that doesn't surprise me," Faye said with a sigh. "Still, she does beautiful work. There's nothing wrong with a fairytale wedding, you know?"

"Yeah well, there's nothing wrong with being single, either."

No one said a word.

"You know what? I think I'm done here." Imogene put her napkin down.

"Immy, come on, don't be like that!" Chrissy said.

"No really. Go ahead and vote for Lindsay's show. You seem to think that everybody else will!" Imogene stood up and shoved her chair, making the whole table shake, nearly spilling the drinks. She winced but refused to apologize. "You guys go ahead and talk about your husbands and your children and, you know, all the stuff that's *important* in life. Obviously, I have nothing to say that's of any interest to any of you."

Imogene grabbed her purse and headed toward the door. Her father called after her, "Imogene, hon, please don't go."

Guilt surged through her, but she refused to give in. She left her father's house, slamming the door on her way out.

Imogene's hands were shaking with fury and it took her a few tries to get the key in the ignition. The engine roared to life and she revved it a few times for good measure. She jammed her cell phone into the car dock and put it on speakerphone. She hit speed dial, and then raced out of the driveway, tires screeching.

"Hey, hey!" Matt answered the phone cheerfully like he always did. She felt better already just hearing his voice.

"I need a vent session. You up for it?" Imogene asked.

"Let 'er rip, baby doll. What's up?"

"So, I just told my family about the whole reality show deal."

"And they thought it was a terrific idea and supported you wholeheartedly like families are supposed to do, right?"

"Oh, yeah. That's just how it happened," Imogene scoffed.

"Families suck sometimes, Immy. They mean well, but they still suck." Matt always knew just the right thing to say. He didn't tell her not to feel bad. She had every right to feel bad and he knew it. He was awesome about just letting her rant when she needed to. They hadn't known each other long, but this was hardly the first time he'd been there to listen when she needed it.

"They just think I'm throwing my life away because I'm not married. I mean, it's not like…" she stopped herself before she said *it's not like I don't want to get married.* She still thought about getting married someday, but nobody needed to know that. Not even Matt. "It's not like your life has no meaning if you're single. I know that and I really want other people to know that, too. I want people to know that they matter, married or not. I really think this show can make a difference!"

"I think so, too, Immy. For what it's worth, I'm proud of you even if your family's not."

"Thanks, Matt. That's worth a lot. They just think the show is trying to convince people not to get married, and that is so not it."

"Look, I know it's important to you to get your family's approval. I mean, everybody wants that, but you can't force it. Concentrate on what you're doing because it's important. It'd be great if you had their support, but you don't need it to succeed."

Imogene thought about that for a moment. It was true, but her family still pissed her off. "They don't think we stand a chance against Lindsay's show."

"Then they're in for a surprise now, aren't they?"

Imogene smiled. "You're the best, Matt."

"I am, you know? I really am."

Imogene laughed. "I'll see you Thursday night."

She sighed heavily as she hung up the phone. It would have been so nice to be able to tell her family about her friendship with Matt, but they wouldn't understand it at all. They'd grill her on why she didn't want to date him. They weren't capable of understanding how much she cared for Matt as a friend. It pained her to the core that her family didn't seem to care about anything she did unless it had to do with dating. It hurt so much, especially since Imogene really did care about her sisters, her dad, and her nephews. She was genuinely happy that they had good marriages and good lives. Was it so much to expect them to feel happy for her successes?

Imogene groaned in frustration. She flipped on the radio and tried to calm herself. She pictured Susan, Kate, and Adrienne, and reminded herself that not all couples were so damned self-righteous. She listened to a few upbeat songs, which made her feel a little bit better. She also heard a few love songs that made her feel a little melancholy, though she hated to admit that to herself. She found it confusing sometimes how she could be so happy being single, yet still be a little sad that she was unmarried. Feelings like those were especially difficult to deal with because she couldn't confide in her sisters or her Solo Power group about it. They were on such opposing sides of the issue of marriage, Imogene wondered if it was possible to be somewhere in the middle.

Imogene's thoughts were interrupted by a radio advertisement that mentioned Valentine's Day. She groaned again. She'd almost forgotten the dreaded holiday was coming up. Still, it was bound to be easier on her this year, given all the new single friends she had around her.

"Planning on proposing on Valentine's Day? You'll want the very best diamond to give her on the most important day of her life," droned the jewelry store ad.

"Oh, gimme a break," Imogene said. That advertisement didn't even make her feel sad. It just made her mad. She was so tired of being told that engagements and weddings were the most important things in a woman's life. It was pretty damn sexist. Nobody ever said that about men! She found herself gripping the steering wheel as she endured the rest of the commercial. So much for calming down.

The next advertisement was for a flower delivery service. "Make her feel special this Valentine's Day. Sending her flowers at work will make your sweetheart the envy of all the girls in the office." Imogene heaved a deep, annoyed sigh.

"Because that's what love is all about. Making the other girls jealous," Imogene said aloud. She banged her fist on the steering wheel as she got stuck at a red light, which only compounded her aggravation. Imogene was again reminded of what a total lie the whole idea of romance was. All those love stories that told you some handsome, strong man would come sweep you off your feet bearing roses and jewelry while declaring his undying passion were a joke. Nobody acted like that in real life. Valentine's Day was a total farce. People bought overpriced flowers and candy, and went out in public to show off that they had a significant other. Imogene's chest tightened as she thought about Lindsay Saga's contribution to the hype. She proclaimed to be a champion of love and true romance, but all she really cared about were money, power, and fame. She and her flashy, extravagant weddings had nothing to do with real love.

The light finally turned green and Imogene screeched out of the intersection, tires squealing. Much to her relief, the next radio advertisement was about oil changes.

"Right now, get a free brake-check when you come in for an oil change at Jiffy Jeff's Auto Shop. Give your sweetheart the gift of safety this Valentine's Day…"

Just when Imogene's heart rate had slowed and she beginning to calm down, all that pent-up fury came flooding back through her system.

"That's it!" Imogene screamed. "That is it! Enough with all this

Valentine's Day shit!"

She pulled over to the side of the road. She was so damned furious that she didn't trust herself to drive safely. Enough was enough. Something had to be done about Valentine's Day, that insipid, insulting, degrading, sexist, wretched, pathetic excuse for a holiday. And Solo Power was just the group to do it.

CHAPTER FIFTEEN

What will be the next exciting reality show on The Estrogen Network? YOU GET TO DECIDE! We're letting our viewers tell us which show they want in our lineup. Cast your vote NOW! The first show to receive 250,000 votes will be put on the air! Choose from the exciting potential candidates below:

__BEAUTIFUL BRIDE__ – Have you ever dreamed of having your own fairytale wedding? Of course you have. Who hasn't? Brides-to-be, now's your chance to win an all-expenses-paid dream wedding planned by none other than wedding guru Lindsay Saga! Lindsay will be the judge of the lucky brides who compete to make their princess wedding dreams come true!

__SINGLE, NOT ALONE__ – An uplifting program to inspire single men and women to love themselves and their lives. This show will feature never-married, divorced, or widowed people who need some support and direction in their lives. See them transform from lonely-and-single to single-and-loving it! Feel like you're all alone? Watch this show and realize you're not!

Jillian Jeepers let out a shrill scream that sent her fiancé, Derek, flying into the room expecting to see an axe murderer.

"What's the matter?" Derek looked around wildly to find the source of Jillian's horror.

Jillian pointed at the TV. Derek looked at the television, probably expecting to see an axe murderer on the news. One who bore a striking resemblance to one of their neighbors.

"They just said that Lindsay Saga is going to do a reality show for brides!" Derek stared blankly at Jillian. "The first prize is going to be an all-expenses-paid wedding planned by her! Lindsay Saga!"

Derek continued to stare blankly. How could he not know what she was talking about? Jillian had been fascinated by Lindsay Saga since the day she'd seen her on a local talk show five years ago. As soon as she and Derek got engaged, Jillian had studied every magazine, every website, every TV show that had anything to do with Lindsay's work, trying desperately to figure out how she could afford to have a wedding as lovely and elegant as the ones Lindsay designed. Truth be told, she had started this planning before she and Derek officially got engaged. Well before. Jillian had pretty much been planning her wedding for her entire life.

It was fitting that she lived in Orlando, the Disney capital of the world, since she had been obsessed with princesses since she was six years old. Even as an adult, she dressed up as a different princess every year for Halloween and whoever she was dating at the time was her prince. She trotted out the same prince outfit every time because, let's face it, the princes in Disney movies and fairytales were pretty much interchangeable. On the wedding day, nobody looked at the prince anyway. It was the girl in the gown who got all the glory.

"Derek!" Jillian said. She punctuated her words with punches, "Lin! Say! Sa! Ga!"

"Ow! Ow! Ow! Ow!" Derek said, rubbing his shoulder. "Who is Lindsay Saga and why are you beating me up?"

"She is *the* greatest wedding planner around! She's been on *Oprah, The View, Good Morning with Kaynein and Sampson*, and-"

"Oh, yeah, yeah, yeah. Her. I remember now. Still don't know why you're hitting me…" Derek grumbled.

Jillian couldn't tell if he actually remembered who Lindsay was or if he was just trying to avoid a fight. It was so annoying. He should know exactly who she was talking about. Did he know his future bride at all?

"Don't you know what this means?"

Another blank stare. Jillian wanted to hit him again. Harder this time. She flipped her long, blonde hair in annoyance.

"It *means* that I could win a Lindsay Saga wedding! As in the really fancy, expensive, gorgeous wedding I've always wanted!"

"Oh yeah?" Derek said, finally showing some interest. "That would be pretty cool."

Jillian figured Derek would be interested once he found out they might have a big, swanky wedding. He definitely had expensive taste. He loved things like fancy microbrews and thick steaks and wearing nice business suits. It was a shame that he didn't have a high-paying job to go with his caviar dreams. He did okay financially, but not great. He worked for some boring investment firm. Jillian had always hoped to marry a really rich guy so she wouldn't have to work. At this point, she was lucky to have anybody. She was twenty-nine years old, which was an embarrassing age to still be single. Most of her friends had gotten married years ago. She'd been a bridesmaid, meaning slave to The Bride, more times than she cared to count, and it had seemed it would never be her turn. When she'd met Derek, she'd liked his thick, brown hair and dark brown eyes. He had a nice build, which was a bonus. And he was pretty good husband material. He did what she wanted, most of the time, and didn't give her grief about how much she spent on shoes.

Now that she had Derek, she would finally have the chance to get revenge on all her friends who had forced her to wear ugly bridesmaid gowns and treated her like a lowly peasant on their wedding days. Her days of being pre-wedding Cinderella were over. Not only was it Jillian's turn to be queen for a day, but she was gonna have a Lindsay Saga affair that would put all her friends' weddings to shame.

Jillian jumped up and went to the computer to pull up The Estrogen Network website. It was totally laughable that Lindsay's show was up against some show about single people. As if people would prefer to see a bunch of lonely hearts over a Lindsay Saga reality show. Obviously, Lindsay's show would win hands-down. It was merely a formality, but the quicker the results were in, the quicker the show would air. Jillian and Derek had a tentative wedding date, but naturally it could be pushed back if –no, *when*— Jillian got on Lindsay's show. There wasn't anything in the world that Jillian wouldn't do to have a Lindsay Saga wedding. She got chills just thinking about the wedding she would have; one that would surpass even her six-year-old self's princess dreams. And this would be real.

Jillian cast her vote for *Beautiful Bride*. She tried to vote again, but the website recognized her computer and wouldn't let her do it. She pulled out her cell phone and loaded the website, and then did the same on her iPad. She would get Derek to do the same on all his electronic gizmos.

The next step was to get in on the ground floor with Lindsay. Jillian had no intention of waiting until Lindsay's show won the contest and they started advertising for potential contestants. Oh, hell no. Jillian was intimately acquainted with Lindsay's website and she knew there was an email address she could use to write to Lindsay herself. Jillian had thought about contacting her a million times to tell her how much she admired her work and now she was kicking herself for not having done it before. It would have been great if Lindsay already knew who she was.

Oh, well. It didn't matter. Lindsay would soon see that Jillian was the most determined bride-to-be she would ever meet. Jillian was not only going to get on that reality show, she was going to win.

CHAPTER SIXTEEN

Imogene asked Matt, Paula, and Hannah to meet at Talmer's Sports Bar and Grill for dinner so they could discuss strategy on how to win the fight for the reality show. It was the perfect place to meet. The grown-ups could order adult beverages if they chose to imbibe, and it was before 9pm, so Hannah could still sit near the bar. In addition, Paula and Matt could watch whatever sports they followed. They both seemed to follow every sport there was; hockey, football, baseball, and more. Imogene had no interest in sports, but it amused her to see Paula and Matt shout at all the different televisions when something good or bad happened.

It was nice having a small meeting here. The Solo Power group was growing with each new meeting, but Imogene liked the idea of Matt, Paula, Hannah, and herself being the core members who made decisions about the group. As far as Imogene was concerned, they were all founding members.

"Yes!" Both Matt and Paula yelled suddenly. Good thing they both supported the same team.

"Which game are you watching?" Imogene asked, scanning the televisions.

"Miami Heat," Matt answered. "Basketball," he added after seeing Imogene's blank look.

"Sorry, honey. We're being awfully rude, aren't we? We really are listening to you," Paula said.

Imogene laughed. "No, I know you are. You're fine. I want this to be fun, not like some boring business meeting." She noticed that Hannah was also amused watching Matt and Paula. Hannah wasn't interested in sports either, but it was entertaining for her to see the others get all fired up. "So anyway, we've come here today with one purpose in mind. How the hell are we gonna beat that bitch Lindsay Saga and her evil, mean-spirited Bridezillas-from-hell reality show?"

Matt blinked. "No one could ever accuse you of mincing words, Imogene my sweet."

"I tell it like it is," Imogene informed him. "Ugh, I can't help it. I guess it's supposed to be a professional competition, but I can't help but make it personal. I can't stand that woman. She's just so fake, and all the stuff she says is really harmful. Especially to women."

"I know. I mostly want to win for our sake, but part of me wants to beat that woman just for spite." Matt said. "It's not only single women she hurts. Did you know she refuses to plan gay weddings?"

"No, I didn't know that," Paula grumbled. "But I'm not surprised."

Matt made a face. "Yeah, she claims it's for religious reasons, but that's bull. I think it's just that it doesn't fit into her image of the perfect fairytale wedding. No prince if it's two women, and I'm sure she figures if it's two men, what's the point if there's no bride?"

Imogene shook her head. "Yeah, what's a wedding without a bride? It's not like weddings are about two people who love each other."

"Not to her, they're not," Matt said, shaking his head. He stabbed a French fry into a pile of ketchup, probably imagining it was Lindsay's face.

"Well, one thing that works in our favor is that Lindsay's pretty much counted us out. She figures it's a foregone conclusion that her reality show will win hands down. We can use that to our advantage, and kind of sneak up on her," Imogene said.

"So what do we do?" Hannah asked.

"Well, the first thing to do is to drum up as much support as we can. We keep the blog going of course, and reach out to as many people as possible. That strategy is working, but really slowly. Little by little, we're getting more people to join, but that's not going to be enough. The next step is to reach out to all our family members and friends and get them to support us. They don't have to go to meetings, though it would be nice…" Imogene thought of her family and how they would never show up to a Solo Power meeting in a million years. No rule said you had to be single to join. You just had to be supportive of the idea that single people should be treated like human beings. So far, her father and sisters didn't seem to think they should. They just wanted Imogene to get married already.

"But we do need to get them to vote," Paula said.

"Yes. The very least they could do is vote for our cause," Imogene said.

"Still no progress with the family, huh?" Paula asked. Imogene shook her head. "I know it's hard, but you can't let it get to you. My ninety-five-year-old mother still bugs me about being single."

Imogene's jaw dropped. "You're kidding."

"Nope. She worries that I won't have anyone to take care of me in my old age," Paula said with a laugh.

Matt shook his head. "Really, Paula. It *is* about time you settled down and got responsible. When are you going to let me make an honest woman of you?"

Paula took his hand in hers. "You do make it tough to resist…" Matt batted his eyelashes, making Imogene laugh heartily.

"You're a fickle little beast, aren't you," Hannah said, shaking her head.

Matt kissed Paula's hand, then dropped it and turned to Hannah.

"Oh, I haven't given up on winning your heart yet, Hannah," Matt said. He raised his eyebrows.

"Good luck with that," Hannah said, looking him in the eye instead of looking at the ground. She smiled, and Imogene could finally see a glimmer of confidence in her.

"Watch out for that guy," Imogene said. "I hear he gets around…."

Matt laughed and shrugged his shoulders. He didn't argue with her assessment. "Anyway, yes, at the very least we should be able to get our family members to cast their vote for us, even if they don't entirely agree with what we're doing. I mean, my mom isn't a fan either," Matt shot a sympathetic look at Imogene. "But like I told you, my brother and his fiancé are totally on board. They figure I support their cause, so they're going to support mine. That's the thing; you don't have to be single to support the idea that single people should be treated with respect."

"So true…I just wish more people understood that," Imogene said.

"Well, that's part of what we're doing here. Raising awareness. Unless you happen to be single, you don't realize how badly we're treated. Hell, even the people who treat us like crap don't always realize what they're doing," Matt said. Imogene nodded.

"Unless you're Lindsay Saga. She knows exactly what she's

doing," Paula said. "She preys on women's fears about being alone, being an outcast if they don't have a man."

"Yep. Job security. The more women she can pressure into getting married, the better," Hannah said. "She's like the evil leader of the Stepford Brides."

"Exactly..." There was a tone of mischief in Imogene's voice.

"Uh-oh," Matt said. "She's plotting something..."

"Damn skippy, I am. Okay, tell me if this idea is crazy. Like most single people, I'm sick of hearing about Valentine's Day. They start putting all that red and pink garbage on the shelves the day after Christmas and it's nonstop pressure on men to get their women jewelry, flowers, overpriced dinners, and all that. And, if you're single, naturally you're a complete loser," Imogene said bitterly. She couldn't help but think of her sisters. They were great at making her feel horrible about being single.

"True, all true..." Paula said as she leaned forward, eager to hear what Imogene had in mind.

"I think we should stage a boycott of Valentine's Day!" Imogene said. "We could plan a Solo Power boycott of restaurants, movie theaters, flower shops, and all that on February 14." She looked around to gauge everyone's reactions.

"Hmmm..." Matt said, stroking his chin. "I like the idea of a boycott, but the problem is that it's not single people who patronize those places on Valentine's Day. It's all couples who buy that stuff."

"Well, we do have some married people who are Solo Power members," Imogene said.

"Yeah, but not too many," Matt said.

Imogene couldn't help but feel disappointed. She was so damn fired up over the insulting nature of Valentine's Day, and it felt good to think they could try to do something to stop it, or at least make it less popular. Point out how cruel it was to singles and how degrading all that fake romance could be to women.

Matt seemed to notice Imogene's disappointment. "Well, now hold on. Don't give up on the idea just yet…We could still picket the places on Valentine's Day. If we made Solo Power signs and stuff like that, we could probably at least get on the local news. Get us some more publicity."

"Yeah, you're right!" Imogene said, brightening a bit.

"I say we go for it!" Paula said.

"I don't know," Hannah said softly. Imogene shot her a look. "I don't know!" Hannah said much louder.

"That's better," Imogene said, winking at her.

"Don't you think a boycott might make us look bad? Like we hate happy couples? I know we don't, but making a big deal out of how we don't like Valentine's Day might make us look mean, and that's not what we're about."

Imogene considered that for a moment, but she couldn't bear to let go of the boycott idea. "I don't know. I think if we do it right, it could be really great. I just hate the idea that there's this day that's reserved just for couples and that it makes people feel bad if they don't have a date. I really want to put an end to it. I think if we're positive and upbeat, then it could be a great success."

Hannah nodded. "Makes sense." She paused for a moment. "Imogene? I've been meaning to thank you."

"For what, sweetie?"

"For forcing me to speak up. I just…for so long I found it easier to try to stay hidden. Not easy, you know, considering…" She gestured weakly at her heavyset physique. "But you made me start looking up. Looking people in the eye. I tried it at school."

Imogene's eyes widened with hope. "And?"

"And, well, I can't say people are all of a sudden nice to me or anything. But it's like…like when I look them in the eye, I can see them thinking twice about whether to say something mean to me, you know? It's like they're not sure what I'm up to and they don't know if they should risk it. So, you know, thanks," Hannah said.

Imogene reached over and clasped her hand. "That's wonderful, Hannah. That's the strong, confident girl I always knew was in there. You can't change overnight and I know it's still gonna take some effort, but you're doing great."

"Agreed!" Matt said. He grabbed his drink and held it up. "To Hannah finding her voice!" They all clinked glasses and Hannah smiled warmly at Matt. He looked around at Imogene, Paula, and Hannah. "Damn, I love being a single guy. I get to be surrounded by beautiful, single ladies all the time."

Imogene blew him a kiss. "Okay then, darlings. I'll put together info about the boycott and get it on the blog ASAP. And I have another idea I wanted to run by you guys…"

Matt rubbed his hands together in anticipation. "What else you got going in that brain of yours?"

"I've been thinking…what if Lindsay agreed to go on TV with me? Like on a talk show or something?"

"You mean like a debate?" Hannah asked.

"Yeah. Something like that. We could appear on one of those daytime talk shows she's always on. We could say it's to promote the network and the contest, but yeah. It would kind of turn into a debate of sorts…" Imogene said grinning.

"Ah, I see. Trap her! Make her think she's just getting more publicity for her show but you're really getting a chance to get your side out there. Very clever!" Matt said.

"Yeah, she'd never turn down a chance to be on TV. Besides, she really doesn't think our little group is a threat to her. I'm not famous, so there's no way I could get on a talk show without her, but if we went together…"

"That's a great idea!" Paula said.

"You think she'll go for it?" Imogene asked.

"Yes," Matt and Hannah said at the same time.

"Yeah, Immy. I really do. It's publicity. And Lindsay Saga is all about publicity," Paula said, smiling.

"I hope she does. Not only can we tell the world about Solo Power, but can you imagine if we could announce the boycott of Valentine's Day on television? It could be huge!" Imogene said. She couldn't help but picture her sisters' judgmental faces. They would hate the idea of the boycott, which made Imogene even more eager to do it.

CHAPTER SEVENTEEN

Dear Ms. Saga,

   I can't tell you how excited I was to hear that you will be hosting a reality show on The Estrogen Network! I have no doubt whatsoever that you will get 250,000 votes in no time. Every woman alive will be looking forward to watching Beautiful Bride*! I am writing to tell you that I want to be one of the contestants on your show. I've always dreamed of having a fairytale wedding like the ones that you plan for all those lucky brides out there. I never thought that I would actually have a chance to have a wedding like that, even though it has been my lifelong dream! I will do anything and everything that it takes to be a contestant. I know you won't regret having me on your amazing show. I simply can't wait to meet you in person! Please remember my name when you are choosing contestants – Jillian Jeepers.*

Lindsay grinned as she read the email. Within minutes of The Estrogen Network announcing the contest, Lindsay began receiving emails from potential contestants for her show. She loved receiving messages from brides-to-be who were desperate to have their fantasy wedding and become the envy of not only their friends, but women everywhere. And the hero worship was incredible. These women would do anything for her. Anything to get the wedding of their dreams. If they were sucking up this much now, Lindsay could only imagine what it would be like on the actual reality show. It would be incredible, especially because it would be broadcast nationally. All that power, all that control over the lives of these women. She held their dreams in her hands. They would practically be her slaves.

Lindsay chuckled out loud as she wondered what effect the contest was having on that sad little singles group. A few dozen more hits on Imogene's blog? A few sad sacks reaching out to her, hoping that her reality show would help them? What a thought. Her show would never see the light of day. Even if it did, what good could it possibly do? No show can help you when you're leading a lonely, pathetic life. If you were single, it was probably for a good reason. You were fat or ugly or both. You had only yourself to blame. You couldn't expect some little makeover show to fix your life.

An unexpected email popped up in the midst of her adoring fan mail. It was from Imogene Hart. What could that woman possibly want?

Hello Lindsay, it began. The message was not off to a good start. Lindsay had received so many emails from women wanting to be contestants that she'd starting deleting those that failed to address her as *Ms. Saga.* Those girls were obviously unaware of how much power she held over their futures, so they wouldn't be as much fun as the other ones. She wanted groveling, and that was what she deserved.

> *I am so excited about the opportunity to work alongside you, even if it's only for a short while!*

Short while was right. Imogene would eat her dust. The contest couldn't possibly drag on for more than a few weeks at the most.

I was wondering if you would be interested in appearing together on one of those daytime TV talk shows you always go on. I thought it might be kind of fun to go on TV and talk about our shows. We could promote the contest for the network. I'm sure a little publicity would be great for both of us, and we could speed up the vote a little (. Obviously, you are the big star (nobody really knows who I am) so you pick the time and place. Thanks and good luck!

Lindsay shook her head and laughed. This was hysterical! It was clearly a desperate bid for publicity for Imogene's singles show. Everybody knew Lindsay Saga didn't need much promotion. Lindsay grinned just thinking about how Imogene had had to swallow her pride big time to send that email. The girl hated her. That much was apparent from when they had met at The Estrogen Network office. It must have been painful for Imogene just to type the words "you are the big star". Though her first instinct was to delete the email, she didn't. As she stared at the computer screen, Lindsay found herself tempted by the idea. Publicity was always a good thing and maybe it really could help speed up the voting process.

Anyone could see that the singles idea was embarrassingly pathetic. Why not go on TV with Imogene and let her hang herself? There was no way to make the singles show appealing, especially when compared to Lindsay's wedding prize. The singles didn't even have anything tangible to offer. They were peddling what, self-esteem? Compared with having a lavish, dreamy wedding? Good luck…

Lindsay began a new email. *Imogene, so nice to hear from you. What a lovely idea!*

CHAPTER EIGHTEEN

"Good morrrrrning!" crooned Jerry Kaynein of *Good Morning with Kaynein and Richards* crooned. His hosting style was far more game show than talk show. The sound clip of a barking dog was played every time his last name was mentioned. The show had been *Kaynein and Sampson* for years, but Kimberly Sampson had recently left to pursue an acting career. Now the show was comprised of Jerry Kaynein and his new co-host, Polly Richards. In fact, this was the very first show after Kimberly's departure. "I'm Jerry Kaynein," he said, pausing for the dog bark effect. "And please give a warm welcome to my sparkly new co-host, Polly Richards!"

The studio audience applauded wildly for Polly. She flashed her best Colgate smile. "Thanks, Jerry. It's very exciting to be here!" She sounded nearly as perky as Jerry. After a few minutes of the usual daytime talk show banter, they moved on to the guests. "We're very happy to have Lindsay Saga on the show today!"

A huge round of applause and some hoots and hollers from the women in the audience.

"Yes, Lindsay's back on the show for the what, fifth time or so?" Jerry asked. "She's always a favorite with the ladies out there planning their weddings. Come on out here, Lindsay!"

Lindsay Saga strutted out onto the stage, clearly loving the attention. She looked glamorous as always, in a cream-colored suit, her too-long-for-her-age brown hair flowing freely down her back. Her nails were done in a French manicure and a diamond pendant adorned her neck. She was the epitome of elegance and grace, just like her over-the-top weddings.

"Also joining us this morning is the founder of a new group for single folks called Solo Power. Please welcome Imogene Hart!"

Scattered, polite applause greeted Imogene as she walked across the stage and took her seat next to Lindsay. It was about what Imogene had expected. No one knew who she was yet, but that was about to change. She heard Paula's cheers rise above everybody else's. That made her smile.

"These two ladies each have their own idea for a reality show for The Estrogen Network, but *only one will win!*" Jerry said mock ominously, like an ad for a horror movie. "Lindsay Saga's show would feature bridal beauties competing for the grand prize of an all-expenses-paid fancy-dancy wedding planned by Lindsay herself!"

Loud cheers from the crowd. Imogene saw both Paula and Matt in the audience, arms folded. Hannah was there as well. She said she'd gotten her mother's permission to be there, but Imogene seriously doubted it. Imogene hoped Hannah wouldn't get in trouble for cutting school. Still, she figured Hannah was better off with the Solo Power group than she was at school with a bunch of mean teenagers or at home with her mom.

"And Imogene's show is all about encouraging single people to lead happy and fulfilled lives!"

Polite applause, but the audience clearly had little interest.

"Well, it's just wonderful to have you two ladies here with us today!" Polly said. Suddenly, Perky Polly disappeared as her inner reporter personality took over. She turned to Lindsay Saga. "Ms. Saga, there are those today who feel the wedding industry is anti-feminist and degrading to women. What is your response to that?"

Jerry looked surprised at the sudden change in his co-host. This was supposed to be light and fluffy television, not hard-core journalism. "Whoa now, hold on there, Sally-Super-Serious. We're not here to interrogate these ladies."

"I do feel the wedding princess mentality greatly undermines the credibility of women," Imogene said.

"Well, I can't say that I agree with that at all," Lindsay said, trying to recover from the shock of the sudden shift in the interview. No doubt she was used to talk show hosts fawning all over her and kissing her ass.

"Oooh, catfight!" Jerry said, clearly smelling ratings. A catfight-inspired REAARRRR! soundbite played.

Imogene smirked at Lindsay, who was not amused in the slightest.

"There's nothing at all wrong with a little romance and fantasy. Everyone needs some of that in their life. A fairytale wedding is a dream come true for every girl!" Lindsay said.

"Not every girl, Ms. Saga," Imogene said. "Some of us have loftier goals in life than that."

That remark got some applause from the audience. Imogene grinned as she heard Paula's familiar "Hear, hear!"

"A wedding is not a goal, Ms. Hart. It's a dream. A dream that many women have. Women who aren't hard-hearted and still believe in love and romance. I make it my business to make those dreams come true. And my show will give one lucky winner the chance to do just that."

Louder applause on that one. Jerry looked thrilled as he watched the fight brewing.

"Oh, no doubt having a fantasy wedding is a wonderful thing," Imogene said. "But I think it's extremely damaging to women, and to society in general, to sell the idea that women are pathetic losers if they don't get married. The pressure to get married in today's society is quite severe, and singles are often so afraid to be alone that they rush to marry. They end up marrying the wrong person, and that's one reason why the divorce rate is so high."

"That's an interesting perspective, Miss Hart," Polly said.

"Oh, quite," Jerry added, probably hoping to prolong the argument. "And what do you have to say to that, Lindsay?"

"Well, it's not like I'm forcing these people to marry," Lindsay snapped. Imogene loved seeing Lindsay's cool demeanor unravel. Imogene had shown up today fully prepared to do battle against the Queen of Weddings, while Lindsay had clearly shown up expecting to be adored by the hosts and to lord over Imogene, the "nobody." She wasn't prepared for an ambush. "Couples who are in *love* come to me to help plan the most important day in their lives!"

"And by 'couples,' you mean The Bride, and she comes to you expecting you to help her put on a big circus show so she can be Princess for a Day. Sorry, but a lot of the weddings I've seen lately seem to have very little to do with love. I'm appalled at how some of these women treat their friends and family members. They're not called Bridezillas for nothing!" Imogene replied.

That garnered a lot more applause than Imogene had expected. Apparently, the audience was comprised not only of brides-to-be and hopeful singles, but also women who'd had their share of bad bridesmaid experiences. She glanced out at the audience in surprise. Matt grinned and gave her a thumbs-up sign.

"Well, of course you're going to have some women who take the whole thing a bit too far, but I assure you, they are in the small minority," Lindsay said stiffly. Laughter from the audience made it clear that they did not agree with her assessment of bridal behavior. Lindsay sounded more defensive by the second. "Well, none of you have seen anywhere near as many weddings as I have. I've witnessed so many beautiful, romantic weddings, it can make even the most hardened cynic," Lindsay looked pointedly at Imogene, "believe in love again."

"There's nothing wrong with beautiful, romantic weddings, but weddings in general have gotten way out of hand lately," Imogene said. "Marriage isn't about designer gowns and pricey champagne. If you're really in love, a small church wedding or even a courthouse wedding would suffice."

Lindsay gasped at that idea, which didn't help her case.

"And furthermore," Imogene saw Matt pump his fist as she continued her rant, "is it really wise to spend thousands and thousands of dollars on one day, when the money could be used for a down payment on a house? Or to go back to school? To start a new business?"

Polly and Jerry were both silent, apparently content to let Imogene and Lindsay have at each other. They seemed afraid to say anything, lest the women stop fighting.

"Perhaps so, but some things in life transcend dollars and cents. The photos and memories of the happiest day of your life are priceless."

"Except for the price you charge for your wedding services," Imogene said. Matt pumped his fist again.

"So what do you suggest, Miss Hart? Staying single and alone and miserable for the rest of your life? That's what you're advocating, isn't it?" Lindsay said.

"Single and miserable are quite separate things, Ms. Saga. Single simply means unmarried or without a partner or significant other.

Single does *not* mean you are alone or miserable. Single people have families, friends, hobbies, and passions just like everyone else. I, for one, have lots of friends, and I am never alone unless I want to be. That's why I started the group Solo Power, so like-minded single people can meet new friends and hang out together without being pressured, bullied, or otherwise harassed about their single status!" Imogene turned to the camera. "You can find our group at www.solopower.org."

"Well, that's very cute that you have a singles support group," Lindsay said.

"It's not a support group, because being single is not a disease!"

"Hear, hear!" Paula shouted. She started applauding and a fair amount of people joined in.

"Look, I think it's very nice that you have formed a lovely little friendship group," Lindsay said, trying her damnedest to come across as even remotely sincere, "but I think it can be very harmful to convince single people that they're better off being alone than finding someone to settle down and start a family with. You're going to end up with a bunch of people with terrible regrets about their lives! Sure, it can seem fun and exciting to come and go as you please and to worry selfishly only about your own needs, but then you just end up dying all alone in a houseful of cats!"

"Really?" Imogene asked. "You're gonna drag out the cat lady stereotype? See, this is exactly what I'm talking about. You know, a lot of well-meaning family members and friends try to talk us singles into getting married because they're genuinely worried about us. They don't understand that we're fine the way we are. We can take care of ourselves. We have jobs, homes, friends, and lots of things to make our lives meaningful, even if we remain single. But people like you in the wedding industry aren't worried about us. You prey on people's worst fears about growing old alone and you do it just to make money off weddings! Not every woman is a bridesmaid on the sidelines just waiting for some man to save her. I know I'm not. I'm a lot stronger than that!"

That last part got the loudest applause so far for Imogene. Maybe even louder than the applause that greeted Lindsay when she first strutted onto the stage.

"Wow, a real liberated woman!" Jerry said. "That's great! Sooo, Lindsay…" He leaned toward her. "What do you think of all this?"

Lindsay shook her head and tried to give Imogene a look of pity, but the fury bubbling underneath was seeping through. "I think it's very sad. Very sad that we've reached a point in our society where people would rather pursue their own interests than raise a happy family. Makes you wonder what will become of the world if people just stop having children. Then what?"

"You are aware of the massive overpopulation problem on this planet, are you not?" Imogene asked. "So how about if the people who want to have children—and there are a *lot* of people who do—can go ahead and get married and have kids, and those of us who don't—won't. Problem solved!"

"So you don't find anything wrong with people just living lonely existences, wasting away in some apartment by themselves?" Lindsay asked. "I mean, you always hear of those people living alone who die and nobody knows they've died until weeks later and–"

"Oh, okay. So we're back to the whole dying alone scare tactic. I'm so glad you brought that up…" Imogene said. She whipped out a newspaper from her back pocket. Jerry and Polly looked nervous. This was live TV after all, and they weren't sure where Imogene was going with this. "See this newspaper obituary?"

Lindsay nervously scanned the page. "Yeah, what about it?"

"This is the obituary from the *Orlando Sentinel* for a woman named Georgina Simon. Imogene read from the listing, "*Georgina Simon, 92. Lifelong resident of Katesville, FL. Never married. She is survived by brother, Carl.*" She put down the newspaper and said somberly, "This lady did die in her home, all by herself. So yes, some single people do end up dying alone."

Lindsay clucked her tongue. "So sad."

"But…" Imogene said, picking up another newspaper article. "Check out this obituary, also for a single woman who died in her nineties. *She was beloved by all who knew her. She worked at the local grocery store for nearly fifty years, having begun work there as a teenager. She never married and lived alone, but was never short on visitors of all ages. Especially fond of the neighborhood children, she baked more than a dozen varieties of cookies and knew the preferences of each child, sure to always have the right kind on hand when they paid her a visit. When she grew too old and infirm to bake any longer, the now-grown children would return to her house time and again, and now they were the ones bringing the cookies and other treats for their favorite adopted aunt. She never set foot outside of her small town in Florida, but folks who moved far and wide often came back just to pay her a visit. Her funeral was held at St. Matthew's Church, where she had been a choir member since she was six years old. More than 700 people attended the service, forcing the pastor to move the ceremony outside into the sunshine, which mourners say she would have loved.*"

"Wow, that's really beautiful," Jerry Kaynein said. His snarky game-show attitude had disappeared for the moment. He actually looked like he might cry.

"It is," Imogene said. "It really is. And as for these two obituaries?" Imogene picked up the first one from her lap and held it up next to the second one. "Guess what? They're for the same person! One was from the city newspaper, which made her sound lonely and pathetic. The paper from her hometown told the real story."

Lindsay, Polly, and Jerry all looked quite surprised, which thrilled Imogene.

Imogene turned and addressed the camera directly. "Listen up, Single America! Don't buy into the threats of dying alone. Don't believe that your life has no meaning if you don't get married and have kids. Life is what you make it. We singles need to band together. Stand with us! I would like to take this opportunity to urge all the single people out there to make their voices heard loud and clear. Join Solo Power and band together in a nationwide boycott of Valentine's Day!"

"Wait. What?" Jerry asked, perplexed.

"That's right. My fellow Solo Power members and I have decided to launch a boycott of Valentine's Day this year. And the boycott is not just for single people. For all you married couples out there who support singles rights, join us by not patronizing restaurants and movie theaters on Valentine's Day. Forget the candy and flowers, and donate the money to your favorite charity instead."

Lindsay rolled her eyes, and Polly shot her a look of disapproval. "Why a boycott of Valentine's Day?" Polly asked, sounding intrigued.

"Because it is a discriminatory holiday that glorifies fake love and makes single people feel like there's something wrong with them," Imogene said. "Valentine's Day really only has two purposes: to jack up the prices on roses and fancy dinners, and to let couples feel superior to single people. It's time to put a stop to that *now!*"

"All right, then," Jerry said with enthusiasm. "You heard it here first. There's going to be a nationwide boycott of Valentine's Day!"

Lindsay just sat there, speechless, as she watched the show take off without her like a runway train.

"That's right, single America. Refuse to be pressured into being part of a couple just because everybody says you should. We've got a lot of living to do! We're not gonna be treated like lonely outcasts anymore!" Imogene looked out at the audience and shouted, "HOW DO WE RUN?"

"SOLO POWER!" Matt, Paula, and Hannah shouted back. Relief flooded through Imogene. Though she trusted her single allies in the audience, part of her was afraid they would miss the cue they'd practiced.

"HOW DO WE RUN?"

"SOLO POWER!"

"Check out our website for more information on the group and the boycott. More importantly, all you singles out there *and* all you married folks who believe singles should be treated with dignity and respect instead of pity and scorn, go to The Estrogen Network website and vote for our show *Single, Not Alone!*"

"All right!" said Jerry Kaynein. "Could we pull up the site and get a tally?"

A few seconds later, The Estrogen Network tally was cued up on a large display screen just behind where they all sat.

Beautiful Bride: 14,736

Single, Not Alone: 9,248

"Well, it looks like Lindsay's show is clearly in the lead for now…" Jerry said. "But can somebody hit "refresh" to see if anything-"

Beautiful Bride: 14,812

Single, Not Alone: 12,116

"Whoa! It looks like maybe today's television appearance is having an effect on the voting!" Jerry said.

Lindsay's jaw set, and she looked like she was grinding her teeth into dust.

"So there you have it, folks," Polly said in her best serious correspondent voice. "A battle between the Singles and the Bridezillas. Will independent-minded women win out, or is there still room in today's society for old-fashioned fairytale weddings? Keep watching The Estrogen Network's website to find out. This is Polly Richards."

"And I'm Jerrry Kaynein!" The dog bark sounded. "Be sure to get out there and vote for your favorite show. It's your civic responsibility!"

*****

After the show, Imogene bounded eagerly into the studio audience to greet her fellow Solo Power members. It made her sad that none of her family members was there to support her, but that was mainly because she hadn't invited them to come. Sure, they knew about the show and were watching at home, but there was no point in bringing them here. They didn't understand what she was doing and weren't supportive; it was best to bring along people who were.

"Imogene Hart, you were amazing! You did us proud," Paula said, hugging her.

"You *owned* Lindsay Saga!" Matt said.

"Yeah, she did," said an audience member, chuckling as she walked by.

"Seriously, Imogene. You were fantastic," Hannah marveled. Imogene was especially touched at Hannah's approval.

They heard a loud clacking noise and they all looked up to see Lindsay stalking toward them, high heels pounding on the studio floor, bracelets jangling, and earrings swinging. Fire blazed in her eyes. Imogene was quite pleased to see the rise she'd gotten out of her. Lindsay was always so cool and put together. Not anymore.

"Well, I certainly hope you enjoyed the show today," Lindsay said tersely, straightening her blouse.

"Oh, I really did," Imogene said, grinning at her.

"Good, cause it's the last show you're ever gonna be on," she said the words so menacingly, it sounded like she meant that it would be the last thing Imogene ever did...

Paula rolled her eyes. Lindsay noticed and shot her a fierce glare. Paula countered with an equally steely one, which seemed to catch Lindsay off-balance for a moment. She was used to brides admiring her and other people fearing her. She didn't seem to know how to handle people she had no power over.

"I'm the 'name' here. The celebrity. They only let you tag along on the show because I let you. It was my idea."

"The hell it was. It was my idea, you fell for it, and it worked out exactly as I planned," Imogene said, smirking. Lindsay took a deep breath and exhaled before responding. It was a visible struggle for her to keep her cool.

"You can call it Solo Power or Singles Pride or whatever you want. It doesn't change the fact that you are the leader of the nobodies. The head loser of the loser club." Lindsay looked at Matt, Paula, and then actually grimaced at Hannah. Matt stiffened and put a protective arm around Hannah's shoulder. Still looking at Hannah, she said "You're a bunch of losers who *can't* get married because nobody wants you."

Hannah swallowed hard and tears filled her eyes. Matt looked like he wanted to punch Lindsay. He'd have to get in line, because Imogene wanted to do it first.

"Back off, Lindsay!" Imogene shouted in her face. Lindsay barely flinched. By now, she was getting used to Solo Power's counterattack on her. "Your fight is with me, not her. Like all bullies, you're too afraid to pick on people your own size."

Lindsay laughed harshly and opened her mouth, no doubt about to say something vicious about Hannah not being close to "her size".

"Watch your mouth, Saga," Matt said menacingly. He was usually so laid back; Imogene had never seen him so angry.

"I don't know what we're all fighting about here. This whole silly contest is going to be over before you know it. The bottom line is that every woman wants to get married and they all want a dream wedding. It's in their DNA! I'm sure you'll get a few more votes for your sad lonely hearts club after your little performance today, but after that, the votes will go my way." Lindsay looked straight into Imogene's eyes. "And I think you know it." Lindsay turned on her heel, then clacked and jangled her way out of the studio.

Seeing Hannah's devastated expression made Imogene's anger dissipate. Her heart ached for the girl. So much for keeping her safe from bullies. Imogene couldn't bear to let Lindsay destroy Hannah's delicate self-image. She put her hands on Hannah's shoulders and looked into her eyes. "She's just lashing out because she's scared. She'd counted us out and now she knows we are a force to be reckoned with. And we're only gonna get stronger."

Hannah nodded, but didn't really look like she believed her.

*****

Imogene headed to her car and slid behind the wheel, trying to steady her nerves. She'd been running on adrenaline all morning from having been on live TV. It was one of the most exhilarating and terrifying things she had ever done. It was great.

Her phone rang.

"Holy crap, you're famous!" was Chrissy's way of greeting her.

"Damn, that was fun," Imogene said, leaning back in the driver's seat, still coming down from her rush. "I need my own talk show."

"You've got the mouth for it, that's for sure. You almost had me convinced it's good to be single."

"It *is* good to be single. Not better than being married, not worse, but just as good."

"Uh-huh," Chrissy said, not sounding convinced in the slightest. "Well, now that you've gone on television extolling the virtues of being single, what happens if you get married?"

"I'm probably not getting married. I mean, if I'm not by now-"

"See, I knew it! You're just doing all this because you're afraid it's too late to get married."

"I am not!" Imogene exploded, surprised by her own anger. "I'm doing this because it's not fair the way single people are treated and it's horrible the way people get pressured into marrying some idiot they don't even love. Maybe I won't get married, but I won't get divorced either!"

"Immy, I'm just saying you went on TV and now you're practically the spokesperson for single people everywhere, so what happens if you do get married? You'll look like a fool."

"Yeah, well, let's worry about that if it happens," Imogene said. She had to admit that the thought hadn't occurred to her. "I'm over thirty and have had no luck in the marriage department so far, so it's high time I made other plans."

"I still don't like that you're giving up on getting married," Chrissy said with a sigh. "It depresses the hell out of me." That sounded so stupid that Imogene didn't know where to begin. Chrissy was acting like Imogene had just been diagnosed with a fatal disease.

"But I'm happy! Why can't anybody understand that?"

"Immy, you've always said, your whole life, that you wanted to get married and have kids. I'm just worried that you started all this single stuff because you've given up on your dream of having a family of your own. And that's not the same as wanting to be single."

Imogene fell silent for a moment. There was a ring of truth to that statement, though she could barely admit it to herself, let alone to anybody else. She really had pretty much given up on the idea of getting married, and that was what had sparked her singles movement. But so what? The way she saw it, she could either sit at home and pine over the husband and kids she didn't have, or she could get out and live her damn life! You didn't see men sitting alone eating ice cream and crying in the corner because they didn't have a spouse.

"You just don't understand me at all," Imogene said wearily.

"I'm sorry, Immy. I'm not trying to upset you. Seriously, you should be proud of what you did today. You really were amazing."

"Thanks," Imogene said dully. As if a lame compliment like that could make up for her sister's ridiculous comments about how she was crazy to like being single. She sighed. "Talk to ya later."

Imogene was about to drive off the lot, but decided to call her father first. She hoped he had seen the show. She hoped he would be proud of her.

"Dad? Did you see it?"

He sighed heavily. "Yeah, I saw it."

Imogene realized too late that it has been a gargantuan mistake to call her father.

"Chrissy still thinks I'm crazy and I suppose you do, too."

"No, I don't think you're crazy, sweetheart," her father said, sounding tired.

Imogene realized she had been wise to not have any of her

family at the show, and she wished like hell she hadn't spoken to any of them on the phone. Moments earlier, she had been on an incredible high from her appearance on *Kaynein and Richards*. It had been scary to take on Lindsay Saga on live television, but she had done it. She'd done it for Matt, Paula, and Hannah and for singles everywhere so they could stop feeling alone and stop feeling bullied by idiots. It made her so damn angry that she couldn't count on her own family to support her. They might as well join forces with Lindsay.

"Mom would have been proud of me!" Imogene burst out angrily.

"Your *mother* was my *wife* for 26 years before she was taken from me!" Her father yelled, startling Imogene. He rarely talked about her mother and sometimes Imogene forgot how badly her death had hurt him. "I don't understand what you suddenly have against the institution of marriage. We had a wonderful family and life together. I don't understand why you want to turn your back on that."

"I'm not turning my back! I just want to be a single woman without being tortured and mocked because of it!" She pressed the End Call button. Imogene felt horrible about hanging up on her father, but she couldn't take one more minute of this.

Her eyes filled with tears. She was hurt and angry, and desperately wanted to talk to somebody who would understand. She was about to pick up the phone and call Matt when she saw that he and Paula were just now walking toward their cars.

She jumped out of her car and ran over to them.

"Hey now, what's the matter?" Matt asked softly, seeing her tears. His kindness only made Imogene cry harder. Matt wrapped his arms around her. "What happened? You're not upset about Lindsay, are you?"

"No. It's my family. I made the stupid mistake of talking to them on the phone. I was an idiot to think they would support me in all this."

Matt rubbed her back as he hugged her. Imogene felt Paula's hand on her shoulder. "Oh, honey, I'm so sorry. You should be so proud of what you did in there today. I know we are," Paula said.

"Damn right," Matt said. He released Imogene so he could look into her eyes. "Screw them. Look, I know they're your family and all, but they just don't get it. Maybe they never will. Just know that we're really proud of you. You handed Lindsay's ass to her on live television!" Matt's eyes lit up. "You know how long I've waited for somebody to do that? And to think I know you personally!" Matt lowered his head and feigned shyness. "Can I have your autograph?"

Imogene laughed. "Thanks, guys. I really appreciate it."

"Seriously Immy, don't let them ruin this for you. You were so great in there. I bet we'll get a ton of votes now. I really think we have a shot at this!" Paula said.

Imogene nodded. She was almost afraid to hope, but she felt that way, too. For the first time, she actually felt like they might have a chance to beat Lindsay Saga.

CHAPTER NINETEEN

Jillian stared at the television, eyes blazing. She had DVRed Lindsay's appearance on *Kaynein and Richards* from that morning. She had seen just about every show Lindsay had ever done— she had the woman's interview on *Oprah* from several years ago practically memorized — and this was by far the worst appearance she'd ever seen. Lindsay was usually so cool, so poised. Not today. She'd clearly been blindsided by this Imogene woman. Sure, the bridal show was probably still a lock, but Jillian didn't want to take any chances. She was going to win that dream wedding prize, and she wasn't about to let some jealous, single girl ruin it.

Derek came into the living room and did a double-take at Jillian's furious expression.

"Um, watcha doin'?" Derek asked, sounding a little nervous. No doubt he was trying to figure out if he'd done anything wrong. Typical clueless man.

"I'm watching *Kaynein and Richards*," Jillian responded angrily.

"Who's that?" he asked, looking at the screen.

"Are you kidding me?" Jillian said, turning her furious face toward him. "You seriously don't know who that is? Do we have to have this conversation every day? It's Lindsay Saga!" To his credit, his face did light up a bit with recognition at the name.

"Well, yeah. I know her. The wedding bit…I mean, lady. I meant the other one."

"You mean the one who's humiliating Lindsay Saga on live TV? She's some crazy singles advocate nut. She's the one who has the reality show that's competing against Lindsay's wedding show that I'm gonna to be on. It's stupid and I'm sure nobody's gonna vote for some depressing singles show instead of a wedding one, but we can't take any chances."

"We?"

"Lindsay and me."

"Oh, I see. You're best buds, now?" Derek said, chuckling. Jillian shot him a death stare and he clammed up. Wise choice.

"Well, I've been emailing her every day since the network announced the contest and I'm sure she knows who I am. If she wants to win this thing, she'll need my help." Jillian grabbed a handful from her snack bowl and started crunching.

"Is that…are you eating ice chips?"

"Yes. It's my dinner. I need to lose weight if I'm gonna win *Beautiful Bride*. And I *am* going to win."

Derek eyed her critically.

"You don't need to lose that much weight. Maybe a little around the thighs."

Jillian nodded. The criticism hurt, but she knew it was for her own good. If she was going to have the wedding she had always longed for, she would have to be tough and do whatever it took.

Derek grabbed a beer from the fridge and a bag of Cheetos from the cabinet. He flopped down in the easy chair across from where his bride-to-be sat crunching ice chips and glaring at the television.

"I dunno. Seems like an awful lot of work to be on the show," Derek said.

"You know a better way to have a nice wedding? Not like you're gonna pay for it!" It was a low blow, but Jillian couldn't help it. It annoyed her that Derek didn't make more money.

"Well, it's not like your parents are chipping in."

"Don't remind me." That annoyed her even more. Since she was nearly thirty, her parents figured she was a grown woman and should pay for the wedding herself. Talk about adding insult to injury. As if it wasn't bad enough that it had taken her this long to land a husband. "I don't care what it takes. I'm gonna have the perfect wedding if it kills me."

Derek popped a Cheeto in his mouth. "Sometimes I think you're only marrying me so you can be a bride." He said this almost as a statement of fact. A fact that really didn't seem to bother him.

Jillian hesitated a bit before answering. Of course she wasn't only marrying him so she could have her wedding. He was a nice enough guy most of the time. Not bad-looking. Had a job and all that. She was lucky to find him. Once a girl hit thirty, her odds of getting married went way down. She'd found him in the nick of time. Besides, she often felt he was just marrying her because his parents kept telling him he should settle down. Well that, and he seemed to like the idea of having a wife who would cook for him and do his laundry, so why not get married? Everybody wins.

"Well, are you?"

"What?"

"Are you marrying me just so you can march down the aisle in a fancy dress?" Derek asked. He still didn't seem upset, but clearly wanted some reassurance anyway.

Jillian pretended to have trouble tearing her gaze from the television, feigning absorption in the show to excuse her earlier hesitation in answering him. "Of course not, Derek. I love you!"

And she did. She was pretty sure she did. "I'm not marrying you just to have a wedding, but you know how important this is to me."

Derek nodded. It was all she'd ever talked about from the day they met, which would have sent most guys running for the hills. Jillian gave him credit for not freaking out when he found bridal magazines in her apartment right after they started dating, or when she stopped and lingered over wedding gowns and engagement rings in shop windows. He took it all in stride.

"I'm telling you, this wedding is going to kill all my friends! It's gonna be so great. All those years of being a bridesmaid and being treated like a handmaiden to the bride. Now it's gonna be my turn…." Jillian tried to ignore Derek's worried look. She knew he was afraid she was going to be some awful Bridezilla, but why shouldn't she be? She'd earned it! She'd suffered through all her friends' weddings. They had been *awful*. Each of her girlfriends had turned into a total nightmare the closer it got to her wedding day. They didn't hold back. Why should she? "HA! You hear that? That's me getting the last laugh. HA! I'm gonna have a wedding like Kate and William's, and it'll make my friends' weddings look like shotgun courthouse affairs."

It would be such a relief to get married. No more pitying looks, no more pressure from her parents, and she could finally get rid of her awful last name. Alone it was fine, but combined with her first name it sounded like an exclamation from a cartoon character. Jillian Jeepers! Ugh. All her life she winced when she had to say it out loud. Jillian Whetson sounded so much better.

The only down side was that she wouldn't get to humiliate her friends with the bouquet toss because all her friends were married now. Whatever. She had something even better in mind. Given her adoration for Disney princesses, she decided that instead of a bouquet toss, she was going to reenact the scene from Cinderella where the prince tries to put the glass slipper on the other girls and it doesn't fit. At the reception, she was going to have Derek pretend to try to fit the shoe on each bridesmaid and then turn each girl down, one by one, until he got to her, the princess, and it would be a perfect fit. Once the shoe was on her foot, he would sweep her up into his arms, leaving all the jealous bridesmaids behind.

Jillian couldn't wait.

But first, she was going to dispatch this Imogene woman. Jillian cringed as she watched Imogene wrap up her insane tirade about single people with a call to vote for her show. There was no question that Jillian and Lindsay were going to have to act quickly to do damage control.

CHAPTER TWENTY

Lindsay smiled when she saw yet another email in her inbox from Jillian Jeepers. The woman was clearly desperate to have her fantasy wedding, and desperate women were Lindsay's favorite kind of bride. This Jillian woman had emailed her every single day since the contest was announced. She definitely had the killer spirit. There was no doubt in Lindsay's mind that Jillian would make the short list of brides to compete on her show. An email from Jillian was just the ego-stroking Lindsay needed after that awful television appearance.

> *Hello Ms. Saga,*
>
> *Sorry to be blunt, but you gotta do better than today's* Kaynein and Richards *show if you're gonna get* Beautiful Bride *on the air. I promise you, I'm the only one in the world who wants this show to happen even more than you do. If you're smart, you'll work with me and we will crush Imogene Hart.*

The harshness of the email took Lindsay completely by surprise. It was yet another blow to her injured ego, but the idea of crushing Imogene appealed to her so much that she was willing to overlook

Jillian's rudeness. Besides, it was precisely that cutthroat attitude that made Jillian the potential Head of the Bridezillas. If Jillian could help her win the reality show and get revenge on Imogene for embarrassing her on national television, then Lindsay was all for it. She emailed Jillian back immediately and they agreed to meet in person to discuss their next move.

They decided to meet in a local coffee shop. Lindsay arrived a bit early to allow time for people at the shop to recognize her. She was not disappointed, as two teenage girls nervously asked for her autograph. That kind of attention never failed to thrill Lindsay and she couldn't wait until the reality show aired and even more people would recognize her. The whole fame thing was very hit or miss. Sometimes she would have a dozen people recognize her in a day, while other times a week or more would go by with nobody knowing she was famous. *Beautiful Bride* would change all that.

Lindsay recognized Jillian the moment she set foot in the door. Jillian had given her a physical description of herself: thin, blonde, and petite, but it wasn't necessary. Lindsay could tell who she was by the forceful, determined way she walked. It fit the attitude from her emails perfectly.

Lindsay felt a surge of jealousy as she looked at Jillian. It had been a long, long time since she had been that beautiful, that young. Sometimes it was hard to believe that she was pushing fifty. She didn't feel that ancient and she certainly didn't dress that old. She'd done all she could to turn back the clock, but she wasn't a young bride anymore. If she couldn't be The Bride and the center of attention, she would have to settle for being Queen of the Brides on the show.

Jillian's eyes lit up, recognizing Lindsay immediately. "Oh, my gosh, it's really you..." Jillian said, rushing over to where Lindsay was sipping her black coffee. It seemed Jillian had, at least for now, reverted to her gushing attitude from her earlier emails. Jillian held out her hand and Lindsay shook it, bracelets jangling. "So wonderful to meet you finally! I'm such a huge fan of your work!"

"Yes, so you've mentioned..." Lindsay said, a bit coolly.

"I'm so excited about your show and finally being able to have the wedding of my dreams! I mean, I can't believe it could really happen!" Jillian's expression suddenly turned darker, more determined. "Not just 'could happen.' It will happen. When this show gets on the air, I'm gonna be the last Bride standing. I can promise you that."

Lindsay laughed. "I must say, I'm impressed with your attitude." Jillian reminded Lindsay so much of herself. So ambitious, so determined. Lindsay had little doubt that she would get what she wanted.

"So, before we begin, do I have your word that when *Beautiful Bride* gets on the air, I will be one of the contestants?" Jillian asked. From the moment Lindsay started getting the emails from Jillian, it was clear that she would not only be a contestant, but she likely would end up being the winner. Her fierce determination was evident from the very beginning. Still, there was no reason to let on that Jillian was already a lock to appear on the show.

"And what exactly do I get in return?" Lindsay asked, playing hard to get.

"Like I told you before, not only will I help you win The Estrogen Network contest, but I will help you destroy Imogene Hart in the process. What more could you ask for?" Jillian asked, smiling. It was funny how Jillian seemed to hate Imogene as much as she did. Lindsay liked to think it was because she was Jillian's hero and she didn't like what Imogene had done to her on television. However, she knew it probably had more to do with Imogene's disdain for weddings and the way she essentially made a mockery of women who longed to be a princess bride. Whatever the reason, it was delightful to have such a strong ally in this fight.

"Fair enough. If you help me beat Imogene down, then you are guaranteed a spot on *Beautiful Bride.*" Lindsay offered her hand and they shook on it. "So, what's the plan?"

Jillian leaned in eagerly. "Okay, here's the deal. You gotta play down the wedding stuff." Lindsay was about to argue, but Jillian held her hand up. "I know, I know. It's counterintuitive, but hear me out. Imogene is saying what a lot of people are thinking these days. That it's dumb to have a big, expensive wedding in this economy. I'm sure your business has suffered recently because of that."

Lindsay nodded. The economy *had* negatively impacted her business as people were forced to scale back on the extras. Lindsay tried to reason with them, telling them that their wedding was a once-in-a-lifetime thing (or it was supposed to be…) and that long after the economy recovered, they would look back and regret not going all out for their big day. That tactic worked often, but not always. The Bride would start second-guessing her higher-budget wedding, and that's when Lindsay would start guilting the groom. She'd say she understood how pressed for money they were, and they wanted to have a wedding they could easily afford, but he wouldn't want the woman he loved to be disappointed on the day she'd been dreaming of her whole life, now, would he?

Worked like a charm. Even so, most couples still spent way less on weddings than they had just a few years ago.

"Both you and I totally get how important a wedding is. It's the most important day of your life! I mean, it's even better than the day you give birth, because you're not in agony all day."

Lindsay nodded, though Jillian couldn't possibly know how bad childbirth could be. Yet.

"But we'll come off as shallow and superficial if we focus on releasing live doves and having crystal vases at the reception. It's not fair, but that's the way it is. If we talk about how important it is to have everything you want at your wedding, a lot of people will think we're just being irresponsible or whatever," Jillian said, rolling her eyes.

Lindsay knew Jillian had a point, but it wasn't exactly news. She had certainly heard a fair amount of criticism over the years about having expensive weddings, but it was rarely directed at her personally and it certainly had never been on live television. Still, her business was weddings, so what else was she supposed to talk about?

"Instead of talking about the actual weddings," Jillian continued, "you need to play up the whole marriage angle. Love and marriage and family and all that crap."

"That makes sense…"

"You're damn right it makes sense. Who's gonna argue against Holy Matrimony and having sweet little children? It's gonna make the singles thing look totally anti-love. All you gotta do is say Family Values and it's checkmate!" Jillian said, throwing her hands up.

Now *that* was a very good point. If they showed that Imogene and her singles were a bunch of selfish, individualistic people who thought it was better to do whatever they pleased instead of raising a family, people would undoubtedly vote for the wedding show, hands down. Plus, it would make Imogene look bad. A total win-win.

"And we have to make sure Imogene doesn't get to go on television again. I hate to admit it, but she's a great public speaker," Lindsay said. Her stomach lurched in protest, like her whole body was fighting the idea of saying anything positive about that awful woman. "But that shouldn't be a problem. The only reason they let her on the show in the first place was because of me. Because I'm a celebrity."

"Very true," Jillian said. "I know her little appearance caused a temporary spike in votes for her ridiculous show, but it'll peter out the longer she's out of the public eye. That's why you need to stay visible." Lindsay nodded. "How soon do you think you can book another television appearance?"

"Well, with Valentine's Day coming up, it shouldn't be too hard at all. Now's the perfect time for me to guest star on lots of shows because everybody's talking about romance."

"Perfect!" Jillian said. "I really do think this is gonna be an easy fight. She won one little battle on TV, but that's as far as she's gonna go. We just gotta stay proactive to make sure."

"Right!" Lindsay said. "And speaking of proactive..." She dug in her purse to find her cell phone. She scrolled through the photo gallery until she found the picture she was looking for. Lindsay handed the phone to Jillian. "I took this picture outside the studio after the *Kaynein and Richards* show. For somebody who's supposedly all about being single, Imogene Hart seems awfully cozy with this guy."

Jillian grinned as she examined the photo of Imogene hugging the man. "Great! You never know when this might be useful. You think he's her boyfriend?"

"I have no idea. Doesn't really matter though, does it? As long as it looks like he is, that's all we need. She wants to be the poster girl for independent women who don't need a man, but that's kinda hard to do if you have a boyfriend," Lindsay said.

"You're right. Awesome!" Jillian squealed. Lindsay couldn't help feeling caught up in Jillian's enthusiasm. It was actually going to be fun working with her to take Imogene down.

CHAPTER TWENTY-ONE

Jillian was ecstatic after her meeting with Lindsay. Now that she'd spoken with the woman in person, her dream of a Lindsay Saga wedding was so close she could taste the Moel & Chandon Dom Perignon, (which only the bride and groom would get to drink, of course). She was also excited about the picture Lindsay had gotten of Imogene hanging all over some guy. That was gold. Maybe she should find out where Imogene lived, to see if this guy ever showed up at her place. She could even follow her around to see if she went out on any dates with him. It would be fun. She would be like a spy! It was perfect because Imogene had no idea who she was. It wasn't like Lindsay could stalk Imogene without being noticed.

It really worked in their favor that the contest was taking place around Valentine's Day. Everybody would be thinking about romance, even sad-eyed single people. Valentine's Day was torturous enough to make even the most independent-minded single woman desperate for a date. It would be so easy to play up the whole love and marriage angle around this time of year. There were flowers and candy and romantic things everywhere. People would be reminded of all the reasons it was wonderful to be in love. It was the worst time of year to be anti-love and anti-romance. Anybody working that angle would just come across as lonely and bitter, which was obviously what those ridiculous Solo Power people were. Imogene's Valentine's Day boycott was insane and would end in certain disaster. Jillian couldn't wait.

CHAPTER TWENTY-TWO

Join Solo Power as We Fight Back on Valentine's Day!
If you're a single person, you know how awful Valentine's Day can be. It's not that you're necessarily lonely. You could be perfectly happy being a swingin' single, but that doesn't stop your friends, family, and society in general from treating you like you've got the plague if you don't have a date. Everybody knows that Valentine's Day has little to do with real love. It's just an excuse to jack up the prices on roses and force people to spend a ton of money they don't have on candy and expensive dinners out. Besides, the whole idea of romance is degrading to women, if you really think about it. The notion that women turn completely to mush just because we're given a bouquet of flowers is insulting! We are grown adults with lives and careers and minds of our own. You don't see men parading around, acting like princes and demanding to be adored, do you? And who says a woman is incomplete without a man anyway? You don't see single men sitting around on Valentine's Day, eating chocolate and crying over sappy romance movies, do you? Hell, no! They're out having a beer with the guys, watching sports, or doing whatever else it is they usually do. Men

simply don't fall apart if they're without a partner. So, if you're single on Valentine's Day, DON'T sit around lamenting your life. This February 14, WE'RE FIGHTING BACK!!! So come to our next Solo Power meeting and join the cause as we fight for dignity and respect for singles everywhere!! JOIN OUR BOYCOTT OF VALENTINE'S DAY!!

— *Imogene Hart, Solo Power blog*

Until until recently, Imogene hadn't realized how demeaning the whole concept of romance was to women. The Disney princess thing was pretty damaging to little girls. According to those stupid fairytales, all you had to do was be pretty and thin and stand out in the woods singing with a bunch of forest creatures and your dream man would come and literally sweep you off your feet! Imogene hated to admit to herself how much she had bought into the princess fantasy as a child. It was even worse that she had bought into it as an adult.

She was also guilty of indulging in romance novels, and had committed the very sin she had railed against in her most recent blog. Yes, she had definitely gone through a box of chocolates while tearing up over romance movies. Ugh. What had she been thinking?

Still, as much as Imogene hated to admit it, a big part of her missed the idea of romance. Sure, her past boyfriends weren't exactly great in that department. She usually received the obligatory gift and flowers on Valentine's Day and her birthday, but nothing that really required a lot of thought or effort. No, it wasn't the reality of romance that she missed. It was more the fantasy of it. The part that didn't really exist. Ever since she'd made the decision to embrace being single and to give up on romance, she hadn't read a single romance novel and she avoided any movies or television shows that were even remotely romantic.

And she found that she really, really missed it.

Imogene knew it was stupid. She knew that she'd been buying into all the garbage, the fantasy notions, the harmful stereotypes that she was fighting so hard against, but she couldn't help but miss romance, even when it existed solely in her imagination. It was fun to fantasize about it; that's all there was to it. Like lots of women, she loved looking at magazine photos of gorgeous guys like Ryan Reynolds, Ryan Gosling (even the name "Ryan" was sexy…), Channing Tatum, etc. It was fun to look at them and fantasize. It was fun and exciting to read a story about a romantic hero, the kind you wouldn't ever meet in real life. Romantic comedy movies could be sweet and funny and uplifting. You didn't have to watch them and mope about being single. Sometimes watching films like that could actually boost your mood. If the mousy little girl in the movie could find true love, maybe it was possible in real life.

Imogene also knew that those same stories could be harmful. They set everybody up for failure, not just women. Seriously, what real-life guy could be as buff as Ryan Reynolds? What man could live up to all those ridiculous romantic fantasies women had, especially if he was on a budget? That's why people like Lindsay Saga had to be stopped. Nobody could afford that type of crazy, overblown wedding anymore, but she kept parading them around on TV as if a two hundred thousand dollar wedding was something that every Bride "deserved." Imogene imagined that Lindsay probably berated the poor grooms, telling them that if they really loved The Bride, they'd make her every stupid fantasy wedding idea a reality.

Yeah. No doubt about it. Something had to be done about Valentine's Day. And Solo Power was just the group to do it.

*****

Between Imogene's television appearance, the blog, and the recruiting efforts of the original Solo Power members, there were a lot more people at the next Solo Power meeting. It seemed like they would soon outgrow the library conference room, which was a wonderful problem to have.

It wasn't hard to figure out who had come with whom. There were a bunch of older folks, no doubt coerced to attend by Paula. There were a few more men this time, including several who were most likely gay, in attendance. This time Imogene wasn't just making blanket assumptions. Some of them actually had their arms slung around each other. They must have been friends of Matt and his brother. There were a few teenage girls there, too, but it was hard to tell if Hannah had brought them or if they had just heard about the group on their own.

It didn't matter where all the people had come from. Imogene's heart soared just looking at the crowd. "I'm excited to see so many new people joining our group. As you know, Valentine's Day is fast approaching…"

Groans greeted her announcement. Imogene grinned. It was wonderful to be surrounded by so many like-minded people. Nobody here would be pressuring her to find a date anytime soon.

"That's right! The meanest, most demeaning, most discriminatory day of the year is almost upon us!" Imogene continued. This time, her words were met with boos. "I think that Valentine's Day is the perfect time of year to spread the word about Solo Power. We want every single person out there to know that they may be single, but they're not alone."

"Hear, hear!" Paula shouted. There was some scattered applause.

"Valentine's Day isn't just about romance and couples; it's about making single people feel bad about not having a significant other. How many so-called romantic comedies and sitcoms about Valentine's Day show single people as sad, lonely, and pathetic if they don't have a date?"

Lots of tsking and shaking of heads. Though Imogene did enjoy romantic comedies, much more than she would dare admit to any member of Solo Power, the ones that portrayed single people as lonely spinsters really got her blood boiling. Those shows turned out all happy and sappy in the end, the lesson being that you were lost and unhappy until you met that special someone. Not all single people sat at home feeling sorry for themselves on Valentine's Day!

"So the time has come to boycott Valentine's Day. It's time we fought back against the day that makes us all feel unworthy if we don't happen to have a mate. So we're going to boycott and picket all the places that support this annual forced-love, fake romantic, anti-singles, overly commercialized, useless day!" Imogene shouted with flourish. The crowd burst into applause. "We will boycott flower shops, restaurants, card stores, candy stores, and any other business that profits from this discriminatory so-called holiday. If we really band together, we can make our voices heard!" More applause, but she wasn't done. "Don't forget why we're doing this. This is for every single girl who sits at home on a Saturday night feeling like there's something wrong with her. For every woman who's reached the age of thirty and, no matter how accomplished she might be, feels like a failure because she doesn't have a wedding ring!"

Louder, more enthusiastic applause.

"This boycott is for every little boy who didn't get a Valentine card at school! It's for every teenage girl who didn't go to the prom and was told she would regret it for the rest of her life!"

Applause, and some hoots and whistles on that one. The prom thing had clearly struck a chord.

"We're fighting for every bridesmaid who was made to feel like a desperate loner and a slave to The Bride!" Imogene shouted.

People got on their feet and cheered.

"We're fighting for the futures of all those high school girls who are more worried about having a boyfriend than about going to college!" Hannah cheered especially loudly on that one, which warmed Imogene's heart. It really drove her crazy the way so many teenage girls worried so much about who was dating whom while the boys were busy playing sports and getting ready for college. It was a crime to raise girls that way. Things were definitely improving, as many girls played sports and were college-minded, but there was still a lot of work to be done in that area.

She looked out into the crowd and saw that Matt had his arms crossed, tapping his foot in an exaggerated manner. He was grinning, though. Imogene got the message.

"And we're fighting for every single guy who's treated like he's irresponsible and lazy because he's not married. For every guy who's told he needs a wife to take care of him!" Matt cheered and whistled for that, and even the crowd of mostly women cheered. That was another cool thing about this group. It opened your eyes to issues that you might not have thought about before. Single women rarely thought about how single guys were treated. Imogene surely hadn't until she met Matt.

"And just because you're a single dude doesn't mean you're gay!" a man shouted out. Matt laughed and put his arm around the guy and squeezed him. Imogene realized that he must be Matt's brother, and the man sitting next to him must be his fiancé. She shot him a thumbs-up. She thought it was especially cool that they were here, given that they were getting married soon. Just as there were plenty of straight allies in their fight for equality, it would help singles to have some married and engaged people on their side.

"That's right!" Imogene shouted. "And it works the other way, too. Just because you're gay doesn't mean you can't get married!"

"Damn straight!" Matt shouted. His brother cheered and gave his fiancé a quick kiss. Imogene thought they were too cute for words.

"We're fighting back against the day that makes everybody feel bad. Men feel compelled to spend a great deal of money on their girlfriends—or boyfriends—even if they can't afford it. Even women who are dating someone are disappointed on Valentine's Day if their dates don't measure up to some ridiculous, impossible, romantic ideal. And worst of all, people who don't happen to have a date on that one particular day in February are treated like they're rejects of society! Are you single?"

"Yes!" People shouted.

"Are you a reject?" Imogene yelled back.

"No!"

"Are you ready to fight back?"

"Yes!"

"Are you tired of being treated like you're pathetic?"

"Yes!"

"Are you ready to make your voice heard on Valentine's Day?"

"Yes!"

"Then let's get out and fight!" Imogene shouted, sounding a like a coach at the Super Bowl. "Now, are we ready?"

"Yes!"

"How do we run?"

"SOLO POWER!"

"How do we run?"

"SOLO POWER!"

The room thundered with applause and cheering. For the first time, Imogene realized that the hapless librarian had been trying to get her attention for quite some time, but Paula had been holding her back so that Imogene could finish her rallying speech.

Imogene also realized that this would be the last time she would be allowed to hold a Solo Power meeting at the library. In fact, she would be surprised if they let her back into the place to borrow a book.

It didn't matter. Solo Power had already outgrown the room and was ready to move on to someplace bigger and better.

*****

"You think this boycott will actually work?" Imogene asked Matt when he came over to her place for their Thursday night TV ritual.

"Hope so," Matt said. He set his beer down on the coffee table. Imogene lifted the beer and put a coaster underneath it. It amused her how much they were like an old married couple. However, it was still just a friendship thing. A best friendship thing and they both were grateful for it. "I figure worst-case scenario, the boycott doesn't make much of an impact, but you haven't really lost anything. We'll probably pick up a few votes, a little publicity, maybe some new Solo Power members. If nothing else, you're reminding single folks that they're not alone."

Imogene nodded. She felt better, like she always did when she talked to Matt. He had a point when he said there really wasn't anything to lose.

Imogene unpaused the TV and they both fell quiet, but not for long. Neither one could resist making snarky comments at the show.

"What a dumbass," Matt said. "Everybody knows that guy's in on it. He's obviously blackmailing the girl. Look at that guy. Would you sleep with him unless he had some dirt on you?"

Imogene shuddered. "Uck. Hell no. Now his assistant is another matter…"

"Yeah, he ain't bad on the eyes," Matt agreed. He noticed Imogene's amused expression. "Shut up." He took a swig of beer while Imogene laughed. Her favorite question to tease him with was *"Are you SURE you're not gay?"* This time, she didn't even have to say it out loud. She loved to tease him about how clean his house was and about being a snappy dresser.

Imogene leaned back on the couch and put her feet on the coffee table. "You know what you are, don't you?" she asked him. "You're like my gay best friend!"

Matt groaned. "I know. Don't think that hasn't occurred to me."

"It would be so much easier if you were gay. It would explain our relationship to other people. Might get the family off my back about not dating you. They don't get it. I don't think even I get it." Imogene looked into his eyes. "Matt, why aren't we dating?"

"I don't know. Do you want to?" Matt asked.

"No," Imogene said, laughing gently. She knew her response wouldn't hurt him because she knew he felt the same way. She asked him the question anyway. "Do you?"

Matt shook his head, laughing. Theirs was an easy, fun relationship with no complications. They hung out and laughed and drank, and there was no pressure because they were totally on the same page with their friendship. It was wonderful, but their opposite sex best friendship seemed to baffle the outside world.

"We're like some anti-romantic comedy," Imogene said, laughing. She said mock-dreamily, "Oh, Matt. I love how you finish my sentences. You understand every reference I make from *Family Guy* and *The Simpsons...*"

Matt batted his eyes at her. "And I love that it takes you a half hour to order a sandwich," he said. Then he scrunched up his face. "Nah. I'm glad you don't do that. That would drive me nuts."

Imogene nodded, laughing. "Matthew," she said, kissing his hand, "Will you be my platonic, non-gay, super-awesome, best friend without benefits forever?"

Matt wiped an imaginary tear from his eye. "Oh, yes, Imogene. Yes, yes, yes! I can't wait to tell our families!"

"Yeah, right," Imogene scoffed. Matt's family was as baffled by their friendship as hers was. They hadn't even met her yet, but they wanted him to date her as much as her own family did.

"Hah! He totally deserved that," Imogene said as one of the villains on TV got bludgeoned with a crowbar. Matt grinned at her and clinked his beer with her wineglass. He always seemed impressed with her lack of squeamishness. No matter how bloody or gory the show was they were watching, she never turned away. She usually laughed instead.

Imogene and Matt ended up drinking more than they should have that particular night. It wasn't the first time that Matt had too much to drink to drive home safely. When it happened on the weekend, sometimes Matt would crash on the couch. Since this was Thursday, he really needed to get home so he took a cab. He'd carpool with a buddy to work. They would figure out what to do about his car later. Sometimes they'd meet for lunch on Friday and Imogene would bring his car and then he'd drop her off at her apartment to get her car back. They were having so much fun together that it was worth the hassle. Imogene wouldn't have traded her platonic, non-gay BFF for anything. So what if nobody else understood their relationship? It was nobody else's damn business.

CHAPTER TWENTY-THREE

Imogene *was* sleeping with that guy, just as Jillian had suspected. The man had shown up at her apartment last night and, sure enough, his car was still there in the morning. Jillian got pictures of him arriving and got photos of his car. She wasn't exactly sure what she was going to do with this evidence, if anything, but she had it just in case. If Imogene's stupid singles show started to take off on the website for some inexplicable reason, Jillian would be ready with evidence that Imogene wasn't as single as her little disciples would have liked to believe.

Plus, Imogene was publicizing that stupid boycott of Valentine's Day. It was a dumb idea and it was hard to imagine that it would have any impact, but Jillian warned Lindsay that she might want to do some kind of counterattack just in case. If the singles pride folks wanted to be all anti-Valentine's, fine. Let them. They would just look like angry, bitter people who didn't have dates and were trying to ruin everyone else's fun. The best countermeasure was to show how Lindsay Saga was totally pro-love and pro-romance. Jillian convinced Lindsay to do a matchmaking thing to find people dates for Valentine's Day. Who better to help you find your perfect Valentine than the queen of dream weddings, Lindsay Saga herself? Jillian had even helped write the copy for her website:

Valentine's Day is the most romantic day of the year! We here at Lindsay Saga Weddings want to help you find your soulmate. You never have to spend another Valentine's Day alone! Now is the time to find that special someone your heart has always longed for. We want to help you find love and realize your wildest romantic fantasy! From now until Valentine's Day, Lindsay Saga Weddings is offering a free matchmaking service. We want to help as many lonely singles as possible to find love before February 14. After all, love is what life is all about!

It was hard to say how this whole thing was going to work. No doubt they would get a ton of single women, but it would probably be harder to get guys to sign up for the service. After all, it wasn't men who were checking out the Lindsay Saga Weddings site on a daily basis. Still, if they could match up a few couples who would share their stories on the website, that might be enough to keep the votes pouring in. All they needed was a few women to shoot some teary-eyed videos for the site. That would remind everybody that no one wanted to be single, and that you could find somebody if you didn't give up. Seriously, wasn't that a much better message than convincing single people to stay single and lonely? Sure, they might feel all empowered and whatnot after hearing Imogene's rah-rah Solo Power speeches, but where would Imogene be when these people were holed up in their apartments all alone, surrounded by cats?

Shacking up with that skinny guy. That's where she'd be.

*****

Jillian's idea of a matchmaking scheme for Valentine's Day was brilliant, but it was tough for Lindsay to find the time to keep up with it. She was still running a business after all, and February was a popular time for weddings. She had three scheduled for Valentine's weekend, and had to attend to a million details. She knew she would have to scale back temporarily on planning weddings once *Beautiful Bride* went into production. After that, the real fun would begin. When the show ended, she'd be more famous and popular than ever.

There was a huge, positive response to the matchmaking idea, which resulted in lots of votes for Lindsay's show. At last check, the votes were:

Beautiful Bride: 130,677

Single, Not Alone: 98,230

The initial spurt of votes for Imogene's stupid show seemed to have finally died out and been surpassed by votes for Lindsay. Even though Lindsay had to grudgingly admit that Imogene had put in a spectacular performance on that talk show, not everybody had seen it. Nobody knew who this Imogene was. She was a minor blip on the radar, and now Lindsay's show had almost half the votes she needed to win the contest.

It was time Lindsay tried to get herself booked on some shows for Valentine's Day. She started making calls to see who would be interested in putting her on the air to talk about the matchmaking thing and, more importantly, the reality show. Lindsay knew that it would only take a few more television appearances to seal the deal for The Estrogen Network contest. The sooner she won, the sooner she could start living the celebrity life. Then all those television producers would be calling her and begging her to appear on their shows instead of the other way around.

Lindsay booked an appearance on *The Ladies Room,* a daytime talk show for women. It was the perfect venue to sell her matchmaking services, promote Lindsay Saga Weddings, and, of course, drum up more votes for her show. She'd already been on this show a few times and it was always successful. It would certainly be a lot more fun than her television appearance with Imogene. Right now, Imogene Hart was at home where she belonged, wallowing in obscurity.

The Ladies Room featured three women of varying ages. There was Vivian Adams, who was in her late fifties, Susan Stratford in her forties, and Angel Ming, the token twenty-something. Angel was the only one who was single (or at least, unmarried). She was a pretty girl, so she probably had a boyfriend. The other two women were married with children, so it wouldn't be hard for Lindsay to get them on her side.

"Good morning everyone, and welcome to *The Ladies Room!* We're here today with celebrity wedding planner, Lindsay Saga!"

Lindsay adored being referred to as a celebrity wedding planner, even though it wasn't exactly true. Yet. That would come after the success of *Beautiful Bride.* Loud applause and even some squeals greeted Lindsay, which pleased her immensely.

"Thank you so much for having me!" Lindsay said cheerfully, putting on her best faux-humble face. She glanced out at the eager audience. Her audience. Her fans. The thought of all the new fans her reality show would give her was exhilarating.

"So you have an upcoming reality show on The Estrogen Network," Vivian said.

"Well, hopefully…" Lindsay said, crossing her fingers and sticking with the humble act. Sure, she was out to crush Imogene Hart, but she wasn't about to be as in-your-face as Imogene was. Well, she had *wanted* to be, but Jillian had talked her out of it. Jillian had convinced her that it was best to stick with the whole love, marriage, and family routine and let Imogene out herself as being anti-family and all of that. Lindsay had to admit that would probably work best. "If the show gets enough votes, I will!"

"Right, there's some kind of contest going on for this?" Susan asked. "There's another show that the network is considering?"

"Yes. They're considering doing a show for singles as well. I mean, that's nice and all, but I just really, really hope that I'm able to get my show, *Beautiful Bride,* on the air because I am so excited about having the opportunity to give away a dream wedding. I know it costs a lot of money to have a fantasy wedding and I just love the idea of being able to grant that wish for some girl who otherwise couldn't afford it, you know?"

Vivian, Susan, and Angel all nodded. So far, so good. All three women seemed on board with Lindsay's show.

"Yeah, so what's up with this other show? I know it's something about single people and aren't they trying to get rid of Valentine's Day or something?" Angel wrinkled her nose. "That lady who runs it sounds crazy."

Lindsay's heart leapt with excitement. She couldn't have said it better herself, and yet here was the young, single girl who'd realized that Imogene was nuts. Still, recalling Jillian's advice, Lindsay played it cool.

"Well now, I wouldn't call her crazy," Lindsay said gently in her best motherly tone. "Just sort of confused and well…lonely. Look, nobody wants to be alone. We all want to find that special someone to add meaning to our lives. A soulmate, a friend, a lover who will share our life journey with us.

Vivian, Susan, and Angel sat there, enraptured by Lindsay's words.

"And I think it's really great that she has this singles support group now where people can get together and know that they aren't the only ones going through this. It takes time to find The One, and I'm sure it helps to have a group of people who can lean on each other during the lonely times." Lindsay could practically hear Imogene screaming back at the TV if she was watching. Well, if not now, she'd be screaming later when she watched the show on her DVR. Imogene would get all worked up, insisting that she wasn't lonely, she was just *fine*. Wow, was that girl ever in denial. Lindsay decided to lay it on even thicker, just to spite her. "And, of course, I would be more than happy to do a free matchmaking profile for Imogene. If you haven't seen her yet—I know a lot of people haven't heard of her—she's just lovely and I'm sure she wouldn't have the slightest trouble finding a man. If she had a boyfriend, I'm sure she would stop trying to promote this crazy single agenda of hers and embrace love instead of anger and bitterness. It breaks my heart the way she seems to have given up on true love!"

The Ladies Room co-hosts leaned forward as if to soak up every word.

"After all, it's love that matters the most. Love is what makes life worth living. Having a family is what makes you whole."

"Oh, that is so true!" gushed Susan. "I didn't understand what life was about until I had children."

"I know," Lindsay said dreamily, putting her hand over her heart. "I feel the same way. My Cody and KellieAnne are my whole world. You just don't *get it* until you have kids, you know that I mean?"

"Oh, absolutely!" Vivian agreed. "Life takes on a whole new meaning when you have children. And now my children have their own children and I see them experiencing the wonder of parenting, and it just takes my breath away." Vivian was near tears. Lindsay smiled at her as serenely as the Blessed Mother herself.

"Exactly. And it all starts on your wedding day! All that joy, the wonder of love and family. It all starts on that amazing day when you get up in front of God and all your loved ones and say those sacred vows. That's why my true passion in life is giving people the wedding of their dreams. That's the day that it all begins. The first day of your life as a real family. I mean, when I think of when my little Cody took his first step, it just…." Lindsay was overcome. She simply could not go on! And yet somehow, she did… "And when KellieAnne looked up at me for the first time and said "Mommy, I wuv you!"

Susan wiped away a tear. "I remember when mine were that little…"

"And then you get to see them grow…to see the young man and young woman they become…I mean, I know everybody talks about how terrible teenagers are, but mine? Mine are amazing. You can really talk to them, you know? You can relate to them on an adult level. I'm just so proud and blessed that I can have that kind of relationship with my kids, even though they're older now. I know not everybody is that lucky. I'm just so proud of my babies!"

There was barely a dry eye in the house.

Take that, Imogene Hart.

CHAPTER TWENTY-FOUR

Finally, the big day came. Imogene had done all she could to galvanize her side into making noise on Valentine's Day. Though she'd notified every press outlet she could think of, both local and national, she had no idea if there would be any coverage of the Solo Power protest. She and Matt had spent hours in her apartment coming up with slogans and painting protest signs. It was funny how they always hung out in Imogene's apartment instead of Matt's house, which was decidedly roomier. Knowing how anal Matt was about cleanliness, Imogene knew better than to even suggest painting over at his joint. They made as many signs as possible to ensure that anybody who was willing to carry a sign would have one. People were also free to make their own, too. They could write whatever expressed their personality best. Within reason.

Imogene also printed out flyers, which she, Matt, Paula, and Hannah plastered all over town. They pinned them on every public message board they could find: in grocery stores, drug stores, and gas stations. They posted them on Valentine's-related businesses, like candy and flower shops, knowing full well that the owners would just rip them down the next morning. Imogene took particular delight in covering up matchmaking service flyers with

Solo Power ones. Her flyer read 'DEFINE YOURSELF BY YOUR CHARM, NOT WHO'S ON YOUR ARM!' She also had flyers that simply said 'SINGLES POWER! BOYCOTT VALENTINE'S DAY!'

Matt took special pleasure in plastering the flyers over romantic comedy posters. Those movies annoyed him because he felt they always gave men too much to measure up to. He said they made his dates expect him to be witty and sweet and handsome and charming all the time. Imogene had told him he was all of those things, but he'd waved her off. She wouldn't dare admit to him how much she used to love movies like those.

Judging from the response that Imogene was getting on her blog, the Solo Power boycott of Valentine's Day could actually end up being a huge success. If things really went well, *Single, Not Alone* could be the winner by the end of the day on February 14. Lindsay Saga wouldn't know what hit her.

Lindsay had also been working overtime to get attention for her side. She'd made a huge deal of her matchmaking crap, putting her "new couples" front and center on her website. These newly-matched people were suspiciously photogenic. Imogene wondered if Lindsay had simply hired models to pose for her website. Oh, well. She didn't have time to ponder what Lindsay was up to. She was preparing for battle.

Imogene, the original Solo Power members, and a few others agreed to meet in front of a local Hallmark store at about 3pm. Good thing they lived in Florida. It made an outdoor protest in February bearable when the highs would reach 65 degrees. That was freezing by Florida standards, and Imogene did her share of complaining every time the "frigid" wind blew, but she knew they had it good. She couldn't imagine there would be too many protestors today in, say, Minnesota.

Imogene's brightly painted protest sign read *'SINGLE AND PROUD!'* on one side while the other side read *'UN-COUPLED DOES NOT MEAN UN-HAPPY!'* Paula proudly marched with a sign with the words OLD MAID slashed out in red and then the words *'BEING SINGLE MEANS I'M <u>NOBODY'S</u> MAID!!'* Matt's sign read *'CONFIRMED BACHELOR DOESN'T MEAN GAY, IT MEANS <u>HAPPY!</u>'*

They marched around in circles like union workers on strike and chanted things like 'SINGLES ARE PEOPLE, TOO!' and 'VALENTINE'S DAY IS UNFAIR TO SINGLES!' whenever people walked by. They never prevented anybody from walking into the store, but Imogene was pretty sure their presence scared off more than a few potential customers. It was great. What better place to boycott than a stupid Hallmark store? That idiotic corporation probably invented Valentine's Day and raked in the dough year after year, forcing poor guys like Matt to empty their wallets for schmaltzy cards and overpriced chocolate. They started stocking the shelves right after Christmas, forcing everyone to be assaulted by huge displays of red and pink fake-love garbage for months.

Imogene laughed out loud when she saw a new protester join the march with a sign that read *'YOU KNOW THOSE FLOWERS ARE PRE-PAYMENT FOR SEX, RIGHT?'* Imogene went over to talk to her and thank her for joining them.

"Oh, wow. You're Imogene, right? I saw you on *Kaynein and Richards!* You were awesome!" the girl told her.

"Thanks," Imogene said, smiling. It never ceased to amaze her when somebody recognized her from television. It had only happened a few times, but it was totally surreal.

Imogene looked up to see a local television news crew arriving.

"Oh, my gosh. Matt, look!" Imogene said, gesturing at the news crew.

"Sweet!" Matt said, hoisting his sign higher, hoping to get it on TV.

Imogene was excited that there would be some coverage of the boycott. She had been sure to mention in the press release where she would be protesting and at what time, figuring that if any newspaper or TV people did want to cover it, they would want to interview the ringleader.

Imogene recognized the reporter as Donald Velts from Channel 9, WFTV. It was so weird to see the TV reporter up close after seeing him on television and on all those billboards.

"A number of protesters are already out this afternoon in support of the Valentine's Day boycott spearheaded by Imogene Hart and her Solo Power group," Donald said into the camera. Imogene kept an eye on him as she marched in circles with the others. She figured he would approach her when he was ready to talk to her.

Donald walked over to a goth-looking girl who carried a sign that had *FEBRUARY 14 VDAY* painted in red, drippy, bloodlike letters. "So, why did you decide to boycott Valentine's Day this ye-"

The girl turned directly toward the camera. "Because I refuse to be bound by the bloody, torturous shackles of contemporary matrimony," Goth Girl said. Donald's eyes opened wide. "Besides, men SUCK! You hear me, Adam Worley?" With that, she held up her middle finger directly at the camera.

"Whoa! We'll have to blur that out later," Donald said, stepping away from Goth Girl.

Imogene frowned. That wasn't exactly the message she was hoping to get across. There were already enough people who thought that singles who were against Valentine's Day were just bitter about being alone. That wasn't what this was about at all. It was about fair treatment. Imogene deliberately marched closer to the reporter, hoping he would talk to her instead. He took the bait.

"Oh, look! And here we have Imogene Hart, the leader of Solo Power. Ms. Hart, would you like to say a few words about why you're here today?"

"Yes, I would. Thanks! We're here to show the world that people are fine with or without a partner. We believe that it's possible to lead a very full, meaningful life without necessarily getting married and having children. It's so important to remember that everybody has something to contribute to the world. God made us all individuals for a reason. We can each make a positive difference in our own way."

"Okay," Donald said. "So why boycott Valentine's Day?"

"We're protesting the pressure that society puts on people to get married," Imogene said, using the speech she'd pre-rehearsed, just in case she was interviewed. "We're fighting back against the idea that you have to have a spouse or a boyfriend or girlfriend, especially on Valentine's Day. We feel that it's that kind of pressure that leads people to settle. You know, marry the wrong person and that's why the divorce rate is so high. People would rather marry the wrong person than be single, and we're trying to change that." Imogene felt relieved that she had gotten a chance to say all that on camera. It was critically important that she was able to get the right message across. She was worried about Goth Girl's words and bad attitude. Imogene was determined to keep the fight for singles equality positive, but she had no control over how others behaved.

After a while, Imogene, Paula, and Matt left the flower shop and set up their protest in front of a fancy restaurant. It was around dinnertime and it was very crowded. Imogene felt a little disheartened at the fact that the boycott hadn't made much of a difference, as both the flower shop and the restaurant seemed to have the usual, heavy Valentine's Day attendance. Still, the noisy protestors were at least getting some attention. These things had to build momentum, right? This year, they were setting the groundwork and getting the word out. Next year, the boycott might have a much bigger financial impact on the whole Valentine's industry.

Hannah joined them in front of the restaurant with a sign that said '*MY LIFE PLAN DOESN'T INCLUDE A MAN*.' Imogene heard quite a few people make some very ugly comments under their breath concerning Hannah's weight and how that was the reason she didn't have a man. She hoped to God Hannah didn't hear them. It seemed that the ignorant people who made those comments at least had the decency to speak out of Hannah's earshot.

Imogene couldn't resist talking back to some of them. One guy said something about "fat chicks can't expect to have dates on Valentine's Day". Imogene marched right up to the guy and looked his date up and down. "So, this is true love, huh? Sure hope you don't get fat…" The girl did shoot her date an annoyed glance. He quickly ushered her inside. Imogene was satisfied that she had given them something interesting to talk about on their date.

It didn't take long for another news van to pull up in front of the restaurant. They were unpacking their equipment just as the irate store manager came running out.

"Will you guys get the hell out of here?" the sharply dressed female manager shouted. This was a crazy expensive restaurant and this was, no doubt, one of their busiest nights of the year. The night when people who usually couldn't afford to go to places like this actually splurged and were counting on a night of being pampered. Having to step over protestors to get inside wasn't part of the plan.

The news crew scrambled to get their cameras ready to catch the unfolding drama. Imogene knew she had to make sure that the protestors were respectful but also got their point across.

"Hello, Ms. Pinders," Imogene said, reading the manager's name tag. "I'm Imogene Hart. I'm the one who started the protest."

"Good! Then you can end it!"

"Well, no. I mean, yes, I guess I could…but we're here for a reason. We're just doing a peaceful demonstration against the unfair treatment of singles in society," Imogene calmly explained.

"I'm running a restaurant. A business! A business that serves everybody, regardless of race, creed, color, or whatever else there is. We don't discriminate against anybody, so why are you trying to wreck my business?" Ms. Pinders shouted as the news cameras rolled.

"It's not that we have anything against your restaurant. It's just that we're trying to make our voices heard that Valentine's Day is a discriminatory holiday that marginalizes single people and puts too much pressure on everybody to get married."

Ms. Pinders stared at Imogene like that was the craziest thing she'd ever heard. "Look, lady. All I'm trying to do is run a business. Yes, tonight happens to be about couples. Couples who spent a lot of money to hire a babysitter and have saved up for a long time to have one night out without yelling and screaming and whining!" The manager yelled as she looked around and glared at the protestors. This lady must have kids of her own. "Maybe they're here on their first date, or celebrating their anniversary. I've got a couple in there now who've been married forty-seven years and they've come here every Valentine's Day since we opened fifteen years ago. Don't they deserve a peaceful meal?" Imogene honestly didn't have an answer for that.

"And in this economy…as bad as everything is right now, do you really think my restaurant or any of the other businesses you're harassing really needs this kind of hassle?"

Matt came over to help. "We're not trying to cause trouble here, okay? We're just trying to get our message out. We're not preventing anybody from going inside and we'll keep the noise down so we don't bother people, okay?" he said, looking at Imogene to see if she would agree. She nodded and the manager stormed back inside to take care of her customers.

One of the news reporters came over to interview Imogene and she gave a similar speech to the one she had given the other reporter about why they were protesting, but she knew it was too late. She knew how the news report would end up looking like later that night on TV, and it wasn't good.

*****

No. The news wasn't good. Imogene sat at home alone on the couch and watched the coverage of the day's events. Matt had offered to stay with her and watch, but she'd decided she just wanted to be alone. She was already hugely disappointed in the way the Valentine protest had gone, and she knew the news coverage would confirm what a disaster it had been. She couldn't help but think that the restaurant manager was probably right. These businesses really didn't need anything to take away from their income right now. And it wasn't like they were racist and wouldn't serve certain people, so did they really deserve to be boycotted? It wasn't their fault that Valentine's Day made half the population feel like dirt. Imogene guessed there was a better way to get their message across, but she was damned if she knew what it was.

Channel 9 featured some of the protesters and most of them came across as angry and bitter. They showed Goth Girl and also interviewed some singles who complained that Valentine's Day made them feel like there was something wrong with them because they didn't have a date. Though that was exactly the kind of attitude that Imogene wanted to change, protesting Valentine's Day clearly wasn't the way to do it. This campaign obviously wasn't going to inspire anybody to embrace being single. It would simply reinforce the notion that if you wanted to be happy and fulfilled, you needed a mate.

"Days like this are just really cruel to people like me. There's just some people that nobody's gonna want to marry," Hannah said to the camera.

"Oh, Hannah," Imogene said aloud to the TV. As always, she felt terrible that Hannah felt that way. She also worried that Hannah's words reinforced the lonely stereotype of singles, and that she would have a negative impact on the campaign. Imogene hated herself for even thinking that, but she couldn't help it. Couldn't anybody be upbeat about being single? Anybody at all?

Mercifully, the news segment about the Solo Power boycott came to an end. But then things got even worse.

"Valentine's Day was a lot brighter for the happily coupled…." The reporter said brightly. Imogene groaned as Lindsay's smug face appeared on the television. "Lindsay Saga and some friends handed out roses in front of Dufresne's Restaurant to celebrate Valentine's Day."

The news report showed Lindsay smiling and handing out roses to couples entering the restaurant, an obvious and stark contrast to the Solo Power protestors outside the other place.

"With all the bad things going on in the world today, it's so wonderful that we have this one special day set aside to celebrate love, you know? It warms my heart. It really does," Lindsay said sweetly to the camera.

Imogene felt rage start to boil up in her. It was just so damn unfair. Lindsay was just so awful and manipulative. That woman didn't give a shit about love, she cared about being famous and pressuring couples into spending way more than they could afford on some stupid, extravagant wedding that had little to do with love.

"Indeed, Lindsay Saga brought together more than 200 new couples with the free Valentine matchmaking campaign on her website. Speaking of campaigns, if you'd like to vote on the reality show contest between Lindsay Saga and Imogene Hart, just go to The Estrogen Network website and–" Imogene shut off the television.

Imogene took a deep breath as she thought about the contest. She'd once been confident that the protest would bring in lots of votes for *Single, Not Alone* but now she was afraid to look at the score. She knew she would have to look sooner or later, so she checked the site.

Beautiful Bride: 195,060

Single, Not Alone: 128,240

Pretty much what she'd figured. Imogene's stomach knotted and her chest ached. She thought about calling Matt or Paula, who would do their best to cheer her up, but she couldn't bring herself to do that. She felt like she had let them down. She felt like she had let everyone down. She knew she certainly couldn't talk to her family. They had never supported her in this fight and now they had more ammunition against her. It would be one big "I told you so." They would say that it really was best to get married and raise kids. That was what made people happy and that's why there were so many unhappy single people.

The worst part was that Imogene was starting to fear that they might be right…

She stretched out on her couch in defeat. She was starting to be sorry she'd ever started this whole singles fight. Though she had met some wonderful, single friends who were devoted to the crusade, she was the face of the movement. When it failed - and it was failing - she was the one who would look bad. For one awful moment, she felt that Lindsay was right: Imogene was the head loser of the loser club. But then she pictured Matt, Paula, and Hannah and felt terrible for even thinking such a thing. They weren't losers. They were her friends.

Still, she felt differently than she had when she'd first started Solo Power. For a short while, she had been happy about being single. That excitement was fading.

Maybe being single was nothing to celebrate after all.

As she fidgeted on the couch, something stuck right into her backside.

"What the -" she said, as she reached underneath the couch cushion. "So that's where you got to!" she exclaimed as she finally stumbled across the stupid library book that she'd had to pay for when it went missing months ago. She stared at the cover. *His Own True Love.*

A romance novel.

Imogene laughed bitterly as she flipped through the pages. Hesitating for just a moment, she settled back to read. She lost herself in the story, the fantasy of a dashingly handsome loner who fell completely and utterly in love with the beautiful heroine. He abandoned his lifestyle of remaining alone to avoid being hurt, and surrendered himself to the girl he loved in a world where everyone was beautiful and couples made mad, passionate love on a daily basis.

She didn't go to bed until she'd finished the entire thing.

CHAPTER TWENTY-FIVE

Imogene drove to work feeling more conflicted than ever. There was no denying how reading that romance novel had made her feel.

Happy.

Excited.

Hopeful.

Hopeful that it could happen to her. So where the hell did that leave her with the singles movement? What if her family, her married friends, and the rest of the damn world were right? Was she out of her mind to be single? Was she crazy to wait for the right guy to come along? Was her dad right to say she was too picky? Was she nuts to have broken up with Nathan?

Camille eyed her with concern when she walked into work.

"You all right?" she asked.

"No." Imogene said.

"I know you're disappointed the Valentine's Day thing didn't go the way you planned."

"Yeah, you could say that." Imogene sighed, and then asked with uncharacteristic softness, "Am I crazy to be doing this?"

"I want you to see something," Camille told her. "Wait here." She left the room for a moment and then returned with some photographs. "I love my husband, and I really can't imagine what my life would be without him. We've been together so long it's just, you know, hard to fathom what my life would be like if I'd never met him. Marriage, when it works, can be a truly wonderful thing in life. Here, I want you to see these."

They were wedding photos. Imogene expected to see photographs of Camille and her husband, Mark, but it was a couple she didn't recognize. The bride and groom were gorgeous, like something out of a magazine. The man had rugged good looks, not unlike the guys you saw on romance novel covers. The woman looked like she'd just stepped out of a bridal magazine, except she was actually smiling, while the models in those magazines always looked ridiculously serious for some reason.

"Wow, she's beautiful!" Imogene said, feeling a stab of jealousy. Sometimes she wondered if maybe you really did have to be model beautiful to land a husband. She couldn't help but think of Hannah.

"Isn't she just lovely?" Camille said as she flipped through the photographs. "I don't know that I've ever seen a better-looking couple in my life! They look so happy, don't they? I guess your wedding day really is one of the happiest days of your life." Just as Imogene was forming the decision in her head that yes, perhaps she should go back to her old life of searching for a husband, Camille said quietly, "He killed her."

"What?" Imogene asked, shocked.

Camille nodded somberly. "Sure, there were warning signs before they got married. He didn't like her to see her friends. He always had to know where she was, and he was prone to jealous rages. That sort of thing. But then sometimes he would be so sweet to her that she always went back to him. Elena. That was her name. Elena." Camille spoke her name with reverence. Imogene sat perfectly still, willing this story to have a different ending than the one she had already heard. "Somehow, she eventually got up the nerve to leave him. I was processing their divorce when…" Camille stopped for a moment, trying to compose herself enough to get the rest of the story out without choking up. "He beat her too hard one time and…and then it was over."

Camille blinked back tears as she looked up at Imogene. "My point is that weddings can be beautiful. Marriage can be beautiful. But things are not always what they seem. Couples can sometimes put on a front to the world and make it look as if marriage is wedded bliss all the time. Even in good marriages, it's not always easy. If you meet a great guy that you feel you could spend the rest of your life with, great! Go for it! Get married! But if you *don't*, then you shouldn't be pressured into marrying the wrong one. You cannot force a good marriage. You either find the right one or you don't." Camille took Imogene's hand in hers. "You keep up this fight, you hear me? If you get this reality show on the air, you'll show millions of people that they don't have to settle for the wrong person. They don't have to be afraid to be single, and they're gonna be just fine on their own." Camille sighed deeply and said. "Do it for all the Elenas out there."

All day long, Imogene thought about Camille's words. Elena's tragic story was an extreme example, but Imogene knew Camille was right about settling for the wrong person. Even if you didn't marry some horrible abuser, it was still a sad thing to tie yourself down to somebody you didn't love. She thought of her friend, Kate. Imogene could see that she wasn't happy in her marriage. Robert would never hurt Kate physically, and he wasn't verbally abusive. It seemed it was a lot of little things, and little things quickly turned into big things. Robert never seemed to consider Kate's feelings, and he wasn't especially affectionate. They didn't really seem to enjoy being together.

Imogene thought about the romance novel she had just read. She couldn't help but imagine how soul-crushing it must be to read books like that, or to watch sexy romantic movie heroes, and then turn around and see some belching slob on the couch, drinking beer in a smelly T-shirt. At least while you were single, the fantasy was still alive. Nothing like a slovenly husband to kill romance for you. That really was worse than having no one at all.

There weren't any perfect, romantic movie heroes out there and she wasn't a size zero heroine with golden blonde hair. Still, fantasizing about romance could be fun. Okay, so maybe Lindsay was right about there being nothing wrong with a little romance in life. Still, Imogene knew that those perfect, fantasy weddings of Lindsay's were as fake as those romantic heroes in books and movies.

And she was going to prove it.

CHAPTER TWENTY-SIX

Valentine's Day was a complete and utter success. Lindsay couldn't have planned it any better. Of course, she *did* plan it, but even the things she couldn't control had gone better than she could have imagined. She'd planned a peaceful sort of counterprotest to Solo Power's hateful, anti-love campaign by happily handing out roses to couples - kind of like a 60's war protest. Quiet and peaceful beat angry and bitter any day. Between the furious, love-scorned protesters and Imogene's on-air fight with that restaurant manager, Solo Power had practically done themselves in. It was fabulous.

Jillian had been right. Just play up the love and marriage angle, and you simply couldn't lose. Seriously, who could root for people who were against white weddings and cute little babies?

Lindsay had gotten several calls to be on more talk shows, which was exciting and fed her already healthy ego. The offers were pouring in! Well, trickling at this point, but it was a start. The pouring would begin once her reality show hit the air. She would become a real celebrity, instead of someone that some people recognized but more people didn't.

Being a talk show guest was fantastic. Each appearance brought the votes closer and closer to 250,000. It wouldn't be long at all before the reality show was officially hers. It was just a matter of time. Perhaps the best part was that each show offered Lindsay the chance to slam Imogene Hart over and over again, and there wasn't a damn thing that little nobody could do about it! Sure, Imogene had been really cocky and self-assured when she appeared on the *Kaynein and Richards* show, but nobody wanted to hear from her now. Lindsay could say anything she wanted. Of course, Lindsay rarely mentioned Imogene by name, making it seem as if she was taking the high road, but everyone knew who she was talking about when she said things like, "It's such a shame that some people would rather wallow in selfish misery and take others down with them instead of embracing the joys of love." Lindsay had all those talk show hosts eating out of her hand, especially when she got to talking about her own husband and kids. That trick worked every time.

Lindsay figured that by now, Imogene should be ready to admit defeat. Even if she wasn't, who cared? She was going to be defeated anyway. Even if for some crazy reason, Imogene decided to keep up this losing battle in which she was humiliated on a daily basis, Lindsay still had one more weapon at her disposal. Jillian had gotten several more incriminating pictures of Imogene and that guy friend of hers. It would be so easy for Lindsay to simply release the photos, taking the high road as always, and announce how happy she was that her foe had finally found true love.

CHAPTER TWENTY-SEVEN

Both Matt and Paula eyed Imogene warily when she breezed into Talmer's bar to meet with them. The last time she had spoken with either of them, she'd been really depressed about the Valentine's Day debacle. They'd probably realized how close she'd been to giving up. They didn't know how close she'd been to returning to her former man-seeking lifestyle, and she saw no reason to tell them. Ever. She still felt like she was betraying the cause in her own thoughts, but they didn't need to know that, either.

"Where's Hannah?" Imogene asked as she put her purse on the floor and sat down at the table.

"She's in the restroom. She looked kinda, you know, upset," Matt said, looking worried.

"Why? What's the matter?" Imogene asked.

"The kids at her school are giving her a hard time," Matt answered.

"Oh," Imogene said, feeling her anger rise. "What else is new?"

"Well, it's kinda because..." Paula began gently.

"Because of what? Oh, you mean...."

Paula and Matt both nodded grimly. "The kids at her school saw her on the news and, you know, were giving her a rough time because of all the bad press..."

"I see. You mean they're bullying her because she's on the losing side," Imogene said bitterly, her heart sinking. She hated to think that Hannah was suffering because of Solo Power. "Well, we haven't lost yet!" she said, summoning the positive energy that she'd been working hard to maintain. Paula and Matt looked at her with a mixture of bewilderment and pity. Clearly, they thought the fight was over.

Hannah returned to her seat. She looked tired, battle-weary. Imogene felt terrible to be the cause of Hannah's current misery, but that would make it all the better when they won in the end, right? And they could still win.

"Hey, beautiful," Matt said to Hannah as she took her seat. That coaxed a small smile out of her.

"All right, let's get to work. We're not beaten yet, guys. Now is not the time to give up!" Three pairs of eyes stared at Imogene and none of them looked convinced.

"Look, Imogene. There's plenty more work to be done with Solo Power. There's so much we can do with the organization and I'm looking forward to helping in any way I can, but I think the reality show thing is kind of a bust at this point," Paula said, leaning wearily back in her chair.

"How can you say that? You're just gonna give up?" Imogene asked.

"I don't know, Immy. It does seem kinda hopeless," Matt said, running his hand through his hair. He looked tired, too. It was exhausting, losing. It sucked.

"It is *not* hopeless! It's not over until it's over, right? If Lindsay wins…" Imogene struggled not to choke saying those words aloud, "then there's nothing we can do about it. But it's ridiculous to give up now! She hasn't won yet. We can't give up. And I'll tell you why…" With that, Imogene took a deep breath and relayed the

Elena story that Camille had told her. She told the story exactly the way Camille had, starting by describing how beautiful the wedding photos were and ending with the tragic death of the bride.

Matt, Paula, and Hannah seemed as stunned as Imogene had been when she'd first heard the tale.

"There are worse things in life than staying single," Imogene said gently but firmly. She looked at Hannah, who nodded somberly. Imogene turned to the rest of the group. "We can't let it end like this. And not just for us. I just…I just think we need to *do* something to help the single people out there who feel so down for not being married. It's just not fair. It's not fair for them to feel bad when they've done nothing to deserve feeling bad about themselves, you know? Not being able to find the right guy or girl, or preferring to be alone, is nothing to be ashamed of!"

Paula and Matt nodded, but Hannah just looked down at her plate. A surge of determination shot through Imogene. She was going to make Hannah be proud of being single, make her literally hold her head up high, if it was the last damn thing she ever did. Hannah was a prime candidate to wind up in a miserable marriage, or even a deadly one like Elena, because she didn't think she was good enough or pretty enough to attract a good guy. She'd settle for anyone who would have her. Not on Imogene's watch, she wouldn't…

"Look, we all know Lindsay is full of crap, right?" Imogene said. Nods all around. "She goes on and on when she's on those talk shows about the glory of love and marriage and…" Imogene put a finger down her throat and made a gagging noise. Matt raised an eyebrow. "Look, I'm not saying that there's anything wrong at all with love and marriage and romance…" An image of the hot romance novel guy flashed through her mind. Damn, that was a good book. "But does anybody here really think Lindsay Saga cares about any of those things?"

"Sure she does!" Hannah said. "Until the check clears. Then she wouldn't care if she had to drop the wedding video off at the divorce lawyer's office." Imogene smiled at her, happy to see that Hannah was speaking up again.

"Exactly!" Imogene said, slamming her hand on the table, jarring the drinks. "Sorry. Lindsay stands for fancy, extravagant weddings that are all for show. Just like Elena's wedding, they all look so pretty on the outside. Lindsay doesn't care about love and marriage and commitment. She cares about fame and money."

"True, all true. But what can we do about it?" Paula asked, leaning forward. She seemed as eager to get Lindsay Saga as Imogene was. Good. Because Imogene was going to need her help.

"Well," Imogene began, leaning forward conspiratorially. "She keeps using the media to slam us, so we're gonna do the same to her."

"Can you get us on one of those talk shows?" Paula asked hopefully.

"Well, maybe. I mean…" Imogene began, but then decided the truth was best. "No. No, I can't. I tried. A lot. But that's okay! I've got an even better idea. I know damn well that Lindsay and those bridezillas are obsessed with looking good and having the perfect wedding just to show off and act like they're better than everybody else."

There were more nods all around. An especially enthusiastic nod from Hannah, which encouraged Imogene even more.

"I'm sure there are plenty of people who get married for the right reasons and I guess now I can see how boycotting Valentine's Day wasn't the best way to support our cause…" More nods, which hurt a little. Imogene had half-hoped to hear encouraging statements about how it wasn't her fault that Valentine's Day was a bust, but none were forthcoming. She knew it was her fault, but there was no use crying about it now. Lesson learned. On to the next. "But we all know damn well that those brides of Lindsay's are all about showing off. Those crazy, expensive circus weddings have nothing to do with love, and it just makes me so angry that everybody believes all her crap about how she only does it because she loves *love*!" Imogene raised her right arm dramatically as she spoke, and her fellow singles laughed. It was barely even an exaggeration. Lindsay really did get that dramatic when she was up on her high horse about the wonders of love and marriage. And there was no way in hell that she meant a single word of it.

"Yeah, she's full of crap. So how do we prove it?" Paula asked.

Imogene took a deep breath before revealing her plan. "We're gonna follow Lindsay to some of those weddings of hers and get some of those awful brides on video. We're gonna show the world that it's not just single people who can be angry and bitter. Sometimes the brides—or bridezillas—are too, and we're gonna prove it! We'll get some footage of brides being mean and then we'll post it to YouTube!"

Imogene felt slightly guilty as she announced the plan out loud. It really wasn't fair to tape those women without their knowledge. Then again, since when did Lindsay fight fair?

"That's an awesome idea! You just know some of them are horrible bitches," Matt said, shaking his head. Imogene grinned at him, recalling his words about why he never wanted to get married, and how some of his friends' wives were so mean.

Imogene felt bolstered by Matt's support. "Matt and I can get all dressed up and act like we're together and crash the weddings, but we have to make sure Lindsay doesn't see us. Paula, you can sneak in, too. You know, act like you're a relative of the family or something. Too bad Lindsay met you guys at the TV studio. She knows what you look like. Still, the brides won't know us, so we should be able to use our phones and get video of them."

"Sounds like fun!" Paula said. Imogene had known she would be on board. Paula was the adventurous type and was always up for something new.

"And Hannah, you can help, too," Imogene said. "You could be-"

"I don't know. I'm not sure about this," Hannah said, looking very uncomfortable with the whole idea.

"Hey, no problem. This is totally voluntary. You don't have to do anything that makes you uncomfortable, okay?" Imogene said gently. She felt awful about it, but part of her was relieved that Hannah wouldn't join them on this little venture. Hannah would be very conspicuous, due to her size. Lindsay had met her at the TV studio, too, and if she saw her at one of the weddings, they'd be done for.

"Yeah, she better not come with us," Matt said grimly. "If she shows up all dressed up, nobody's even gonna look at the bride." He winked at her.

"You're crazy," Hannah said, smiling and waving him off.

Matt looked Paula up and down. "Maybe you better stay home too, sexy."

Paula burst out laughing. "Well, if I show up and the groom starts checking me out, it'll piss off the bride and we'll get some great video of her having a meltdown."

"That's a good point," Matt said. He pointed his fork at her. "Wear something with a slit up the side."

Imogene, Paula, and Hannah laughed uproariously. Even in her sixties, Paula would probably look good in a gown with a slit. She was brazen enough to do it, too.

Matt rubbed his hands together deviously. "This is gonna be great!"

CHAPTER TWENTY-EIGHT

They crashed an outdoor wedding first. It took place at Sherwood Gardens, a popular wedding spot in Orlando featuring a gorgeous mansion that looked like a castle. The flowers in the sprawling garden were perpetually in bloom, and their fragrance was as strong as perfume. It was absolutely picturesque, like something out of a fairytale or a romance novel, which made it the perfect spot to prove their point. Everything looked perfectly lovely, but that didn't mean that was the way it really was.

"Now remember, the trick to getting in is to act like you belong here," Imogene said and Matt nodded. It was kind of fun to have a reason to dress up for once. Imogene wore a light, pale blue spring dress that flattered her figure. She loved this dress because it always made her feel beautiful, like a princess. Ugh, how she hated to admit that to herself. That was what brides-to-be were forever saying, how they wanted to be a princess on their wedding day. Jeez, they were grown women. What was wrong with them? Still, Imogene adored this dress and the way it made her feel. She would sleep in this dress if she could.

Okay. Sometimes she did sleep in it. But that was beside the point.

Right now she had a legitimate excuse to wear it, which was

cool. Matt looked incredibly handsome in a suit and tie and it was great fun to walk around on his arm. Imogene had forgotten how much she missed having a boyfriend. It still irked her that she could not seem to summon any romantic feelings for Matt. It would be so easy if they could just fall in love. He was single, she was single. He was a wonderfully fun, sweet guy and she cared deeply for him, but she just saw him as a friend or even a big brother type. She couldn't explain it, but that's the way it was. Disappointing as it might be, it worked out great that Matt saw her the same way. If he liked her in a different way, they really couldn't be friends. And that would suck.

Getting into the wedding itself was a breeze. Nobody really cared who attended the wedding. You could pretty much walk in off the street. It was when you entered the reception hall that things got dicey. She and Matt would sit inconspicuously in the back once the wedding started, but for now they wandered around to see what they could find. Imogene was careful to get some good video of the grounds before the ceremony. She loved the idea of starting the YouTube video by showing the gorgeous, palatial setting and then smash cutting to the bridal bitchfest. That would be such a powerful image.

The weather was absolutely perfect and Imogene was having fun just strolling around, taking in the sights. She felt like she was on an adventure, and having Matt by her side as her partner-in-crime was great fun. They wandered down over a hill and spotted a gazebo where Imogene caught of glimpse of a white dress.

"Paydirt!" Imogene said, feeling like she was in a spy movie. This was more fun by the minute. "Come on!" She lifted the hem of her dress as she ran toward a bunch of trees nearby. If they could stay hidden in the little wooded area, they could get some video of the bride getting ready. Once they got settled behind a tree,

Imogene saw that Lindsay was in the gazebo as well. She turned on the video camera on her phone and zoomed in. It was when she watched the action through the zoom lens that she first realized the bride was crying.

"That's not good..." Matt said, looking concerned. Imogene felt bad as well. She hated to see a bride cry on her wedding day. These did not appear to be tears of joy, that was for sure.

"I just...I don't think I can go through with it...it just doesn't feel right..." The Bride sobbed. She looked beautiful in her wedding gown with her blonde hair done up in a fancy French twist. Only her tears marred her lovely features.

Lindsay put her arm around the girl and spoke with surprising tenderness. "It's all right. Everything's gonna be all right, Patricia." Imogene had never seen Lindsay be nice before. She hasn't thought she was capable of it. Imogene felt a stab of guilt for not only witnessing this scene, but recording it. She knew she should turn off the camera, but she wanted to see if everything turned out okay.

"It's just...I thought I could go through with it at first...but it just feels wrong!" With that, Patricia burst into a fresh round of tears. Imogene noticed that her bridesmaids didn't exactly seem sympathetic. One actually rolled her eyes. "I mean, look. Just look!" The Bride gestured at the pink ribbons that were tied to the gazebo. "The ribbons, the streamers, not to *mention* the seat coverings for the guests are Cotton Candy Pink. They are *not* Baby Powder Pink!"

Matt broke into a grin and Imogene smiled wryly back. It was a good thing she'd kept filming...

Later, by hiding behind some pillars at the mansion, Imogene got some great video of the bitchzilla screaming at her bridesmaids, and even better...or worse...screaming at her groom. Imogene was thrilled that they were getting the footage they were after and was also happy to see how right Camille was. Things really weren't always what they seemed. This was proof that a lot of people really did get married for the wrong reasons. The groom from this wedding seemed like a nice guy and Imogene couldn't imagine what he was doing with that awful shrew. She guessed guys could be pressured into getting married, too. Imogene wondered if he was afraid to be alone or maybe he was tired of being treated as irresponsible or gay or all of the above.

Not all the weddings they crashed were like the first one. Many of them were actually very nice and the couples did seem to be very much in love. Still, the extravagant Saga weddings seemed unnecessary and way over the top. Like many women, Imogene had sometimes fantasized about what her wedding might be like, but she couldn't imagine going to all the trouble and expense of these crazy affairs. Mostly, she'd fantasized about wearing a pretty dress, feeling beautiful, and having a sweet, handsome man by her side. It always amazed Imogene how women could think of themselves as "princesses" while screaming their heads off at everyone around them. Not exactly feminine and delicate, these broads.

Imogene and Paula nearly got busted at one wedding when they were doing the "act like you belong there" thing. Matt was on a fishing trip with his buddies that day so it was just the girls. At the grand church wedding, the usher actually asked for their names as they entered. That was the first time anybody had bothered to do a name check at the actual wedding ceremony.

"Name?" The guy asked, eyeing Paula and Imogene suspiciously. This caught Imogene completely off guard. She froze.

Paula shot the poor usher a fierce death stare that could have melted his face. "Did you *seriously* just ask me my name? Do you live in a tunnel under the L.A. Freeway?"

"Uh-um…I'm sorry…Sorry! I wasn't paying attention and didn't recognize you at first. Right this way, Madam!" Imogene bit her lip to stifle her giggle as the man offered his arm to Paula. The women managed to be seated before they dissolved into a fit of giggles.

"Paula, that was amazing!"

Paula shot a sympathetic glance toward the usher. "Poor guy. Yeah, I did a little theater in college." Imogene fist-bumped her. She had almost as much fun crashing these weddings with Paula as she did with Matt. It turned out that the bride was a news anchor on a local TV station, thus the extra security at the door.

It was a good thing they were able to get into this particular wedding, because it ended up being very worth their while. Imogene got some good footage of the ceremony itself, which was actually quite lovely. The bride teared up and the groom seemed on the verge as well. Everybody was all smiles and love and laughter and all that good stuff. Picture perfect, or so it seemed…

"Come on. Let's get movin' here. I don't feel like spending my whole reception doing these damn pictures," The Bride said irritably. It was utterly fascinating to see how rapidly she could switch from bitch to princess when the photographer took her picture. She smiled her most serene, woman-in-love smile for the camera, but the moment the flash went off, she shouted to her beloved, "God, would you MOVE! You're on my dress!" The groom jumped back as if avoiding a snake, which he kind of was.

Paula wiped away a mock tear while watching the drama unfold. "Weddings are just so beautiful."

"I can't believe this is what I wasted half of my life waiting for," Imogene murmured to herself. Lindsay stalked over to the altar and started yelling at the photographer to hurry up. Imogene ducked behind a church pillar, but was still able to get some great video of both the blushing bride and the pseudo-celebrity wedding planner berating the poor photographer.

The photographer did his best to get the photos he needed, and then finally released the bridal party.

"About damn time," The Bride said as she waved her bridesmaids over to hold her dress as she walked back down the aisle. The groom trailed behind her, already forgotten.

Two teenagers who were clearly not dressed for a wedding walked into the church. Lindsay hurried toward them as Paula and Imogene lowered their heads so as not to be seen. They still had a good vantage point from the back row and Imogene kept filming with her phone, just in case there would be any more fireworks from Lindsay and the bridezilla-du-jour.

"What are you two doing here?" Lindsay hissed at the teenagers. She glanced around nervously, hoping no one was watching. Paula and Imogene were, but they were discreet about it.

"You promised us you were gonna drive us to the dance tonight but dad told us this morning you were working late," the girl said.

"Your dad's right. Sorry," Lindsay said, not sounding the least bit sorry. She just looked annoyed and embarrassed at the presence of her children.

"I told you," the boy said to his older sister. "Didn't I tell you? We shoulda never trusted her. She never comes through. Why are we surprised?"

"Cody! You show some respect!" Lindsay said to her son, her voice harsh but barely above a whisper. God forbid she be seen talking to one of her kids.

"Mom, we told our friends you were gonna drive us to the dance in the Mercedes. You promised us. We promised them!" the girl said, sounding desperate. Imogene felt terrible for her. It was hard enough being a teenager without the added stress of having unsupportive parents.

"Ask your father to do it," Lindsay said, not even looking at her kids. She was trying to keep her eye on the bride. She clearly didn't want to leave her side for too long.

"He's out golfing and then he's going out with his stupid friends. He won't answer his phone when he's out. You know that," the girl said. She looked tired. She knew she was going to lose this argument, and it was clearly not the first time she'd had this conversation with her mother.

"Can KelliAnne at least drive us in one of the cars?" the boy asked.

"Get serious, Cody." Lindsay told him. "No way. Get one of your friends to take you."

"You know," Cody said, his voice rising, "Sometimes I really hate you!"

Lindsay looked horrified, but it was clearly because her son's statement was made so loudly, so publicly. "Yeah, well, sometimes I hate you guys, too!" Lindsay hissed back.

Imogene gasped. Teenagers frequently said they hated their parents, but parents weren't supposed to say it back! Lindsay's home situation was sadder than Imogene had realized. It made her angry to think of all those talk shows Lindsay had gone on, acting like the perfect, loving mother.

"Let's get the hell out of here," KelliAnne said angrily. She stormed out. She would have slammed the door if she could, but all she could do was leave the back church door swinging wildly upon her exit.

Cody shot his mother another disgusted look and followed his sister out the door. Rather than go after her children, Lindsay hurried toward the bride to make sure everything was all right with her. She looked relieved that her children were out of her hair.

"Wow," Imogene said softly. She turned off her cell phone camera.

"That's quite interesting," Paula said. "The queen of love and family has children who can't stand her." Paula gestured at the camera. "And you got all that?"

Imogene nodded, but she couldn't imagine actually using the video against Lindsay. Sure, it proved that Lindsay was a terrible mother and it was concrete evidence that her "love and family" schtick was complete garbage, but Imogene couldn't bring her kids into this fight.

Could she?

By this point, they had gathered pretty much all the evidence they needed to prove that Lindsay and her photogenic brides were not all fairydust and sugared roses. Still, there was a fair number of nice brides among the ones they had seen. Some of the couples did seem to be truly happy together. One bride had stumbled on her high-heeled shoe when they were outside getting photos taken. Her new husband rushed to her rescue and was so tender and sweet when he applied the bandage to her ankle. She put her arms around him and kissed him; then he pulled her to her feet and held her arm carefully so she wouldn't fall again. It was such a simple, sweet moment. It had made Imogene tear up just watching it.

Truth be told, Imogene had witnessed a lot of tender moments like that between many of the newly-married couples. Each time they encountered one of those couples, Imogene felt a familiar twinge of longing. Though she was learning to really enjoy her life in a way that she never had before, she still felt a desire to have someone to share her life with. She hated feeling like that, and she hated the guilt that came along with it. She couldn't imagine what Matt and Paula would think if they knew how she sometimes felt about being single.

No sense in thinking about that now. The most important thing was that they had gotten more than enough footage of brides and of Lindsay acting like total bitches. Enough to put together a fantastic YouTube video that showcased how Lindsay really felt about love and marriage.

CHAPTER TWENTY-NINE

Solo Power had officially outgrown the library conference room. Imogene found a church hall that was at least twice the size and held the next meeting there. She couldn't wait to show off the YouTube video, which had turned out even better than she had hoped. It was one thing to see all those brides in person acting like total bitches, but when you saw all of the screaming and yelling and tantruming back-to-back-to-back, the effect was truly horrifying. It was fantastic.

Imogene felt guilty about taping these women without their knowledge, but she reasoned that it really was for the greater good. Lindsay was getting people to vote for her show by convincing everyone that the program would be all about beautiful, romantic love, whereas Imogene knew the actual show would be nothing but petty, mean-spirited bridal drama. The YouTube video was just a warning about what people were actually voting for when they chose Lindsay.

"Thank you all for coming today! I know that the whole Valentine's Day thing didn't work out the way we hoped it would," Imogene said. She was relieved to see so many supportive faces at the meeting. People looked sympathetic, like they didn't blame her for the fiasco. "I'm excited to share with you the next phase of our plan for getting our message out and our show on the air! I know that Lindsay Saga has an awful lot of votes, but I want you to know that we are not out of it yet. It's not over until somebody gets 250,000 votes. There's still time."

Imogene looked out at all the people gathered for the latest meeting. It was heartening to see that this was the biggest crowd yet. She'd been worried that some people would abandon the group after the Valentine's Day debacle. Though the protest may not have gone exactly the way she had planned, it had certainly gotten them some publicity. More people than ever had heard of Solo Power, and there seemed to be a lot of people who wanted to get involved. She took a deep breath as she looked out at all the faces that were still filled with hope.

"We're not giving up, but we are kind of changing tactics. I'm starting to think that Lindsay Saga is right that love and marriage are some of the most important things in life."

Some gasps and murmurs of annoyance. Imogene grinned. That reaction was to be expected. They weren't sure where the hell she was going with this. Yet.

"What better way to show you what I mean than a visual demonstration of what a wedding is really all about. Paula?"

Paula hit the lights and Imogene cued up the YouTube video. She hadn't posted it online yet. She wanted to screen it for the Solo Power group first before releasing it out into the world.

Soft, sweet, instrumental music began to play. It was the kind of music that you hear at the beginning of a subdued, fancy church wedding. Imogene watched the group with great interest as they viewed the video. It was obvious that people thought Imogene had lost her mind, or perhaps was just throwing in the towel. She couldn't wait until they saw the punchline of the video. It was almost literally a punch...

With the romantic music playing as the soundtrack, the bridezilla, who just moments ago had been smiling sweetly at her new husband, suddenly slapped a bridesmaid. Shocked gasps came up from the crowd. Matt grinned and squeezed Imogene's shoulder. He had gotten that particular shot and had almost dropped his cell phone when The Bride hit the poor girl.

The video went on to show wedding after wedding, bride after bride, first beginning with shots of the beautiful church or venue and still photos of the lovely Bride and groom, and then cutting to The Bride showing her true colors.

"It's *my* day!" professed bride after bride after bride. That was one of the funniest parts of the video. The sheer number of times they had heard that particular phrase was hysterical. They had edited them all together so you could see them shouting it over and over again. After that, they spliced together all the times Lindsay had agreed with the bridezillas that they should have anything and everything they wanted on *their* day.

"Of course. You do what you want. It's your day!"

"Those caterers are total morons. I can have them fired if you want."

"It's your day, so you should be able to do whatever you want. Who cares what Greg thinks? It's not about him."

"It's ridiculous! You're right to be mad. It's the bridesmaid's responsibility to lose weight before your day. Nobody wants a fat bridesmaid. No wonder she's still single."

Imogene glanced over at Hannah and was pleased to see she was simply shaking her head at Lindsay's words. She had thought long and hard about including that last part about the "fat bridesmaid," but Lindsay's words were so cruel, she knew including them would be a good way to get their point across. Marriage was only for the thin and beautiful, according to Lindsay Saga.

Bride after bride ranted and raved and looked anything but princess-like on her magical fantasy day.

"This is supposed to be about *me*!"

"Who *cares* what you want?"

"You are not going to screw this up for me. You had your turn, now get outta my face!"

"I am the *bride*, so I make the rules!"

That last line amused Paula and Matt so much that Imogene repeated it throughout the video. Whenever a bride did something particularly crazy, she would repeat the clip "I am the *bride*, so I make the rules!" It was hilarious and amazingly affective. Imogene also put together a bunch of crying, tantruming brides, starting with the gazebo lady.

The laughter in the room was uplifting, infectious. It felt so good to see all these single people gathered together and embracing this cause. It was wonderful to be able to show them that maybe they weren't missing out on as much as they thought by not getting married. It seemed to be an eclectic group of all ages, backgrounds, and opinions. Some, like Paula, were defiant about being single and were totally cool with it. Others, like Donna, seemed to be depressed about it and were really down on themselves. Those were the people Imogene really wanted to help. She hoped this video would show them that weddings and marriage weren't the mystical key to happiness that society said they were.

Best of all, the video would expose Lindsay Saga for the fraud she was.

The last segment was a fabulous, silent bitch montage of brides screaming and fighting. One even threw a shoe at her groom. It ended with a voice clip of Lindsay from one of her talk show appearances saying, "After all, it's love that matters the most. Love is what makes life worth living."

The final image was a still photo of a screaming bride coupled with Imogene's voiceover saying, *"If you want to vote for Lindsay's version of "love", by all means go to www.theestrogennetwork.com and vote for* Beautiful Bride. *If you want to vote for an uplifting show that helps single people live happy and fulfilling lives, vote for* Single, Not Alone. *Remember, you're never really alone if you have friends. Join Solo Power and be alone—together!"*

Imogene had been unable to resist adding the words, *"Even if you are alone, that's better than living with this…"* and the final still image of the video appeared. It was the woman aiming, ready to fire her shoe at her wide-eyed groom.

Everyone burst into wild laughter and applause. To Imogene's amazement, people started standing up. It was a standing ovation! There was no way that Imogene could bask in this glory alone. She stood up and grabbed Matt and Paula, dragging them to the front of the room. The three of them bowed together as if they had just appeared in a play. As they dissolved into laughter, Imogene realized she could not remember the last time she'd had so much fun. Her heart was so filled with joy and hope for the future, she could burst.

"So!" Imogene had to shout to be heard. The crowd quieted down a bit so they could listen. "Are we ready to go live with this baby?"

Wild cheers and applause. Imogene let Matt do the honors since he was the computer expert. With the touch of a few buttons, the YouTube video was locked and loaded.

"So…" Imogene said, cueing up The Estrogen Network vote count up on the big screen. "This is where we're at now…"

Beautiful Bride: 223,275

Single, Not Alone: 147,130

Boos from the audience.

"We'll check back and see what happens once our little video gets out."

CHAPTER THIRTY

Derek walked into the living room to find his lovely bride-to-be sitting in front of the computer watching a Lindsay Saga video.

"Jeez, you're obsessed with that lady," he said, shaking his head.

Jillian whirled around and Derek actually took a horrified step back when he saw her expression. Jillian was in such a rage that her hands were shaking.

"I am going to kill that bitch."

"The wedding lady? I thought you liked her," Derek asked cautiously.

"Not her!" Jillian shouted, and Derek backed even further away. "That Imogene bitch!" She could see the wheels turning in her fiancé's brain as he desperately tried to recall who the hell Imogene was. She wanted to smack his face. He should know who she was talking about by now.

"Oh, um. The singles lady, right?"

"Yes, the singles lady! She must have followed Lindsay around to a bunch of weddings and she videotaped the brides yelling and stuff. She did it to try to get votes for her stupid singles show!"

Derek glanced over at the computer screen and watched as bride after bride yelled, screamed, ranted, and raved. He bit his lip to keep from laughing.

"Derek! It's not funny!" Jillian shouted, near tears.

"I'm sorry, honey," Derek said, actually sounding a bit contrite. "You don't really think it's gonna work, do you? Isn't your show like way ahead?"

"Well, yes. It is," Jillian said. "It's just so awful. She's making Lindsay Saga out to be the bad guy. It's not her who's bitter and hates marriage. What if it does work? What if everybody starts voting for her stupid singles show?"

"Now come on, hon. That's not gonna happen," Derek said. Jillian rushed over to him and he put his arms around her.

"This is all I ever wanted, you know? All I've ever dreamed of since I was a little girl. I wanted a really nice, beautiful wedding. Is that really too much to ask?"

"No, honey. Of course not. I'm sure you have nothing to worry about," Derek said. His words were kind, but Jillian couldn't help but notice that he already sounded bored with the conversation. Didn't he care about her at all? "So, um, have you thought about what's for dinner tonight?"

Jillian shoved him away. "Are you kidding me?" She glanced at the computer screen. The video had just gotten to the part about voting for Lindsay's brand of love versus voting for that sorryass singles show. This was the third time Jillian had viewed the video, and it enraged her more each time she saw it. She grabbed her cell phone and started dialing.

"Lindsay! Have you seen it?" Jillian drew in a deep breath and tried to stifle the urge to strangle Lindsay over the phone. Of course she hadn't seen it. Lindsay wasn't tech savvy at all, whereas Jillian had Google Alerts set up to notify her every time Lindsay was mentioned on the Internet. She had found out about the video pretty much as soon as it went live. Muttering under her breath, Jillian plopped back down in her seat and quickly emailed the link to Lindsay. "Imogene and her group of man-haters put together a video of you."

"What kind of video?" Lindsay asked, sounding horrified. Truly, was there anything scarier than being told there was some kind of video of you going around on the Internet? "She must have followed you to a bunch of weddings and taken video of some of the brides acting like bridezillas." Just saying the words out loud made Jillian's blood pressure skyrocket. It was bad enough that Imogene was making Lindsay and her wedding business look bad, but she was also making a mockery of Jillian's most treasured dream. For as long as she could remember, Jillian had fantasized about wearing a fancy, white gown and drifting down the aisle to beautiful music with candles everywhere and a handsome prince waiting for her at the front. The church would be like a palace with everybody attending the service just to see her, the beautiful bride. Imogene was making her dream look stupid. Jillian hated her for it.

"I cannot believe she did this," Lindsay said slowly. Jillian could hear the dreaded video playing on Lindsay's computer. Lindsay didn't sound nearly angry enough. Sure, she was watching the video for the first time and was still in shock, but Jillian could tell that Lindsay wouldn't have a clue about how to handle this.

"So what are you going to do about it?" Jillian demanded.

"What *can* I do about it?" Lindsay asked, sounding defeated already. "It's already out there! I guess I could go on some more talk shows and-"

"That's not enough anymore, Lindsay!" Jillian screamed into the phone. Derek glanced over at her, looking worried. She hated when he looked at her like that. Like he wasn't sure what he was getting into by marrying her. Well, too bad. He had proposed, she had accepted. They were going to have a wedding, and it was going to be the wedding of her dreams. Too late to back out now. Not when she was this close. "You've been on every talk show out there, going on and on about the importance of love-"

"Which is what you told me to do!" Lindsay shouted. It pissed Jillian off that Lindsay was yelling at her, but at least she was getting fired up. That was more like it.

"But now Imogene's taken your words and used them against you. She's trying to prove that you didn't mean a word you said about marriage and love."

"So what am I supposed to do?"

"There's nothing you can do," Jillian said bitterly. "But I can. I'm gonna do the same damn thing to her that she did to you. To us. I know she's dating that guy she's always hanging around with. I've already got photos, but I'm gonna get video this time. Fight fire with fire. She doesn't know who I am, so I can follow her wherever I want. How was Imogene able to tape you at all those weddings without you noticing?" Lindsay might be a brilliant wedding planner, but she didn't seem all that bright otherwise. It kind of sucked. Jillian had liked it better when Lindsay was her celebrity hero.

"I don't know!" Lindsay said defensively. "She probably got some of her little followers to do it for her."

"Whatever," Jillian muttered. "It doesn't matter now. The damage is done."

"Maybe it won't be that bad. Who's gonna see this video anyway?" Lindsay said. "I never even would have known about it if you hadn't told me."

That's because you've got your head up your ass, Jillian wanted to say, but she bit her tongue. Lindsay had a point. Maybe it would just sit on YouTube and only a few people would see it. There were thousands of videos out there. Dancing cats would probably get more hits than Imogene's stupid video.

No such luck. The damn thing went viral. As it turned out, lots of people found the video of a bunch of brides freaking out amusing enough to forward to their friends and post on Facebook and the like. Not to mention that Imogene and her sad, single cronies were posting it everywhere they could. It wouldn't have been so bad if it was just the brides, but even Jillian had to admit that Imogene had been savvy when she put the thing together. It was rather damning evidence to have Lindsay Saga all over the video, egging on the brides and telling them they should be able to do and say whatever they wanted because it was their day.

Well, it *was*, wasn't it? Seriously, people were always complaining about the bride wanting things her own way, but did they really think the groom gave a crap about what color the napkins were, or if the flowers were arranged properly? Of course not! All the guys wanted to do was get drunk at the reception, so let them. There was no reason why the bride shouldn't have one day—just *one* day—that was all about her. Was that really so unreasonable?

Jillian didn't think so. And there was no way she was letting anybody stop her from getting the wedding of her dreams. She was going to expose the fact that Imogene was dating that guy and that she was an even bigger fraud than she'd made Lindsay out to be. The queen of singles pride wasn't even single, and Jillian was going to prove it.

CHAPTER THIRTY-ONE

Getting the goods on Imogene was even easier than she'd thought. Jillian sat in her car outside Imogene's apartment at about 4pm on a Saturday, figuring that if she and that guy were dating, they'd be going out on a Saturday night. Sure enough, he showed up around 4:30. Dressed in a tuxedo. Where in the world were they going? Jillian got some great pictures of him walking up to Imogene's apartment building. While she waited for the two of them to come out, Jillian reviewed the photos of him on her phone.

He was kind of hot.

She felt a flash of jealousy toward Imogene and hated herself for it. It was stupid. That girl was nothing to be jealous of. Jillian was the bride-to-be, which meant every single girl in the world should be jealous of *her*. Especially when they saw her amazing, fantasy wedding broadcast on television.

Still, Jillian couldn't help feeling a flutter of attraction when she looked at the photos of the guy in the tux. It had been a long time since she'd felt that kind of attraction toward Derek. Or had she ever really felt that way about him? He wasn't bad looking. He was average. Maybe slightly above average. He was kinda cute and all, but they'd been dating almost a year. You couldn't expect white hot attraction to last forever. Jillian tried not to admit to herself that she'd never felt white-hot about Derek. She couldn't ever remember her heart fluttering at the sight of him. He was good enough in bed, but it wasn't like she ached for his touch. After all, it was just *Derek.*

Jillian felt another flash of jealousy as Imogene emerged from her apartment building wearing a lovely pale blue dress. She was actually kind of pretty. She and the guy looked good together. Jillian eagerly started filming the two of them walking toward the guy's car. She was hoping to catch them in a kiss, but they'd probably already done that when he'd first arrived at her apartment. Right now, they were just joking around with each other. Jillian was hoping to get his full name so she could look him up on the Internet and try to get some dirt on him, but all she got was "Matt" when Imogene said it as she punched him playfully on the shoulder. They certainly seemed to enjoy each other's company.

They got into his car and Jillian followed them. She hoped they were going someplace where it would be easy for her to spy. Probably some fancy restaurant or something, given that they were all dressed up.

A bolt of excitement shot through Jillian as a delicious thought occurred to her. What if this was some kind of anniversary or something, and he was going to propose? Even if by some miracle Imogene decided to stick to her principles and stay single, it would be devastating to her cause if a video of the proposal leaked. Jillian would just edit out the part where she said no...

She followed them to a church. No way...they weren't going to a wedding, were they? That would be awesome! Showing them snuggling all night and having fun at a wedding would be almost as good as a proposal! The Head Singles Pride Nerd enjoying a wedding, which was supposed to be her most hated event. This was gold. Not only that, but Jillian would get to attend a wedding, which she absolutely adored. She would crash them all the time if it wasn't so pathetic. She loved going to weddings because it gave her a chance to critique what was tacky and get good ideas for what wasn't. It also got her really excited about her own wedding. Weddings had always had that effect on her, even long before she'd ever had a specific groom in mind. There was nothing in the world that she enjoyed more than going to weddings, and with her own nuptials so close, she could barely contain her excitement.

She tried not to think about how it would feel going to weddings after she was married. In fact, she avoided thinking about anything that would happen after her wedding. She'd worry about that later.

Jillian parked the car and eagerly went inside. Yes, definitely a wedding. There were white pew bows on the first few rows. Jillian wasn't as dressed up as she should have been to attend a wedding, but her khaki pants and pale pink silk blouse were passable. An usher rushed up to her and offered his arm.

"Which side?" he asked pleasantly.

"Um, the groom?" It was best to sit on the groom's side so you faced the bride and got a better view of her in her gown.

He laughed inexplicably and took her arm. The usher seated her on the right side of the church. Once he walked away, she got up and re-seated herself right behind Imogene. She was sitting alone now with Matt nowhere in sight. Well, given the tux, it was likely that he was in the wedding party. Jillian had gotten some still photos of them walking in together, and she would likely get a good video of them at the reception. The drunker they were, the better the video would be.

An older woman came in and sat down next to Imogene.

"Hey, Paula. You look great!" Imogene said, greeting the

woman like she was a good friend, even though the lady was old enough to be her mother.

"So do you!" Paula said. Nothing good was happening now, so Jillian turned off her camera. She'd been pretending to take pictures of the altar, but she could only do that for so long without seeming suspicious.

Jillian tuned out Imogene's boring conversation with the old lady as she impatiently waited for the wedding to start. She was eager to see what the bride's dress would look like. That was the best part. Sometimes seeing other gowns gave her ideas about what she would wear, but she had already decided on the type of gown she wanted. It would be bright, gleaming white and none of that ivory crap. She had the rest of her life to wear ivory. Your wedding day was the one time that you could get away with wearing straight-up white, which was what made you stand out from the rest of the commoners on your day. Anybody could wear some boring, understated, off-white dress. On her day, there would be no mistaking that she was The Bride. Her dream gown would be trimmed with white roses and silky smooth, with none of that tulle stuff. At least, none that was visible. The dress wouldn't be poofy like those huge gowns some brides wore, but it would be bigger than a normal dress. Again, a dress that only a bride could get away with wearing in public. When she won the *Beautiful Bride* contest, Jillian would be able to get one of the best designers around to make her dress. It would blow every other bridal gown away, which was another reason she was eager to see today's bride. So she could compare how much better her own gown would be.

The wait was interminable, but finally the ceremony started. *Pachelbel's Canon in D* began. Jeez, could they be any more predictable? Still, the music was beautiful. They had a string quartet playing the song and it was quite stirring.

The bridesmaids emerged wearing midnight blue dresses. A little dark for a wedding, weren't they? Well, it was still technically winter, so Jillian figured the color made sense. Still, it was bright and sunny here in Florida and didn't exactly feel like wintertime. Once the bridesmaids and groomsmen were all settled in, it was time for the big moment. Everyone stood to the bride as the music swelled. Jillian could feel her heart thunder in her chest. She'd seen so many weddings and spent so many years fantasizing about them that she could hardly believe how close she was to her own day. Soon, that would be *her* walking down the aisle, and it wouldn't be just the congregation watching her. It would be a huge television audience. She couldn't wait.

Jillian turned toward the back of the church. For some odd reason, the groom's father was walking the groom down the aisle. Weird. Jillian guessed they were just trying to modernize their ceremony and put their own spin on it. Whatever. Why any bride would want to share the spotlight and let the groom walk down the aisle was beyond her.

As the men neared her seat, she realized that they were both about the same age, so it couldn't be the groom's father. She realized what was happening when she noticed the rainbow-colored handkerchiefs neatly folded inside each man's black tuxedo.

"Oh, ick," Jillian said aloud, but fortunately the music covered her comment. A gay wedding. Were they kidding with this? Jillian could hardly contain her disappointment that there would be no bride, no gown. Seriously, what was the point? She didn't have any strong feelings either way about gay marriage. She didn't care what gay people did; she just found the idea of two men together utterly boring. Two brides would have been better. But how weird would it be if you weren't the only bride on your wedding day? Talk about sharing the spotlight. Jillian couldn't help thinking that even if she was gay, she would still want a straight wedding. At least once. Just to do it.

Jillian rolled her eyes and sighed deeply as the ceremony began. She knew she'd better hide her annoyance if she didn't want to draw attention to herself. She was supposed to be a family member or friend of one of these guys, so she'd better start acting more supportive.

Well, at least the men were attractive. That would make the ceremony and reception a little more interesting to watch, though it was hard to get too excited about guys who were only into other guys. Boring, boring, boring.

"Thank you all for joining us on the happy occasion of joining two hearts, two families, two lives," the minister began. The minister prattled on and it was pretty much your standard wedding service. Jillian had every intention of making her wedding way more memorable, right down to the Bible verses. She was going to scour the Good Book to find some cool passages that nobody would think to use in a wedding. None of that boilerplate "love is patient, love is kind" stuff.

"Seth and David have composed their own vows," the minister said. Finally, something different to jazz up the proceedings.

The two men joined hands and looked into each other's eyes. Yes, they were definitely cute. And they looked cute together.

"Seth, you are the very best friend I've ever had," David began. He stopped for a moment as he began to choke up. Seth grasped his hand tighter as he struggled to continue. "Wow, I got further than I thought I would before I started to cry…"

Gentle laughter rippled through the congregation. David paused a moment to compose himself before continuing. The church fell silent. People were riveted, waiting to hear the rest.

"I never even dared to dream that I would meet a man like you.

I didn't think happy endings were for people like us. Standing here today, I can't believe that I get to spend the rest of my life with you." David started to tear up again.

Jillian noticed that Imogene had placed her hand over her heart as she watched the ceremony. Then she moved it to her mouth and stifled a small laugh. She nudged the old lady next to her and pointed to Matt up at the altar. He was crying like a baby, silent tears streaming down his face. Jillian realized that one of the grooms was probably his brother.

"Is he adorable or what?" Imogene whispered to the old lady, shaking her head and smiling.

"He is a cutie," the lady responded, smiling.

Jillian considered turning her cell phone camera on again, just in case Imogene said anything else about the guy, but decided against it. She told herself it was because Imogene wasn't likely to say much else until after the ceremony, but the truth was that Jillian was so caught up in the wedding vows, she didn't want to miss a word.

Now it was Seth's turn to speak. Before he did, he reached over and wiped a tear from David's eye. This small gesture was so beautiful, so touching, it made Jillian's heart ache. She couldn't fathom having anyone love her like that, and she could scarcely imagine being that much in love with someone. She felt a heavy sense of dread when she thought of Derek, which scared her. It would be completely different when she and Derek were up on the altar saying their vows. Not like this wedding at all.

"When I first met you, it was like coming home," Seth began. Jillian watched Imogene wipe a tear from her eye. Jillian didn't even feel her own tears until they were dripping onto her blouse. "I think we both knew that we belonged together right from the start."

David nodded and squeezed Seth's hand.

"And today is only the beginning of our life journey together. I promise to love and support you through it all. From bad hair days…" More laughter from the crowd. "To when the Dallas Cowboys lose."

"Go, Cowboys!" David interjected. Seth grinned at him. Jillian could feel the love between them. She'd never seen anything like it, and she wondered if she ever would again.

"And any time your heart is broken," Seth continued. "I will always be there to hold you. I will be there in happiness and sadness, through wealth and through poverty. I will be by your side, and I will love you until God calls one of us home. And even then, I will wait for the day when I am home with you again."

Sniffling and rustling for tissues could be heard throughout the church.

When the minister pronounced them husbands, both Seth and David broke into adorable grins and embraced and kissed each other for the first time as a married couple. The congregation exploded into applause and people actually stood up.

It was the best wedding Jillian had ever seen, and there wasn't even a bride in sight.

The moment she had that thought, Jillian banished it away as completely ridiculous. They were a sweet couple. That was all. They were happy. Good for them. Jillian would be happy with Derek, too. Of course she would be. Everybody always said marriage takes work, right? So that's what they would do. They would work on their marriage and make it a good one. But that was a worry for later. Much later. What mattered right now was making sure she got the wedding she deserved. And that meant crushing Imogene Hart into dust.

CHAPTER THIRTY-TWO

Imogene sat in the pew after the ceremony, tears streaming down her face. It took Paula a moment or two to realize that Imogene wasn't just crying from the emotion of the ceremony, and that something else was wrong.

"Hey now, Immy," Paula began gently. "What is it?"

"That was just…you know, so beautiful," Imogene said, wiping her eyes.

"Yes, it certainly was. They make a lovely couple, don't they? But come on, Imogene. What else is going on?"

Imogene thought about what to tell her. She couldn't tell her the truth, could she? That watching this incredibly moving ceremony had just confirmed her worst fears. That getting married and sharing your life with someone really was the only way to truly be happy. She had never seen any two people as happy as Seth and David were. She recalled Camille's words about how things weren't always what they seemed, but their love was real. There was no doubt about it. These two men were lovers, best friends, and soulmates. And Imogene realized how desperately she still wanted what they had. It was what she had always wanted.

"I'm scared," Imogene said softly.

Paula silently took her hand and waited for her to finish. For now, she just sat with her. Being a good friend. One of her best friends.

"I'm scared that people are right when they say that getting married is the only way to be really happy in life," Imogene finally admitted. There it was. The founder and leader of the singles pride movement wanted to get married. She was terrified to look up at Paula now that she knew what a traitor she was to the singles cause. "I-I'm sorry. I know that's a terrible thing to say. You must hate me for feeling like that. Almost as much as I hate myself for it."

"Oh honey, you can't be serious!"

"It's true. I know it's awful, but sometimes I feel-"

"No, sweetie," Paula said, laughing softly. "I mean you can't seriously think I would hate you or think any less of you for feeling that way."

Imogene looked up at Paula with amazement. "Really?"

"Sweetheart, of course not. There's nothing wrong with wanting to get married."

"Really?" Imogene asked again, shocked and relieved at Paula's response. "Did you ever regret not getting married?"

"Well, no. Not really," Paula admitted. "But I'm different from you, Imogene. Marriage is just something I never wanted. Sure, it's crossed my mind what my life would be like if I'd gotten married. Don't we all wonder how our lives would be different if we made different choices? But really, no. I've never regretted it. I love being single. Always have." Paula squeezed her hand. "You still want to get married someday, don't you?"

Imogene figured she might as well spill her guts. She sighed heavily. "Yes. I do still want to get married. I'm a traitor to my own cause."

"Oh, Immy. Of course you're not! Honey, the purpose of Solo Power is to show people that getting married is a choice. A conscious decision. It's not something to be bullied into because society makes you feel like you're wrong if you don't get married."

"I guess. I know I shouldn't…but sometimes I really worry about winding up alone."

"I know you do. Lots of people feel that way. But believe me, lots of married people wind up lonely, too. They drift apart. Some cheat. Some just end up feeling trapped for the rest of their lives, which is so much worse than being by yourself. This singles group you've created…it's going to help people not to make that mistake in the first place. You're helping people see that they're gonna be okay even if they don't get married."

Imogene wiped her eyes and started to feel better. Married or not, with friends like Paula, would she ever truly be alone?

"If you learn nothing else today, know this," Paula said forcefully. Imogene leaned in to listen to what her friend had to say. "You *cannot* force a happy marriage. You can dress it up all you like. You can have a fancy gown and an expensive wedding, and make it look like a fairytale, but unless you happen to meet the right person—not the perfect person, but the *right* person—it just *won't work*," Paula said.

Imogene thought about that for a moment, remembering that Camille had said the same thing. She'd said you couldn't force a good marriage, and that you either met the right person or you didn't. Imogene glanced toward the back of the church where Seth and David were greeting and hugging their family members and friends.

"Exactly!" Paula said, following Imogene's gaze. "Unless it's love like *that*, it's just not worth getting married."

Imogene watched Seth and David stand side-by-side as they greeted their guests, now joined together forever. Matt stood next to them, his eyes still red from crying. He was taking some good-natured teasing from his friends about his tears. He laughed and took it in stride.

Imogene thought about what Paula had said. She knew Paula was right about why she was still single. She hadn't yet found her David. Or Seth. Imogene had dated a lot, but had never found someone she knew she could love for the rest of her life. She thought about Seth's beautiful words about the way he'd felt when he met David; it was like coming home.

Her parents had had a marriage like that. They were really, truly in love. When she was growing up, both her parents had worked full time. Every single day when they got home from work, they reached for each other right away. They hugged and kissed and asked each other how their day was. Her dad brought her mom flowers several times a year. No occasion. They were "just because" flowers. Imogene recalled lazy Sunday mornings when her parents slept in. Sometimes she and her sisters would jump in bed with them to wake them up. Imogene remembered how they would sneak into their parents' room and find them asleep, always snuggled together in the bed. The memory of it filled her with warmth. She guessed that was why her fathers and sisters were so worried that she was still single. They remembered those beautiful, happy days and they didn't want Imogene to miss out on that kind of relationship.

Imogene watched Matt in the back of the church. As much as she loved him—and she really did love him—it was just as a friend. She could imagine why some women settled for marrying guys that they loved, but weren't in love with. It was comfortable. It was safe. Matt would be a good provider. A good husband. A great father. But if they were to get married, it would be a marriage of convenience. Easier. Less scary than being alone, but ultimately unsatisfying.

It would be a mistake.

Just the kind of mistake that Imogene wanted to help others to avoid. Paula was right. That was the point of the Solo Power group.

"Look Immy, I can't promise you that you'll meet the man of your dreams. But I can promise you that you can have a truly happy and fulfilled life, married or not."

Imogene nodded and felt heartened by her words. But there was something else that was bothering her.

"That makes a lot of sense," Imogene said. "But what about having children? Lots of people say having kids really is the only way to be truly fulfilled in life."

Paula actually laughed at that. "Oh, honey. I'm sorry, I don't mean to laugh. Look, having children can be very fulfilling. So I'm told. It truly is an amazing thing to think of bringing new life into the world. Looking at these little people and thinking they wouldn't even be here if not for you. That's incredible. Or even if you adopt, you know, you get to raise them and shape them and help them grow to be wonderful people. But..." Paula shook her head.

"What?"

"Look, I've seen most of my friends get married and have kids. Some happily married, some not so much. One thing I can tell you is that having children is way, way harder than all those books and TV shows tell you. My friends loved their kids, loved being mothers, but I still remember what they went through, especially when their kids were little. It truly was a 24-hour-a-day job. Even though fathers help out a hell of a lot more now than they did before, let's face it. Moms still do most of the work!"

Imogene nodded. That had certainly been the case in her family until her mother died. And even though her sisters had married great guys, the men were forever watching football while Faye and Chrissy chased the little ones around the house. At least that's the way it was at family dinners, and she doubted it was much different at home.

"Children need constant looking after. You just don't realize how big of a commitment that is until you go through it. You spend the majority of your time with them, tending to their needs, keeping them entertained. When you're not with them, you feel like you should be. Guilt is a constant companion with mothers," Paula said.

Imogene nodded and sighed.

"Oh, it's not all bad. I love being an aunt, honorary at least. I don't have nieces and nephews by blood. And I see how much fun it is for parents—the birthdays, Christmases, school field trips, school plays. It's just that it's damned hard work. Harder than anybody ever tells you and it's *all* the time. I'm tired just thinking about it," Paula slumped against the pew for effect. "You really don't get to have much of a life of your own while your kids are young. You can lose yourself if you're not careful. I've seen it happen."

Paula squeezed Imogene's hand. "There are a million ways to be happy. It's different for everybody. You just have to find your way. And never forget, Imogene my darling, you are single by choice. I know you don't feel like it, but you're single because you've chosen *not* to settle."

Imogene nodded. She was starting to see that she had been right all along about that. People had pressured her to stay with Nathan, and now they wanted her to be with Matt. But neither one of them was right for her. She imagined what would happen if she had settled for a man she wasn't really in love with and then went to a wedding like the one she'd witnessed today. She would have realized she'd had married the wrong guy.

And it would be too late.

Imogene felt emotionally drained, but she also felt a whole lot better. No matter how many people told her she was crazy to be single and wrong to embrace being unmarried, she knew in her heart that what she was doing was right. She wouldn't settle. Ever. She would have love like Seth and David, or she would remain single forever.

And either way, she was gonna be just fine.

CHAPTER THIRTY-THREE

Jillian decided not to go to the reception after all. She told herself it was because it was two guys and no bride, and the reception would be totally boring. She refused to admit to herself the real reason. That it depressed her horribly seeing Seth and David so happy together. She and Derek had never been that happy before, not even close, so it was crazy to think that would change after they exchanged vows.

Oh, well. No sense worrying about that now.

Besides, there really was no need for Jillian to bother with the reception anyhow. She had already gotten all the evidence she needed against Imogene Hart.

Jillian had recorded every word of Imogene's conversation with the old lady.

Imogene had gone on and on about how much she wanted to get married and how she was afraid to be alone and single. Jillian could barely contain her excitement when she thought about how devastating it would be when she released the video of the Solo Power Queen whining about how much it sucked to be single. So what if Imogene's little bridezilla video had been bad PR for Lindsay's cause? That was nothing compared to what Imogene had said. Not only was this video going to clinch *Beautiful Bride* as the winner of The Estrogen Network contest, but it would be enough to collapse Imogene's whole movement. None of her little followers would stay with her once they realized what a total fraud she was.

That would teach Imogene to make fun of brides like Jillian.

CHAPTER THIRTY-FOUR

Imogene stared at the computer in utter disbelief. Her hands shook wildly as she watched the YouTube video of herself taken by one of Lindsay's bridezillas. Jillian Jeepers had emailed her the YouTube link this morning, explaining that it was payback for making Lindsay and her brides look bad.

The video of Imogene was much, much worse than the bridezilla video had been.

At least Lindsay hadn't been caught on tape saying something that was in total opposition her own cause. Sure, the bridezilla video had proved that some brides were mean and cruel, especially to their grooms, but that didn't mean they opposed marriage. It wasn't like Lindsay Saga had been caught saying something about single life being great or that she didn't believe in marriage. But Imogene had been outed in front of the whole world saying that being single could be lonely and that maybe marriage was better.

Imogene felt faint as she watched herself on video saying things like:

"I'm scared that people are right when they say that getting married is the only way to be happy."

"Yes. I do want to get married."

"I'm a traitor to my own cause."

"Sometimes I really worry about winding up alone."

"...having kids really is the only way to be truly fulfilled in life."

Jillian had also included still shots of Imogene and Matt together. The photos themselves weren't really that incriminating. After all, she and Matt really were just friends, but combined with Imogene's own words about not wanting to be single, the evidence was quite damning.

And just like that, it was all over. Everything she'd fought so hard for. Her fight for dignity and respect, not just for herself but for single people everywhere. Her quest for equal rights and fairness, the right to be treated like a person and not a lonely hermit. The worst part of all was that she had felt that she finally had it all figured out. Sure, Jillian included all Imogene's statements about wanting to get married and being afraid to be single, but she'd neglected to include the conversation with Paula that followed. The pep talk that had convinced her that she wasn't crazy to want to be single after all was entirely missing. The whole video had been carefully edited to look like Imogene had completely abandoned any degree of singles pride. Instead, Imogene just looked like a woman desperate to get married.

For the first time in her life, Imogene had found her purpose; to run Solo Power and help other single people find their way. Like Paula said, it might not always feel like it, but people were often single by choice. Sure, those people wanted to get married, but they chose not to settle. Not only was that okay, it was so much better than the alternative; a depressing, unsatisfying marriage.

Imogene had felt so happy, so excited after her talk with Paula. She'd felt that wonderful sense of renewed hope that she'd had when she first decided to quit looking for a man and embrace her life as a single woman. She didn't have to give up on romance and she could read all the sexy novels she wanted. It didn't mean she was a traitor to her cause after all. She'd felt free, relaxed, happy. And all through the reception, the more she watched Seth and David laughing with each other, dancing together, and looking into each other's eyes, she knew without a doubt that she was doing the right thing. She would get married *if and only if* she met the right guy. In Paula's words, not the perfect guy, the *right* guy. The right one for her. And if Mr. Right didn't show up, then so be it. Her life would still be wonderful. It felt so good to finally feel validated after having her family and society as a whole tell her she was too picky and that she was crazy for not marrying Nathan or Matt. She wasn't crazy dammit, she was *right*. And she wasn't ever going to let anybody make her feel bad about her decision to be single ever, ever again.

But that epiphany had come too late. She should have been able to use her sudden realization to help other single people. She should have been able to take her resurgent energy and conquer the world, or at least win the network contest. But that was all over now. Just like that. She would lose not only the contest, but the whole Solo Power group. Nobody would believe in her now.

Thinking about how this video would affect the other Solo Power members was too much to bear. They would feel so disillusioned with her, with the whole cause. Imogene had led them to believe they could actually win. She'd given them hope that things could change. That single people wouldn't have to feel degraded any more. Now she'd made things worse for single people than they had ever been before. Now every smug, married person would believe that all single people secretly wanted to get married, no matter how loudly they protested otherwise.

Imogene checked the contest votes just to see how close they had gotten before it was all over.

Beautiful Bride: 230,280
Single, Not Alone: 179,995

They had gotten closer than Imogene had thought possible.

Her heart ached when she thought about Hannah. The kids at school gave her such a hard time already about the singles group. They'd crucify the girl over this video, and it was all Imogene's fault.

Paula and Matt had both left a bunch of concerned voice mail messages but Imogene didn't return their calls. She didn't want to talk to anybody ever again.

It was time to go see her stupid family for stupid Sunday dinner. She seriously considered blowing them off, but she figured she'd have to face them sooner or later, and she might as well get it over with. It would be one less thing to worry about.

*****

"I don't want to talk about it," Imogene said definitively when she arrived at her father's house. She'd deliberately shown up late so that everyone would be there by the time she arrived. She wasn't kidding when she said she didn't want to talk about it, and she didn't want to repeat herself. If people knew what was good for them, they'd leave her alone.

Imogene's father looked fairly grim and her sisters just shot her worried, pitying looks. Liam and Richard were better at making small talk. Either they were sensitive enough to avoid the subject of singles or they were simply oblivious to the matter. Knowing men, that latter was probably true.

Having little kids around was also useful for avoiding awkward conversations. Marcus wandered in and Imogene picked him up and chatted with him for a while. Four-year-olds were very talkative and easily amused, so that ate up some time.

Imogene loved her nephews dearly, but they really could be tiring. She sometimes felt completely drained after even a short visit with them. Imogene babysat for the kids once in a while to give Faye and Richard a break, and it was exhausting. It was especially hard watching them during the day when you couldn't put them to bed. Naptime was always hit or miss, so she often found herself dealing with them for eight hours straight. It made Imogene smile to recall Paula's comments about her friends who were parents. Sure, it could be fulfilling to be a parent, but it could also be straight-up awful sometimes. It was hard for Imogene to imagine what it was like to be a full-time parent. She felt happy about being single for just a moment, but then remembered the YouTube video and came crashing back down to earth.

Dinner was more awkward. Things got quiet. Even little Allen quit babbling for a while since he was concentrating on his food. Nobody seemed quite sure what to say.

"Sooo, Imogene…" Faye began cautiously. Everyone looked up nervously. They almost seemed afraid for her, like she was the first person brave enough to approach the dragon. Imogene found herself already getting annoyed, defensive. "Does this mean you've, you know, changed your mind about getting married?"

Utter silence. Everybody seemed scared to move. *Good.* Imogene was half-tempted to drag out the silence just to make people uncomfortable for as long as possible. Why should she be the only one suffering?

"No…" Imogene began slowly. "I have not changed my mind. Not in the slightest. In fact, I'm more convinced than ever that I'm not crazy for refusing to settle for some guy I don't love. And, for the record," Imogene said, her voice rising, "I never said that I didn't want to get married. I said I refuse to be forced, coerced, and bullied into marrying somebody just to get certain people off my back…"

"Okay, that makes sense," Faye said, clearly backing off. Good thing. "I just, you know, thought I'd ask."

"Are you okay, Imogene?" her dad asked. He looked worried instead of accusatory.

"Of course. Why wouldn't I be?"

Nobody answered that, but the answer was obvious. She might not be okay because some horrible bridezilla bitch from hell had totally humiliated her, completely ruined her reputation, and single-handedly destroyed her life as she knew it.

"Just, you know…asking…" her father said, still looking worried. He was a good dad and it was impossible to be mad at him right now. At least he wasn't ragging on her for being single. Or worse, saying I told you so. He knew better.

They all did. God help anybody at this table who dared tell Imogene they told her so…

"Soo, what are you gonna do now?" Chrissy asked. Everyone looked at Chrissy, then turned to Imogene, waiting for her response. Now they were concerned for Chrissy's safety and wellbeing.

"What do you mean?"

"Well, um, I mean…now that, you know…there's that video of you admitting that you were wrong-"

Liam sucked his breath in through his teeth and shook his head. He loved his wife, but even he realized that was an awful thing to say.

"Admitted that I was wrong? Is that what you think I did?" Imogene's blood pressure shot up faster than the rocket at nearby Cape Canaveral. She'd already been on edge and ready to blow, and now Chrissy had lit the fuse. It made her so damn angry that everybody was taking that bridezilla's side. Her father and sisters should have been ranting and raving about how awful that Jillian woman was. How evil it was to take a video of her without her knowledge.

It didn't matter that Imogene had done the exact same thing to Lindsay and her bridezillas. This was different. Well, maybe it wasn't different. Maybe Imogene had been just as wrong, but her family still should be on her side. Imogene recalled all of Lindsay's gooey, saccharine words about the importance of family, and started to realize that family really didn't seem to mean anything to anybody these days.

"Well, um, didn't you?" Faye asked cautiously. Now it was Richard who shook his head. He looked at Liam, who shot him a wide-eyed look.

Imogene took a deep breath, determined to at least make a good faith effort to keep her temper in check. "Look, just because I expressed concerns, *private* concerns, about spending the rest of my life being single doesn't mean I've changed my mind. When that video was taken, I had just witnessed the most beautiful wedding I've ever seen. And it had nothing to do with the flowers or a fancy dress or anything else. I could see how much they loved each other. I mean, really, truly loved each other and I was scared that I might never get to have that in my life."

Nick looked at Imogene somberly, and Faye and Chrissy nodded as if Imogene was finally agreeing with them.

"But I haven't changed my mind about anything!" Imogene said, her voice rising again. "I still say I will *only* get married *if* I meet the right person, and if I *don't* meet the right person, then I will be *just fine!*" Allen's eyes opened wide upon hearing Aunt Imogene yelling. His expression was so comical, Imogene was afraid she would start laughing. She fought the urge, though. She really wanted to be taken seriously right now.

"Wow. Whose wedding was this?" Chrissy asked, genuinely curious.

"Matt's brother's."

"Ohhhh, you mean the um...."

"Gay one. Yes, Chrissy. The wedding was with two men," Imogene informed her. Chrissy held up her hands as if to say *hey, who I am to judge.* Liam winced, clearly uneasy with the idea of two guys getting married. Like a lot of men, he was a touch homophobic. Imogene couldn't help wondering how he would have reacted if he'd heard those vows. Seth and David's vows were so powerful, so moving, they'd make a believer out of even the staunchest anti-gay activist. Which Liam wasn't. Two dudes together just made him a little uncomfortable.

"Just seeing them together and how happy they were reminded me of the real reason that I'm still single," Imogene said. Everyone stared at her, riveted, as if she were about to reveal a huge secret. The reason she was, in their estimation at least, a freak of nature. "Because I refuse to settle for just anybody! I love Matt, but just as a friend. And Nathan wasn't right for me. That's why I told him no when he proposed." Everyone gasped. Imogene almost gasped herself once she realized what she had just admitted out loud.

"He *what?*" her dad roared. He actually roared like an animal. Imogene had never heard him sound like that. It caught her off guard at first, but then her own anger returned with a vengeance. Nobody here had any right to tell her how to live her life and if they tried, well, they'd best be ready for a fight. "He proposed? He actually proposed? I thought you said he just moved away."

"He did move away, but he proposed first. I turned him down!" Imogene said defiantly.

"Why?" Chrissy cried. "He was so nice! And cute. God, he was so cute!" Liam shot Chrissy a surprised, wounded look. Chrissy had always talked about how hot she'd thought Nathan was, but she never said it around Liam. Until now.

"Seriously, Immy, why did you say no?" Faye asked, genuinely perplexed.

"Did you think he was cute?" asked Richard. The insecurity of her sisters' husbands was oddly endearing. Faye shook her head, but she was lying. She'd said Nathan was hot, too.

"No. I mean, not really. Not my type anyway. But he was perfect for Imogene!" Faye said.

"Really? Why?" Imogene asked.

"Well, you know, he was nice and he was single and…"

"Male. He was a single, eligible male and I was single, therefore he was perfect for me, right?" Imogene waited, triumphant, for anyone to come up with a rational reason why Nathan was so perfect for her. "See? Nothing. You got *nothing*. He was a nice guy, but I didn't love him. At least not enough to spend my life with him."

"Unbelievable," Chrissy muttered to Faye. "All this time we've been feeling sorry for her, and she coulda got married a long time ago."

"Mmmm hmmm," Faye agreed, shaking her head.

Imogene felt like standing up on the table and screaming to get their attention. To somehow make them understand, but it was hopeless. They didn't get it and they never would. Faye and Chrissy seemed happy with their husbands, but Imogene couldn't help wondering if they'd settled or if maybe they'd just gotten lucky and met the right men for them. It didn't really matter. What they did was up to them. This was Imogene's life and she would decide what was right for her. Screw everybody else.

"Oh, so you think I should just grab the first single guy who comes along? Since I'm so old and desperate, I should marry whoever happens to show up?"

"Of course not, Immy. But Nathan was a good one!" Chrissy wailed, earning another sidelong glance from Liam.

"Yes, he was. He was a good one. And so is Matt. They're both good husband material. But not for me!"

Chrissy and Faye rolled their eyes and Imogene fought the urge to bang her fists on the table.

"It would just be nice if you had somebody to settle down with. You know, somebody you could bring with you to Sunday dinner. A husband, some kids, you know. Be like a part of the family," her father said, obviously irritated that his daughter hadn't married a man she didn't love when she'd had the chance.

Of all the hurtful things that people had said to her lately, that one stabbed her heart the most.

"You want me to get married so I can be a part of the family," Imogene said, her voice getting dangerously quiet. Her anger evaporated instantly and was replaced by a horrible, aching pain in her chest. "You think I'm not a part of this family because I don't have a husband and children?"

"Of course not!" Nick said, alarmed at his daughter's sudden change in demeanor. He tried to backpeddle but it was far too late. "That's not what I said."

"That's exactly what you said," Imogene said, her vision almost completely obscured now by her tears. Imogene wiped her eyes and slowly stood up. Poor little Allen looked up her, worried. He wasn't used to seeing Aunt Imogene cry. Imogene tried to keep her voice steady. She looked at her father. "I am your daughter." She looked at Faye and Chrissy. "And I am your sister. How dare you suggest that I am less of a person and less of a family member because I don't have a family of my own."

Everyone fell silent, finally penitent. But it was way too late for any of that.

"So I guess I will just come back to *family* dinners when I have a *family* myself. So, I guess I'll see you all, you know…*never.*"

Instead of storming out, Imogene silently gathered her things and left. She knew that would have a much more profound impact.

The last thing she heard as she left was little Allen calling after her. That just made her want to cry harder.

CHAPTER THIRTY-FIVE

Imogene fled to the safety of her apartment. She turned off her phone and refused to go on the Internet, where her video was no doubt circulating all over the place. She curled up on the couch and started catching up on some of the TV shows she had DVRed during the week. She watched only sitcoms, both to cheer herself up and because she had to save the crime dramas to watch with Matt later.

She took comfort in being alone. That awful scene with her family was further proof that being alone was way better than being with people who were unsupportive. She thought of her friend, Kate. What did Robert do when she was upset? Probably nothing. Imogene looked around at her empty apartment and thought about how much more painful being upset and depressed would be if she were stuck with a husband who just didn't care.

Imogene tried to focus on the television but it was hard. There was just so much going on in her life right now. Just a few days ago she had been so sure that Solo Power was what she was meant to do with her life. Even if there didn't seem to be a way of making money with it or doing the Solo Power blog and support group thing for a living, it still gave her a purpose in life. She hadn't made a cake in weeks, having almost forgotten about the business she had wanted to start. She'd been so caught up with Solo Power and her quest to win the reality show. She still believed strongly in the group's mission, but there was no way anyone would believe in her now. Her credibility was completely destroyed. It was all over. So now what? She was more confident than ever that being single was the right thing for her. The trouble was, she needed a passion, something to pursue, in order to have a wonderful, fulfilled life. She had found one, but it seemed like it was slipping away from her almost before it had begun.

Without Solo Power, which would likely fold because of the fallout from the video, she was back to square one. No husband, no kids, and a dead-end job. She'd have to figure out something. Go back to school, find a new career. She could try to make the cake business work, but it was hard to imagine being as passionate about anything as she was about the singles group. She had made so many mistakes with it, but there was still so much she wanted to do. There were so many ways that single people were discriminated against and so many benefits they were robbed of because they weren't married. She had started to do some research into things like that, but now there didn't seem to be any point in continuing her work.

Imogene realized she'd zoned out and hadn't heard any of the TV show she was watching. She started rewinding it to watch it again when there was a knock at the door. She still didn't feel like talking to anyone, and there was no way in hell she was speaking to her father or her sisters. It was doubtful that it was one of them at the door anyway. Her family rarely visited her in her apartment since it was too small in their estimation. They always insisted that Imogene come to one of their houses since there was plenty of room. Just another way the spinster sister was treated as inferior. They would hardly have recognized the apartment anymore if they did visit. Imogene had made a lot of changes to it since any of them had come over. She'd made it more her own and she found she really loved it.

Whoever it was knocked again, louder, and Imogene knew she couldn't ignore it forever. She groaned. She paused the TV and got up. She looked through the peephole and was relieved to see that it was Matt. He always made her feel better. Always.

Matt didn't say a word when she first opened the door. He just reached out and hugged her like the best friend he was. He held her tight for a few moments, then finally released her. They both flopped down on the couch in their usual spots.

"Are you okay?" Matt asked her, his eyes filled with concern.

"No," Imogene said truthfully, trying to fight back tears.

"If I ever find out who did this…" Matt said menacingly.

"I *know* who did this. Some bridezilla wannabe crony of Lindsay's. She emailed me the link to the video herself."

"What's her name?" Matt asked, ready to draw his sword on her behalf. It was unbelievably sweet. Imogene realized if she told him Jillian's name, Matt would probably kill her. She also realized this was not necessarily a bad thing….

"It doesn't matter. It's done. It's over."

"What's over? You're not giving up, are you?"

"There's no way we can win this thing and nobody's gonna want to be a part of Solo Power now that they think their leader thinks it's bad to be single," Imogene said glumly.

"Well…what *do* you think?" Matt asked, genuinely curious.

Imogene explained all the things she'd been feeling lately. How she used to secretly worry that maybe the bridezilla camp was right that marriage was the only way to be happy. She told him how deeply his brother's wedding had affected her, and Matt seemed quite touched. Imogene explained how she realized now that she really was doing the right thing by not settling. She admitted she still might want to get married, but no way in hell was that going to be the focus of her life. "I have better things to do! I'm just not sure *what*."

"You know damn well what!" Matt told her. "I know how much this singles group means to you. You gonna let that bitch bridezilla, not to mention Lindsay Saga, stop you?"

Imogene honestly wasn't sure what to think. It seemed obvious to her that it was hopeless to continue with Solo Power, but Matt didn't seem to think so.

"You're not gonna just let them win, are you?" Matt demanded. Imogene had never seen him so worked up.

"What can I do, Matt? Just act like nothing happened?"

He didn't seem to have a response to that. It would be impossible to come back from the damage that video had done to her reputation. How could she possibly explain it? Other than Matt and Paula, nobody ever seemed to understand her explanations of the taped conversation.

He opened his mouth to answer but there was another knock at the door. "I'll get it," Imogene said. "You keep trying to think of a good reason for me not to give up." Good luck. Solo Power was on life support and there didn't seem to be any way to resuscitate it.

Imogene checked to see who it was before opening the door. She was still determined to avoid her family at all costs. Still, she was a little disappointed that it wasn't Faye or Chrissy or even her dad. Her father owed her a big time apology even if she was too angry to want to hear it right now. Did they really think of her as less of a family member because she wasn't married?

Paula greeted her with a hug just like Matt had.

"Hey girl," Imogene said. "Come on in. Join the party."

Paula followed Imogene into the living room and saluted Matt when she saw him.

"Hey, sexy," Matt said to her. "We're getting a hunting party together to go tar and feather the bridezilla bitch who made this video. Want in?"

"Hell yeah!" Paula said, sounding even more pissed off than Matt was.

"Nobody's hunting anybody down," Imogene said. She felt too tired to fight anymore, and she hated the feeling. It was much better to get all fired up and try to change the world, but she felt too beaten down by life to fight this losing battle anymore.

"Well, we have to do *something!*" Paula exclaimed.

"I know, right? Imogene's ready to give up," Matt said.

Paula looked disappointed in her, which was so not what she needed.

"Seriously, guys. I really don't need a lecture right now."

"No. You don't need a lecture. You need a pep talk. A mini Solo Power rally. And that's what we're here to do. Right, Matt?"

Matt grinned at her. "Absolutely."

"We're gonna get Lindsay back for this!" Paula said.

"Well, technically it wasn't Lindsay who did this. It was some bridezilla named Jillian Jeepers who wants to be on her stupid show," Imogene said.

"Jillian Jeepers…" Matt said, obviously making a mental note of her name so he could exact his revenge.

"Look, it's pointless to go after her. What's done is done. Besides, she's not important. It won't do any good to get revenge."

"It would do *me* good," Matt said.

"I know what you mean…" Paula said, still looking pretty pissed off. "But Immy's right. Lindsay's the one we need to go after. So that's what we'll do."

"Guys, I just want to forget this whole thing. It's over,"

Imogene said.

"It is *not* over!" Matt shouted.

Paula vehemently shook her head. "Nope."

Imogene sighed wearily. She knew her friends meant well, but right now she just wanted to be left alone. She leaned her head back on the couch and put one of the pillows over her face. Matt ripped the pillow from her hands and tossed it across the room. Imogene sighed again.

"We're not letting them win, Imogene. *You* are not letting them win."

Imogene looked at Matt as if to say *convince me...*

"Just picture Lindsay's smug, smarmy little face," Matt said. Imogene could feel her blood pressure begin to rise just thinking about Lindsay Saga. "She thinks you're a loser, Imogene. She thinks we all are. She thinks Hannah is pathetic."

"Come on now. That's not fair," Imogene said.

"It's true!"

"I know..."

"Lindsay thinks it's every woman's dream to get married. That's all women should want out of life," Matt said, knowing damn well that was the perfect way to goad her into action. She hated the way Lindsay always said the bride was the envy of the world.

"Lindsay says none of our lives matter because we don't have kids," Paula said.

"I know. I know! I know all of this," Imogene replied.

"Then don't give up on the group," Paula said softly. "Please."

"What if they give up on me?"

"We haven't," Paula said. Imogene wasn't convinced. The idea of showing up at the next Solo Power meeting and having nobody attend was too much to bear. Sure, Paula and Matt were on her side. What if nobody else was?

"My father said that if I got married and had kids then I would finally be a real part of the family," Imogene said quietly.

"He didn't…." Matt said softly. Imogene nodded.

Paula shook her head. "Think about how you're feeling right now," she said, "and resolve to work as hard as you can to keep other people from going through it. Don't quit on us, Imogene. Please." Imogene was shocked at the sadness, almost desperation in Paula's voice. "I've waited my whole life to finally be able to show my friends and my family that there is *nothing wrong with me* just because I never married. I can't do it alone. You can't do it alone. But as a group—a big group—we can show the world that we're united and we won't stop until we get the respect that we deserve."

"We've come too far to give up now, Immy. I mean, can you imagine if we did win that contest?" Matt said.

"But how can we-"

"But if we did!" he said. "It would be the underdog story of the year if we could beat Lindsay and her band of bitchy bridezillas. Don't you see how awesome that would be? I mean, somebody's got to stand up to people like that. They can't be allowed to win all the time!"

Matt spoke with such forceful passion that it took Imogene by surprise, but she understood why he felt that way. Imogene knew he was thinking about all his best buddies who married shrews who ordered them around and never let them do anything they wanted. Some of his best friends were whipped by women who'd started out as bridezillas and ended up being awful wives. Matt was right. Why *should* the bad guys be allowed to win?

"You're right," Imogene said, hating how tentative her voice sounded. "You're right!" She repeated more forcefully, sounding more like her old self. Paula and Matt grinned at her. Their encouragement reminded her that she wasn't the only one struggling as a single person in a couples' world. She would keep up this fight. It was an uphill battle, but they had to win sometime, right? So why not start by defeating Lindsay Saga and getting their show on the air where they could reach hundreds of thousands of people? The last vote count was closer than she had ever expected. There was time yet.

"So what do we do? I mean, how do I even begin to fix this mess?"

"Well, the video of you was bad because it made it look like you were saying that being married and having kids is what life is all about," Paula said. Imogene winced and Paula patted her shoulder. "We both know that's not what you said. Or at least not what you meant. Anyway, the best way to take Lindsay down—and quickly— is to do the same thing to her that her bridal bitch did to you." Imogene looked at Paula, wondering where she was going with this. "The bridezilla video we did showed that Lindsay's brides don't know a thing about what love really is, or what makes a good marriage. We have to prove that Lindsay herself is even worse than her bridezillas."

"How do we get proof of that?"

Paula held up her cell phone. "We already have." She cued up a video of Lindsay on her phone. "Remember?"

Imogene gasped as she looked at the video of Lindsay and her teenaged kids. She had forgotten all about that.

"For all her preaching about the importance of love and family and saying kids is what life is all about, her own children can't stand her!"

"Whoa, unbelievable!" Matt said, leaning over to take a look. Matt hadn't been at that particular wedding and didn't know about the video.

"I know! I also got some footage of her yelling at her husband on the phone. She kept calling him an idiot and then ended up saying 'I hate you!' before hanging up on him," Paula said smiling.

"Oh, she's just dreamy, isn't she?" Matt shuddered.

"She's awful. No doubt about that. But we can't use that video," Imogene said.

"What?" Paula asked.

"Why the hell not?" Matt demanded.

"Because it involves her family and her kids. It's just…it's too personal. I can't do that."

"Oh, and what she and Jillian did wasn't personal? She videotaped a private conversation of yours and released it to the whole world!" Matt said, getting fired up all over again.

"Yeah, but we did the same thing!"

"No way!" Paula shouted. "It was not the same thing!"

"It really wasn't, Immy. Those brides were yelling, screaming, and being downright abusive and it served them right that we outed them for the cruel bitches they are!"

"She had no right doing what she did to you, Imogene. She took the whole thing completely out of context," Paula said. "Besides, this is the only way to really prove to everybody that Lindsay Saga is full of crap. She claims marriage is so sacred, yet she treats her husband like garbage. She makes single women feel like they're society's rejects because they're not married. She tries to stir up jealousy among women by making them compete to see who looks the prettiest and who can spend the most on their ridiculous weddings. I mean that's what her reality show is all about. The prettiest bride is the best and screw everybody else!"

It did make Imogene incredibly angry thinking about that stupid *Beautiful Bride* idea and all the shallow garbage it stood for.

"Exactly. And now think about what our show stands for. Supporting single people and helping them feel good about themselves. Finally! After years of being mistreated and ostracized, we can build single people up instead of letting society tear them down. Give them the courage to say *no* to marriage if that's what they want!" Matt said with conviction. He was a great speaker. He could have been a politician or an attorney.

"Come on, Imogene." Paula said. "You have to do this. Do it for us. Do it for Hannah and everybody like her. Do it for single people everywhere. And if for no other reason, do it to wipe that goddamn, smug, self-righteous smirk off Lindsay Saga's face!"

They were right, dammit. This was war, and war wasn't pretty.

"You're right. You're right! Let's do it!" Imogene said, snatching the cell phone out of Paula's hands.

CHAPTER THIRTY-SIX

Imogene finally got up the nerve to check her emails. The news wasn't good. As she'd predicted, there were a lot of people mad at her for what she'd said. Hardest to read were the ones who said they had believed in her. That they had been so happy that somebody finally had the courage to get up and defend single people against all the crap they had to put up with day after day. And now things were even worse because Imogene's words had given the impression that single people really did secretly want to get married. Now it would be harder than ever to gain any respect.

Imogene called another Solo Power meeting, saying that they would be discussing the next phase of the plan to try to win The Estrogen Network contest. That is, if Lindsay's show didn't win first. She planned to show the videos of Lindsay fighting with her children and screaming at her husband. She'd announce that they would be releasing those videos to show how hypocritical Lindsay was, and how mean she was to her own *loving family* that she constantly prattled on and on about. Somehow Imogene knew this video wouldn't get the same excited reaction that the bridezilla video had. That one was funny, a real crowd pleaser. This one just seemed kind of sad.

Winning the contest seemed hopeless at this point and Imogene felt horribly beaten down. She'd thought about giving up a million times, but couldn't bring herself to do it. There was still some fight left in her. Even if she lost, at least she would know she had done the best she could.

It occurred to Imogene that maybe nobody would show up. The video of her talking about wanting to get married had definitely gone viral. It was everywhere. Imogene had kind of hoped that she would get some calls from the media asking her to go on one of those talk shows to discuss the video, but none came. People were still only interested in Lindsay Saga and her tiresome wedding talk.

She considered having the meeting in the old conference room at the library in case the group was small, but decided to be optimistic and hold it at the bigger church hall.

Imogene knew she could count on Matt and Paula to not only show up, but to be there early just in case they were the only ones to come. She wasn't sure if Hannah would show up, but Imogene really hoped she would. She hadn't heard from her in a while.

As it turned out, Imogene could have held the meeting in the smaller library conference room. Easily…

There were about 50 people there. It wasn't too bad, but it was a huge difference from the last time. Still, it wasn't as awful as it could have been. After all, the group had started out with just four people. She had built it up from there and maybe she could do it again. It would take time, though. Time they didn't have if they still wanted a real shot at winning this thing.

Imogene waited a few moments longer to see if anyone else would show up. No one did. She took a deep breath and began speaking.

"Thank you all so much for coming. I know we've been through some really hard times lately and I really appreciate your loyalty to the cause." Imogene looked out at the faces gazing back at her. She tried hard to read their expressions. Some looked sympathetic, while some of them looked like they were waiting for an apology or at least an explanation for what she had said on the video. Fair enough.

"I want to make it clear that now is not the time to give up. I'm not giving up on winning The Estrogen Network contest and I don't want you to give up either." Imogene saw that most people looked doubtful, which was understandable. "I know it's not likely that we'll win, but we still have a shot. It's not over until it's over."

"Damn right!" Paula shouted. A few people applauded. Very few. Matt nodded encouragingly at Imogene.

"We have a video of Lindsay Saga," Imogene said, holding up her iPad which had the two videos that Paula had sent to her. "They show very clearly that she is far from the perfect wife and mother that she claims to be."

Murmurs from the audience. People definitely started to perk up and look more hopeful.

"She wanted to try to show that I didn't believe in my own cause, which isn't true by the way," Imogene said softly. She would explain that later. "Lindsay claims that love and marriage are the most wonderful things in the world and she thinks single people are selfish and evil for not getting married. By showing these videos to the world, we can prove that she hates her husband and her own children can't stand her."

Louder murmurs and some laughter.

Imogene hesitated a moment. "But we're not gonna do that," she said, putting the iPad down. She hadn't really even known she was going to say it until the words came out of her mouth. She had fully intended to use the video, but suddenly realized she couldn't do it. Paula sighed heavily and groaned. Matt looked a little disappointed. He sighed, then nodded. Deep down he knew she was doing the right thing by not releasing the video.

"We can't just be thinking about Lindsay here. I mean, these are her kids." Lots of people nodded in agreement. "We caught her on tape arguing with her teenage children, refusing to help them and be there for them when they needed her. She clearly puts her career and her own interests ahead of her kids and that's really sad. It's a reminder that just because you're a parent doesn't mean you're a good parent. Just because you have a family doesn't mean your life is meaningful or fulfilling. Single or married, life is what you make it!" Imogene pounded the podium for emphasis and was pleased to see the smiling faces looking up at her.

"Anyway, I hope you can all understand my reasons for not releasing the video. It's not just about the kids, but that's the most important part. I mean, it's hard enough being a teenager without all the drama of being put in the public eye. And I really think it's high time we stopped all this sneaking around and videotaping and stuff," Imogene said, laughing. "I know I kind of started it and, well, as entertaining as the bridezilla video was…" That comment got lots of laughter from the crowd. They were definitely warming toward her. "I suppose it really wasn't the best way to get our message across. And neither was the Valentine's Day thing. Look, I admit that I haven't handled this contest and singles pride thing as well as I could have and I know I've made a lot of mistakes, but I think we have a great group and I want to keep it going. We still have an important message to get across, don't we? We're single, we're proud, and we're not going away!"

Cheers erupted. Maybe not as loud as at previous meetings, but cheers nonetheless.

"Since I have a lot of you gathered here, I want to take the opportunity to explain about the video of me that I'm sure you've all seen by now." Matt nodded and Paula smiled. It helped so much to have them here for moral support. "I actually wrote my response as a blog article that I'm going to put up later today. I just…I wanted to share it with you first." Imogene glanced down at her paper and began to read:

I've spent the majority of my life assuming I would get married and have kids. That's what people are supposed to do, right? I figured I would get an ordinary day job to pay the bills while I waited for my future husband to come along. I've been at that ordinary day job for five years now….

Over the past few years, I've become increasingly worried about still being single. I turned twenty-five. No big deal. Lots of women are still single at that age. Then I turned twenty-six, then twenty-seven. By age twenty-eight, I started to get scared. Where was Prince Charming? Twenty-nine came and went. Then, I turned thirty years old. That's when shit got real. I was thirty years old. Husbandless, childless, alone, and still stuck in a dead-end job. Worse, I had just broken up with my boyfriend. He asked me to marry him. I said no, and I wasn't sure why. Was I crazy not to marry him when I had the chance? According to my family, I'm certifiably insane.

After breaking up with him, I had planned on going back on the dating websites, going back on blind dates, and starting the exhausting process all over again. Then, I had a sudden realization. I didn't have to do that. What if I stopped focusing on finding a man to complete my life and started making my life complete on my own?

And that's just what I did. I started taking cooking

classes and I found out I'm pretty good at it. I learned to bake and decorate fancy cakes. Best of all, I met a new friend at the cooking class and I reconnected with old friends by inviting them over for a meal. Next, I started the Solo Power group and met a bunch of new friends. My life has never been happier. My only regret is that I didn't realize sooner that I was putting my life on hold while I waited to get married. Despite the fact that my father and my sisters make me feel like I'm making a terrible mistake by enjoying being a single woman instead of spending all my time looking for a husband, I know in my heart that I'm on the right path.

I love my friends and my new life, but I still get scared sometimes. Sometimes I get sad when I realize I might never get married. And that's what's happened with that video you all saw…

Shaking a bit, Imogene looked up from her paper to see dozens of warm, empathetic smiles. Her eyes filled with tears. She was overcome with emotion, with the understanding that she had all the love and support she would ever need right here. Her family didn't have to understand her because she had plenty of other people who did.

But you know what? It's okay to be scared sometimes. Everybody gets scared. We all wonder what would happen if our lives had turned out differently. And there's nothing wrong with that.

I really don't think there is anything wrong with getting married, and I'm sorry if I ever gave the impression that I felt otherwise. It was a mistake to try to boycott Valentine's

Day. This world needs more love, not less. I'm sorry to any stores and other businesses that I have may caused to lose money on Valentine's Day. I'm also sorry to all the brides who I recorded without their knowledge. All I wanted to do was get the message across that there is nothing wrong with being single, but the protest and the bridezilla video were wrong ways to go about it. Yes, we came across a lot of brides who were mean to their new husbands and their friends, but we also saw a lot of couples who were wonderful together. We were wrong to leave that part out. Sure, some weddings and marriages are superficial, but some are beautiful. I used to think that romance was a total lie, a made-up fairytale. Now I understand that it's real. I've seen it with my own eyes at some of those weddings. Sometimes you go to a wedding that's so touching that you know in your heart those two people are going to love, honor, and cherish each other for the rest of their lives.

Being in a romantic relationship is a wonderful thing, but it's only one way to have happiness in your life. For all you couples out there who are genuinely happy, I want to say that I am happy for you. I wish you a long and wonderful life together. I respect your relationships and your marriages. All I'm asking is that <u>you extend me the same courtesy and respect</u>.

Imogene read that part with great emphasis and her words were greeted with cheers and applause.

Even if you are married, you're still an individual. You have your own life to lead, too, both separate and together with your spouse. You may be a husband or a wife, but you

286

are a person first. And guess what? So am I.

Everybody should have the right to live their lives in the way that's right for them. Though everybody seems to say that you can't possibly be fulfilled without getting married and having kids, I'm here to tell you that YES, YOU CAN!

More applause. Imogene was getting more fired up by the minute.

And one final note that I want to make very, very clear…

Imogene paused for dramatic effect and looked up to see that people were leaning forward, eager to hear what she had to say.

Love really is the most important thing in life, but couples don't own love. Love is not confined to people who are in romantic love with each other. Love is for best friends, sisters, brothers, cousins, aunts, uncles, parents, and grandparents. It's in the helping hand of a loving stranger who offers a supportive smile or a kind word when you need it most.

And for all you single people out there, it's okay to feel lonely sometimes. We singles don't have the market cornered on loneliness any more than married folks do on love. Everybody feels lonely sometimes. There's nothing wrong with you. First, figure out IF you want to get married. Don't do it because you're scared to be alone—you're not alone. Don't do it because you decide to settle for the wrong person—you're better than that. If you want to get married, don't give up on the hope of finding love, but don't make that the focus of your life. You have so much to bring to the world. There are so many things to see and there's so much to do in life, don't waste a second waiting for your life to begin. Life doesn't begin when you find a partner. It's already begun. So make it a good one.

Imogene looked up and shrugged quietly as if to say *that's it.* Paula whistled loudly and started applauding.

"Well said, Imogene!" Paula stood up and winked at her while applauding. The rest of the small but dedicated group stood up and applauded as well. Imogene let out a sigh of relief as that familiar feeling of happiness and peace washed over her.

Imogene realized that life was simply too short to waste being around negative people like her family and Lindsay Saga. She was determined to live her life on her own terms. There would be no more waiting for the approval of others. Despite their numerous voicemail messages, emails, and texts, Imogene hadn't spoken to her father or sisters since the day she'd walked out of Sunday dinner.

If her family couldn't see her point of view, then they simply wouldn't see her at all anymore.

CHAPTER THIRTY-SEVEN

Imogene hadn't seen or spoken to her family in weeks. She missed seeing them, especially her sweet little nephews, but she was bound and determined not to let Faye, Chrissy, or her dad hurt her ever again. What she really missed were the *old* Sunday dinners, the ones when her mother was still alive and Faye and Chrissy were still single, too. Back then, there wasn't so much talk about husbands and kids and all that. Nobody judged her for being single in her twenties, but that had all changed the older she got. Imogene wanted nothing more than to have a life filled with both friends and family, but that wasn't going to happen as long as her family continued to treat her badly.

Faye and Chrissy had emailed her a few times, but Imogene refused to answer. Their messages weren't exactly contrite. They were more along the lines of "quit throwing a hissyfit and come back to Dad's house." No way.

Imogene's father was harder to ignore. He'd left her several pleading voicemails telling her how sorry he was for making her feel bad and how much he missed her. Imogene played his messages over and over, and cried every time she listened to them, but she wasn't ready to go see her family. She knew damn well what would happen. Everybody would be nice at first, tiptoeing around her, and then someone would say something stupid and mean and she'd just have to leave again. Imogene could admit that things with Solo Power had gone poorly, but she was working hard to make the group strong again. The bottom line was that her family neither accepted nor respected what she was doing with her life, and they had no problem telling her that.

After posting her latest blog entry, the one she'd read aloud at the Solo Power group after Jillian's video went live, she received an email from her dad.

Hi, sweetie. I wanted to write and tell you that I've been thinking a lot about you and what you're doing with your life. I realize that it's not enough to just tell you how much I love you and how much I miss you. But I really do….a lot… :(I know that you need for us to understand you and the choices you're making for your life. I've been talking to your sisters and we realize that we've been pretty bad about all this. Please know that we meant well and we never meant to hurt you.

Your mother was the most precious person in the world to me. When she died, it felt like I died, too. Despite that pain, I wouldn't have traded a moment I had with her or the life we shared for anything in the world. I guess it's that kind of love that I wanted for all of my daughters, and I was scared at the thought that you would wind up all alone.

I really liked your last blog article. You're right that husband and wife love is just one kind of love. And I think you are right that you can't force a happy marriage. I was lucky to find the perfect woman for me, but lots of my friends weren't so fortunate. I have more divorced friends than happily married ones, that's for sure. You probably saved yourself a lot of heartache by not marrying somebody who wasn't right for you.

We're not so different, me and you. I'm single, too, now, and it occurred to me that I'm kind of sitting around the house like you used to do. Instead of waiting for someone to show up like you were, I was acting like my life was over because my wife died. I'll miss her every day of my life, but I can't bring her back. The highlight of my week was seeing you all at Sunday dinners, but I've got to have more going on to fill the other six days of the week.

You inspired me to pick up some of my old hobbies, ones I haven't done since before I got married! I even got in touch with some friends I haven't seen in a while, and we've gone fishing a couple of times. I feel like there's so much to look forward to now. I just wanted to tell you that you've inspired me, and I can't imagine what you've done for other single people. It would be amazing if your show could beat that awful Lindsay woman, because there's no telling how many people you could help!

Now please come home to dinner, sweet girl. I can't handle seeing two empty chairs at the table…

Love,

Dad

Imogene grabbed the tissue box on her desk and wiped away the tears that were flowing freely. She missed her family so much, and her father's support meant more to her than she could possibly say. The idea that she could be an inspiration to anyone amazed her, and the fact that she'd gotten through to her father was nothing short of a miracle! She'd made such of mess of Solo Power, but her father's words made her feel that maybe it wasn't too late to fix it. Imogene hadn't seen or heard from Hannah since that awful video from David and Seth's wedding was released. She'd been worried that it was too late to help the poor girl, that the negative publicity of Solo Power had destroyed Hannah's already delicate reputation at school. Imogene reasoned that if she could get her father to change his mind, there was hope for everybody.

CHAPTER THIRTY-EIGHT

Lindsay rolled her eyes as she read over Imogene Hart's latest, whiny blog. She had to come up with something to explain that video of her going on and on about how much she wanted to get married and how she was afraid to be alone, but it was obviously too little too late. The damage had been done.

Lindsay loved the part where Imogene ate crow and actually admitted that the whole Valentine's Day thing had been a mistake. She was only saying that because it had been a total disaster and admitting it might make her look slightly less stupid than acting as if it had been a good idea. Lindsay scanned the rest of the blog to see if Imogene would apologize personally to her. That would be sweet.

No such luck.

Lindsay clicked off the ridiculous Solo Power page. She had work to do. Important work that didn't involve Imogene or her stupid group. *Beautiful Bride* would be the reality show for The Estrogen Network any day now, so she had to be prepared for it. She decided to check the webpage to see how close she was to winning. Lindsay wasn't prepared for what she saw.

Single, Not Alone: 243,500
Beautiful Bride: 236,997

Single, Not Alone was in the lead for the first time in the contest.

"What the hell?" Lindsay said aloud as she looked at the latest vote count. The last time she'd checked, the count was nowhere near that close. There was no way that Imogene's trite little apology on her stupid blog could have resulted in that many votes. What in the hell had happened? The singles were within 6,500 votes of winning and were actually *ahead* of *Beautiful Bride!*

Lindsay happened to glance at her cell phone, which was set to silent. There were five missed calls. All from Jillian Jeepers.

CHAPTER THIRTY-NINE

Jillian had been ranting and raving for hours and Derek knew better than to even attempt to talk to her when she got like this. He'd seen her get nuts like this before, but it wasn't usually this bad. He didn't ask what was wrong. Instead, he tried to piece together what had set her off based on her lengthy rants.

It seemed to be something about The Estrogen Network, Lindsay Saga, and of all people, Jennifer Arlington.

Derek figured he'd best give his bride-to-be her space, so he snuck quietly out of the house.

*****

Jillian seethed as she watched the entertainment news segment. She'd rewound and watched it three times, growing more furious every time she saw it. She contemplated calling Lindsay again but it seemed pointless. Where the hell was she? This was an emergency, dammit!

Jennifer Arlington, as in *the* Jennifer Arlington, the movie star, had spoken out on national television in favor of Imogene Hart and her sorryass club of lonelyhearts. There was no doubt that way more people saw Arlington's news segment than ever saw the videos of the bridezillas or of Imogene. The videos had made the rounds on the Internet, but this was national television.

"I just, you know, I normally don't speak out about these things," Jennifer Arlington had said during the interview, "but I feel like I have to say something about this Estrogen Network contest thing that's going on. Look, I have nothing against weddings. I had one once, in case you didn't happen to hear...." The reporter laughed politely. Everyone knew about her $4-million-dollar wedding and the subsequent divorce, which had probably cost a lot more. "But there are an awful lot of wedding shows out there already, especially on The Estrogen Network! It's supposed to be a network for women but it's not. It's become the all-bridal network and I think it's really insulting to women to assume that's all we care about. A wedding and landing a man."

She seemed to hesitate a moment. Arlington had always been intensively private about her personal life, despite the fact that the tabloids were hellbent on watching her every move. She rarely spoke about her love life. Why did she have to open her fat mouth now? "It really is a double standard. Ever since my divorce, people have been trying to set me up with this guy or that guy. The tabloids are constantly pairing me up with whatever current costar I'm working with. It's just—it's really ridiculous. Everyone thinks I'm a sad lonelyheart...and then you look at George Crawford! Who's great, by the way. He's a hugely successful actor, and since he's male everybody thinks of him as this freewheeling bachelor, while I am somebody to be pitied because I'm alone. I can really identify with Imogene Hart. I rarely feel lonely, but everybody expects me to be."

"So does that mean that her reality show *Single, Not Alone* has your vote?" the reporter asked.

"Oh, my gosh. Absolutely! I actually voted a while back when I first heard about it. I think the whole idea is really cool, you know?

It's about time that there was a show about single people that has nothing to do with matching them up, you know?" Jennifer rambled on.

"Really, no love for Lindsay Saga's show?"

"Oh, please," Jennifer said, making a face. "That crazy lady, I swear...I can't tell you the number of times I've wanted to strangle her. She's like the ringleader of the people saying that I'm sad and lonely. How I've never recovered from my divorce and I'm sooo sad. I'm such a tragic case, you know?" she said, shaking her head.

The reporter laughed. Oh yes, the two of them enjoyed a big, hearty laugh at Lindsay's expense.

Where the hell was she? That stupid singles show was within a few thousand votes of winning. Jillian's hands shook as she saw her dream wedding slipping away before her very eyes. She couldn't let that happen. Not when her fantasy wedding was so close she could almost touch it.

Jillian practically jumped when her cell phone rang. Her nerves were totally shot. If it wasn't Lindsay, she didn't know what she would do.

Caller ID confirmed it was her.

"Where in the hell have you been?" Jillian shouted into the phone. She was long past the point of sucking up to Lindsay. Jillian was already a lock to be a contestant on *Beautiful Bride,* and at this point Lindsay needed Jillian more than the other way around. Once the actual reality show started, Jillian was gonna have to kiss her ass hard. Fine. She could do that. But they had to secure the show first.

"What is going on with the voting? Why is it so close all of a sudden?"

Jillian fought the urge to scream at Lindsay to crawl out from whatever rock she'd been living under and turn on the damn news once in a while. She took a deep breath. "Jennifer Arlington went on national television in support of Imogene's show."

"She *what?*" Lindsay screamed into the phone.

Jillian simply did not have the patience to wait through Lindsay's range of emotional reactions to the Arlington fiasco. She had already been through disbelief and rage and fear and she did not have time to hold Lindsay's hand right now. This was the time for action.

"She said she thought Imogene's pathetic singles show is a great idea and that she hated you for all the things you've said about her over the years," Jillian told her. Okay, so maybe Jennifer hadn't exactly said she hated Lindsay, but she sure wasn't happy. Jillian couldn't help but be pissed off at Lindsay. If she hadn't insulted the woman, maybe this never would have happened! Still, it did seem awfully pathetic that Jennifer was still alone while her ex-husband Brandon and his new wife were shacking up and popping out kids left and right. Then again, with Jennifer's constant parade of hot guys, she seemed to be doing all right.

"Oh, no. Really? That's awful!" Lindsay said, sounding worried and even a little depressed. "Wow, I kind of always hoped that maybe someday she would meet some nice man, maybe another celebrity, and, you know…"

"You thought you could plan her wedding!" Jillian said mockingly. "Well, that's pretty much out."

"You don't have to be so snippy about it!"

Jillian realized she had better take it down a notch. Lindsay would definitely make her a contestant on the show, but she still had to win. If Jillian pissed her off, Lindsay could choose another bride to win the prize. That thought made Jillian shudder.

"I'm sorry, Lindsay. I'm just scared, you know? We have to fix this, okay? We only need a few thousand more votes, but we need them now!"

"So what do we do?" Lindsay said, sounding defeated. "It's not like I have time to do more talk shows or anything. The vote will probably close—one way or another—in a matter of hours."

"I know. Here's what we do. We have to make a bunch of emergency phone calls. Contact every religious group and every family values type place you can think of. *Focus on the Family*, the *Christian Coalition*, stuff like that."

"Right!" Lindsay said, sounding heartened. "The whole family values deal."

"Exactly. Tell them that we're fighting to get our show about marriage on the air. Remind them that our competition is a group that doesn't believe in the sanctity of marriage. Make sure you use those exact words. *Sanctity of marriage.* They use that phrase all the time to get people to vote their way and it works every time."

"Got it!" Lindsay said, sounding enthusiastic. Lindsay might be great with planning weddings but when it came to doing anything else she needed an awful lot of instruction. Jillian listed a few organizations for Lindsay to call and said she would handle the rest of them.

"Do it right this second, okay? Seriously, this could all be over today so we don't have a minute to lose." Jillian hung up without saying goodbye.

CHAPTER FORTY

Lindsay let out a breath as she hung up the phone. She quickly logged onto the Internet to find the phone numbers she needed. That's when she noticed a new email with the subject heading WE GOT ANOTHER VIDEO OF YOU, LINDSAY SAGA!

Her heart lurched in her chest. *Oh God, what now...*

The sender of the email was Paula Flandey. Lindsay remembered that the old lady that Imogene was talking to at the gay wedding was named Paula. Hands shaking, she opened the message.

> *Just wanted to let you know that we have video of you screaming and yelling at your kids and your husband. Though it would be the perfect way to show the world how completely full of crap you are when it comes to "love and family, the most important thing in the world!" we're not going to release the video. I just wanted you to know that Imogene refused to release it because she didn't want to hurt your family and she didn't even want to hurt YOU. Imogene's a way classier broad than you are because she actually believes in her cause.*

Lindsay's heart sank as she watched the video that Paula had attached to the email. It really did make her look horrible as it showed the way she treated her kids. Familiar Mommy guilt flooded through her. She felt less guilty when she saw the video of herself yelling at her husband on the phone. Barry deserved yelling when he was being a pain in the ass, but KellieAnne and Cody? They might be obnoxious teenagers but they were still her children. She had the urge to go up to their rooms to see them. To just check in to see how they were doing. It had been a while since she'd really sat down and talked with them. Lindsay made a mental note to go talk to them just as soon as she could.

First, she had some phone calls to make if she was still gonna win that contest. She'd have plenty of time for her kids once she made sure her show would be on the air.

CHAPTER FORTY-ONE

Imogene called a Solo Power meeting once she realized how close the tallies were to reaching 250,000. The vote would be over any time now. She wanted to be able to see the results live with as many members of the group as possible, so she sent out a blast email to everybody telling them to meet at the church hall. She also wrote another blog post that she'd posted on Facebook, Twitter, Google Plus, and everywhere else she could.

The attendance was incredible; it was standing room only. Imogene could hardly believe it. She was so grateful that she hadn't given up after Jillian's video went live. People seemed to understand her explanation about what she'd said and many of them actually agreed with her sentiments! She was stunned to find that lots of members still had an interest in getting married someday. After all, Solo Power was made up of people who were single for a million different reasons and it helped that she was able to address those who were not necessarily single by choice. It was people like that—people like her—who needed the most encouragement to go out and live a fantastic, adventurous life with or without a partner.

Imogene set up the projector so they could see the results on a giant screen on the wall. It was incredibly nerve-wracking to see how close the vote was. They could actually win this thing!

And she owed it all to Jennifer Arlington of all people. If they did win this contest, maybe Jennifer really would want to be the host just as they had hoped. She'd already spoken out in support of *Single, Not Alone,* so maybe The Estrogen Network would approach her about being on the show.

It had seemed utterly impossible that Imogene's singles group could win, especially when they had to go up against a quasi-celebrity like Lindsay Saga who held all the cards as far as the media was concerned. Except for Valentine's Day, nobody wanted to interview Imogene if Lindsay wasn't right there next to her. The only media coverage Imogene ever seemed to get was negative.

Speaking of media, Imogene noted with astonishment that a camera crew had actually shown up. It was a local news station; they must have gotten wind of the meeting online. She'd sent countless press releases in the past that were always ignored. Having a real celebrity endorse you apparently made a big difference.

Imogene walked over to speak to them quickly before the meeting started.

"Hello, Ms. Hart," reporter Donald Velts said. "Hope you don't mind, but we'd like to get some video of your group for the evening news. You know, just in case the contest is decided tonight."

"No, of course not. Go ahead!"

"Okay, well don't mind us. Just go do your thing and maybe we'll have time for a quick interview afterward."

Imogene nodded and then hurried back to the front of the room.

"Wow," she said, looking out at all the people. "Thank each and every one of you so much for coming out tonight on such short notice. Looks like we could actually win this thing!"

Cheers erupted. Imogene turned around and hit refresh on the computer.

Single, Not Alone: 249,322

Beautiful Bride: 248,900

More cheers. Imogene's heart thumped. It was so close. So unbelievably close. She hardly dared to hope that they could actually win.

"Shouldn't be long now," Imogene said nervously. "And, you know, again I just want to thank everybody for their support in all this. We've really come together as a group and we're starting to have a voice in the public arena. As you can see, we have a news crew here." Heads turned to see. "This group started with four people and just look how we've grown. We are single, but we're certainly not alone!"

More applause and Matt gave her a grin and a thumbs-up. Imogene hit refresh again.

Single, Not Alone: 249,588

Beautiful Bride: 249,200

More applause as people saw the new figures. It got quieter now as people waited, holding their collective breath. Imogene had auto-scheduled tweets to go off every few minutes, urging people to vote and vote now. She didn't know what Lindsay's tactics were, but for sure she was pushing her side just as hard. It would only be a matter of minutes now. It took all of Imogene's willpower not to hit refresh again right away. She knew she had to give it more time. She waited as long as she could stand and then hit refresh again.

It took a few seconds for her to register what the screen said.

CONGRATULATIONS TO BEAUTIFUL BRIDE, THE WINNER OF THE ESTROGEN NETWORK'S REALITY SHOW CONTEST!

The number 250,000 was flashing in huge font all over the screen. It took a few seconds for the audience to read the words and let the truth sink in.

Once it did, there were gasps around the room. Then silence. Just a few moments before, Imogene had been so hopeful that the room would be filled with cheers and applause and laughter when they won.

It was all over. Just like that. Lindsay Saga had won. The news cameras were there to capture Imogene's stunned expression, which was sure to delight Lindsay when she saw it on the news.

Imogene simply couldn't believe it. They'd been so close. The sheer unfairness of it all overwhelmed her. Lindsay wanted this show solely to please herself. She craved celebrity, fame, money, power. She wanted to lord over the brides, torture them, boss them around, and make them her slaves as they begged her to give them the superficial, shallow wedding of their dreams. Plus, the show glorified physical beauty. Only beautiful women got married and the most beautiful of them all got to have her dream wedding just for being the prettiest. Well, for being the prettiest and probably the most cutthroat and horrible. It was a contest that encouraged backstabbing and cruelty, so most likely it would be the bitchiest bride who won. The meanest girl of them all would end up in first place, rewarded for being cruel to everyone around her.

No doubt Jillian was a lock to win that prize.

Meanwhile, *Single, Not Alone* would have helped people. The whole point of it was to reach out to people who felt shunned because they were single, or divorced, or widowed, and to show them how exciting their lives could be. The contestants would have been rewarded with scholarships or trips around the world and it would have gotten single viewers at home excited about their lives. It would have helped change the perception of single people everywhere, giving them the courage and strength to stand up to anybody who said they were less important because they were single. People would stop settling for the wrong person and maybe some really unhappy marriages could have been avoided.

It was so damn unfair that Imogene could hardly stand it.

She shook with anger when she thought about Lindsay's quest for celebrity and fame. The singles show had nothing to do with making Imogene famous. She hadn't really even expected to be on it! If the producers had asked her to, she'd have been happy to do it, but she hadn't assumed anything. They could do what they wanted with the show, so long as they presented singles in a positive light.

Imogene was filled with renewed rage when she thought about Lindsay's smug face and how thrilled she must be right now. No doubt she'd go on the air and start talking about how she had no hard feelings and still wanted to set Imogene up on a date or something.

Imogene was suddenly seized with an almost uncontrollable urge to go to her computer and upload the video of Lindsay with her husband and kids.

She was wrenched away from her vengeful fantasy when Matt stood up and approached her. He looked devastated, which made Imogene feel even worse. She had let her best friend down by losing. She had let everyone down.

"Oh honey, I'm so sorry," Matt said tenderly as he took her in his arms. She embraced him and her tears started flowing. It just hurt so much. It hurt to come so close only to lose out to Lindsay. She was mean and selfish and a bully. It wasn't fair. It just wasn't fair.

Paula got up and wrapped her arms around both of them, and a few others joined in the group hug. The dramatic scene was all captured for the evening news.

A few people started clapping and soon everybody was clapping. And standing up. She heard a few whistles, too. Normally, it was Paula or Matt who started the applause and other people joined in. This time, they'd had nothing to do with it.

"Yeah, Imogene!" Somebody shouted out.

"Thanks for everything you've done!" shouted another.

Imogene looked out at the hundreds and hundreds of people who were gathered in the church hall. Smiling, cheering, applauding. It was just how she had imagined it would be, except they'd lost. But they were still cheering.

Imogene scanned the crowd and saw a lot of familiar faces. She'd been getting to know some of the regulars who came to the meetings, but there were a lot of new faces here as well. The group was really taking off.

Kate walked up to her and wrapped her arms around Imogene. "I'm so proud of you, Imogene. You've done such an amazing job with all of this." Kate's eyes welled up with tears. "I-I wanted to tell you that…that Robert and I have separated."

"Oh, Katie, I'm so sorry," Imogene said, hugging her tighter.

"No, it's okay. It's a good thing. I mean, it's not easy but…He's not a bad person, but we've been unhappy for a really long time. I just thought that's how my life was going to be, but you showed me that it doesn't have to be like that." Kate smiled through her tears. "I mean, I'm scared, but I feel like it's gonna be okay, you know? You showed me it was gonna be okay. In some ways I'm relieved. I know this is the right decision and I never could have done it without you."

Imogene embraced Kate again and whispered, "You're so brave, Kate. I'm so proud of you. You're gonna be just fine." Kate pulled back and nodded. Imogene could see the relief on her face. The change in her appearance was remarkable; she looked calmer and more at peace.

A sudden, new hope surged through Imogene. She realized she didn't have time to waste on trying to get revenge on Lindsay. She also found that she didn't really want to anymore. Lindsay was a selfish bully who didn't care if she hurt people in the process of getting what she wanted, but that didn't mean Imogene had to be the same. The only time you really lose to the bad guy is when you start turning into one yourself.

Imogene wiped her eyes and waited for the noise to die down before she spoke. "Thank you all so very much for your support. It's been a long road and I really wish this had ended differently. It's really, um…" Imogene wanted to say unfair, unjust, and *total bullshit,* but she decided to take the high road. Besides, the camera was still rolling. "…disappointing that our reality show didn't win."

Boos from all around.

"Saga sucks!" someone shouted. It might have been Paula.

"Well, it's a shame that our reality show didn't win, but I want to make sure everybody understands that this is not the end of Solo Power. We're still standing!"

Loud cheers and applause rose up from the room.

Imogene paused for a moment, contemplating her next move. She had the overwhelming urge to *do* something. She wanted to do something concrete, something positive for the group that had absolutely nothing to do with Lindsay Saga or her band of psycho bridezillas.

"It's important to remember that as much as we wanted to get our singles show on the air, that wasn't the reason I started this group. *Single, Not Alone* was just one possible project. The point of this group was to band together and show the world that you can be single and happy and, well, not alone."

She bit her lip as she looked out at the crowd. "I really wanted to win that reality show because I wanted to reach out to single people on a national scale. Maybe that's not going to happen, but we can still reach out to people. I was so busy trying to beat Lindsay Saga that I think I lost sight of the point of Solo Power. The point of the group shouldn't be to make married people accept us, the point is to accept ourselves! If there's one thing I've learned, it's that you can't force people to change their minds." Imogene shook her head as she thought of her sisters.

She also thought of Hannah, whom she hadn't seen since before Jillian's video went public. Her heart ached to think that Hannah had given up on the idea of singles pride. Hannah would never be able to force her classmates to accept her, nor could she make her mother support her membership in Solo Power. But that didn't matter. All that mattered was that Hannah accepted herself so she wouldn't end up as an unhappy wife or worse, another domestic abuse victim.

Imogene continued, "I think the most disappointing thing about not getting the reality show was that we won't get the chance to tell our story. I mean, we won't get to show how amazing we are and all the incredible things that we do with our lives." She nodded her head, as if confirming to herself what she wanted to do. "So we're gonna tell our story anyway. Not to convince married people of our worth, but to convince single people that they're worthy."

People leaned forward expectantly. Imogene was thrilled to see that they were still with her, excited about the next phase of the group. She wasn't giving up so neither were they.

"Okay, so I know I said that we were done with all the YouTube videos and stuff, but I say we do one more. I think we should create our own. Tell our own stories in our own words. Tell the world why you're single, what you love about your life, what you've done, what you want to do with the rest of your life. I think it would be a great way to reach out to all our fellow singles out there. Anybody who wants to contribute is welcome. Whaddaya think? "

People applauded and called out things like "I'm in!" and "Let's go for it!"

Using Imogene's cell phone camera, they ended up filming late into the night.

It was an incredibly emotional experience for Imogene. For everybody, really. It was inspiring to hear all the stories from people's lives. All the good they had done, the places they'd been, and the love they'd shared. Imogene could scarcely imagine that *Single, Not Alone* could have been any more inspiring than the simple video that the Solo Power group made. Sure, the video wouldn't get the audience that *Beautiful Bride* would get by airing nationally on The Estrogen Network, but the Solo Power video would have a positive influence on anybody who happened to see it. If it helped just one person feel great about herself, it would be totally worth it.

"I always wanted to be single," Paula said to the camera. "I've kind of always done my own thing. I like my house to be just for me, my sanctuary where I can relax and unwind. I have a simple life but a really good one. Before I retired, I worked as pediatric oncology nurse. It's a hard thing to do, you know, be around kids with cancer all the time. But it could be amazingly rewarding. The best part was the end-of-chemo parties we had. When a kid got done their last chemotherapy session, we threw them a party with their parents and all the nurses and everything. It was…really amazing," she said, her eyes shining. Imogene shook her head with wonder. How dare anyone say Paula's life as a single woman was meaningless?

Paula went on. "It wasn't always easy of course. So many times the kids lost the battle. You get to know them, you know? Their siblings, their parents. You know them all personally and it never gets any easier when, you know…" Paula stopped for a moment. Imogene had to wipe her own eyes and she wasn't the only one. "There was this one kid. Six years old. We all knew she had just a few months to live, if that. So we sent her home to be with her family." Paula's eyes filled with tears. "I got a card just the other day. From her six-year-old daughter," Paula laughed through her tears. "Her daughter is now the same age she was when she was expected to die. I really do believe in miracles!"

"You're killing me, Paula," Imogene said when Paula was done taping her segment. She embraced her friend, both of them crying.

Next up was Donna, the woman from the law firm who was going through a divorce. Imogene remembered what a mess she'd been the last time she saw her. How the poor woman felt her whole life was over because she was getting divorced.

"So what's good about being single?" Imogene asked.

Donna smiled and answered, "Freedom. I'm just getting out of a bad marriage and I was terrified of being single at first. But now I feel like I'm getting another chance to do all the things I've always wanted to do. I'm going back to school to study journalism. I can't wait!" Donna said, her eyes lighting up. She looked so excited. She was like a different person, hardly recognizable from the sobbing mess in Camille's office.

"I wanted to have kids, though. I really did, but I've decided that I don't want to be a single parent. I don't think there's anything wrong with it, but it's not for me." She paused a moment, contemplating. "I can see how having children with my ex-husband would have been very difficult. So, I'm kind of glad it happened this way. If I meet somebody else, great. If not, I'll be okay. I'll be better than okay. I've have my journalism degree!" Donna's excitement was infectious, inspiring. It made Imogene want to take a class in journalism even though she hated that kind of thing.

Imogene asked other people what they liked about being single and she got some great responses.

"I love that I can travel wherever, whenever I want," answered a single man in his 50s. "I've saved up a fair amount of money, so if there's someplace I'm curious to see, I can just go. I once took a trip to Australia—*Australia!* Pretty much spur of the moment. I met the most fascinating people and saw amazing things. Imogene's inspired me to maybe start a singles' travel blog. Might be fun," the man said, grinning at Imogene. She felt honored to think she'd inspired anyone to do anything. The thought was incredible to her.

"Are you lonely?" Imogene asked some of the participants.

"No!" Paula had answered enthusiastically. "And that's something I really wish people could understand."

"Single people don't just sit around our apartments, you know," said one woman, shaking her head.

"Single people aren't hermits. Do I look like the Unibomber to you?" asked one man.

"I was more alone when I was married," Donna said quietly.

People had lots to say when Imogene asked how they felt about the way singles were treated by society.

"Hah!" Paula answered. "Pull up a chair. This might take a while."

"I'm so, so tired of the pity," said one woman in her late 20s. "I was the only single bridesmaid at a wedding once. And I was *fine.* I was having a blast. Dancing, drinking, toasting my best friend. It was the pitying looks, the so-called reassuring comments like 'don't worry, you'll find somebody' and 'it'll be your turn soon, I promise' that made me feel bad."

"Right now I've got a career that I love, hobbies, friends and I'm happy! And nobody believes me!" said a woman in her 30s, sounding just like Imogene at Sunday dinner.

"What pisses me off the most is people who call me selfish because I don't want kids," said a lady in her 40s. "They think my life has no purpose, no meaning because I don't have children. Like nothing else I do matters. Look, that's great if you're a mother. It really is. But is that all you are? Do you cease to exist when your kids aren't around?"

"It's like people think your life begins when you get married. What the hell were you doing before that?" demanded one woman angrily. "Lindsay Saga loves saying that a woman's life begins on her wedding day. So a woman was worth nothing at all before she had a man? Hah. Maybe *you* weren't."

"Having kids doesn't automatically make you a better person. I know a lot of jerks who have kids. Their kids are jerks, too. That's your contribution to the world? Thanks for nothing!" said a woman in her 20s.

"I have a lot to give to the world," said a woman in her 40s. "Gifts God gave me. I'm just not meant to have kids. That doesn't make me worthless," she said, her voice quaking a little. "Even though people make me feel that way sometimes."

"I am single and lllloving it!" Matt said with a grin. "I work hard and play hard. I have everything I need. Good food, good beer, good friends. What else do I need?"

Imogene was overwhelmed with pride at people's responses to her questions. These people inspired her so much that she began to wonder why she ever thought it was bad to be single. She asked

Kate if she wanted to speak on camera.

"Not yet," Kate replied quietly. "I'm still kind of working things out. Later, though. When I'm through the worst of it, maybe I can tell people how I got divorced and that everything worked out okay. Because I really think it will."

One older lady shyly came up to speak on camera. Imogene had seen her somewhere before, but couldn't place her at first. She mentally ran through all the places she frequented. Talmer's bar, her dentist, her pharmacist, the nail salon. She racked her brain and still she couldn't figure out how she knew the woman.

"My name's Judy," the woman said softly to the camera. *Judy!* Finally, Imogene recognized her as the librarian who was always annoyed at the noise from the Solo Power meetings. "I kinda always felt bad about being single. All my friends are married and I kinda just sit home on weekends with my two cats."

Imogene bit her lip. Judy was an *actual* cat lady.

"But being here kinda makes me feel like it's okay, you know? Maybe there's nothing wrong with me after all." Judy fell quiet and kind of shrugged. She smiled. "That's all I had to say."

Somehow Judy's quiet confession seemed the strongest of them all. Such a simple statement that summed up the whole point of Solo Power. *Maybe there's nothing wrong with me after all.*

Of course, Imogene answered her own questions on camera.

"I'm single because it's right for me. I haven't found the right person yet and if I don't, I'm staying single. Having people harass me about it, like family members, won't change my mind. It just hurts me," she said, fighting back tears. "I'm only alone when I want to be. I think people don't get that. There are so many more relationships in life than just husband and wife. There's parents and siblings," she trailed off a bit, thinking about how long it had been since she'd spoken to any of her family members. "Friends, co-workers. You surround yourself with people you love. Even if you're married, you don't just share your life with one other person. All the people you're close to make your life meaningful."

When Imogene edited the video later, she added some still photos of single people. She included photos of past meetings and one from the night they lost out to Lindsay. Imogene superimposed words at the bottom of the photos:

"I am single…I don't have to be somebody's parent to care for others." She included a photo of a group of single women laughing at a meeting. "I don't have to be someone's spouse to be a shoulder to cry on." She included a photo of Matt, Paula, and herself hugging and crying after they'd lost. "I am someone's child and someone's grandchild." More photos of various Solo Power members of all ages, shapes, and sizes. "I am a brother or a sister. I am someone's aunt or uncle. I am somebody's best friend. Whether or not I choose to marry, I…am…*someone*."

Imogene was very proud of the finished video. Just as she had with the bridezilla video, she premiered the finished product at a Solo Power meeting before she uploaded it to YouTube. Everyone loved the video and they were thrilled to finally get a chance to tell their stories. They knew they wouldn't reach anywhere near as big of an audience as Lindsay would with her nationally televised reality show, but it didn't matter. What mattered was that they were making a difference to those they did reach.

The video also brought in some new members and, judging by the emails and blog comments, it was really making a difference in people's lives. There were a lot of single people out there who had bought into the notion that there was something wrong with them because they were single, but they were slowly starting to change their minds. Lots of people had emailed Imogene to tell her that they had decided to go back to school, start a new hobby, join a new club, go on a trip they'd been putting off, or otherwise had just stopped waiting and started living. Imogene didn't even bother to check the number of hits the video got. It didn't matter. The messages she received were enough to convince her that the video was reaching the right people and impacting their lives.

Imogene still hadn't seen her family, though she had emailed her father a few times. She knew she couldn't keep this up forever and she had pretty much made her point, but she was still angry. She couldn't help it. She was sick of being treated like there was something wrong with her and that she wasn't a "real" member of the family until she had kids. Imogene much preferred hanging out with Matt, Paula, and her Solo Power friends because they didn't judge her.

It was always the most judgmental people who couldn't see that *they* were the problem, not the ones they were shunning. If everybody would just figure out what worked for them and mind their own damn business when it came to other people, the world would be a much better place.

CHAPTER FORTY-TWO

Lindsay was so excited she could barely stand it. It had been a horribly close call, but she had won. Imogene Hart could suck it! The victory was so glorious, in a way even better because it had been so close. For a few seconds, Imogene must have actually thought she could beat her. The last-minute phone calls to the religious groups had put them over the top. Those people knew how to rally their troops when they put their minds to it. Jillian was right. If there was one thing they got all up in arms over, it was the "sanctity of marriage." They got their followers to vote quickly and en masse, making *Beautiful Bride* the winner.

Lindsay immediately suspended all her wedding planning to focus on the upcoming reality show. She got her hapless assistant, Melissa, to handle the weddings that were already on the books. Sure, this resulted in a bunch of pissed-off brides, but whatever. She had way more important things to attend to. Planning weddings for nobodies was all in the past. With the fame she would gain from the reality show, she would be strictly celebrities and multi-millionaires. Oh, yes. Her time had definitely come.

Her first meeting at The Estrogen Network was a dream come true. There were assistants fawning all over her, responding to her every whim. Sometimes she would ask for a glass of water just to watch the production assistant go run for it. It was incredible.

Meanwhile, Imogene's fifteen minutes of fame were coming to a close. News cameras had captured her stunned expression at the exact moment she realized she had lost out to Lindsay. That was great, but then the stupid news reporter had turned the whole thing into a feel-good story. They showed everybody crying and hugging Imogene and all that garbage. Then the crew went on and on about how some of the Solo Power members had stayed until two in the morning, making some ridiculous YouTube video about how great it was to be single. Pathetic, but what else could they do? They sure weren't going to get to spread their single propaganda on The Estrogen Network. Instead, they had to do it the poor man's way by doing a homemade movie and putting it on the Internet. It made Lindsay smile to think about how embarrassingly pitiful that was.

CHAPTER FORTY-THREE

Jillian was just as excited about *Beautiful Bride* as Lindsay was, if not more so. The look on Imogene's face when she'd lost was *priceless*. That would teach her to go up against the Head Bridezilla. There was absolutely no way in hell Lindsay would have won this thing if it hadn't been for Jillian, and it was that same competitive streak that was going to win her the entire competition.

Jillian's dream wedding was so close that she could almost taste the $10,000 wedding cake. She'd come this far and she was going to win the whole thing, no matter what it took. Sure, the other brides-to-be at Lindsay's casting call were attractive; some much prettier than she was, but that wouldn't be enough to win. You had to want it. *Really* want it. And nobody on the planet wanted to win more than Jillian. Not only that, if she really made a name for herself on the reality show, maybe she could somehow channel her fame into a career. Write a book or be on *Celebrity Apprentice* or something. Derek sure as hell didn't make enough money for both of them, so she'd be stuck doing something. Besides, she hated the idea of hanging around the house all day with him.

Yes, no doubt about it. Jillian's wedding was going to be one of the prettiest, most expensive weddings the world had ever seen. And she would be the star.

CHAPTER FORTY-FOUR

Just as Lindsay and Jillian no longer paid any attention to what Imogene was doing, Imogene had largely forgotten about the whole, well, saga with Lindsay. Sure, it sucked to lose out to her, but Imogene had way more important things to do with her life and particularly with Solo Power.

Imogene made a special effort to reach out to Solo Power members and figure out exactly what they wanted to do with the group. Unlike Lindsay, Imogene had no desire to be a dictator. She was open to suggestions and she had gotten some great ones.

One of the best suggestions was to expand the social aspect of the group outside of meetings. People had started making friends and yes, some even began dating one another, which was fun. Imogene certainly had no objections to that as she had always proudly welcomed married people as members of Solo Power. Some people had suggested that they schedule outings to go on together. Not match-making, just friendship outings. If there was a movie out that people wanted to see or a new restaurant somebody wanted to try but had no one to go with, they could schedule a group trip. It was understandable that some people weren't comfortable going to movies alone and it was stupid to sit around and wait until you got a date. Why not go with a group of fun people who had similar interests?

It was wonderful. With Matt's technical help, Imogene started a kind of online bulletin board where people could sign up for outings or suggest new ones. People were talking about putting together a trip to Las Vegas and even to Aruba! Aruba was a popular honeymoon spot, but plenty of other people wanted to see it, too. Imogene couldn't quite afford the whole Aruba trip yet, but she was totally in on the Vegas deal, especially when she found out Matt and Paula were going. It would be such a blast.

Another great idea came from a young woman who had just started her first real job after finishing college. In her early twenties, she lived with her mother who was in her fifties and not in the greatest of health. Kimberly had found out that she could not take a leave of absence under the Family and Medical Leave Act to care for her mother the way married people could for a spouse. She also realized that if anything happened to her, her Social Security benefits would just go back into the system. Despite paying the same amount as a married person, she was not allowed to name a non-spouse as the beneficiary.

Imogene decided to look into other issues that singles faced and she found there were a lot of inequities. Despite the fact that there were about 124 million single Americans —slightly more than half the population of the U.S. — they had yet to come together to fight for their rights or even be aware that they were being deprived of them. Imogene started posting facts on her website to help create awareness.

DID YOU KNOW?

- Single people are frequently paid a lower salary than their married colleagues

- Though you pay the same amount into Social Security and pension benefits as married people, you can't name a beneficiary if you aren't married
- Singles typically pay more for car insurance, gym memberships, and travel packages

The more facts like these that Imogene uncovered, the more she wanted to do something about them. It wasn't enough to raise awareness. That was just the first step. Now that people knew exactly what rights they were being cheated out of, the time had come to fight for them.

That's when Imogene decided to organize a March on Washington.

She wanted it to be a spirited, positive rally. She couldn't help but fear that it would turn out to be another disaster like the Valentine's Day protest, but she still wanted to try. She figured that maybe a few hundred people would show up this year and maybe they'd do it again next year. Sort of build up the group of protestors over time. Solo Power, which now consisted of over a thousand local Florida members, wasn't built in a day. After losing the reality show and the huge audience it would have meant, they'd have to build their group the hard way. But that didn't mean it couldn't be done. It would be a lot of hard work, but Imogene wasn't afraid of hard work—at least not now that she had found her purpose and something important to work for.

Imogene got the word out about the march as best she could through the usual channels: the blog, Facebook, Twitter, Instagram, Google Plus, and she sent out the usual press releases to the media, which she knew they would ignore like they always did. Still, every little bit helped.

She really liked the idea of the march being both a political rally to help raise awareness to get discriminatory policies changed and also as a kind of pro-singles parade kind of event. Much like gay pride parades weren't anti-straight, this parade would not be anti-marriage. It was just about embracing who you are and welcoming anybody who supported you. The most important thing that Imogene was sure to emphasize to everyone was that this was to be an upbeat rally. It should be peaceful. Bitter, angry, people should not apply. This shouldn't be anti-love at all. In fact, it was pro-love. She wanted this to be a celebration of friendship and love in all their forms.

Imogene just hoped to hell that it worked and, if nothing else, put a positive spin on Solo Power's image, which had been so badly battered in the past.

At first the idea of holding a march was incredibly exciting. The more she thought about it, though, the more terrified she became. What if it was another total disaster? What if just a handful of people showed up? Now that Jennifer Arlington had drawn attention to her cause it was possible that they might get media coverage. Imogene was terrified to be humiliated on TV again if their march ended up as nothing more than a tiny gathering.

A few days before the march, Imogene happened to drive past the cemetery where Aunt Maddy had been buried. On a whim, she decided to pay a visit. But not to Aunt Maddy.

Imogene knelt on the ground and ran her fingers over Agnes' epitaph.

Here lies Agnes McCann,
A lady who never had time for a man,
She had a good life,
Was never a wife,
But how fine did she sing with the band.

Imogene closed her eyes. Born in 1882, Agnes had died in 1954. Imogene could almost see what Agnes had looked like back in her heyday, singing in a 1920s band. She envisioned Agnes wearing a snappy flapper kind of dress with short, sassily cropped hair. She probably went on stage and sang her heart out with all the passion she had in her body.

Imogene's eyes flew open and she suddenly knew what she had to do. She'd not only march in that rally, but she would shout at the top of her lungs and she'd do it even if only four people showed up. So what if people thought she was crazy? She was gonna make her voice heard, just like Agnes had done. Agnes must've had fire in her and by God, so did Imogene. Sure, she was still scared. But she wasn't about to let the fear stop her.

Imogene, Matt, Paula, and a few others made the trip for the rally together. They took a flight to D.C. and then took the Metro to get to the Mall where the march would take place. Imogene was so nervous she felt she might throw up. Good thing she hadn't eaten anything yet. Every time she felt her courage waning, she pictured Agnes and felt better. She wondered if Agnes was looking down on her from Heaven, cheering her on.

It was a battle to find seats on the Metro. Imogene had only been to D.C. once on a family trip and she remembered that it was crazy crowded back then so she shouldn't have been surprised.

"Maybe it wasn't the greatest idea to plan this during the Cherry Blossom Festival," Imogene muttered. The festival ran from March through the end of April. Singles Day, as Imogene had declared it, was April 5 during the height of the beauty of the trees that famously lined the Mall in D.C. Then again, at least lots of people would be gathered for the festival, which would increase Solo Power's visibility. Wasn't that better than gathering during a time when nobody was around to see them?

"Umm, Immy?" Paula said, snapping Imogene out of her thoughts. "I don't think all these people are here for the cherry blossoms…"

Imogene took a closer look at the people crowded onto the early morning Metro train. She saw that a lot of them were holding posters. It was so crowded, she was only able to lean forward far enough to see one of the posters.

It read: SINGLE AND SASSY.

A surge of excitement shot through her. All these people couldn't be here for the rally…could they?

Imogene wriggled past Matt and Paula to talk to the woman. "Excuse me," Imogene began. "Are you here for-"

The woman's eyes widened. "You're Imogene Hart!"

Imogene blinked and nodded.

"Oh my God, I'm so glad to meet you! I'm Carly Martins. I came all the way from Oregon to be here."

"Oh my…you're kidding!" Imogene exclaimed.

Murmurs of excitement rippled through the train as the people who were there for the singles rally realized that Imogene Hart was there in person. Before she knew it, she was signing autographs and posing for pictures, which was a completely unreal experience for her.

The people who actually *were* on the Metro for the Cherry Blossom Festival observed the scene with interest, realizing there was some kind of celebrity in their midst even if they had no idea who she was.

As it turned out, thousands of people showed up for the rally. *Thousands.* And they came from all over the country.

Imogene, tears in her eyes, couldn't stop shaking as she looked out at all the people who had gathered in support of singles rights. She was overwhelmed.

"It's okay, hon," Matt said gently, laughing. He put his arm around her as he, too, looked around in amazement.

At first, Imogene couldn't understand where all these supporters had come from. There were way more than 250,000 people there. Had the Estrogen Network voting taken place today, *Single, Not Alone* would have won by a landslide. What happened?

Two things had happened. The first was Jennifer Arlington. Having an A-list celebrity speak out about the contest had introduced a hell of a lot of people to Imogene Hart and her singles group. Secondly, as a supporter from Iowa informed her, the last YouTube video had gotten over two million hits.

Two million.

And here Imogene had avoided checking the numbers because she didn't want to be disappointed.

There were so many people gathered at the rally that Imogene had to battle her way to the front so she could address the crowd. She had secured a microphone and podium ahead of time, but hadn't actually expected to need to them. She had envisioned a sorry group of a few people walking in a tiny circle carrying singles rights posters.

Clearly, the idea of singles rights had really touched a nerve. The uncoupled people of America were ready to stand up and fight.

Paula squeezed Imogene's shoulders. "Somehow, I think this is gonna get more media attention than some dippy reality show on a second-rate cable network," she said, looking equally as stunned as Imogene. "Holy crap!"

Imogene nodded numbly as she watched news crews setting up. These weren't local D.C. networks, either. She saw CNN, CNBC, MSNBC, and FOX News.

One of the best parts was reading all the signs. Imogene

snapped as many photos as she could. They were as varied as the people who held them:

One had a drawing of a hand that read *I don't WANNA put a ring on it!*

JOHN 3:16....has nothing to do with this. Still, Christians for equal rights!

Another in the same group read: *JESUS WAS SINGLE.*

I WISH I WAS AS "MISERABLE" AS JENNIFER ARLINGTON, read a poster that was pasted full of photographs of Jennifer and the many sexy co-stars whom she was rumored to have dated.

It wasn't just single people in attendance, either. Imogene saw a sign that said: *Wedded for Equality: Marrieds for the Fair Treatment of Singles.*

Imogene liked the signs from Matt's brother and new brother-in-law most of all. Seth and David had flown to D.C. a day earlier. They had never been to Washington before and wanted to sightsee before the rally. Their signs read, respectively: *MY BROTHER MARCHED IN MY PARADE SO I'LL MARCH IN HIS* and *MY BROTHER-IN-LAW MARCHED IN MY PARADE SO I'LL MARCH IN HIS.* Both signs depicted the rainbow symbol on them. Matt stood between them with a sign that read *SINGLE, STRAIGHT, AND SEXY. EQUALITY FOR ALL!!*

The three of them together were about the cutest thing Imogene had ever seen. She made sure to get a good photo of them to post on Solo Power's website.

Imogene looked around in wonder, taking it all in, as she thought about what to say when she got up to speak. It was all just so overwhelming. Overwhelming in a really good way.

In the distance, she saw someone marching toward her with great purpose. People were milling around all over, but this person was definitely walking directly to her. Imogene could not have been more shocked when she saw who it was.

Hannah.

How in the hell did she make it from Florida to Washington, D.C. alone? From what Hannah had told Imogene about her mother, she never would have let her go to something like this. Really, what parent would let a sixteen-year-old attend a rally by herself hundreds of miles away?

Hannah strode with purpose, her head held high. Imogene had never seen her stand up so straight, so confidently. She marched right up to Imogene, smiling. Imogene lifted her eyes to read the sign that Hannah held up proudly. It read:

DID IT EVER OCCUR TO YOU THAT MAYBE THE FAT CHICK DOESN'T WANT YOU?? I AM POWERFUL, SOLO!

Imogene smiled and hugged her warmly. "I can't believe you came. How in the world did you get here?"

"Used my babysitting and part-time job money. My mom thinks I'm at a friend's house," Hannah said, smiling deviously.

"I can't believe you made it!" Imogene exclaimed. She looked at the sign again. "Good for you. Good for you! I love it!"

"Thanks for everything you've done, Imogene. Really, it's made me feel so much better. It was just…it was so cool seeing that video. I must have watched it a million times. It's a relief to know I don't have to wait around for somebody who may or may not show up."

"Exactly!" Imogene said, knowing just how Hannah felt. The same way she had felt in the cemetery when she first saw Agnes' grave. That sudden exhilaration, the realization that really anything was possible and her happiness wasn't up to fate anymore. It was up to her.

"My mom's fat, too, ya know," Hannah said quietly. "I guess

that's where I get it from. She has this boyfriend. He's kinda cute and all, but he's a total asshole. And I guess my mom thinks she can't do any better, so she keeps him around. I'm just, you know, I'm *not* gonna end up like her."

"I'm glad. I'm so glad, Hannah!" Imogene said, tearing up again. Hannah wasn't going to end up like Elena with her abusive husband. No way.

"Hey, beautiful!" Matt called out to Hannah, looking equally shocked to see her.

"Hey, Matt!" Hannah said cheerfully.

"I hope that sign doesn't refer to me," he said, looking sad.

"Of course not," Hannah responded, nudging him playfully.

"Doesn't refer to you either. I don't see any fat chicks around."

Hannah rolled her eyes but smiled. She punched him gently on the shoulder.

Matt sighed dreamily. "I'll never wash this shoulder again."

Hannah laughed.

"Immy, you better get up there," Paula said, as nearby protestors had realized that Imogene Hart was in their midst and began chanting "Speech, speech!"

Nervously, Imogene stepped up to the podium. Her presence resulted in wild applause which was exhilarating and humbling at the same time. It was surreal, looking out at the thousands of people who had gathered on the Mall.

"Wow, this is amazing!" she said into the microphone. "How many of you out there are single Americans?"

People cheered and waved their signs.

"Now take a minute to look around you," Imogene said, then paused for a moment. "Are you alone?"

"No!" The roar of the crowd was deafening.

"I didn't think so! I really want to thank each and every one of you for coming out today. Today, we stand together. We are a nation of individuals, whether we are married or not. So I urge everybody out there to keep fighting for our rights as single people. We demand fair treatment under the law! We each have the right to live our lives the best way we know how- free from judgment. Just because we are single does not mean we are selfish loners. We are sons, daughters, brothers, sisters, cousins, and friends. Just like married people, we share our lives with many others. Love really is the most important thing in the world, but it is not confined to romantic love. Love is wherever you find it. And I see it everywhere here today!" Imogene choked up a bit as she looked out at all the supportive faces.

The applause was deafening. Hannah was jumping up and down excitedly, trying to applaud and hold her sign up at the same time. Imogene gestured for her to come up next to her. Hannah hesitated for only a second before walking up to the podium.

"Love your sign, girl!" shouted a woman in the crowd. Hannah grinned and held it higher.

Imogene whispered to Hannah. Hannah nodded and shouted into the microphone, "HOW DO WE RUN?"

"SOLO POWER!" Came the thunderous response from the crowd.

"HOW DO WE RUN?"

"SOLO POWER!"

Imogene squeezed the girl's shoulders and the crowd went crazy all over again.

Imogene stepped down, adrenaline still pumping. She still couldn't get over the sheer number of people who were there! She thought of all the cameras that had been rolling and how many more people she would be able to reach with her message once the news segments aired.

Imogene took out her phone and started snapping more pictures of all the creative signs people had brought. She noticed that some were actually from family members of singles who came out to support their loved ones. *Must be nice*, she thought. The signs read:

That's No Spinster, She's My Sister! And she deserves equal rights.

Single Aunts Are the Most Fun.

I'm Proud of My Single Daughter!

Imogene nearly dropped her cell phone as she saw through the lens who was holding that last sign. Her eyes filled with tears.

"Dad?"

Her dad rushed over to his daughter. He dropped his sign and wrapped his arms around her. "Sweetie, I've missed you so much." He held her like he never wanted to let go. Imogene glanced over his shoulder to see that Faye and Chrissy were there, too.

Imogene had been saddened at the distance between her and her family, but it had probably been good for all of them. She couldn't bear to deal with them until they were truly good and ready to accept her just the way she was.

"I'm sorry I made you feel like you're not a part of the family. Of course you are."

Love and affection swelled in Imogene's heart.

Nick looked around, utterly stunned to see all the people. "Look at what you've done!"

Imogene sighed contentedly. She was overwhelmed at the outpouring of support.

Chrissy tentatively stepped forward. Imogene eyed her suspiciously, telling herself to give her sister the benefit of the doubt. She'd give her one chance to speak, to say something nice and supportive about her successful singles rally. One negative word, and Imogene vowed to herself to turn and walk away. This was Imogene's moment, and she'd be damned if she let any try to ruin it.

"Immy…Faye and I wanted to say that we're really sorry for the way we treated you." Chrissy glanced at Faye, who nodded.

"Look, I don't think we're ever really gonna see eye-to-eye on this," Chrissy said. Imogene sighed wearily. She might have known…

"You're our sister," Faye said, "and we're always gonna worry about you. We want you to be happy and we're still afraid that you're gonna live to regret staying single and—"

"Okay, you know what?" Imogene began angrily, determined not to take any shit from her judgmental sisters.

Faye held up her hand. "But—*but* we realize how mean it was to keep saying that over and over again. We're gonna worry about you, but we promise we will never rag on you for being single again. We *promise*." Faye held up her hand as if swearing in a court of law.

Chrissy did the same. "We can disagree on this, but we don't have to be bitches about it. And we were, Im. We really were."

Imogene nodded. She wasn't going to argue with that. Her dad watched the conversation with great concern. He looked terrified that Imogene would run off again.

"Immy, you have always been there for us," Faye said, looking genuinely contrite. "Through bridesmaid dress fittings, baptisms, kids' birthday parties…that time you stayed up all night with me at the hospital for Marcus' emergency appendectomy…" Faye choked up as she recalled that awful memory. Imogene had held her weeping sister though the night, telling her to hold on and that Marcus would be fine. Which he was, thank God.

Chrissy nodded. "You have a point when you say it's wrong when people say single people are selfish. You're the most selfless person I know."

"You have always, *always* been there for us and we've never supported a damn thing you've ever done," Faye said. "And we're really sorry."

"Thank you," Imogene said softly.

"And this?" Faye said, looking around at the thousands of people gathered. "This is beyond incredible."

"I know, right?" Imogene agreed excitedly. She reached out to hug Faye, and Chrissy joined in. Her father's sigh of relief was audible.

"Imogene, honey, I want to show you something," Her dad said. He pulled out his cell phone and cued up a picture. Imogene squinted in the sun to see it. It was a photo of a beautiful, wooden clock. It was quite a showpiece with intricate, delicately-carved designs. It was clearly hand-crafted and probably very expensive. "I made this."

Imogene gasped. "You...how?"

Her dad smiled shyly. "Oh, just something I used to do a long time ago. Before you girls were born. I just thought, you know, I might try doing it again. You know, like a hobby. I put together a little woodshop area in the garage. Maybe I'll even sell some of them."

Imogene realized that her father wasn't kidding when he'd emailed her about the changes he'd made in his life. "Dad, this is amazing! I mean...wow! I want one for my apartment!"

"You got it, sweetie."

Imogene looked up and saw Matt and Paula standing nearby, watching.

"Oh, I want you to meet my friends. This is Paula." Nick shook her hand warmly, as did Imogene's sisters. "And this is Matt."

"So nice to finally meet you!" Faye said.

"Heard a lot of good things. Nice to put a face with the name," Nick said, shaking Matt's hand.

Matt looked Nick directly in the eye. "Sir....I'm so glad to have the opportunity to meet you because...well...I'd like to ask for your daughter's hand in marriage." Matt let the words sink in for a few seconds, and then grinned. "Just screwin' with you. Nice to meet you!"

Nick laughed and pumped Matt's hand harder. The two of them hit it off, and before Imogene knew it, they had plans to go fishing together. It was wonderful to have *all* of her family together in one place: her biological family and her dear friends who were as much family as her blood relatives were.

Before they left, Imogene was sure to get a few final photographs. She had her dad take a picture of her, Paula, and Hannah leaning back-to-back-to-back: kickass women from three different generations ready to take on the world. Then she had a fellow Solo Power member get a picture of her, her dad, her sisters, and Matt, Paula, and Hannah. The photograph came out great. A testament to a single lady surrounded by family and friends, the people she loved most. Single, yet far from alone.

Take that, Lindsay Saga.

CHAPTER FORTY-FIVE

The fallout from the singles rally was immediate—and wonderful. The support she got from fellow singles made her feel less alone than ever.

Well that, and now she had her adorable cat, Agnes, to come home to every night...

The rally in D.C. had made the national news, turning Imogene Hart into an instant celebrity as the pioneer and leader of the singles rights movement. She was appeared on all sorts of television programs, and not just fluffy morning talk shows either. She appeared on *CNN*, *MSNBC*, and *ABC News*, among others. She also was preparing to testify before Congress on singles rights and had been approached by several publishers to write a book.

Within a few weeks, Imogene had made enough money from her television appearances, public speaking engagements, and book deal to quit her job. This ride might not last forever, but for now she didn't need her day job. She gave her resignation letter to Camille, who accepted it graciously with best wishes to her for her future.

Imogene also organized a big, celebratory party for Solo Power that was almost like a wedding, but instead was to celebrate the beginning of the new, improved singles group. With Adrienne's help, she prepared a fabulous buffet dinner for everyone. Naturally, Imogene put her baking skills to good use and made a cake. She decorated a fancy, four-tiered cake that sort of resembled a wedding cake. On it, she scripted the words *Single and Loving It!* in bright red frosting. Imogene invited Matt, Paula, and Hannah to help her cut it. They all held their hands on the knife and cut it together like a bride and groom would. Everyone laughed and applauded, and Imogene felt as full of love and life as she would if she were getting married. After all, good weddings were a celebration of life and love, and so was this amazing party.

Imogene, Matt, Paula, Hannah, and about a dozen other Solo Power members made it a habit to gather every Sunday night at Talmer's bar to watch *Beautiful Bride,* a trashy but surprisingly addictive show. Tonight they were watching the season—and maybe the series—finale. It was the night of the wedding. Jillian's wedding.

The show had premiered to acceptable ratings, but plunged steadily downward. The critics' reviews of the show were not kind and even the viewers didn't seem all that crazy about it. The singles rally had attracted a lot of attention and people became aware of The Estrogen Network contest even if they had never heard of it while it was going on. It was too little too late to save *Single, Not Alone*, but people seemed rather annoyed in hindsight that Lindsay Saga's superficial wedding program had beaten out Imogene's show. The rally had been so high-spirited, fun, and positive that it kind of resulted in a backlash against Lindsay's type of cutthroat reality show. A lot of women started to realize how offensive it really was to say that a woman's life began on her wedding day. This was the 21st century, after all. Romance was great, but there was a lot more to a woman than just having a man in her life.

Beautiful Bride *seems to be a concept whose time has come…and gone,* wrote one reviewer. *In these tough economic times, the waste of an extravagant wedding seems especially ill-advised and irresponsible. It's also a somewhat disturbing concept that the prettiest, most devious contestant is rewarded with a fantasy wedding. Wouldn't it be better if the best couple won the prize? The couple who seemed most likely to succeed in their marriage? Admittedly, watching the bridezilla behavior can be a guilty pleasure. It's entertaining for a while, but it soon grows thin. The yelling and screaming sometimes borders on the abusive, making it uncomfortable to watch. It begs the question: What are these grooms-to-be thinking? In retrospect, it does seem that Imogene Hart's singles show would have been a better choice. The whole point was to take single people and help set them on a positive path toward a brighter future. You can't help but wonder what the future holds for these bridal terror queens. I'd love to see the follow-up to* Beautiful Bride…Divorced and Depressed?

Imogene struggled to take the high road, but after how awful Lindsay had been and after all the times that she had offered her matchmaking services for poor, lonely Imogene, it was hard.

"Well, if any of them does end up divorced, Solo Power is always here for them!" Imogene could not resist saying in a television interview.

In the end, Jillian Jeepers had won the prize. It was definitely interesting to see the final product: Jillian in a huge, over-the-top, princessy gown and jewel-encrusted tiara, with candles and tulle and flowers as far as the eye could see. It was a huge, overblown affair that took place in an actual castle. It was definitely something to see. The part where she reenacted the shoe-fitting scene from Cinderella had everyone doubled over with laughter. Jillian's bridesmaids couldn't refrain from rolling their eyes at the ridiculousness of the whole thing and the groom looked so awkward and uncomfortable that it was more like a cheesy prom than a fairytale scene.

"It's MY DAY!" Jillian screamed on the television suspended above the bar.

"MY DAY!" repeated Imogene and her Solo Power group as they all took a drink. *Beautiful Bride* ended up being the ideal show for a drinking game. Any time a bridezilla said it was "It's my day," "It's all about me," or "I'm The Bride!" they took a drink. Imogene had learned the first week that it was best to take a cab to the bar if you played that game. Hannah played along with her Coke, matching them drink for drink.

Hannah looked thoughtful as they all watched Jillian and Derek take their vows.

"It's funny, you know…" Hannah said in a quiet, introspective voice.

"What is, beautiful?" Matt asked her.

"It's kind of sad." Hannah said, still watching Jillian. "I mean, she got what she wanted, but what happens when she wakes up tomorrow morning? Everything she wanted…everything she worked so hard for her whole life…it'll all be over. Then what? She's not gonna be happy with that guy. It's just kind of sad, you know?"

Everyone at the table nodded. Jillian was a real bitch, as they'd seen from all those weeks on the show, but it really *was* kind of sad. They couldn't help feeling a bit sorry for her. When her wedding was over, she'd just be married to some guy she didn't seem to care much about. It truly was a depressing thought.

Imogene honestly felt sorry for Jillian. She was clearly going to have a miserable marriage. Still, she couldn't help giggling when a thought occurred to her. "Now this is a switch…a bunch of single people sitting around feeling sorry for the bride!" Imogene raised her glass and they all clinked and drank.

Imogene was filled with emotion as the group went on laughing and talking and drinking. She thought about all the things they'd done together and were going to do in the future. The trips they'd take, the adventures they would go on, and the new friends they would make. Together. They truly were single, yet not alone.

Camille had put it best when she signed the farewell card presented to Imogene on her last day of work:

To Imogene: Lots of luck and love to you on this, the first day of your happily ever after.

Acknowledgements

Heartfelt thanks to all who contributed to making this book happen. Thanks to Beth Miller, Kendall Bailey, Leighta Bennett, and Robert Thomson for their helpful and honest beta reads. Thanks to Lisa Winders and my sister, Zann Wasiljov, for providing their expert editing services. Thanks to my family and their unfailing support. Lucky for me, I never had any of the problems with family that Imogene did.

Thanks to my husband, Bill, and my children Celia and Noah, for their love and support.

To all the sassy singles out there – never settle for anything but the best in life.

Thank you for reading this book! I would be so grateful if you would take the time to leave a review of *Singles Vs. Bridezillas* on Amazon, Goodreads, and so forth. Reviews are vital to any author's success.

I hope you will check out my other book, *Queen Henry*

** All proceeds from *Queen Henry* go to the Harvey Milk Foundation to help further LGBT equality **

To stay informed about my upcoming books, you can join my email list at http://www.wannabepride.com/contact.html. Be sure to choose the READER'S list.

I would love to hear from you! You can contact me in any or all of the following ways:

Email
lindafausnet@gmail.com

Facebook
www.facebook.com/lindafausnet (author page)

Twitter
@LindaFausnet

Writers – Check out my educational and support website for writers at www.wannabepride.com. Join the WRITER' email list at http://www.wannabepride.com/contact.html You'll get writing advice and articles, as well as information on my upcoming books and other book recommendations.

You can also join my writer support Facebook group at https://www.facebook.com/groups/369053709961293/. I am always looking for good books to promote! Once you join the group, feel free to post your blog or book links at any time.

www.ingramcontent.com/pod-product-compliance
Lightning Source LLC
Chambersburg PA
CBHW030014180626
46810CB00001B/38